SEE THE HANDSOME FACE AND THRILL TO THE GOLDEN VOICE OF TV MINISTER ARTHUR BACH.

JOIN WITH ALL THE OTHER PEOPLE, YOUNG AND OLD, BLACK AND WHITE, RICH AND POOR, WHO HAVE MADE HIS UNIVERSAL MINISTRIES SUCH A SENSATIONAL SUCCESS.

COME TO HIS HEAVENLY COMMU-NITY WHERE ALL PRAYERS ARE ANSWERED AND ALL NEEDS FULFILLED, AND DON'T WORRY ABOUT THE FAITHFUL AROUND YOU WHO DISAPPEAR. . . .

ONE LITTLE WORD OF WARNING, THOUGH. IN THIS CHURCH, IF YOU WANT TO BE SAVED, YOU'LL NEED A DO-IT-YOURSELF KIT— COMPLETE WITH A FORBIDDEN CROSS AND A SET OF SHARP STAKES. . . .

"Delivers chills and shudders . . . a writer to watch."
                    —Robert R. McCammon, author
                    of *Swan Song*

NIGHT PROPHETS

a novel by
PAUL F. OLSON

AN ONYX BOOK

NEW AMERICAN LIBRARY

A DIVISION OF PENGUIN BOOKS USA INC.

NAL BOOKS ARE AVAILABLE AT QUANTITY DISCOUNTS
WHEN USED TO PROMOTE PRODUCTS OR SERVICES.
FOR INFORMATION PLEASE WRITE TO PREMIUM MARKETING DIVISION,
NEW AMERICAN LIBRARY, 1633 BROADWAY,
NEW YORK, NEW YORK 10019.

The author gratefully acknowledges the following permission:

First stanza of "Winter Remembered," copyright   1924 by Alfred A.
Knopf, Inc., renewed 1952 by John Crowe Ransom. Reprinted from *The
Selected Poems of John Crowe Ransom*, 3rd edition revised and enlarged.
Reprinted by permission of Alfred A. Knopf, Inc. and Methuen London
Ltd.

ONYX TRADEMARK REG. U.S. PAT. OFF. AND FOREIGN COUNTRIES
REGISTERED TRADEMARK—MARCA REGISTRADA
HECHO EN DRESDEN, TN, U.S.A.

SIGNET, SIGNET CLASSIC, MENTOR, ONYX, PLUME, MERIDIAN
and NAL BOOKS are published by New American Library, a division of
Penguin Books USA Inc., 1633 Broadway, New York, New York 10019

First Printing, December, 1989

1 2 3 4 5 6 7 8 9

PRINTED IN THE UNITED STATES OF AMERICA

For Erin

From 210½ to 223 to 155, to 527,
it's been a long, strange trip.
But your belief helped pave the road.
I love you.

Author's Note

The following work is fiction. The people and events described in its pages are wholly products of the author's imagination. Any similarity between them and people or events in real life—living or dead, past or present—is coincidental and unintended.

There is no such church as the Universal Ministries described in these pages, nor such a place as the Universal Ministries compound. There *is*, of course, a Los Angeles, California. There is also a Winfield, Illinois; and several other places mentioned in the book do exist in the real world. But I have used such places fictionally, and with no purpose beyond entertainment in mind.

—PFO

Prologue

For I must to the greenwood go,
Alone, a banished man.
                    —Anonymous
                    (15th century)

Winston's Tap was located just off the intersection of Highway M-28 and County Road 118, two miles north of Granger, Michigan. It was a workingman's bar, patronized by the pulp cutters, mechanics, gas jockeys, and truckers from town, who usually came around only every other weekend after payday, and otherwise left the place pretty much alone.

When the young man who had recently become his best customer arrived on a Wednesday evening in the middle of June, Jordie Winston was nursing his second beer of the evening and testing out a video game he'd purchased several months before, during the midst of a failed campaign to attract a younger crowd. The game was called Comet. It involved trying to maneuver an electronic blip that was your spaceship through thirty or forty other electronic blips that represented a meteor shower. Jordie's blip had just been blown to colorful, computer-generated smithereens for at least the fifth time when the door opened and the young man came in.

"It's you," he said, abandoning the joystick and taking his beer back to the bar. "The usual?"

"Please."

Jordie nodded and took two chilled mugs from the freezer chest. He filled them with Pabst from the first of four taps, letting the foam settle for a while before topping them off and sliding them across the bar, one at a time.

"Hot enough for you?" Jordie said. In the time-honored tradition of most barkeeps, he always fell back on the weather for an opening. Sometimes the weather was all he and his customers would talk about. Tonight, being a Wednesday in between paydays, he was hoping to parlay the opening into something more substantial.

The young man nodded. "Is it always so hot this early?"

"Never. 'Least, not often. Last year, I don't remember us getting much above fifty till after the Fourth of July."

"Northern Michigan," the young man said with a grimace. "You freeze or you fry. God's country, isn't it?"

Jordie took a half-step back, surprised. First of all, in all the time this fellow had been coming into the Tap, he'd never strung together more than five or six words at a time. And he'd *never* given Jordie any indication that he wasn't happy with the town of Granger, or with the whole Upper Peninsula, for that matter.

He studied the young man closely. Although he had first appeared almost six months ago, and been in almost every night since then, Jordie knew only that he always drank PBR on tap, wasn't a sports fan, and that he worked as a janitor/maintenance man/jack-of-just-about-everything at the Northern Paradise Hotel on Granger Avenue. He knew the fellow's name was Curt Potter or Porter or some damn thing. Beyond that he didn't know where the fellow came from, or why or how he had come to town. He didn't know if the fellow had bought a house somewhere, or if he rented an apartment. He didn't even know how old the fellow was, although he guessed somewhere between thirty and thirty-five. The truth was, simply, that his best customer, the only person in the entire town of twenty-nine hundred people who could be called a "nightly," was the most tight-lipped, unsociable, self-contained man Jordie had ever run across.

He stared at the fellow—the shaggy black hair that fell to just above his shoulders, the face with the eyes set just a little too far apart and the nose just a bit too flat, the unshaven stubble that miraculously always seemed to be just two days long—and knew what was coming next. He would drink his first beer in silence, staring at the worn bar top, and as he was starting on his second mug, he would ask Jordie to turn on the television.

"God's country," Jordie mused, trying for just a little conversation before having to turn on the tube. "That's what they call it, all right. But I ain't never been what you'd call religious. Oh, I went to church on and off when I was a boy; my folks, they made me go. But once I was of age, I just kinda drifted away from it. Y'know what I mean?"

The young man nodded, but as always he seemed distracted, and Jordie couldn't be certain if the nod was a genuine answer or just a polite response.

He sighed. "Yeah, Jesus, it's been hot this year. Y'know Bart McIver? Works over to the Shell station on Truman Street?"

"I'm afraid not."

"Well, Bart, when he was in here last night, he says that his shoes were sticking to the sidewalk on the way over. Like in the middle of summer, when the asphalt melts in little circles and you can't hardly walk without planting your shoes down in the middle of one of 'em. That's hot. And here it is barely past Memorial Day. What's gonna happen in August? That's what I wanna know."

The young man drained his first Pabst and set the mug down with a thump. "Why don't you turn on the TV?" he said, without looking Jordie in the eye.

Jordie sighed again. On nights like this, when the real customers were too damn broke to come in and all he had was half-assed regulars like this fellow, he wondered why he'd ever bought this place. Four or five nights a month of real business, and the rest of the time he was stuck with this clown.

"Whaddya wanna watch?" he said, turning to the big color Zenith mounted above the bar.

The young man shrugged, as he always did, and said, "I don't care. Whatever's on."

Jordie punched the On button and lifelessly flipped through the channels. There were a couple of those issue-of-the-week movies on the regular stations, and on cable it was mostly fishing shows, news, and box-office bombs so obscure they hadn't even made it to the Granger Cinema during their regular releases. He was about to settle on one that seemed to be showing a little more tits and ass than the others when the young man startled him by leaning forward.

"Stop. Go back."

Jordie turned, puzzled. "What?"

"Go back. To that other station." His eyes were flashing ebony fire, and his lips were stretched in grim determination.

"This one?" Jordie said, dialing back to the seventeenth showing that month of Michael J. Fox trying to find his way *Back to the Future*.

"No, no. More. Back more."

Puzzled and more than a little irritated, Jordie flipped back again, this time finding a rerun of the day's activities in Congress. "You wanna watch this? This C-SPAN crapola?"

The young man slammed a fist down on the bar. "Dammit, no! Go back some more. I'll tell you where to stop."

Jordie turned around to stare fully into the young man's face. "Now, look here, friend. I know you're a real good customer and all, but it's just too fucking hot to play games. Now, tell me straight. What the hell do you wanna watch?"

This time it was the young man's turn to sigh. He lowered himself back on his stool and took a sip of beer, as though trying to calm himself. When he spoke again, his voice was soft and clipped: "The church service. Go back to the church service."

"This?" Jordie said wonderingly, finding one of those loudmouthed televangelists speaking before a large crowd in some football stadium.

The young man nodded. "Yeah. Just leave it here for a minute."

Jordie shrugged. "You're paying the bill. Jesus, I didn't know you were one of those. Hope I didn't offend you or nothing, you know, with what I said before about not going to church and all."

The young man held up a silencing hand, but didn't say

a word. His dark eyes were boring into the screen like lasers.

The preacher was tall and ruggedly handsome in a way that reminded Jordie of a 1940's movie star. He was dressed in a plain blue suit and was holding a small black book clenched tightly in one fist and raised high over his head. With his other hand he was pounding a lectern, draped in garish rainbow-colored cloth. The pounding punctuated his sermon, which to Jordie sounded like all the usual hogwash about a better world, a better place to live, mankind, brotherhood, love, bullshit-bullshit-bullshit.

The camera panned from the man's face across the vast audience, and suddenly Jordie, a baseball fan, recognized Dodger Stadium in Los Angeles. The place was packed to capacity, and he noticed that the crowd was mostly under thirty. They were clean-cut, for the most part, but there was a scattering who looked grimy and worn, poor and broken. Many were leaning forward with rapturous interest. Others were leaning back in their seats, eyes closed, swaying slightly in time to the sermon and the constant pulpit banging.

Then the camera took a dizzying zoom from the outfield back to the evangelist for a close-up. The handsome face was firmly set, the jaw muscles working furiously, the tendons in the neck moving up and down like smooth piston rods. The evangelist was perspiring heavily, and his eyes roved from one side of the crowd to the other. At periodic intervals his gaze locked on some audience member, and for that moment he would be speaking only to him. At slightly longer intervals, the evangelist would stare into the camera, and Jordie felt a chill go walking down his spine, despite the eighty-degree heat outside and the broken air conditioner that was a jumble of loose wires and broken parts on his stockroom floor.

"Reverend Bob," the young man murmured, and Jordie jumped, nearly screamed, he was so startled.

"What's that?"

"Reverend Bob," his recently acquired best customer repeated softly. "Bob Kaye."

"You *know* that guy?"

"Yes. In a manner of speaking, I do."

Jordie grunted. "I don't care if he's your damn father. He's giving me the creeps. I'm gonna turn on Babe Winkleman."

He reached for the dial, but the young man said, "No."

"Screw you, pal. You wanna watch this shit, you go on home. Or take your business over to the Hiawatha."

"Leave the dial alone, dammit!"

Jordie hesitated, staring at the screen. The camera had pulled back a bit and was showing the entire stage area. Behind the man his customer had called Reverend Bob he noticed several other seated men in blue suits, looking up at the evangelist with the same intense interest of the Dodger Stadium crowd. And behind those men was a choir of perhaps two hundred robed men and women—or kids, more precisely; to Jordie, not one of them looked more than twenty years old.

Lettering appeared on the bottom of the screen: "UNIVERSAL MINISTRIES***LIVE***LOS ANGELES."

It hung there for a moment and then dissolved into: "TWENTY-FOUR-HOUR PRAYER LINE***1-800-555-0637*** CALL NOW!!!"

"Fuck it," Jordie mumbled to himself, and snapped the set off.

He wasn't prepared for the blow when it came. It took him on the back of the head and sent him staggering forward against the back of the bar. He struck his neat array of bottles, knocking several of them to the floor. They shattered, sending glass shards into the air. Brown and clear liquids trickled out and mixed together in a colorless puddle, and the cloying juniper smell of lost gin filled the air.

"What the—"

Jordie pulled himself up and spun around. The young man had leapt across the bar at him. Even now, as Jordie tensed himself for the brawl he was sure would follow, the young man had his fists clenched, one arm drawn back and ready to strike. But the hell of it was, he wasn't paying attention. His eyes were riveted on the television.

"You're crazy," Jordie said, shaking his head. "You're fucking certifiable, pal. I want you out of here, okay?

And if you don't get out of here right now, I'm gonna call Otto McKerchie and have him come *drag* you the fuck outta here. You hear me?"

The young man whispered something Jordie didn't catch. He whispered it softly, almost to himself, and he never looked away from the television while doing so.

"What did you say?"

"Please," he repeated, louder. "Just let me watch. Won't you just let me watch for a minute?"

It wasn't until two days later, as Jordie was closing up after a satisfyingly busy Friday night, that he realized what it was about the young man's expression that had stopped him from calling the police chief.

The young man who had been his only regular customer for nearly six months and whom he never saw again after that night, had been watching the television and crying. The tears had been positively coursing down his cheeks.

I
Gathering Together

Whenever God erects a house
of prayer
The devil always builds a
chapel there;
And 'twill be found, upon
examination,
The latter has the largest
congregation.

—DANIEL DEFOE

1

Juan Jimenez awoke in the night to the crackle of flames and the smell of hot smoke in his car.

"Jesus Christ!" he cried, sitting bolt upright in the driver's seat. "Fire!"

But the night was calm, quiet except for the rasping sound of his own breath. He leaned back and felt perspiration trickling down his forehead. He made no move to wipe it away.

A sudden tapping at the window made him whirl to his left, heart hammering. For a moment he saw nothing, but then an elderly man rose in front of him. His face, inches from the glass, looked wise and kind, not in the least bit threatening. There was something about the face that spoke to Juan, that awakened something dormant within him, that made him wish he knew his own father. The elderly man smiled, and Juan instinctively smiled back.

But there was something wrong. The man's face suddenly was streaked with dirt, and there were dark shadows under his eyes. Juan blinked and saw a thin line of blood trickling from the corner of the man's mouth.

"You—" Juan started to say, and as he spoke, the man's face appeared to melt. Before Juan could react, he was not looking at a figure of gentle, ancient wisdom anymore but at a face much harder. The friendly eyes were now dark-crystal drill bits that seemed to bore right into him.

"Who—" he blurted, but that was all he got out before the man outside the car raised his fist and brought it down on the Chevy's window, inches from Juan's face. The glass shattered with a tremendous crash. Shards flew everywhere. He felt a stabbing pain in the center of his forehead and several pinpricks in his cheeks. Dimly he realized that something wet was running past his eyes.

The man reached in through the gaping hole and seized Juan by the collar, pulling him toward the opening. Juan struggled, but the pain was worse than he had thought at first and he felt himself beginning to slip away. Battling against it, he nevertheless sensed a huge blanket of gray rushing toward him. The man's mouth opened and Juan thought he saw flashing light glinting off sharp fanglike teeth.

Before he passed out he made one final feeble effort to ward off the attacker. He clenched one hand into a fist. He raised it. He marshaled the last of his fleeing energy and . . . woke up.

He sat up with a start and looked around, his chest heaving convulsively. The street was empty, silent. He checked the windows. They were intact. He checked the doors. They were locked.

"Oh, Jesus, a nightmare," he whispered. "Oh, Mother of God . . ."

The hand that woke him two hours later was gentle, but when Juan felt it he snapped upright, coiling immediately into a fighting posture. His eyes focused on what he took to be his would-be killer, but he saw only a pleasant young man in his early twenties, smiling harmlessly and making no move to threaten him.

"Whaddya want, man?"

"I want to help you," the young man said in a cool, easy voice.

"Help what?"

"Help you take a good look at yourself. Help you discover what you're doing sleeping in a beat-up car at four thirty in the morning."

"Four-*what*?" Juan's adrenaline was still surging, but his fear was trickling into a pool of anger. "You tellin' me it's four-thirty in the fuckin' mornin'? You fuckin' woke me up at fuckin' four-thirty? Jeezus, man! What's the matter with you?"

"There's nothing the matter with *me*, son. I just want to—"

"Get outta here with your bullshit, man. I ain't your son. I ain't nobody's son, so just get outta here. Go fuck with somebody else, you fuckin' asshole troublemaker!"

The young man didn't seem fazed at all. He continued to smile and asked, "Can you tell me what you're doing out here, sleeping like this?"

"Wha'fuck's the matter with this guy?" Juan inquired of his steering wheel. "I tell him get lost, he just keeps talkin'. What is he? Deaf?"

"I'm not deaf. I want to know what you're doing here."

"You a cop?"

The young man shook his head solemnly.

"Well, then lemme alone, okay? I don't gotta answer none o' your bullshit questions."

"But all I asked is what you're doing out here sleeping in your car like this."

"Okay! Okay, man. I tell you, you lemme alone, right? Is that a deal? I sleep here 'cause this is where I passed out. Got that?"

"You were drinking," the young man said.

"Well, yeah. What the fuck you care, anyhow?"

"I care because I'm your friend."

"Jeezus, now he's my friend. *Mi amigo grande.* He wakes me up at four-fuckin'-thirty, makes me tell him somethin' that ain't none o' his business anyway, and now he's my goddamn friend. Ain't that sweet?"

"Why didn't you go home after the party?" the young man asked.

"Because I don't got a home, man. That okay with you? I don't got a home. Now, will you—"

"You're a street kid, then."

"Yeah, I'm a fuckin' street kid. My mama's gone and Buddy Vargas' mama kicked me outta her place. You happy? You happy now, you fuckin', lousy, nosy bastard?"

"You can't hurt me with those names. But I don't

believe you want to hurt me. I think you know I'm your
friend. I think you realize that I'm here to help you.
Don't you?"

"I don't know that," Juan said petulantly. "I know
you're a pain in the ass, that's what I know. What're
you? Social worker or somethin'?"

"Of a sort. I do some social work, yes. But my real
business is helping street kids like you find a better way."

"You're a missionary, then. A fuckin' missionary."

"You could say that."

"Ohhh, kee-rist! You guys don't quit, do you? You
ain't never happy! Wha'fuck you—"

"Do you take any drugs? Marijuana? Coke? Dust?
Crack?"

"That ain't none o' your business, missionary man."

"It is if you want me to help you."

"I don't want you to help me!" Juan cried. "Did I say I
want you to help me? You hear me say that? Did I go
wakin' you up in your car at four-thirty? Did I go stickin'
my hand through your window and shakin' you? No way,
man!"

"How old are you?"

Juan groaned. "Sixteen."

"Sixteen years old," the young man mused. "Home-
less, drinking, sleeping in your car. I'll bet you don't even
have a license to drive this thing, do you?"

"That's all you know. I got a license. Got it last month."

"So, you're all legal. Good for you. Does that make it
any easier to sleep here at night? To not have a home to go
to. Did you ever think there might be a better way?"

"The barrio's great," Juan said. "L.A.'s great. Better
way, shit."

"There are things beyond Los Angeles, you know.
Things far beyond the barrio and this kind of life. I could
show them to you, if you'd let me."

"Oh, man, just lemme alone. Go back to your church.
I seen kids saved every day on the street. Kids back to
drinkin' and grabbin' purses and shootin' up in a week.
Go on. I don't need none o' your born-again shit."

"All right," the young man said. "So you don't want
to be born again. How about breakfast?"

"Wh-what?" Juan asked, caught off guard.

"I said, how about breakfast? It doesn't look like you have any other plans."

"I ain't eatin' in no mission, man. I been there before. Food sucks, and you gotta repent or do some other kinda crazy shit 'fore they even let you eat it. So just—"

"I wasn't thinking about a mission. I was thinking of McDonald's. Egg McMuffin sound good this morning?"

Juan laughed harshly. "You buyin'?"

"Of course."

"And you ain't gonna preach at me the whole time?"

"Not if you don't want me to. But I will tell you about some of the things I've seen outside the barrio. I"—he held up his hand to forestall Juan's protest—"won't preach, won't even mention God. We'll just talk about facts, facts about the real world, your world, my world—the world out there." He pointed past a line of houses to a distant something on the smog-choked horizon. "Do we have a deal?"

Juan groaned again but nodded limply. "Okay, man. Deal."

"Good. Now, slide over. I'll drive."

"You know about cars, man? You sure you can drive this thing? She's got a double—"

"I can drive it," the young man said. "I can drive anything with wheels and an engine. I used to race stock cars."

"You—"

"I did. Ever hear of Daytona? The Five Hundred?"

"Aw, go on, man. You never drove—"

"No, I didn't drive at Daytona. I was on Richard Petty's pit crew. That was five years ago. He helped get me started on the circuit. Now, move over, would you? I'm getting hungry."

Juan Jimenez shook his head, looking at the smiling young man in a new light. He hitched himself over to the passenger side of the Chevy, mumbling, "Stock cars. Whaddya know? Shit."

The young man climbed in, started the engine, and gunned it. A moment later they were wheeling down the dark, empty streets, taking the corners at forty-plus. They were on their way to the beginning of something, although neither one of them would have wanted to predict an ending just yet.

2

We can't disgrace the family, Phyl.

"Of course not," Phyllis Meyer said to the darkened predawn living room. "We can't do that."

You're being utterly selfish! You have to stop thinking of yourself for once and consider what this could do to your father and me.

"Selfish," Phyllis said. "Right."

Come to your senses, girl.

And of course she had. She had seen the light, and now, barely more than a week after her second missed period, the baby was gone: her baby, Andy's baby, the living thing that had existed inside her for sixty-nine days, was gone, washed down a drain in a sterile examination room. Her parents' lives could continue as they always had, clean and upright, righteous, and most important, undisgraced.

"But what about my life?" she murmured.

Andy had begged her to keep the baby. He had grand plans. He would marry her. They would run away together. They would forsake their families forever. But in their hearts they had both acknowledged that this was impossible. Seventeen-year-olds didn't elope to a lifetime of happiness anymore. In the end, Andy had cried and so had she, but tears changed nothing. It was time to accept the judgment and cope. But how could she cope with the hollow, dead feeling that was as much emotional as physical? The baby was gone and Andy was gone because he couldn't accept the thought of some scrubbed, gently smiling doctor sucking his child from within her. His unborn child. His *unformed* child. Unformed. She had to keep that word uppermost in her mind. Somehow it made the whole thing more detached, more bearable.

"Shit," she said. The living room gave back nothing but silence.

That was the problem. Things were too quiet. The darkness and the silence left too much room for thinking. A simple distraction was what she needed. She needed another person. Or, barring that, she thought wryly, she needed the modern replacement for people—television.

She rose and snapped on the Sony. Snow. Snow. Old movie. Snow. Monster truck competition. Snow. Old movie: The Sequel. More goddamned snow and—

—and religion.

Phyllis let her hand hesitate and actually took a step back away from the set. She recognized the station—one of the three all-religion stations they picked up locally and off cable—and for a moment she almost saw something familiar in the program itself. Almost, but not quite.

The minister who was standing in the pulpit and speaking to the camera was tall and almost absurdly handsome. He had strong features, strong eyes—what she had once called a "muscular gaze" in a short story she'd written for English class (and promptly been told to stop stretching for her metaphors). But the thing that had caused her to back away from the set wasn't his gaze. It was his voice. A wonderful voice, as deep as a disc jockey's, as enticing as a pitchman's, as inviting as a street corner pimp's. Captivating.

She stared at the set for several moments, mesmerized, before she even heard a word of what the voice was actually saying:

" . . . and, my friends, you can have it. If you hate your life, then seek change. If you want a way out, go looking for it. If you're bored or tired or restless or angry, if you want something better—go for it!"

Phyllis nodded imperceptibly, felt herself relax a little, and then caught herself at what she was doing.

"Universal can offer you a chance to leave the old behind, to shed the boredom, eliminate the hate. Universal can—"

She angrily snapped the set off and went back to the couch, lowering herself onto it with a sigh.

Universal. The local born-agains. No wonder it had looked familiar. In this area it was impossible to turn on a television, dial down a radio, or pick up a newspaper or magazine without hearing something about Universal Ministries. It might be an ad looking for members; sometimes it was a positive article praising the group for the dollars they pumped into the Chicago-area economy or the missions they ran around the world; often the articles were negative. Whatever it was, Universal was a powerful, ubiquitous force in the Chicago area. Or a powerful joke, depending on how you looked at it.

The words of the handsome minister kept running through her head.

If you hate your life, then seek change. If you want a way out, go looking for it.

She hated this life, all right, hated everything about it. She loathed living in this affluent suburb called Barrington, hated attending a private school that trained her for an upscale university, an upscale job, an upscale life—in short, turning her into a stock reissue of her parents. She hated them too, and right now she hated herself for giving in, for refusing to bring disgrace on her family, for visiting the scrubbed, gently smiling doctor Andy had so feared.

Her parents. God damn them to hell.

Upstairs they were sleeping soundly, knowing that their precious reputations were no longer at stake. The dirty little secret was laundered and safe. She thought of them up there in their tasteful twin beds and felt the hate, almost a living thing itself, growing ever stronger within her.

If you hate your life, then seek change.

Uh-huh, right, exactly. First you go back in time about two weeks, and then rig things so you win the Lotto jackpot. With six or seven million in your pocket, you

and Andy run away and set yourselves up somewhere
with—

Stop it! a part of her mind shrieked. *Stop torturing
yourself!*

Phyllis Meyer put her face into her hands and let the
tears break free.

3

Since his plane was due in at five-fifteen in the morning, Curt didn't expect any problems meeting his contact in Chicago. But when he came out the automatic sliding doors in front of the American Airlines baggage claim, all he saw was a handful of idling taxis, their foreign drivers asleep in the front seats. He set his suitcase and backpack down and looked around uncertainly, trying to remember if he'd given the young girl on the phone all the information. American flight 672 from New York, arrival 5:13 A.M. Central Daylight Time on September 29. Yes, he had told her that.

After fifteen minutes he decided he would have to go back inside, find a pay phone, and call the compound, but as he was turning toward the doors again he heard a vehicle coasting to a stop behind him and a voice calling through an open window, "Curt? Curt Potter?"

He turned to see an unmarked Ford van with dark-tinted windows sitting at the curb where he had been waiting before. The driver's door opened and a young man hurried around the van toward him.

"Curt Potter?"

He nodded. "That's right. Yes."

"Oh, thank goodness. I thought we were going to miss each other."

The young man breezed past him, pausing just long enough to pat Curt on the shoulder, a friendly, unassuming gesture that nevertheless conveyed the need to move quickly. Before Curt could offer to help, the young man had hefted his luggage into the back of the van. Curt watched him with a thin smile. The man was dressed in jeans and a white sport shirt open at the neck. The shoes on his feet were expensive runners—Adidas maybe, or Pumas. In the unnatural airport light, his windbreaker seemed the color of dried blood, and his hair, which was dark red, looked much the same.

"Hop in," the young man told him. "I don't want to rush you, but I had a flat on the way here. Not only did I almost miss you, but I'm late for a pickup down the line here, at Air Wisconsin. Hop in, hop in. We've gotta keep moving."

Curt did as he was told, pulling himself up into the front seat beside the driver, who now took a moment and a deep breath to compose himself. When he turned to face Curt he was smiling brightly, looking like nothing so much as a flustered politician in the middle of his first statewide campaign.

"Ernest," he said, extending a hand in Curt's direction. "Ernest Cummings. Director of housing, which lately happens to include making all the airport and bus-station runs, since our regular driver's down with a cold."

Curt smiled, and they shook hands. "You have a title and you still have to do all the work in the middle of the night?"

Cummings put the van in gear and they lurched forward. "Well, 'director of housing' might be a title, but it's not much of one. Basically I'm a troubleshooter around the compound. Right now, our number-one trouble is a nasty cold bug in the air." He turned to Curt with another happy grin. "So guess who gets to shoot it, so to speak?"

"You?" Curt suggested.

Cummings laughed. "You got it. The one and only director of housing. So much for advancement."

A moment later they pulled up in front of the next set of sliding doors, where they picked up a wan young girl who couldn't have been more than sixteen. She had straggly, uncombed blond hair and dark blue eyes, and it looked to Curt as though her white Levi's and short-sleeved checked blouse hadn't been washed in weeks. While Curt waited in the front seat, Cummings hopped out and put the girl's single small travel bag in the back, then opened one of the side doors to let her in. When he was behind the wheel again he said, "Curt Potter, meet Martha Zinn. From Madison, just a short hop away. We paid Martha's air fare so she could get here as soon as possible . . . she's had some trouble lately and needs a little help."

Curt turned in his seat and said, "Hi, there. I guess you didn't have too bad a flight, then. I came in from New York and—"

He stopped in mid-sentence when he realized the girl wasn't paying him the slightest attention. She was staring at the floor of the van, concentrating on a spot between her filthy white sneakers.

"It's nice to meet you," he said awkwardly, and when she still didn't respond, he turned around to face front.

"You guys might as well make yourselves comfortable," Cummings said. "We've got a long drive ahead of us. But if you've got any questions, now's the time to ask. Of course you'll have your orientation tomorrow, and your compound tours, but if you need to know anything in advance, I'm the one to ask."

"How many pickups like this do you do?" Curt said.

"That depends. Some weeks we might get sixty or seventy newcomers. That translates out to at least thirty bus- and train-station runs and at least twenty to the airport. Other weeks, well, there may be only five or six people coming to join us. It goes up and down based on the number of crusades we've been doing, the amount of bulk mailings we get out, and how many folks our street workers come in contact with in their various cities."

"How many are here in Chicago now?"

Cummings laughed. "It's funny, Curt, you'd think I'd know that right off the top of my head, me being the big important director of housing. But the figures change a lot. Our rooms are dormitory-style, two or three to a room. We have beds for sixteen hundred, and the last count I saw showed us at ninety-one-percent capacity.

The lowest it's been since I've been around was eighty-three percent."

"That's a lot of mouths to feed."

"True, but at the compound you work to earn your keep."

They went up a ramp that was marked "294 TRI-STATE TOLLWAY SOUTH." Curt gazed out his window at the industrial sprawl racing past and allowed himself to sink lower into his seat

"What kind of work?"

Cummings chuckled softly. "Another question I really can't answer. There are literally over a thousand jobs available. Once you've settled into the dorm and feel comfortable, you'll be able to look at lists of current openings and decide what's best for you."

"I get to choose?"

"Of course. As long as you're doing something that advances the cause, that helps not only you but the rest of us too, there's total freedom."

"Total freedom," Curt echoed. "What if I wanted to be director of housing?"

He had expected his question to either amuse or confuse the young man next to him, but Cummings fielded it diplomatically. "The chance is there for you. You just have to work your way up through the hierarchy."

They were coming to a bank of toll booths, and Cummings slowed the van to a crawl, choosing one of the automatic lanes on the left and dropping a handful of change into the waiting basket before speeding up again.

"How you doing back there, Martha?" Cummings asked, settling down at somewhere around sixty miles per hour.

There might have been a soft reply, but it was hard to tell. Curt and Ernest Cummings exchanged glances, and the driver whispered to him, "Not unusual. A lot of them come in this way. You'll see what I mean when you've been around a couple of days."

Curt nodded and looked out the window again. He felt the strain of a long day begin to pull him down, settling across his shoulders and into his mind like great dead weight. Sometime over the next half-hour he might have dozed, but he wasn't sure. He was aware of several more

toll booths and a seemingly endless stretch of warehouses,
shipping yards, and office parks. They left the Tri-State
Tollway and got onto U.S. 88 West. The offices became
newer and a few comfortable houses began to appear.

"There was something I wanted to ask *you*," Cummings said at one point, startling him from the edge of a
dream. "That is, if you don't mind."

Curt yawned. "No, I mean, I guess not. What?"

"I was reviewing your paperwork before I left to pick
you up tonight, and it seemed . . . incomplete."

"Oh?"

"Well, usually our newcomers come to us after spending time at one of our satellite bases. But the information
my receptionist took down pegs you as a cold call. No
background at the New York outpost, or even any contact with a street worker."

"Is that a problem?"

"Oh, no! Absolutely not." Cummings sounded suddenly distressed. In the darkness of the van Curt could
see that his fingers had tightened on the wheel. "Don't
misintrepret. You're welcome here, whatever your circumstances. I'm just curious. In my position, I like to get
to know as many of the newcomers and residents as I
can, so I'm . . . curious, that's all. How'd you hear about
us?"

Curt didn't answer right away. For a few seconds he
went back to looking out the window at the landscape,
which was growing ever more rural by the minute. Carefully framing his response, he turned to face Cummings
and said, "My family."

"I beg your pardon?"

"My family, they kind of talked me into coming."

"They have a background with us?"

"Yeah. Kind of. Really, Mr. Cummings, I—"

"Ernest, please. If we can't be on a first-name basis
here, there's not much point to what we're doing."

"Okay. Ernest."

"And you were saying?"

"Well, really, I just felt the urge. I was pulled here."
Curt paused. "Drawn." He paused again. "Does that
make sense?"

The driver smiled like a true acolyte. "Perfect sense. Absolutely perfect."

They exited the highway and raced along a country road. As the last of the corporate sprawl gave way to farms and tree-shrouded housing developments and the sky grew ever lighter, Cummings explained their location. As he spoke, he would alternately speak sideways to Curt and back over his shoulder to Martha Zinn, who maintained her utter silence and continued to look at the floor.

"We're about thirty miles outside Chicago now. The compound is in a place called Winfield. Not too long ago, it was nothing but farmland out here. Now it's practically a suburb. Everywhere you turn, there's a new development going up. Dairy barns are getting torn down and replaced by subdivisions with names like Weeping Willow Estates and Lincoln Shores. More shopping centers, too. Fortunately, the compound is safe from all that. We're bordered on three sides by Forest Preserve land, and on the fourth side by Butterfield Road. Six hundred and thirty acres, with most of the buildings on fifty or sixty acres right in the middle. The rest is woods and parks, walking trails, a couple of manmade lakes. It's beautiful."

"How old is it?"

"Twenty years. The land was donated in the early seventies by a local businessman who became a convert. We were fortunate."

"Have you been around since the beginning?"

Cummings shook his head vigorously. "Not even close. Next month, it will only be six years for me."

"You must like it."

"I love it," Cummings said without hesitation. "Six years. They seem like six short months. I love it . . . just as you'll love it."

Suddenly the van was slowing down, pulling off the road, and coming to a stop before an intricately designed wrought-iron gate set deep into two high hedge walls. Curt had the fleeting impression of a 1930's English-country-house mystery, and was startled when a shiver caught him off his guard.

Cummings parked and climbed out, hurrying over to the gate and opening it with a key he found on a big ring of keys in his jeans pocket. Through the open driver's-side door, Curt could feel the warm air being carried along on a gentle morning breeze, and he smelled the summery aromas of recent rain, mossy earth, and fresh-cut grass.

When they were moving again, Curt's impression of an Agatha Christie novel came back in full force. A few small buildings flashed by in the shadows, and frozen pale figures that he recognized as statuary, but otherwise there was nothing on either side of the winding road but trees and rolling stretches of lawn, shrubs, more lawn, more trees.

In time, a great shape loomed up in front of them, blotting out the landscape and the dawn sky above. It took Curt a moment to orient himself, but by that time the headlights of the van had splashed across the front of the shape and he realized he was looking at a building—a big building, nearly ten stories high, or perhaps as many as fifteen.

"This is where you'll be staying. For residents, it's the nerve center of the entire compound. It's called Van Paris Hall—after R. D. Van Paris, the businessman I mentioned, the one who gave us the land—but you'll probably just call it the Hall; we all do."

"Is it—"

"All the dorm rooms are here," Cummings went on, "men in the west wing, women in the east. The center section is all little offices—mine's there, and a lot of others—plus the cafeteria, the game room, the laundry room, the lounge, you name it.

"Martha, you have two roommates already. I'll have someone take you up and introduce you, make sure you get settled. Curt, I managed to find an open room for you. But don't get too comfortable, because the way things have been going, I can just about guarantee you two roommates by the end of the week."

Curt shrugged. "No problem."

They climbed out onto a sweeping horseshoe driveway that was surfaced with the finest crushed gravel he'd ever seen. The drive was lined with shrubs and flowers in neatly manicured beds at approximately ten-foot intervals; the flowers were either blue or purple; it was impossible to tell which.

He and Martha got their own gear out of the back of the van and followed Cummings up the drive and through a set of wide glass doors. Inside was a high-ceilinged lobby, dimly lit, carpeted, decorated in shades of summer-sky blue and sunshine yellow. A vacant reception desk stood to the right, next to a large bank of mailboxes like those in post offices. Opposite was a lounge area dotted with tall plants and miniature trees in hefty ceramic pots. In the center, to Curt's surprise, was a fountain spewing endless, pretty geysers of water.

He looked around at all of it and at the directional arrows painted on the wall. One to his left read "MEN'S HOUSING." Another on the right pointed to the women's rooms. Still others said "LAUNDRY FACILITIES," CAFETERIA," "MEETING ROOMS A-L," and "OFFICES."

Going to the reception desk, Cummings picked up the receiver of a Merlin telephone set with at least thirty buttons on it. He punched a few of the buttons, spoke softly, and by the time he'd hung up and made his way back to where they were waiting, a moon-faced girl wearing a simple red dress had appeared from the office area.

"Martha? This is Dorothy Andresson. She's going to show you to your room." He paused, as though trying to remember something. "Room 709, Dot. The girls'll probably be asleep, but they're expecting her."

The girl in the red dress nodded, took Martha Zinn's backpack, slipped an arm around her shoulders, and led her away toward the women's wing. As they disappeared, Cummings led Curt in the opposite direction, up a short flight of steps and into a cul-de-sac with eight elevators. He pushed an Up button and ushered Curt inside a waiting car. The doors slid soundlessly shut and they began to rise.

"What's wrong with her?" Curt said.

Cummings shook his head, and for the first time since they'd met at the airport, he stopped smiling. His eyes darkened, and for an absurd second Curt was sure that the man was going to cry. "Our reports from the Madison office are sketchy, but that's because Martha herself hasn't told us much. My guess is it's the all-too-common story. Child abuse. Broken home. Early experiences with alcohol, drugs, probably sex without love. You hate to see someone like her hurting so much, but it's a fact of life. We get people like her every day. A hundred a week. Thousands a year. We take them all, without questions."

They rode in uneasy silence the rest of the way to the twelfth floor. When the elevator doors opened again, they stepped out into a wide, luxurious corridor. The walls were papered with a rich blue highlighted in gold; the carpeting was thick, almost spongy; the lighting was provided by enough stately electric flambeaux to light the White House, although the bulbs were dialed down now to a nighttime setting of maybe ten watts each.

It was called a dorm, Curt thought, but it was like no dorm he'd ever seen. There were no graffiti defacing the walls, no empty beer cans dumped in the corners, no ground-out cigarette butts on the floor or brown burn marks on the carpet, no signs tacked to doorways announcing keggers, album swaps, and basketball games. The place was, simply, immaculate.

They stopped in front of a door with "1290" painted on it in gilt. Cummings took out his ring of keys again, poked one into the lock, and led the way in. "We keep the rooms locked when they're unoccupied," he explained. "But once you're moved in, feel free to leave it open whenever you want. We're one-hundred-percent crime-free."

Curt wondered how that could be, if the church really attracted so many different people from such wildly varied backgrounds. But then he remembered the spotless corridor and the grounds which had looked incredible even in the hazy dawn light. He kept his silence and followed Cummings into the room.

The lights came on and Curt's breath caught in his throat. Then the wind came rushing out of him in a long, admiring sigh.

The walls were paneled in dark wood, the floor carpeted with the same lush shag as the hallway. The furnishings were simple—three beds with a small wooden dresser at the foot of each, two large desks, several chairs—but looked as though they had come from the finest store.

Cummings watched his reaction and smiled again. "It meets with your approval, I take it?"

"What do you think?"

"Well, it's important to us that the rooms are comfortable, you know. If you're not comfortable, you're not happy. And if you're not happy, you can't keep full attention on the work at hand."

"Uh-huh."

"I'm going to leave you now to get settled. When you're ready, I'll make sure you get a private tour of the compound, and there'll be a group orientation after dinner tonight for the newcomers who get in today. In the meantime, if you've got any questions, there are phones in the hallway. If you need me, just dial three; that's my extension."

"Uh-huh," Curt said again, still marveling over his accommodations.

"God bless you, Curt. Welcome to Universal Ministries."

For a long time after he was left alone, Curt simply stood in the middle of the room gazing at everything. Finally he walked to the window and pulled back the drapes, gazed out at the brightening sky and an expanse of woodlands and fields. Beyond, a sprinkling of houses and lights told him that even in this high tower room in the middle of a secluded compound, he wasn't all that far from civilization.

He let the drapes slip back into place, thought briefly of unpacking, and ultimately decided against it. He was much too tired to even attempt that now. Instead he went into the bathroom to wash up. He instinctively turned toward the vanity, but was startled to find that there wasn't a mirror hanging there. He checked the back of the door, with similar results.

"Damn," he muttered, settling for a few handfuls of cold water splashed on his face and a vigorous scalp massage with one of the towels he found neatly folded inside the vanity. Then he went back into the room, stripped down to his Jockey shorts, and dropped, exhausted, onto the nearest bed.

It was then that he noticed the picture.

Funny, with all his admiring examination, he hadn't seen it before.

It was hanging next to the door that led out to the corridor. It was a portrait of a man in his late fifties, still looking young, feisty, healthy. His hair had not thinned at all in middle age and there were no wrinkles. His teeth looked bright, white, almost capped. The suit he was wearing was stunningly clean and pressed. The tie was vivid red, just narrow enough to be fashionable.

Curt stared at the picture and realized with a start that he hadn't taken a breath for several seconds.

"Already," he murmured. "On the first day."

He didn't have to read the brass plate attached to the frame to recognize the man in the portrait, but he squinted to read it anyway.

ARTHUR TALLMAN BACH
FOUNDER
UNIVERSAL MINISTRIES

"Son of a bitch."

And then his exhaustion caught up with him before the emotion could, and he slipped rapidly away into a dream-tossed, restless sleep.

4

By afternoon the smog vanished beneath a low sea of dark, roiling clouds blowing in from the Pacific. Eventually a light gray rain began spattering the streets. But Juan Jimenez was oblivious of the weather as he drove his car in endless circles. An earthquake wouldn't have bothered him at that moment, so relieved was he to be away from the nosy, glad-handing, grinning son of a bitch who had dogged him all morning.

The son of a bitch's name was Keith Pritikin. He'd told Juan over breakfast that he was a street worker for some outfit called Universal Ministries, which was a bunch of religious weirdos dedicated to helping kids like Juan change their lives. Actually, Pritikin hadn't phrased any of it quite that way, but the meaning was clear enough. Helping kids like Juan change their lives. Helping them work for a better world. Helping them serve God and others.

"So?" Juan had asked, grumpily munching his Egg McMuffin and swilling cold, stale coffee. "You wanna fuckin' medal or somethin'?"

After breakfast Pritikin had insisted on walking with him through the barrio, never once shutting up or even easing back for a moment. He just kept hammering and yammering about old lives and new lives, bad ways and good, until Juan felt almost ill. That was when he'd known that he had to ditch the missionary bastard fast. So the guy had driven stock cars. So fucking what? The idiot wasn't even proud of it, said he'd been in a shame-

ful haze of booze, women, and drugs the entire time.
Juan didn't really understand what that had to do with
anything. Just to have the chance to do some real driving, real racing, that was the important thing. But try as
he might, the few words he'd been able to squeeze in
edgewise hadn't changed Pritikin's viewpoint, and they
hadn't made the bastard stop pushing him.

At eleven-thirty they had returned to the McDonald's
parking lot to pick up the car. Thinking he was free, Juan
made a break for the driver's door, but Pritikin blocked
the way. He insisted on taking Juan somewhere else for
lunch. Juan refused. Pritikin demanded it.

"What do you think I am?" Juan had asked. "Some
kinda slave?"

Pritikin had just smiled that sickening, stupid smile of
his, and twenty minutes later they were sitting inside a
crowded Denny's ordering sandwiches.

The speeches that Juan started thinking of as "Pritikin's
amazing bullshit" just went on and on. There were
infinite promises of a better life. There were endless
references to something great lying beyond the boundaries of Los Angeles. There were brain-numbing stories
of Pritikin's encounters with drugs, the law, and even
death before the outfit called Universal had come into his
life.

"I don't care, man!" Juan said for what seemed to him
to be the ten-thousandth time. "I don't give a fuck about
any of this! When you gonna understand that?"

"What are you afraid of?" Pritikin asked. "Is it something outside, out there on the streets? Or is it something
inside?"

"Whaddya mean, afraid? I ain't afraid. Ain't nothin' to
be afraid of. I got a good life."

"Oh, of *course*!" Pritikin had said. "Forgive me, but I
forgot. You're a sixteen-year-old kid with no parents, no
home, and no education. You've got a beat-up old car
you can hardly afford the gas for. Your only friends are
the kind who stick around while the coke's being snorted
or the wine bottles are being opened. A good life. Tell
me another one."

"Hey! You quit knockin' my life, okay? Ain't none o'

your business what the fuck kinda life I got. I'm happy,
man. That's all I need. I don't need none o' that Jesus-is-
the-way shit. I don't need your happy crap about God. I
don't need your fuckin' asshole Universal Whatever-it-is.
So why don't you just lemme alone? Why can't you do
that?''

Shaking his head sadly, Pritikin had said, "Because
you need help. You're not the first kid from East Los
Angeles I've worked with, you know, and I realize that
the people here are honest, hardworking folks. But there's
something beyond Los Angeles. It's beyond California or
even the United States. It's beyond the earth itself. It's
love, Juan. God's love, Christ's love. With it, anything's
possible. We have a saying in our church—God's hand can
touch *you*, too. And it can.''

Juan's memory of what came next got a little fuzzy at
that point. He remembered saying something about sticking a knife in the glad-handing son of a bitch's rib cage if
Pritikin didn't leave him alone. He remembered Pritikin
saying: All right, you can go now, take some time to
think, but I'll be back, I'll be back when you're ready, I'll
be back when you need me most. At least he thought
that's what the bastard had said.

Now, driving, he thought only about how good he felt.
Almost nine hours. That's how long he had endured
Pritikin's bullshit. But now he was free. If there really
was a God, and if he was a God worth thanking, then
that was something to thank him for. But the bastard's
talk about God was insane, of course. There was no
God, and there was nothing beyond the barrio for a
street kid. If he'd learned anything in his sixteen years, it
was that. The streets were rough. Shit, at times they were
pure hell. Smart kids lived with that; only assholes
dreamed of escape.

When the rain began to let up at last, he turned the
Chevy toward his home turf, noticing with a start that the
gas gauge was bouncing along just above E.

*You've got a beat-up car you can hardly afford the gas
for.*

He laughed jaggedly. That much of the son of a bitch's
line was true, anyway. When the big V-8 engine had

sucked its last fumes this time around, he'd have to start panhandling again. In truth, he had tried selling the car several times already, despite the fact that he'd owned it only a couple of months, but the closest he'd gotten to a decent offer had been one hundred and twenty-five dollars from Bobby Tiant at the garage.

"One-twenty-five?" he had said, laughing it off. "You're outta your fuckin' mind. I could get double that, maybe triple."

Now he wished he had taken it. The change in his pockets consisted of three quarters, a dime, and a few pennies.

He pulled into his usual cul-de-sac parking spot and killed the engine. He climbed out, locked the doors, and wondered why. It would be a blessing if someone stole the goddamn thing.

He tucked a cigarette into the corner of his mouth—his last one, the one he'd been saving until he absolutely needed it—and started toward the main drag.

A half-block ahead an elderly lady was struggling to pull a shopping stroller up the front walk to her house. He thought about helping her, thinking she might spare him a quarter for his trouble, but rejected the idea. Her housecoat was torn and dirty, her stockings sagging, her heavy black old lady's shoes almost completely worn out.

Shit, he thought, no money there. She's worse off than me.

The Hideaway was open a good twenty hours a day. It was populated by an endless parade of drifters and dropouts, illegal Mexicans, unemployed workers, and old men on relief. The large front room was the regular bar area, the back was the pool hall and video arcade. In the very back, through a door Juan glanced at every day but had never opened, was a room where the serious shit went down. Back there you could score just about anything, from smack to women. And there were craps and poker and horse betting too. He longed for the day he would turn eighteen and Freddy, the Hideaway's manager, would let him in there.

This afternoon the Hideaway was busier than usual.

Almost all of the bar stools were full, and so were a lot of the tables and booths. Mexican music poured from the old jukebox in the corner. Smoke hung in a thick pall above the empty dance floor and the bandstand that hadn't seen a live act in five years. Behind the bar, Freddy looked up from the beer he was drawing and raised a hand in greeting.

"Juan, hey there, I thought you got busted or somethin'. You're usually here by noon. What's up?"

Juan grinned, shrugged, and said, "Just hangin' out, Freddy, lookin' for action."

"Action, my ass. You sure the cops didn't grab you again?"

He laughed. "I'm too fast for them, *amigo*. Too slick."

Freddy's laughter followed him into the back.

In the dim, smoky light, billiard balls clicked and clacked, video games beeped and flashed. The lousy music from the front, which was piped in through a battered set of Realistic speakers on the wall, echoed crazily, setting up such a din that it was almost unbearable.

A hand touched his shoulder and he spun around, foolishly expecting to see Keith Pritikin standing there flashing his stupid grin. But it wasn't Pritikin. It was only Buddy Vargas, one of his friends.

Your only friends are the kind who stick around while the coke's being snorted or the wine bottles are being opened.

No, he thought, that's not true. Buddy was a good guy, a true *amigo*. They went back to second grade together. They had shoplifted their first candy bars on the same day. They had dropped out of high school together last spring. They had been busted together for minor-in-possession just a few months before. They had been through a lot.

"Juan, man, where the hell you been all day? The cops didn't find you sleepin' in your car again, did they?"

He laughed. "No, the fuckers never come down that street no more."

"So where you been?"

"You wouldn't believe me if I told you."

Buddy Vargas lit a cigarette and said, "Try me."

Juan started to answer but paused. Now that he looked back on his hours with the missionary, it didn't seem so maddening or irritating anymore. What it seemed, in retrospect, was . . . embarrassing. How could he tell his best friend that he'd spent nine hours with a holy-roller. That would be as bad as saying that he'd gone to see someone about the possibility of getting back into school. He could never do that.

"Well, you gonna tell me or not?"

Juan shook his head. "Around, Buddy," he said slowly. "I was around."

"Shit, no kiddin', around. I been around all day too. Around here waitin' for you to show your skinny ass. Gotta talk to you."

"What about?"

"C'mon over to the table and I'll tell you. Ricky's there already. We got someone for you to meet."

They ambled over to the corner, strategically avoiding a shoving match that had broken out at one of the pool tables, and sat down. Ricky Castillo grinned at him, and beside Ricky he saw someone he didn't recognize. The new guy's face was imprinted with several scars, one that ran from below the right eye to the bottom of the right ear, and the other zigzagging down the bridge of the nose. He was older than the rest of them, and nursing a glass of Four Roses instead of a Coke.

"Juan," Ricky said, "this is Peter. Peter Rodriguez."

Juan stuck out his hand, but the new guy didn't budge.

"Peter stopped me in the street this mornin' when I was on my way over here. He told me 'bout this plan he's got. He wanted me and two other guys. I thought of you two right away. Juan and Buddy, *mis amigos*, right?"

"Right," Juan said, and shifted nervously.

"You guys are really gonna thank me when you hear this. Ain't that right, Peter? They're really gonna thank me, right?"

Rodriguez nodded and spoke for the first time. His voice was thick and hoarse; he sounded as though he had been drinking all day. "That's right, Ricky. They really gonna thank you."

"So what's the plan?" Buddy said. "Now that Juan's here, spill it."

Ricky glanced around and lowered his voice, although it was doubtful any of them could be heard more than a foot or so away from the table, not with all the racket in the back room. "It's arson," he whispered. "A torch job."

"Arson! Are you outta your fuckin'—"

"Shut up, man!" Ricky snapped. "We ain't advertisin', you know? Just keep it down."

Juan nodded. "Arson?" he repeated softly. "What the hell you talkin' about, arson? That's crazy shit. Jeezus."

Ricky grinned. "Not so crazy, man. Not crazy at all. It's good money. Three hundred bucks apiece. *Mucho dinero*, huh? Now, you wanna hear about it or not?"

Juan and Buddy exchanged troubled glances, and Juan thought: Arson, holy Christ, these guys come up with a lot of crazy shit, but this has gotta be the worst. Still, they were his friends, and he supposed he owed it to Ricky to at least listen. He would hear him out and then tell him to shove his arson in a nice warm, dark place.

"Okay," Buddy said.

Juan echoed: "Okay, I'm listenin'. Let's hear it."

Ricky grinned, copped a cigarette from Buddy's pack, and said, "You guys know the party store on the corner?"

"The Joint?" Buddy said. " 'Course I know it."

Ricky nodded. "The guy who owns the Joint is Peter's father. Right, Peter?"

"Dear Papa," Rodriguez said dryly.

Ricky laughed. "Peter's old man, he wants out. He's goin' broke. Ain't got no business 'cept for us kids. Hard times, bad news, all that shit. The bank's screamin' for some loan to be paid back—"

"Two loans," Peter Rodriguez interjected.

"Two loans," Ricky said. "And he ain't got the money. He's been tryin' to sell the place for over a year, but nobody's buyin'. Shit, who would? No blood's got the kinda money could bail the guy out, and no Anglo's gonna wanna run a business around here. I understand his problems. I sympathize."

"Would you get to the fuckin' point?" Juan said, although he was afraid he saw the point already.

"Peter's old man wants out," Ricky went on, "and since no one wants to buy him out, he figures maybe a little flame in the night would do the trick." He paused, puffing on his cigarette. "You get it? The Joint's gonna get lit."

"But—"

"Keep listenin'. The guy's got fifteen thousand insurance on the place. He's gonna give us twelve hundred to split up between us if we do the job. That's three hundred each. Not bad money for a little flick of the Bic. Whaddya say?"

Buddy was frowning. "What does he need all four of us for? If it's so damn simple, why don't he just get one poor sucker to pull the job?"

" 'Cause it takes two to light the place and two to report it to the cops. Ain't that right, Peter?"

Rodriguez nodded. "Right." He finished his drink and shoved the glass aside.

"Report it?" Juan said. "What the fuck you wanna report it for?"

" 'Cause it looks cleaner that way," Ricky said, sounding like a teacher explaining the sum of two plus two. "Place burns and no one calls it in, that looks funny, right? But if a couple of kids like you and me, if we go runnin' down to the station and report it, hey, it all looks on the level. Who knows? Maybe we even give 'em a description of some fake guy, tell 'em we seen this clown runnin' away with an empty gas can or somethin'. We'll get 'em on the hunt for some guy doesn't even exist. How's that for a plan? It's fuckin' foolproof, man. Fuckin' *seguro*."

"Sure," Juan said. "Till they look us up on their computer and see our records."

"What the fuck's a record gotta do with anything? Guys can go straight, you know. So we were lousy kids once. So we cleaned up our act and now we're bein' good citizens, reportin' a firebug. And they ain't gonna look, anyway. They're gonna be too busy hittin' the streets, lookin' for the guy who torched the Joint." He laughed. "The wrong guy."

Juan glanced at Buddy. His dark eyes were gleaming and he was nodding enthusiastically.

"You go for this shit, Buddy?"

Buddy shrugged, and his eyes danced merrily. "Why not? Like Ricky said, it's good money."

Juan stood up. "Sorry, not me. I ain't into arson. Count me outta this one."

He started to walk away, but Peter Rodriguez was suddenly on his feet, one hand snagging Juan's shoulder and dragging him back toward the table. "I don't think you unnerstand, Jimenez. You're in this thing, *amigo*, in it with the rest of us."

"Why?" Juan felt his hands begin to tremble as they formed themselves into fists. "What's it to you? Get some other fucked-up kid to torch your old man's place."

Rodriguez shook his head and made no move to release his hold on Juan's shoulder. "You heard the story, man. You can't back out."

"I don't—"

"You unnerstand, Jimenez? You're in."

"The fuck I am!" Juan snapped, tearing away and starting for the door.

Rodriguez caught up with him and threw him against the nearest video game, scattering the group of three boys who had been trying to destroy the universe in three turns or less. With one hand on Juan's collar he groped with the other and came up with a cue stick from one of the racks on the wall. He brandished it like a sword and said, "You wanna think again, *amigo*? You don't, man, I'll kill you right now."

Juan cocked his fist to throw a quick punch, but Rodriguez blocked it with the stick before it had gone six inches.

"Think it over, Johnny. Think good. Your life depends on it. Yes, you walk outta here. No, you die. Seems pretty simple to me. But you make the call. What's it gonna be?"

Juan groaned. "Okay, fucker, okay, man, I'm in. I'll help you. Now, get away from me, will you?"

Rodriguez grinned, and the smile stretched his scars into new, surreal shapes. Instead of releasing Juan, he dragged him back over to the table and dropped him into his seat with a thud. Ricky and Buddy, who had been watching in wide-eyed fear, drew back a little from both of them.

Juan swiped one of Buddy's cigarettes and wiped a shock of black hair away from his eyes. "When?" he said. "When we gotta pull this shit?"

"Tomorrow night," Ricky said, and glanced eagerly at Rodriguez for approval. "We're gonna meet down here at one-thirty. We'll get our shit together and head over to the Joint."

"And what about the money? When am I gonna see my three hundred?"

Rodriguez glared at him. "Couple days. Soon as my old man gets the check. You just gotta be cool till then. You'll get paid."

Juan nodded. "Can I go now?"

Ricky glanced at Rodriguez, who waved tiredly with his right hand. "Get the fuck outta here, Jimenez. Just be sure you come back tomorrow."

Juan was almost to the door when Buddy called after him, "Hey, *amigo*, we gonna cool out tonight? You got any more stuff?"

Your only friends are the kind who stick around while the coke's being snorted or the wine bottles are being opened.

Or when they need something else from you, he thought. When they want you to put your ass on the line and do crazy-shit stunts.

"How 'bout it?" Buddy called. "Any more stuff?"

Juan sighed. "No, man, not tonight. I'll see you later, okay?"

Outside, it was dark and had begun to rain again.

5

Alone in the house, Phyllis wandered aimlessly upstairs and down, in and out of her bedroom, the living room, the kitchen.

You've got to leave, she told herself, you've got to get out.

Yes. Get out. But to where?

Where in the world did you go when you were young and afraid? Hadn't she already admitted that happiness elsewhere was just an illusion? Andy was gone, effectively as dead as . . . their baby. There was no relative who would take her in; the family was too tight, right down to the very last uncle and aunt. No friends would have her either, or at least her friends' parents wouldn't. And she certainly wasn't prepared for a life on the road like an anachronistic fifties beat.

Where, then?

Something in her mind whispered an answer, so softly that she couldn't hear.

She frowned.

The answer was whispered again, and she caught a piece of it. It was nothing but a fragment, really, but it was enough to get her to rise from the bed and stand in the middle of her room, listening to the voice and thinking:

If you hate your life, then seek change!

Yes, yes, the mesmerizing minister. But there was something else the voice was trying to tell her, a dim memory of

. . . what? Something she'd seen recently? Something else she'd heard, perhaps?

If you hate your life, then seek change!

Acting on impulse, she went down to the living room, crossed to the big desk her parents piled things on but seldom used, and thumbed absently through the litter of papers there. Old bills that should have been upstairs in her father's study. Old magazines and newspapers. Old fliers. Old junk mail. Contest offers and giveaway bonus opportunities stared her in the face, and still she didn't know what she was looking for.

At last her hand paused on a large business-size envelope. She tugged it free of the stack and gazed blankly at the return address: Universal Ministries, Winfield, IL. Of course. Her memory of the minister's powerful voice had brought back the memory of seeing this envelope, but what the hell did it—or that annoying ministry—have to do with the price of rice? It didn't matter if they were local celebrities or not, or how captivating their spokesman's voice had seemed to her in the hour before dawn. They were just another TV church group.

She turned the envelope over, still uncertain what it was doing in her hands in the first place. It was unopened, and half out of curiosity, half driven by that whispering voice within her, she tore it open and pulled out the collection of tracts and fliers inside. There were six in all, printed in a rainbow variety of colors. A note at the top of each read "THIS IS NOT A PLEA FOR MONEY!" in dark block letters. And although that was mildly stimulating, the messages themselves were nothing new. They extolled hope through God, faith and love and charity as solutions for all the world's problems, an end to all suffering through the works of the church. It was just as she'd thought—they had absolutely nothing to do with absolutely anything.

But before she put them away again, she found her eyes drawn to a small-print paragraph at the bottom of the final flier in the stack. She brought it closer, squinted a little, and read:

Let us state again that we do not seek financial contributions. We only want your time. We desire only to show you how the power of God's love can change your life and how you in turn can change the world. At Universal, we will give you the resources to carve a better, happier, more fulfilled life out of the residue of gloom and despair. We want to prove that God's blessing hand can touch you too. Give us that chance. Give yourself that chance. To find out more, simply write or call us at:

She crammed the tracts back into the envelope, dropped the envelope on the desk, and walked to the couch. Evening had arrived, but the living room still clung to the day's warmth. Nevertheless, she didn't feel warm at all. She felt cold. Dead. Her hatred for everything around her, for herself, still bubbled away inside.

We want to show you how the power of God's love can change your life . . .

We can't disgrace the family, Phyl . . .

. . . We will give you the resources to carve a better, happier, more fulfilled life . . .

This is Barrington, dammit, not some backwater town. Things like this don't happen here. Not to the Meyer family . . .

We only want your time . . . we want to show you how the power of God's love can change your life . . .

Come to your senses, girl!

If you hate your life, then seek change!

Come to your senses . . .

She groaned and put her hands up to her face to stop the voices. It was all nonsense, of course. But she couldn't deny that she found the very *persistence* of the thoughts tantalizing. Could it really be that rescue was so easy, so close? Could a new life really be just a few miles away? Could hope be just down the road?

A phone call would be all it would take, she supposed. One call couldn't hurt. Perhaps there would be a counselor she could talk to. Or maybe she should visit. Not a *long* visit, mind you, but a quick in and out, just to look things over, to get the lay of the land, as Andy used to say.

Andy. . . .

Before his face could rise up again, she pushed all the memories away. She might be in a turmoil of despair, of frustration and anger and a million unanswered questions, but there was one thing she knew. The past was dead. She wasn't going to get anywhere reliving a hundred yesterdays. The future. She needed to think about that. It was the only way she could get through the darkness and find some measure of light.

She closed her eyes, but opened them again almost immediately, startled. For a moment she had seen an unusual picture: the tall, handsome minister from TV had been standing over her, smiling fiercely, showing her teeth that were strong and bright and sharp and white. In the background had been a decrepit-looking house outlined against a cold night sky.

Odd, she thought, and closed her eyes again. This time there was nothing. No minister, no house. And no answer either.

"You're losing it, girl," she whispered. "Another day or two of this and it's the goddamned giggle factory for sure."

She tried to laugh, but there was no humor in her. Not then. Maybe not ever.

Desperate to come to some kind of decision, right or wrong, insightful or misguided, she got up and went back to the desk. Then she began carefully rereading each of the Universal tracts one by one.

She woke from a long, restless nap in which she had been chased by images of Andy and the gently smiling doctor. Sometimes Andy and the doctor would become one. At those times she would hear Andy's voice shrieking at her through the doctor's lips, chastising her for what she had done. At other times the doctor's face would change into the face of a full-fledged monster. As the flesh ran down the monster's face like melting wax, as the dark eyes rolled crazily and the bestial teeth glinted in the bright dream-light that permeated the room, the monster would laugh and say, "A decision, Phyllis. You've got to make one soon. Now. You've got to decide now."

Dream or not, she knew the monster was right. Soon she would have to go back to school, back into the routine of classes and the debate team and the drama club and fluffing her hair and straightening the hem of her uniform skirt without even being aware that she was doing it. Back to looking her best for boys she would never be interested in, doing her best for teachers she hated.

And she knew that if she went back to class she would never escape.

The knowledge came to her in a blinding flash of incontrovertible logic.

If she went back to school it would be the end of everything.

She went to her dresser and picked up the envelope she had hidden there earlier. The bold return address stared at her temptingly. She pulled the fliers out of the envelope and flicked on the overhead light so that she could read them, look again at all the propaganda and promises.

Well, it was better than nothing, wasn't it? For God's sake, *wasn't* it? It was escape, or at the very least a doorway that would open the way to an escape. A fresh start in another part of the country, in Europe or Asia or Africa, or even right here in Chicago. A chance to forget, an opportunity to wipe the slate clean. A chance to do something good for a change and possibly even atone for the murder in which she had played the pivotal role.

But you don't *believe*!

That was the same argument she'd been coming up with repeatedly. She didn't believe the propaganda. Jesus saves—crap. God is love—bullshit. The strength of youth is the answer to the world's problems—leftover sixties rhetoric and about as relevant today as granny glasses.

She grimaced and dropped the fliers on the dresser. Either way, stay or go, it meant compromising principles. It was just a matter of picking the lesser of the evils. Staying meant God knew how many more months of hating herself, her life. And going meant putting up with born-again chatter day after day. But it also meant hav-

ing at least a small chance to reshape her life according to
her own mold.

"Ha-ha," she murmured. "No contest."

And before her parents could return from their evening round of fund-raisers, Phyllis packed a suitcase and
slipped it neatly beneath the flounce of her bed.

6

Curt was dreaming about a huge room where the walls glowed with unearthly green fire and sounds echoed trickily, confusing and frightening him—when voices in the corridor woke him. He sat up in bed, feeling as though his heart had been jump-started after a long period of dormancy. He blinked at his surroundings and found himself looking directly at the portrait of Arthur Tallman Bach hanging near the door. The minister gazed back at him serenely, wise and ageless, handsome and proud.

Curt's mouth opened and a strangled word found its way out—*fuh*.

He had slept most of yesterday away, awakening once in midafternoon, dozing again for several more hours, and not fully rising until almost dinnertime. Then, suddenly afraid of being in Chicago and having to face up to things at last, he had opted not to go out. Instead he had remained in his room, unpacking, munching the last several candy bars left from the snack bar in La Guardia, and doing just what he was doing now—staring at the picture on the wall and wondering if coming here had been the right thing to do.

Well, of course the decision had really been made long ago. For some reason, the memory of that decision seemed vague and clouded, hard to focus in on, but he remembered pounding heat, anger, and finally a heartbreaking kind of sad resignation. Where had he been at the time? Which stop on his long, long journey?

He studied the picture of Arthur Bach carefully. Perhaps it was a trick of the distance as he looked at Bach from across the room, or maybe it was his drowsy state, but suddenly the reverend didn't appear to be smiling. Suddenly he didn't look so stunningly youthful. Curt saw jagged wrinkles creasing the minister's face, saw deeply sunken eyes above heavy pouches of dark flesh, saw teeth that were chipped and brown.

He shook his head and went into the bathroom, where he tried to clear his mind by taking a very quick, very cold shower. When he came out, he heard soft voices arguing just outside his door. He quickly pulled on his jeans and went out, his damp towel still clenched in his right hand.

Two young men, one black, one white, were hurrying up the corridor toward the elevators, speaking in tense whispers. When they heard Curt's door, they hesitated and turned around.

"Didn't wake you up, did we?" the black man said. He was short and stocky, wearing vivid blue running shorts and a red shirt.

Curt shook his head. "Just got out of the shower."

"Well, hello." They came back toward him, hands extended and smiles spreading across their faces. "You must be a newcomer."

"That's what Mr. Cummings kept calling me, but I'll tell you, it kind of makes me feel like a kid on his first day of school."

The black man laughed. "The new twerp on the block. I know what you mean. Well, new twerp, my name's Brad Taylor. And this idiot"—he jerked a thumb at his companion—"is Scott Matheson."

"Curt Potter, nice to meet you."

Matheson, who was tall, skinny, and had a scruffy brown beard, said, "Where're you from, Curt?"

Curt shrugged and said evasively, "All over, really. What about you?"

"Elizabeth." He saw Curt's bafflement and laughed. "Don't tell me you've never heard of it? My God, none of the cretins around here knows anything about geography. Elizabeth, my friend, is without a doubt the definitive southern small town. Elizabeth, West Virginia."

"Didn't I tell you he was an idiot?" Taylor said. "Now, me, on the other hand, I'm from a place no one in the world's ever heard of. It's a mythical spot nestled at the crux of three mythical rivers. In other words, Pittsburgh."

Curt laughed. "Have you been here long?"

"Almost a year," Taylor said. "We got here late last fall. Both of us rolled in within a week of each other. That's how I got stuck with this bearded fool. The big dreamer."

"It was not a dream," Matheson said. "Didn't I tell you—"

"Hey," Taylor said, cutting him off, "we don't need to air our dirty laundry for the newcomers, now, do we?" He turned to Curt. "Actually, we get along famously. Never had a bad word—well, hardly ever. We even work together, in the print shop. I taught him everything he knows. Seriously, I used to be a graphic-arts professor at Pitt before I came here."

Curt nodded, surprised and a little impressed. "How did a graphic-arts professor end up at—"

"That's a story for another day. Besides, if we don't get our butts down to breakfast, we're going to be late for work. Stop by and see us anytime. It's room 1297."

The three of them exchanged a few more pleasantries before breaking up. Curt was amused to hear them resume their argument before they'd gotten ten feet away. He heard Scott Matheson saying, "It was real, Brad. I swear to God it really happened," and then they were out of earshot.

Curt returned to his room, still a little confused. He was ready to begin his mission, but not sure how to go about it. The picture of Arthur Bach drew his attention once again, just as it always would, he supposed. The picture looked normal this time, which didn't surprise him in the least. He recognized the illusion earlier as just what it was—a trick of distance. The face in the portrait smiled at him with its incredible teeth and airbrush-clear eyes.

Curt swallowed.

"Arthur Tallman Bach," he said. "I'm finally here, you grade-A son of a bitch."

When he answered the knock at his door a short time later, he found himself looking up at an enormous black man with a phantasmagorical nimbus of hair and one of the most infectious grins he had ever seen. The man was at least six and a half feet tall, to Curt's own five-eleven, and had forearms that were bigger than Curt's thighs. His cotton tank-top bore the legend "GOD'S ARMY BOWS TO NONE" in threatening red letters, below which was a mammoth fist clenching a yellow lightning bolt.

"Curt Potter?"

"Yes."

"Good to meetcha. I'm Connie Bishop."

Curt laughed and repeated, "Connie?"

"Yeah, yeah, tell me about it, why doncha? It's short for . . . you ready? Cornelius. That's my folks and their wonderful sense of humor. They wanted a son with a distinctive name.

"I'm your tour guide. Ernie said he looked in on you a couple of times yesterday, but you were dead to the world. He figured you needed your rest, so he told me to take you around this morning. You want to start with breakfast?"

Curt nodded. "I'm starving."

They started toward the elevators, Curt struggling to keep up with Bishop's strides. "How long have you been in the church?"

Bishop chuckled, and his belly shook dramatically. "Well, now. That's a tough one. Off and on, I guess it's been eight years." He sighed. "See, I came here after two years in the Marines. I'd planned on making a career of the service, but they booted me out because of a heart murmur those genius doctors missed when I went in. Tiny little murmur, a *murmur* of a murmur.

"I'd never been religious, not really. I was like a lot of the folks here. I came because I didn't have anything else at the time. My parents were dead, I didn't have a girl, and I sure didn't have a job. So I just knocked on those gates out there and told them to let me in."

They had reached the lobby level and they stepped out into a room that barely resembled the one that Curt had seen early yesterday morning. There were people everywhere, some huddled together and speaking in hushed voices, others running to and fro with folders or stacks of loose papers or Bibles clenched under their arms. Phones were ringing from out-of-sight offices and there was Muzak playing over a sound system. A semi-trailer was pulled up to the front doors, and four or five teenagers were helping the bearded driver unload a mountain of plain brown cartons.

"This way," Bishop said, leading him toward an arrow that said CAFETERIA.

As Bishop continued his story, Curt jogged to catch up and stayed on the big man's heels.

"I stayed about a year that first time. Actually, I guess it was closer to eighteen months. But every once in a while I'd get the feeling that, great as this place was, it wasn't the be-all and end-all. You know what I mean? I lit out and traveled around, looking for something else." He paused in both his speech and his steps, looking at Curt closely. "Three times," he said.

"I beg your pardon?"

"Three times," he repeated. "I left Universal three times in eight years. Restless, I guess. That and the fact that I'm a plain fool."

"You always came back, though."

"Oh, yeah," Bishop said with another chuckle. "I always came back, just like the prodigal. I think I finally learned, Curt, my friend. There is no place like Universal. No place. I'm here for good this time. Been here ten months and I'll be staying. These people care. They love. This place is the best. And remember where you heard that first."

Curt looked into the big man's face, studied the intent, sincere, powerful expression, and did the only thing he could. He smiled and nodded slowly.

*   *   *

They ate in the biggest cafeteria Curt had ever seen. They worked their way through a slow-moving serving line where young people in white aprons ladled out big helpings of omelets and pancakes, hash browns, fresh fruit, oatmeal, bacon, and sausage, and then made their way through a set of wooden double doors and into the dining area. Before choosing a seat, they stopped at a fresh juice bar, lined with every thing from orange to papaya juice. Then they worked their way through a throng of people and found an unoccupied round table for four.

The room was the size of a small football stadium, Curt decided. One wall was entirely made of glass, showing a shaded lawn in which trees were just starting to show the first traces of fall color. There were perhaps five or six hundred people eating breakfast, and damn near all of them were under the age of thirty.

"Big crowd," he remarked.

"Got to have a full stomach to do the Lord's work," Bishop said happily, stuffing half a pancake into his mouth. "Now, come on, eat up. You've got a big tour ahead of you."

Curt dug in, surprised to realize that he hadn't eaten anything but Hershey Bars since leaving New York. Still, he ate slowly, distracted by gazing around at the huge high-ceilinged room and the crowd of people contained in it. Most of them looked as carefree as his guide, and were eating in groups ranging from three to ten or more. But the longer he looked, the more he began to notice others who sat alone and did not look happy or carefree at all. Some of these looked incredibly tired. A few looked flat-out sick. Some were unkempt, with messy hair and dirty clothes, while others had untied shoes and unbuttoned shirts, as though they had forgotten how to dress themselves.

Were they all newcomers? he wondered. Were they people like Martha Zinn, lost in their own private worlds of trouble? Or were some of them long-term residents who had for one reason or another grown disenchanted with Arthur Tallman Bach's movement? Connie Bishop had come and gone three times in eight years. Suddenly he wondered what the church burn-out rate was.

"Eat up, eat up," his guide urged him again. Curt looked up and noticed that Bishop's plate was practically licked clean. He had to forgo gazing around the cafeteria and hurry to catch up, but even so, those defeated faces kept drawing his attention.

7

They toured Van Paris Hall first. Connie Bishop showed him the lounges and game rooms, the three rooms full of Westinghouse washers and dryers, the conference halls, the smaller rooms where weekly prayer groups met, and the corridor full of offices with names like Housing and Transportation and Personnel. Most of them, Bishop explained, were satellite operations for the larger offices housed across the compound in the Faith Center.

"Impressive," Curt said at one point.

Bishop threw back his head, shaking that unbelievable halo of hair, and said, "You ain't seen nothing yet, Curt, m'man. You just wait."

Outside, they took a small footpath surfaced with cedar chips and lined with manicured flowerbeds. It meandered southwesterly, taking them from the Hall into the forest.

"It's amazing," Curt said, gesturing at the trees but meaning the compound in general. "It has to be outrageously expensive to maintain an operation like this."

"Oh, it is. You'd better believe it, my friend. But we don't fund-raise. We do it with numbers. Do you realize we've got a worldwide church membership of over six hundred and fifty thousand people? Some are just casual members, sure, but most are actively giving of their time and their love and asking nothing in return."

"Still," Curt said suspiciously, "you can't buy food for the hungry with just love. Or pay for television satellite links. Or heat Van Paris Hall."

"No, that's true. The fact is, we've been blessed with some generous private donations. Do you know that this entire compound was built by a man named Richard Van Paris?"

"Cummings told me."

"Twenty years ago he was just a guy who'd made a fortune in machinery manufacturing. Then he met Reverend Bach and turned his life over to the church. Gave Universal the land and built the buildings. There are other folks like that in Chicago, and maybe fifty or sixty others around the world. People who came to us of their own free will and gave to us out of love.

"And I'll be honest with you, Curt. When you're not on the tube twenty-four hours a day screaming about financial emergencies and begging for nickels and dimes from little old ladies, you'd be surprised how many people come forward and give anyway, all on their own."

Curt nodded thoughtfully. "The membership is mostly young people," he said, more a comment than a question.

"That's right. It's our programs that draw them. We don't stand up and say, 'Hey, dope addict, hey, alcoholic, hey, poor boy, you'd better hit your knees and accept Jesus as your personal savior or you ain't going to heaven.' We tell them, 'Give us your time, do something for other people, reach out, and help the struggler behind you, the cripple next to you. *Then* you'll turn your life around and feel God's love come back to you tenfold.' " He grinned. "The evangelicals and the fundamentalists hate us for it, and those same little old ladies who sign their welfare checks over to Brother Billy Bob from Tuscaloosa turn us off in droves. But young people, guys like you and me, Curt, we go for it. It's the philosophy that draws us in and keeps us. Work for the good stuff. Work for God. Work for your pitiful brothers. Earn your own blessings."

The trees began to thin out, and suddenly they were standing at the edge of a huge natural bowl set into the earth. Placed into its sides were long wooden benches, amphitheater style. From the valley floor rose two magnificent spruce trees, one on either side of a simple wooden stage beneath an impressive beam-supported roof. On the stage was an altar, and next to the altar a large pulpit, a multilevel platform that looked like a bandstand, and several rows of choir benches.

"This is Worship Park," Bishop said. "It's only one of three outdoor churches in the compound, but it's the biggest—seating almost a thousand. Almost everyone comes here whenever they can, when the weather's being cooperative, that is."

"It's very nice," Curt said.

And he *was* impressed. But his mind was still tracking along other lines, thinking about bigshot tycoon donors and stooping to help your poorer brother when you saw him in the road.

"That's all?" Bishop said. "Just nice? C'mon, Curt, m'man, you've got to be kidding! It's beautiful!"

"Okay," Curt said, smiling. "It's beautiful, then. Do you have to go to church a lot?"

"You don't have to do anything you don't want to. There're fifteen services a week around the compound, one a day Monday through Friday, and five each Saturday and Sunday. But there's no attendance rule, if that's what you mean."

"Actually, I don't think I'd mind coming to church *here* at all." He looked at the long benches, the simple but somehow elegant stage, and nodded thoughtfully.

Bishop clapped him on the back. "Atta boy. How about coming with me this Sunday?"

"I . . . okay, sure. Yeah. I think I'd like that." He paused a moment, startled, and then repeated, "I'd really like that."

An hour later they had toured the massive library and the Prayer Center, housing the headquarters of Universal's various outreach ministries—including free health clinics, food distribution programs, drug and alcohol counseling centers, rape and runaway hotlines, child and spouse abuse centers, and family planning organizations. They had also toured the headquarters of God's Hand International, the radio and television arms of the movement, plus two other churches, and a half-dozen smaller buildings that contained incoming and outgoing mail centers, printing shops, and data-entry/bookkeeping offices.

At last they came to the highlight of the tour. As Curt

looked at it, his breath caught in his throat. He knew immediately why Bishop had saved it for last.

The Faith Center was a work of art clearly calculated to make even the most jaded philistine weak in the knees. Composed of three eighteen-story glass towers, it was linked in the center by an enclosed atrium decorated with immense trees, ornate shrubbery, and marble fountains and statuary. At least two of the fountains had exotic fish swimming in them. Overhead, a huge mobile sculpture spun slowly, powered by a noiseless motor.

Curt and Connie stood in the center of the atrium, amid the babbling waters and hundreds of people scurrying about, and looked past the sculpture, through the skylight, to the towers above them.

"I . . . can't believe it," Curt said.

Bishop tossed out another of his rich, rolling laughs. "This baby houses one hundred fifty offices, two full-size churches, five or six lecture halls, twenty conference rooms, a twin-screen movie theater, an auditorium, a huge reference library, I don't know how many bathrooms, sixteen—"

"Okay, okay," Curt said, grinning. "I get the idea. Whoever built it didn't mess around, did they?"

"Not hardly. It was put up in 1970. By that time, Richard Van Paris was Reverend Bach's second in command, and the two of them supervised the construction together. The way I hear it, they worked around the clock, all the contractors and crews pulling double shifts. There's a story about trying to mount the big cross on top in the middle of a thunderstorm. It—"

"Is Bach's office here in the Center?" Curt said. He was no longer really listening to Bishop, but was gazing at a series of directories and color-coded maps mounted under glass and erected on a small platform near one of the fountains.

"Uh-huh. He's got the penthouse on the eighteenth floor of A-tower. Got the whole floor, as a matter of fact."

"I suppose it's kind of hard to get an appointment?"

Bishop frowned momentarily, then shrugged. "I don't want to discourage you if you've got your heart set on it, but it's tough. First of all, the man's on the road most of the time. It's hard to know when he's even in town. And

I hear his appointment calendar is booked at least a year in advance. Personally, I don't even *know* anyone who's been able to get on the calendar. You could try, but . . ." He trailed off with yet another shrug.

"Who do you go to, then? If you want to see someone in charge, I mean."

"Well, usually Ernie Cummings or one of the RL's—resident liaisons. If you need to see a pastor, there's Reverend Welles or Reverend Tupper. You might—and I do mean might—even be able to see Reverend Bob or Reverend Norris. But I wouldn't go wagering good money on the fact."

"I'd really like to see Bach," Curt murmured, so softly that his words were swallowed by the hum and babble of activity inside the Faith Center's atrium.

"What's that?"

He turned to Connie Bishop. "Nothing. I didn't say a thing."

Bishop studied him uneasily. "We probably ought to get you back to the Hall. We'll stop in Ernie's office, and I'll get you a list of compound services and phone numbers, so you can find things when you need them."

Curt nodded. "Good idea."

"Come to think of it, I might even be able to round up a little pocket map for you to carry around with you, while you get used to things."

Curt glanced at the color-coded maps, at the atrium, and out the big glass doors at the rest of the compound, where no fewer than twelve paths went off in different directions. "Make that an excellent idea," he said.

8

Ernest Cummings saw the girl as he approached the gate. She was a pretty girl—nineteen? no older than that— wearing a white sweater and a flattering yellow skirt. She was standing there with two red suitcases next to her on the ground. He rolled to a stop beside her and cranked down the window.

"Good morning!"

She looked up, and he noticed that her pretty face was streaked with tears; her eyes were red and puffy and a bit fearful.

"Do you . . . do you work in there?"

"Sure do. What do you need?"

She held a piece of paper that he recognized immediately as the print shop's most recent direct-mail flier. "I got this a while back. Or rather my . . . my p-parents got it." She paused, glancing down at the ground. When she looked up again there was a flash of newfound determination in her eyes. "I want to help the church."

Cummings grinned. "What's your name?"

"Phyllis Meyer. I'm from Barrington."

"A hometown girl! Well, c'mon aboard, Phyllis. Climb in back with the others and we'll take you in."

He watched her in the rearview mirror as she opened the sliding panel on the side of the van and crawled in beside the two black teenagers he'd just picked up at the bus station.

"Phyllis Meyer, meet George and Paul Friday, from Detroit. They're newcomers too."

He put the van in gear and drove through the gate. As he negotiated the wide, sweeping curves of the road that led back and forth across the sprawling compound, he felt the familiar swell of pride that always overtook him after an unexpected batch of newcomers arrived. The schedule in his office had listed the first arrivals coming into Midway Airport at one-twenty-five that afternoon, but then they'd received the surprise call from George Friday and his younger brother. And now, on the way home, this pretty girl from Barrington. He knew that there were different ways of gauging the church's success— the number of phone calls received on the various hotlines, the ratings of the televised crusades, the dollars that came into the mailroom—but to him the standard was always the same: the number of newcomers. The newcomers meant that the word was being spread, and they meant that Universal was accomplishing precisely what it had always set out to accomplish, namely, helping people find a better life.

"My name's Ernest Cummings," he told the girl. "I'm director of housing for the church, so I'll be the one who finds you a room and sets up your tour of the compound. Also, I'm the one to come to if you've got any problems. I probably can't answer all your questions, but I can point you to someone who can."

He glanced into the rearview mirror and saw the girl nod.

"How old are you, Phyllis?"'

She hesitated. "S-seventeen. Does it matter?"

"Not at all. Do your parents know you're here?"

Another, longer pause. "Nooooo," she said at last. "But you won't send me back, will you?"

"Don't worry, we'd never do that. And no more questions, I promise. You're with us now. Once you roll through our gate, your past is irrelevant."

He thought he heard her utter a long sigh of relief, and then Van Paris Hall was looming in front of them. He swung into the circular drive, eased up in front of the glass doors, and cut the engine.

Looking over his shoulder at the three newcomers, he smiled at them, pointed to the Hall, and said just one word: "Home."

*   *   *

When Cummings got back to his office, he smiled at Kelly Beckworth, a recent arrival from Detroit who had been his secretary for the last eight weeks.

"Hi, Kel. Any messages?"

"Just one. Reverend Bob's back from Korea. He wants to see you ASAP."

Cummings frowned. If Bob Kaye was back from the Far East already, that meant his trip had been less than successful—he hadn't been due to return until the second week of October—and if the trip hadn't been successful, he was not looking forward at all to meeting with the man.

"I'll head over in a few minutes. Did he say what he wanted?"

Kelly Beckworth shook her head. "Nope. Just that he wanted to see you—"

"ASAP, I know." He turned toward his inner office, but said, "Thanks, Kel. God bless you."

The secretary smiled. "God bless *you*, Ernie!"

After a big breakfast and a tour conducted by a girl named Peggy Huett, Phyllis was left alone in her new room on the sixth floor. Her roommates, Carole Vance and Paula Harpool, were off at work, so she unpacked her bags, putting her things away carefully, and still wondering if she had really made the right choice.

So far her impressions of Universal Ministries were favorable. The people she'd met seemed friendly enough. The size of the compound had been a bit of a surprise, Van Paris Hall made an impressive dormitory, and the Faith Center with its glass towers and atrium had been nothing short of spectacular.

And yet she was still doubtful.

She finished unpacking and went down to the cafeteria for a Coke. With everyone working, the Hall seemed eerily quiet. The only people she saw were several kids in white shirts and aprons wiping down the long cafeteria tables and sweeping the tile floor, getting ready for the lunch crowd.

She filled a large paper cup with ice and soda and chose a table off to one side of the big room, wondering if she had made the right choice in coming here. The church seemed like salvation and damnation at the same

time and she couldn't help worrying about how long she
would last. All too easily she could picture a day when
she would return to Barrington with her suitcases in hand
and her head hung low, begging her parents' forgiveness.

No, she thought. Not that. Never.

Still, the possibility was lodged firmly in her mind and
it frightened her.

"Hi there. You look a little down."

She glanced up at the man standing next to her table.
He was tall and thin, with light brown hair and a thin,
scraggly beard.

"I guess I am. Just . . . thinking."

"Need some company?"

She thought about it, and said, "Yeah, I guess so."

He put his coffee cup down and sat next to her. "My
name's Scott Matheson. Let me guess. You're a newcomer, right?"

"How'd you know that?"

"Simple: the newer the person, the more depressed
they look. It's like a rule of thumb. But don't worry, it's
guaranteed to pass. What's your name?"

"Phyllis Meyer."

"Former home?"

"Barrington."

"Oh, yeah? Isn't that in England someplace?"

She couldn't help smiling. "It's about twenty miles
north of here."

"Ooops. I'm from West Virginia myself. You know,
mountain mama, John Denver, and all that. You mind if
I ask why you're here?"

She found it shockingly easy to say, "My parents."

"Couldn't get along, huh? There's a lot of that around
here. When I was a little kid, the guys on the news used
to call it the generation gap. I haven't heard that term in
years, but I still believe in it. Sometimes I think ninety
percent of the people stuck on the young side of the gap
end up right here at Universal."

"No!" she said, immediately realizing that she'd said it
too quickly, too emphatically. "It wasn't that—it wasn't
just that."

Scott smiled. "You don't have to tell me if you don't

want to, but we're all here to help each other, Phyllis. Sometimes talking about things can . . . well, you know."

She nursed her Coke and thought that the cafeteria was suddenly as quiet as the far corner of a forgotten graveyard. The clankings and bangings from the kitchen sounded light-years away.

"How come you're not working?" she said.

He laughed. "Touché. I knocked off early, actually. I didn't sleep real well last night. I had a bad dream—I've been having them for the last week or so. I decided I better take a day to rest up, or I wouldn't be any good to anyone."

They were silent for a moment. He studied her closely until she turned away from his gaze.

"Don't."

"Aw, come on, try me. I'm a damn good listener, Phyllis. Really."

"I don't—"

"Don't give me that. I'd break the ice by telling you my story, but it's really exceedingly dull. It all goes back to the magic day when I received my final divorce decree and my pink slip within an hour of each other. But you, now . . . I think you have a real tale to tell."

"Don't bet on it."

He shrugged. "I'm not a betting man anyway. But I still want to hear it."

"You're sure?"

"Yeah. If you want to tell me."

"And if I don't?"

He wiped a drop of coffee from his upper lip. "I guess I'd just go back to my room and try to catch some Z's."

She sighed. She wanted to tell him, but dammit, she just didn't know how safe it was. If she kept the story to herself, she was going to lose the friendship of this man before it had even started. Yet if she told him everything, she would leave herself exposed and vulnerable.

He raised his eyebrows and cocked his head to one side. "Well?"

She took a deep breath and suddenly chopped through the Gordian knot with one swift, vicious stroke.

"I had an abortion."

There, it was out. That black, dread word had spilled from her lips. It was out, and Christ, she actually felt better.

But if Scott Matheson was shocked or dismayed, he gave no indication. In fact, his expression never changed.

"Did you hear me? I told you I had an abortion."

"I heard you."

"Well?"

"Well, what? What do you want me to say? It's not exactly the news of the world, you know. There are at least a hundred girls here in the Hall who've had abortions, most of them younger than you. Big story. You got knocked up, had an abortion, and ran away before your parents found out. You didn't want them to know your—"

"No! It wasn't like that!"

"Oh? What was it like?"

She started to defend herself, but suddenly couldn't find the words. What was wrong with him, anyway? First he treated her kindly, applying the grease, and when she finally summoned the courage to tell him, he turned on her.

"Well? What was it like?"

"You bastard! You don't even care about me. You don't care that I wanted to keep the baby, that Andy and I were in love and wanted to work everything out. You don't care that my parents made me get that abortion, that they forced me. You don't care that I lost Andy. You don't care about any of that, do you?"

"I don't know," Scott Matheson said. "Do I care?"

"Ohhhhh, you are a bastard! You're just like everyone else. I wanted that baby, dammit, and I wanted Andy. Now I don't have anyone. I don't have a goddamn thing, and you don't give a fuck! You lousy son of a bitch!"

He reached out to hold her. She melted, sagging against his shoulder while the tears exploded from deep inside her. He nestled her head gently and stroked her hair.

"It's okay," he crooned. "It's all right, Phyllis. You lost something and you hurt. You're breaking up inside. But that's okay. We all have to lose something before we come here—that's why we come. But it's okay, we all care here. I care. I really do."

She tried to raise her head, but it came up only an inch or so before sagging back against the hollow of his shoulder. He held her tightly as she continued to weep, allowing the light cotton of his shirt to absorb the tears and the pain.

"Hey, now," he said after many minutes had passed. "Hey, Phyllis, are you all right?"

This time she succeeded in raising her head and looking at him. Her eyes were puffy and red. She nodded weakly. "I . . . I'm okay."

He smiled. "What do you say we take a walk and chew this thing over some more?"

She sniffed. "What about your rest?"

"Heck, I can rest anytime."

"You're s-sure?"

"Of course. Would I lie to you, Phyllis? Would . . . Hey, look, do you mind if I call you Phyl? No offense, but the name Phyllis gives me the holy shivers."

She smiled, hesitated a moment, and then surprised herself by laughing. "Sure, go ahead. Call me Phyl."

"Okay, Phyl, how about it? Does a walk sound nice?"

"Yeah," she said, nodding. "A walk sounds real nice."

9

Cummings wasn't surprised to find his palms sweaty and the back of his neck crawling. Waiting before the Reverend Robert Kaye's reception desk always did that to him. The receptionist, not a newcomer like many of the compound secretaries and phone jockeys, but a veteran who had been with Reverend Bob almost from the start, hung up her Merlin desk phone and said, "You can go in now."

Cummings thanked her and slipped through the heavy oak-paneled door that led into the inner domain.

"You wanted to see me, Reverend?"

Kaye bounded to his feet, his improbable silver hair bobbing and the heavy cross around his neck swinging from side to side. "Ernie! My number-one man! It's good to see you! Real good! How've you been?" His voice was deep and enthusiastic—not the rich, practiced voice that captivated so many television viewers and brought so many newcomers into the church folds, but still powerful and commanding.

"I'm fine, Reverend. Busy but fine."

"Good, good. Have a seat." He motioned to the large padded swivel chair in front of his desk. "Coffee? I can have Bernice bring some in."

"No . . . no, thanks."

Cummings looked around at the office, which despite his discomfort during these visits never failed to amaze him. The walls were mahogany. Kaye's big desk was walnut and always clean except for an In/Out basket, which invariably had at least one neat stack of papers in it, and the reverend's own Merlin phone unit. Behind the desk was an entire wall of books, which wrapped around the corner and extended most of the way down the side wall as well. Where the bookshelves stopped were two ornate wooden filing cabinets and a buffet that held a Mr. Coffee—something Cummings had always thought odd, since Bernice brewed all his coffee out in the reception area. Finally, on the opposite side of the room, was Reverend Bob's trophy case with his impressive array of plaques and awards—from Little League trophies to plaques awarded by Rotary clubs all over America for services to youth or to the religious community.

"So how're things in the Hall?" Kaye asked him.

"Not bad. Actually, considering we haven't had a crusade in three weeks, it's been surprisingly good. Nineteen newcomers since Monday. And at least three that we know of coming in today."

"Excellent! Anything else to report?"

Cummings shrugged. "Not really. There's a cold bug around, so I've been making most of the pickup runs myself. One of the microwaves in the cafeteria went down yesterday, but that's taken care of. Ditto the HVAC this morning." He searched his memory for other information that might interest the reverend, but came up empty. "That's about it. How was Seoul?"

"Seoul, Ernie? Seoul was a bear trap. About what I expected, actually, but still a disappointment."

"Why? I don't understand."

Kaye shrugged. "Who does? If I had all the answers, there wouldn't be any problems, would there? The government's been cracking down on us for some time. Making trouble for our missions and street workers. Two of them are in jail right now. They've been rotting in a little cell for the last month and a half, and there's nothing the American ambassador or I can do to spring them. And do you know what the charge is, Ernie?"

Cummings frowned and, after a moment, shook his head.

"Sedition. Conspiracy to commit treason against the

Korean people. Have you ever heard such—I'm sorry—such bullshit in your life? They're political prisoners, plain and simple. And South Korea is supposed to be an ally." He grimaced. "But I've got happier things on my mind right now."

Cummings drew a deep breath. "Yes?"

"Yes, Ernie, very happy things. Steve Norris picked me up at the airport last night. He and I were chatting, talking about this and that. Your name came up, Ernie."

"My name?" Cummings repeated. He felt childishly foolish, wondering what Reverend Kaye and Reverend Norris could possibly have had to say about him.

Kaye nodded. "He told me you have an anniversary coming up."

Cummings stared at him blankly.

"Your sixth anniversary with the church and your third as director of housing. I think you know what an important milestone that is. I also hope you realize that there's no way any of us in charge can ever repay such dedication and devotion." He slid open his top desk drawer, reached inside, and extracted a plain white envelope. "But we'd like to try." He handed the envelope to Cummings. "We'd like to offer this as at least a small token of our gratitude."

Thoroughly befuddled, Cummings turned the envelope over in his trembling hands. Then he tore it open and pulled out a Universal Ministries check for five thousand dollars. He stared at it for several moments, trying to get all the zeroes straight in his mind, looking at the two words printed on the stub in the light dot-matrix typeface of the accounting department's computer system. "Performance Bonus," those words said, but they might as well have been in a foreign language for all the sense they made to him. He looked up at Kaye and tried to speak.

"No thanks necessary, Ernie. We don't dish out bonuses lightly around here; I think you know that. They only go to the most deserving members of the flock."

"But—"

"And there's more. Effective on your anniversary date, Steve and I are going to put you on the regular payroll. It won't be a lot to start with, but it'll be something. We feel—"

"Payroll?" Cummings said, having as much difficulty assimilating the meaning behind the term as he was understanding the check itself.

"Yes. You'll be drawing a salary. About time, don't you agree?"

"But that wouldn't be right," he managed to say. His hands were now shaking so badly that the check was like a wounded bird fluttering helplessly in his grasp.

Kaye frowned. "What do you mean, right? All the top people in the movement draw salaries. I do, as I'm sure you know. Steve Norris does. Richard Van Paris does too, and Jim Welles, and of course the Master."

"Reverend Bach?"

"Who else? Now, we've talked it over and it's final. I understand that it may take some getting used to, but—"

"Getting used to? That's an understatement." Cummings had never even dreamed of drawing a paycheck before. Like the kids who roomed in the Hall, like the thousands of street workers around the world, like the ninety-nine percent majority of church members, he had always worked for room and board alone. That had always been the way, and it had always been enough. "I don't think I could ever, ever accept money from the church."

"But the work you do, Ernie—"

"What work? I don't do that much work. You and Reverend Norris, you're the ones who really hustle. You bring the people here. I just get them settled and make sure they're comfortable."

Kaye flashed a sad, sardonic grin. "Good God, Ernie, give yourself some credit. You do much more than that. You keep Van Paris Hall running smoothly. You trouble-shoot more than anyone I know. You're in that crummy office of yours . . . What? Twelve hours a day? Fifteen? You fill in where and when you're needed. Didn't you just say you were making airport runs again? Doing the work of newcomers?"

"But I enjoy all that. I'm not doing it for money."

Kaye sighed. "A paycheck doesn't change anything. It

doesn't make you any less of a true believer. You're management, Ernie, and you deserve to be treated as such."

"But I'm not like the rest of management, Reverend Bob. I don't live off-compound. I don't travel. I live in the Hall. I live with the kids, and I think I ought to live *like* the kids!"

"You're really serious about this," Kaye said. He tented his fingers together and flexed them. "Such a small thing, and yet you're so serious."

Cummings nodded. "It's a matter of principle. It's important to me."

"But we want you to accept—"

"No. I don't think so."

"Will you at least think about it? Will you do that much for us?"

"I don't—"

"Take a few days and study all the angles. Talk to Steve or Jim, if you like. And while you're at it, think about your future, and what a paycheck might mean in that light. I believe you'll see where we're coming from."

"Well . . ."

"That's my last word, Ernie. For today, take the bonus check. For tomorrow, think about what we've discussed."

"I suppose I could think it over."

Kaye stood up. "Wonderful. Take all the time you need. Your anniversary's still a little ways off, and I'm leaving again tomorrow for the Kansas City Crusade. I'll call you when I get back, and you can give me your answer. Until then, just keep up the good work."

Ernest Cummings smiled. The smile was very, very thin. "Yes sir," he said. "I'll try."

10

The face pressed against the driver's window was only that of some sick junkie. His hair was wet and straggling, his eyes glazed over, his hand out for any offering that might come his way, but when Juan awoke from the dreamy half-sleep he'd been drifting in, he thought for a moment that it was some kind of horrible gargoyle come to rip him to pieces. When he calmed down enough to realize the truth, he flipped the junkie the bird. The junkie shrugged and shambled off.

"Jeezus," he breathed. "Fuckin' bum."

He closed his eyes again.

It was nightfall. Since leaving the Hideaway the evening before, he had just been sitting here in his car, wishing for a cigarette, staring out the windows at the rusty dumpsters and dented garbage cans at the end of the cul-de-sac, thinking about arson and about the rest of his life.

Okay, so maybe that bastard Pritikin was right. Maybe his life wasn't so great. Maybe his friends weren't the best. But what could he do about it? Sit in church for the rest of his life and listen to righteous assholes like Pritikin? That seemed even worse than what he had now.

God is a crutch.

Hadn't he seen that somewhere? Spray-painted on the side of a building? It was true. God was just a crutch, an escape. The streets were reality, and reality, as his mother had said so often during her year-long fight with lymphatic cancer, was a hard teacher. The trick lay in becoming a good student, learning your lessons well, and being handed as little punishment as possible. Running to God only let you take a leave of absence. Sooner or later, you had to drag your ass back to your desk and open your school books again.

He sighed. He had been dragged into an arson ring. His previous record consisted of little things—two minor-in-possessions, three or four violations of curfew (read: sleeping in your car at the end of a dead-end street). None of that held a candle to Rodriguez's *loco* plan. If he was nailed for arson, he could be sent away. He knew a lot of guys who looked on a jail term as a way to escape the streets for a while, to get regular hot meals all the time and color TV when you were good. Ha-ha. The joke was that, just like running away with God, going to jail did nothing to eliminate your eventual return.

Arson was bad shit, and he was not a bad kid. Not basically. He was a good kid who was lost and . . . afraid.

"Yes," he murmured.

Afraid.

Afraid not just of Peter Rodriguez's arson plan, but afraid of his entire life, afraid *for* his life, afraid every time he walked down the street. He was afraid of his future.

He closed his eyes, willing those terrible thoughts away. He would come through all right. He had to keep telling himself that. He would be okay. He was a Jimenez. He was a street kid, and good street kids found a way to get through the shit, to snatch at least something positive from the pile of crap that the ball-breaking bitch of a teacher kept shoving at them.

It was still raining, and the steady drumming of the drops on the Chevy's hardtop lulled him back into an uncertain, uneasy sleep.

Juan stepped into the Hideaway at two a.m. The sweat of trepidation made his Los Lobos T-shirt stick to his back. His hands felt cold despite the ninety-degree temperature outside.

"Your friends're waitin' for you in back," Freddy told him. "Ricky come out here a couple minutes ago, said you were late, said you were s'posed to get your ass back there soon as you showed up."

"*Gracias*, man," Juan said. He paused in front of the door to the back, hitched a deep breath, and went in. Two people were playing pool, another two or three were battling the video games. Rock music from a boom box drowned out the piped-in music from the front. He saw Buddy and Ricky sitting with Peter Rodriguez, and realized that it was their boom box that was supplying the music, no doubt to cover their conversation. He sighed and went over.

"Juan!" Buddy cried. "Where the fuck you been? You're late!"

Rodriguez grinned sickeningly. "Thas right, Johnny boy. We thought maybe you ducked out on us. We figured maybe we'd have to, you know, hunt you down. You remember what we tol' you yesterday: you're in this thing—"

"I know. I'm in this thing all the fuckin' way. I remember. I ain't stupid." He sat down in the free chair and reached for one of Buddy's cigarettes, lighting it with a hand that was trembling so much it was embarrassing. "So go on, why doncha? I'm here now, I'm listenin'."

Ricky nodded. "Okay, here's what we got so far. In a few minutes we're gonna leave here and head over to Peter's old man's place. He's been storin' everything there. Three cans of gas and a couple of propane torches. We'll get the stuff from him and go to the Joint. We'll take everything to the alley out back, you know, where they make the deliveries, and wait maybe five, ten minutes, so we know that no one seen us go back there. Then you and me, Juan, we take off, start walkin' to the cops. While we're gone, Buddy and Peter light the place up. They're gonna use his old man's keys to go in the back, get the thing goin', and then lock it up tight as a cunt again. They'll make sure it's goin' real good and then go back to the old man's place. They wait there for the cops or the fire guys to call 'em. Then they run down there, all of 'em, and holy shit, ain't they surprised? 'We was just playin' cards, officer. Who coulda done this terrible thing while we was playin' cards?' And us, when we're done tellin' the cops that we seen someone torchin' the place, we just split. Lay low somewhere for a few days, maybe even a couple of weeks. When it cools down, we come back. We're heroes. Sure, they never caught the bum that burned the store, but that ain't *our* fault. We're just two upstandin' kids who done the neighborly thing. Get it?"

"I get it," Juan said. "But wouldn't it be better if Peter and Buddy kicked the door down or somethin'? Instead of lockin' it up, I mean. That way it don't look like an inside job."

No one spoke for a moment. Juan could almost see the wheels grinding slowly in their minds. Then Ricky said, "See, Peter? I told you we needed Juan in on this. Pretty good thinkin', huh?"

Rodriguez nodded with what, for him, was considerable thoughtfulness. "Not bad, *amigo*. Thas what we'll do. We'll bust the door all to hell, and a couple of windows too. Make it look like it was some kinda fuckin' lunatic that did it."

Ricky beamed at Juan and clapped him on the shoulder. "Good job, m'man. You mighta saved us a real hassle on that one."

Juan pushed Ricky's hand away viciously. "And what're we gonna tell the cops? What description're we gonna give 'em?"

"Who knows. Two skinny Anglos, two fat guys, one old man with a cane. It don't matter. We'll tell 'em whatever we think of. It'll be cool."

There was another moment of silence. Then Peter Rodriguez said, "So, whaddya think, Mr. Brains?"

Juan stubbed out his cigarette. "Really? You really wanna know?"

"Yeah. You're the one with all the smart ideas."

"Well, I think it sucks. Like I said before, man, I don't wanna do it."

"You don't got a choice," Buddy said. "You're our partner, just like Peter told you."

"Yeah. But it still sucks."

"You gonna say that when you get your three hundred? What're you gonna say then?"

"Shit. What good's three hundred bucks gonna do me in jail?"

"*Burrico!*" Rodriguez spat. "We ain't gonna get caught. The whole thing's fuckin' foolproof. There ain't no way we—"

"You're a fuckin' dreamer, too!" Juan said. "You guys are so fucked, you were gonna use the old man's keys, so the cops would know right off he was involved. And what about gloves? You gonna wear gloves? Or are you just gonna leave fingerprints, so they can get 'em off all the rubble that's left? You're so fuckin' stupid I can't believe it! Arson squad's gonna be on all of us before we can say shit."

"Shut up," Rodriguez said.

"Like hell. You assholes couldn't make no fuckin' foolproof plan if it killed you. You—"

"Shut up!" Rodriguez repeated. "Jus' shut your fuckin' mouth, Jimenez. I don't wanna hear no more of your chickenshit, crybaby crap. We ain't gonna get caught, 'less you shoot your mouth off to the investigators." His scarred face twisted itself into a cruel grin and his hands knotted themselves into fists. "And you ain't gonna do that. So jus' shut up."

"Shut up yourself," Juan said, rising and starting across the room. "Fuck you guys, all of you. I quit."

Rodriguez came after him again, but this time he was prepared. He whirled rapidly and viciously, bringing his fist around at full speed, full force, catching the bigger man off guard and connecting with his midsection. With a grunt, Rodriguez stumbled back against one of the booths.

"Sonbitch!" Rodriguez cried, lurching forward. Juan stood his ground and charged his opponent, swinging. Rodriguez swore again, tried to fight back, but he was off balance and off his mark; his fists took air but little else. Grinning wildly, Juan pummeled him with blows to the stomach and chest. One shot connected with Rodriguez' nose, smashing it. Blood sprayed like a fountain, and without pausing Juan shattered the man's jaw with a series of strong rabbit punches.

Buddy and Ricky came running, but by the time they got there Peter Rodriguez was sprawled on the floor in a litter of empty beer cans and crushed cigarette butts, gasping through a frothy mixture of blood, mucus, and vomit. He was out for the count, and Juan was out himself—out the door and racing down the street.

Ricky Castillo went after him, clutching vainly to save the remnants of their beautiful foolproof plan. He chased Juan for more than four blocks, calling his name repeatedly, screaming strangled obscenities. But Juan had a head start and he stayed ahead. Cutting through alleys, doubling back several times, he heard the cries ebb. He had to escape, but where? He couldn't return to his car; they would find him there. And yet he couldn't leave the neighborhood either. His fear of being on foreign turf was easily as great as his fear of Castillo, Vargas, and Rodriguez. So he ran without a goal, ran only for what he knew was his life.

And at last, despite his fear of doing so, he ran out of the neighborhood and into that alien land beyond.

As he passed by some familiar golden arches, he stopped suddenly, gulping in air, looking desperately around. Perspiration ran down his cheeks, mingled with the tears he hadn't even known were there. It was that McD's he had eaten in yesterday, and some uniformed kids were still inside, cleaning up.

Now what? Go back? Out of the question. To go back was to walk into the very trap he'd been fleeing. Go ahead, then? That was worse. He wiped a hand across his face and whimpered a little in fright and despair.

A hand touched his shoulder.

He whirled, a scream breaking from his throat.

But it wasn't Ricky Castillo, wasn't Buddy Vargas or a bloodied and furious Peter Rodriguez. It was the smiling face of Keith Pritikin, the grinning, glad-handing missionary. He thought that he'd never seen a more welcome sight.

"Hi, Juan, you look tuckered."

Juan grinned—Mother Mary help him, he actually

grinned—and took Pritikin's hand in a warm, unsolicited grip. "Yeah," he said, still puffing. "Yeah, you bet your ass I am. How'd you . . . how'd you know I was here?"

Pritikin shrugged. "I told you I'd find you when the time was right. Think you're ready to come check out the church?"

Juan turned for a moment and glanced back over his shoulder at the night shadows of the barrio. Over on the next street a mother was screaming in Spanish at her little girl. Somewhere far away a siren wailed. He rubbed his eyes and nodded.

"Yeah," he said softly. "Yeah, I'm ready."

11

Curt paused outside the door of the personnel office and looked at the computer printout a young Japanese boy named Tommy Daiwa had given him. He was startled to see so many positions listed:

Cafeteria busboy
Grounds crew
Clerk: Printing department
Clerk: Mr. Smith's office
Public tour guide
Clerk: Requisition department
Mechanic: auto pool
Receiver: Van Paris Hall loading dock
Clerk: God's Hand TV
Janitorial/Maintenance: Faith Center
Remedial mathematics tutor: ninth and tenth grades

Curt realized that if he was going to stay in the compound for any length of time, he could have his pick of just about any job.

What kind of place is this? he wondered. The feeling he received by being among these people wasn't at all the feeling he'd expected to have. It was almost as though some kind of inner hole had been plugged, as though he'd stumbled onto something that had been missing from his life. It wasn't religious fervor, exactly, but rather a sense of camaraderie. All the others went out of their way to speak to him in the elevator. They smiled without being prompted, without expecting anything in return. They said hello or offered the ubiquitous "God bless you" even as he averted his eyes.

You're not here for camaraderie, dammit, he told himself. He had only to reflect on his years on the road to remind himself of that. He had only to glance at the picture that hung on the wall near the door, or think of the penthouse office in the Faith Center, where no newcomer dared tread.

Think of that, he told himself.

Think of that.

Don't think about fitting in, for God's sake, that's not why you're here.

"See anything that strikes your fancy?" a familiar voice said.

He turned around and saw Ernest Cummings looking over his shoulder. The director of housing was carrying a hefty stack of plain Pendaflex file folders under one arm, and clenched in his free hand was a printed flier announcing a prayer meeting.

"I'm glad to see you jumping into things so soon. A lot of newcomers wait a couple of weeks before selecting a job. What've you got your eye on?"

"I'm not sure," Curt said, shrugging, rapidly thumbing through the pages. He neglected to mention that he was looking for something along the lines of "Personal assistant: Reverend Bach." "All these clerk jobs, what are they?"

"Ahhh, you've stumbled across one of our euphemisms," Cummings said, laughing. "Are you familiar with the term 'gofer'?"

Curt nodded and winced. He was intimately familiar with it.

"Well, that's about the long and short of it. Clerk jobs are the entry-level positions here. Of course, there's nothing to keep you from advancing. We had a young lady come here from New York about six months ago—Mari Andrico, her name was. She started out as clerk at God's Hand TV, and a couple weeks back was promoted to assistant producer of satellite operations. Think of it this way: when you start as a clerk, there's really nowhere to go but up."

Curt nodded. "The problem is, depending on how you look at it, I'm either qualified for everything or nothing. I've got some college, but no degree. I've bucked boxes into semi-trailers and mopped out airport rest rooms. I've even driven cabs and delivery vans. Kind of a classic drifter, you know?"

"Well, don't worry about it. Take your time, think it over. You'll find something. And if you're still gripped by indecision in a few days, Tommy can put you in touch with a personal job counselor."

They chatted several more minutes, and then Cummings turned to leave. He was almost out of earshot when Curt stopped him.

"Mr. Cummings? I need . . . I mean, do you think I could get a mirror in my room? I don't have one anywhere."

This time it was Cummings who winced. Curt frowned at him, wondering what he had said that was so wrong.

"Come on with me," Cummings said softly. "You can walk me back to my office and I'll explain."

Curt shrugged, tucked the fan-folded pages under his arm, and followed the director of housing down the corridor. A short distance along they passed a group of three quiet young girls in their early twenties, similar to the tired-looking, unkempt people he had noticed in the cafeteria the day before. They huddled closely together and hugged the corridor wall as they hurried along, keeping their pale faces turned downward, their empty eyes averted. Cummings greeted them cheerily in passing, but got no reaction whatsoever.

Curt opened his mouth to ask about them, but stopped at the last moment. Instead he turned and watched their progress down the hall. Something in their awkward, almost shambling gaits rang a distant bell in the back of his mind. For no particular reason he thought of darkness— the pressing, thrilling darkness of an old movie theater, where something comic-dreadful was shambling on the screen with outstretched, questing arms and sharp, glinting teeth. That was odd. It was . . . He stopped himself before these thoughts could go any further and jogged to catch up with Cummings.

They stopped at the end of the hall, away from any offices or doorways. Cummings furtively glanced in both directions, checking for eavesdropping passersby before leaning close to Curt and speaking in hushes tones. "You hit on a sore spot," he said. "Mirrors are one of the Master's quirks."

"The Master?"

"Reverend Bach."

"You call him the—"

"Now, you haven't been here very long, but you've probably already gathered that we're a pretty liberal bunch. We have a saying: We preach *for* things—"

"Not against them."

Cummings smiled. "See? You're learning fast. We don't come out against any of the usual things you find a church preaching against. A lot of newcomers are surprised that we allow residents to listen to rock music. Well, we take a strong stance in favor of freedom of choice, in music and everything else. We don't rail against dancing or dating. We support freedom of the press, *all* press, even books and magazines you'd expect us to be against. We don't even ban smoking, although we do run a clinic for those who want to quit."

"Is there a 'but' in here somewhere?" Curt asked.

"A but. Yes. The but is this: despite all the things we're in favor of, the Master has a strange notion about vanity. It's one of the Seven Deadly Sins, you know, and Reverend Bach never lets us forget it. He claims that if you're obsessed with self, you can't be working for the good of others. Well, I agree with that statement wholeheartedly. I'm sure you do too; everyone does. Unfortunately, the Master takes mirrors to be a symbol of self-obsession. He absolutely forbids their presence in the compound."

"But how—"

"Hold on, Curt. Here's where I put my neck on the line for you, just as I've done for every newcomer since I've been director of housing. It's the one area where I don't toe the Universal line." He glanced around again, satisfied himself that they were completely alone, and continued. "I recommend that you purchase a mirror of your own. There's a mall not far from here, called Fox Valley. You can get one there. Incidentally, Fox Valley's the place to go for whatever you need—clothes, shampoo, Kleenex, whatever. Hitch a ride with someone. Or wait until Saturday. We have a bus that leaves from the front of the Hall every Saturday at ten. It drops you off at the mall and returns here at four. Get a mirror there. Just keep it quiet, keep it a secret. I even have a mirror myself—a little woman's makeup job—that I keep in my bottom dresser drawer."

Curt had to bite his tongue to keep from laughing, not at the image of Cummings using a secreted makeup mirror to comb his hair each morning, although that was comical, but at the sheer absurdity of the rule. It struck him, too, that there was something a bit pat in the whole explanation—Seven Deadly Sins. But he only shook his head and said, "It seems so damn silly to—"

"I know, I know. In my position I get all the complaints. You call it silly, some people use harsher words than that. Personally, silly or not, I consider it a small price to pay for our otherwise exceptional quality of life."

As Ernest left him, Curt found himself more confused than ever. What kind of organization willingly gave its workers and acolytes every imaginable luxury—everything from country-estate rooms to four-star meals—yet forbade them the use of mirrors? For the second time in the last few minutes, that distant bell of image and emotion rang in the recesses of his mind.

No mirrors.

Unbelievable.

Who in the world would outlaw mirrors?

All around Curt, the Faith Center was bustling with activity. The leaves of a huge overhanging plant combined with the steady rush of water in the fountain to his right to make him feel as though he was in the world's busiest and strangest woodland preserve. He crossed the atrium to the bank of elevators servicing B-tower. On the way up to the eighteenth floor he rode with a sullen teenager with a bone-white face. Curt nodded and smiled when he got on, offered a casual "God bless you" when he got off, but the teenager merely slouched in the far corner of the car, his dark, sunken eyes looking at everything and at nothing.

As soon as Curt stepped off the elevator, he was confronted by a wooden sectional wall which had been placed strategically in the center of the corridor, presumably to funnel traffic toward the office of the eighteenth floor's only occupant. A short jaunt to his right and he came up against a set of wide glass doors with brass handles. Gilt lettering on the doors read:

R. D. VAN PARIS
DIRECTOR OF OPERATIONS

Inside, seated at a wooden desk amid a forest of plants and odd-looking trees, was Van Paris' secretary. Unlike most of the secretaries and receptionists in the compound, she was not young, and Curt doubted she was a newcomer. Rather, her gray hair pulled back in a tight bun, well-creased face, black, heavy-rimmed glasses, the gnarled hands with a large pencil callus on the index finger, reminded him of every battle-scarred veteran of the secretarial wars he'd ever seen.

"Yes?" she said with an expression light-years from a smile.

"I'd like to see Mr. Van Paris."

"Mr. Van Paris isn't in today." Her voice was the oral equivalent of her face—flat and lifeless. Had she already repeated that phrase twenty times this morning?

He shifted uneasily. "It's kind of important. I mean—"

"Church business?"

"That's right. Yes."

"You were sent here by someone?"

He took a chance and nodded. "Reverend Welles sent me."

"Yes. Indeed. Well, Mr. Van Paris is in Omaha today, on business. If you'd like to leave your name and message, I'll see that he gets it as soon as he returns."

"That's okay. Thanks anyway. I'll stop in next week."

"Well, for that you'd need an appointment," she said, but Curt was already out the double glass doors and heading back toward the elevator, trying mightily to swallow his frustration. He wasn't sure if he had actually expected to see Richard Van Paris, or if he had just allowed himself to be swept along with wishful thinking, but now he felt that he was never going to have the answers he wanted.

Everywhere he turned in his study of Arthur Bach, he kept coming back to the Van Paris connection. Bach had been an obscure, average pastor in Wisconsin until he met Richard Van Paris. Two years later he rose to the top of the worldwide religious community, with an international network made up of thousands of people, Van Paris at his side—his friend, adviser and partner.

But how?

When the elevator doors slid open, he was startled to see the pale, quiet teenager still slouched in the back of the car. He greeted the boy again, but once more received a blank stare for his effort. The car hummed down toward the atrium, and just before the doors opened again, Curt confronted him.

"Are you okay?" he asked.

The teenager stared at him but didn't speak, didn't even blink.

"You need some help? Are you lost?"

Nothing.

Curt shrugged, sighed again, and got off. He turned around and watched the doors slide shut, waited until the lighted panel up above told him that the elevator was ascending again.

Now, *that* was really bizarre, he thought. Just riding up and down like that, not speaking, barely moving. How long had he been at it? The thought of summoning someone to help the boy crossed his mind, but he dismissed it. Something in his expression had told Curt that he didn't want help.

He decided to forego the other stops he had planned for that morning—the broadcast studios, the accounting department, the print shop—and instead headed back for the residence hall. He carried the image of that sullen face with him all the way.

The majority of Universal residents were young, happy, and healthy. They had bright grins, even beatific smiles. But there were many who didn't fit that mold at all. They seemed tired, sad, and moved quietly from place to place, like ghosts, staring straight ahead or looking down at the ground with dark, vapid eyes. Some of them wore unbuttoned shirts, untied shoes, and most seemed to be using Arthur Bach's odd rule about mirrors as a convenient excuse not to wash their faces or comb their hair.

A boy riding an elevator up and down, up and down.

Jesus. What kind of nonsense was that?

When he got back to his room he paused just inside the door, one hand still frozen on the knob and an ice sliver of momentary fear lodged in his heart.

Two people were sitting on his bed.

"Who—" he began, and relaxed when Scott Matheson turned to face him and flashed a thin, weary smile.

"Hi, roomie."

Curt blinked and shut the door behind him. "Roomie?"

Scott nodded. "At my request, Ernie Cummings made a switch. I've taken up residence."

"But I thought you and Brad were rooming together."

"We were. At least until we had"—he cleared his throat and lowered his voice several octaves—"a Big Falling-Out. But look, if you mind, I can have Ernie change me to—"

"No, hang on. It's fine. Actually, I could use a little company." He crossed to the desk and sat down. "You and Brad had a fight?"

Scott scratched absently at his beard, grinning a little. "A fight, yeah. You know, the two of us were as tight as an oak door until . . ."

"What happened?"

"Nothing."

"It doesn't sound like nothing."

Scott made a show of waving it away. "It was no big deal, believe me. I . . . hey, where are my manners? Curt Potter? I want you to meet my new friend. She just got here yesterday. Phyllis Meyer."

Curt smiled at the pretty young girl sitting next to Scott on the bed and said, "Hi, Phyllis. How are you?"

She shrugged. "I've been better. But thanks to Scott here . . . well, I'm doing okay."

He nodded, distracted, and said, "I'm not sure I like you keeping secrets from me, Scott, at least now that we're roommates. What was it between you and Brad?"

Scott grimaced. "I'm telling you, roomie, it was no big deal."

"But—"

"But nothing," Scott said, and the edge in his voice made Curt and Phyllis pull back a little in surprise. "It's all about a cemetery and dreams and things . . . other things I don't want to talk about right now."

"A cemetery?" Curt said, sure he had heard wrong.

"That's right." Scott nodded. "A cemetery."

And after that, he wouldn't say another word.

12

Saturday the Chicago area got a taste of fall. The temperature had dropped overnight and a chilly northwest wind drove a nasty, sporadic rain across the compound. While Curt continued to investigate the grounds, trying to firm up some of his feelings, Scott and his "new friend" Phyllis took the shuttle to the mall.

When a shivering Curt got back to his room just after noon, he almost stepped on an envelope that someone had slid under the door. It said "SCOTT AND CURT" on it in block letters written by a felt-tip marker, and inside was a note from Ernest Cummings, asking them to stop by his office at their earliest convenience.

He pocketed the letter and went back downstairs. On his way to the housing office he was approached by a short, pretty black girl wanting to know if he was interested in joining a new coed Bible-study group that was metting Sunday afternoon. He wasn't sure how long he'd be able to keep turning these invitations down.

Cummings' office secretary, Kelly Beckworth, was tall and thin, with blond hair so light it was almost white. She was wearing blue jeans and a Universal T-shirt—"GOD'S HAND CAN TOUCH YOU TOO!" in big red letters—and sat at her desk running a seemingly endless string of figures. through her TI calculator.

"Ernie's not here," she said, impossibly chipper for a cold weekend morning. "He's meeting with some men from the maintenance department. What do you need?"

He took the letter from his pocket and showed it to her.

"Oh, you're Curt Potter. Yeah. I've got a message for you here somewhere."

For several comical minutes she searched through a hefty stack of scribbled notes, typewritten memos, and pink "WHILE YOU WERE OUT" slips. She dug through folders and plowed through her desk drawers. Finally, getting desperate, she turned to the PC on her right and tapped in a few commands. Curt leaned over and watched her scroll through several screens of information, settling at last on a page that had his name at the top in capital letters.

She looked up, embarrassed. "Sorry about that. And after all the hunting around, this is all it is: Ernie wanted you to know you're getting a new roommate this afternoon."

"Oh? Who?"

She consulted the screen. "A boy from Los Angeles. Juan Jimenez. He's getting into O'Hare at two-ten on American Airlines." She tapped a couple of things into the computer and then scrolled the page with his name on it out of sight. Several more keystrokes and the screen was blank again, except for a blinking cursor in the upper-right corner, awaiting her next command. "That's it. Sorry it took so long."

He shrugged. "No problem. Thanks for letting me know."

He turned and started out of the office, but was struck by a thought and paused. "Kelly?"

She was already back to the figures on her calculator, and she looked up, distracted. "Hmmmm?"

"I'm having a little problem here . . . I thought maybe you could help me out."

Her eyes widened. "I've only been here two months myself. What is it?"

"I've been trying to see—I have to see—Reverend Bach. It seems impossible to get an appointment, and when I tried to see Richard Van Paris instead, I found out he's out of town. Isn't there any way to—"

"You're really talking to the wrong person," she said. "All I know is what Ernie told me. The Master is booked for the next eight months. Travel, business, tapings of his radio show. There's no way for any resident to get in to see him."

"Well, see, that's what I don't understand. He *is* the leader of the church, isn't he?"

"Of course. Sure."

"But he's completely off-limits to church members. That doesn't make sense."

She flashed a quick frown, and Curt braced himself for a lecture on accepting the will of the boss, or something of that sort. But instead the frown softened almost immediately into a smile. "It doesn't make sense to me either," she said softly. "And you can probably guess that you're not the only one who's asked to see him. A lot of them ask Ernie about it, and he gives them that little speech about being their own personal troubleshooter, you know. But because he's out a lot, they ask me instead. And so many of them have good reasons to see Bach! It really ticks me off to always have to say, 'No, sorry, you can't see him.' "

"Then—"

"But he is the Master, after all. Fighting it, or trying to . . . well, that's just stupid."

Curt nodded. "I guess so."

"What's your problem? Maybe Reverend Welles or Tony Smith could—"

"I doubt it. I . . . I can't really tell you what it is. Seeing Bach would be best, or maybe talking to Mr. Van Paris. Even Reverend Bob."

She grimaced. "Well, he's just as tough as the rest of them."

"Yeah. So I hear. It seems like you need an act of Congress to see anyone higher than Welles."

She laughed. "Maybe an act of God."

Curt looked at her, startled by the joke. Then he was laughing too. "Maybe so," he said, heading back for the door. "Thanks anyway. At least I know I'm not the only one who disagrees with the company line."

Her laughter stopped abruptly. "You're *not* the only one," she said, her voice soft again, quiet but almost shockingly firm. "Whatever you think, Curt, you're not alone."

That last statement echoed in his mind all the way back to his room.

Scott and Phyllis got back from the mall just before three. Curt filled them in on the impending arrival of the boy from California, and they settled down to wait for him, chatting idly. When the newcomer had not arrived by a quarter of four, Phyllis excused herself.

"I'm not sure what I'm letting myself in for," she said, "but I promised to let my roommate take me to a prayer meeting."

"I like her," Curt said when she was gone. "You've got yourself a real winner."

Scott flushed and glanced awkwardly at the floor, although he didn't seem altogether displeased. "You make it sound like there's something going on."

"There's not?"

"No! She's had a bad time, and I'm helping her get over it."

"That's all?"

Scott flushed again, but this time he managed to grin as well. "So far. I'll keep you posted."

There was a light rap on the door, and Scott hurried over to answer it, clearly glad for the opportunity to bring the current conversation to a halt. Connie Bishop was standing in the corridor outside, his hand raised and ready to knock a second time. Two or three steps behind him stood a small boy with dark skin and black hair. He was wearing a pair of crisp new Wranglers and a white Adidas sport shirt with vivid red piping on the sleeves. His gaze was riveted on the floor near Connie's feet.

"Gentlemen!" Connie said with his characteristic grin. "I got something for you. Scott Matheson and Curt Potter, meet Juan Jiminez. Juan, m'friend, these guys are Scott and Curt. You'll be rooming with them."

The boy mumbled something without looking up.

"We'll take it from here," Scott told Connie, stepping out in the hall to pick up Juan's single suitcase, which was as new as his clothes. He patted Connie on the back. "Thanks for bringing him by. I'll see you for church tomorrow, right?"

Connie nodded. "You better believe it." Then, to Juan: "You take care of yourself, m'friend. Don't worry about a thing. And if you need anything these gents can't help you with, you just give me a shout. I'm around."

"Thanks," Juan mumbled as Connie ambled away and Scott shut the door.

Once they were alone, he insisted on taking his suitcase back; he clutched it in front of him like a schoolgirl holding a textbook. "Where do I sleep?"

Curt pointed to the bed in the far corner. He kept silent while Juan crossed the room and dropped his suitcase on the bed. Then he said, "You have a good trip?"

Juan shrugged. "I got here safe."

"Apparently. Did I hear right? You're from California?"

"East L.A. You know what that is? It's the slums."

Curt and Scott exchanged glances, and Scott shrugged, asking Juan, "You ever been to Chicago before?"

"Shit. Chicago. All I ever knew about this place was the Bears. I thought it was near New York or somethin'." He paused and sat down beside his suitcase, looking at the floor again. After almost a minute he looked up, and his dark features had softened just a little. "Where're you guys from?"

"Everywhere and nowhere," Curt said, using the poetic phrase he'd adopted in response to the question almost everyone in the compound asked of everyone else. "I've been knocking around the country for ten or twelve years. And Scott's from West Virginia. A town called Elizabeth."

"Elizabeth? That's a stupid name."

Scott laughed. "You think the name's stupid, you ought to see the town."

They lapsed into uncomfortable silence. So far, their meeting had not been a sterling success.

"Have you . . . have you eaten yet?" Curt asked at length.

Juan nodded. "On the plane. They served us some shit s'posed to be steak. I had better steaks outta the garbage can. And that flight! Jeezus, we musta circled for hours. They said it was the weather. I think they're just a buncha assholes."

"It sounds rough," Curt said. He hesitated. "But I think you're going to like it here."

Juan stared at him with a cool, amused expression. "You think so, huh?"

"Yeah, I do. I mean, I'm pretty new myself, and it does take some getting used to, but if you—"

"Gettin' used to," Juan repeated softly, musing. "We'll see, man . . . we'll see."

The uncomfortable silence settled over them once again.

13

The next morning, Connie Bishop knocked on their door at exactly eight o'clock. Scott padded over to answer it.

"You men ready to go?" Bishop said before the door was fully open.

Scott nodded, and Curt turned from the window, where he'd been using the ghost of his reflection to comb his hair, and said, "You bet."

"What about you, Juan, m'man?"

Juan barely raised his head from his pillow. He was wearing underpants and nothing else. "Not me. I ain't goin' to church today."

"You sure?" Bishop said. "It's a real pleasure having church in the Park. You won't know what you're missin' till—"

"No church," Juan said again, and fell asleep.

Five minutes later the three of them were wolfing down pancakes and coffee in the cafeteria, and twenty minutes after that they were at the tail end of a long line of people filing into Worship Park. The long amphitheater benches were filling up rapidly. As they claimed seats about halfway down, Curt looked to the stage below. It was a bustling swarm of activity. Two young men in jeans and black T-shirts—they look just like roadies, Curt thought—were running sound checks on a couple of P.A. speakers set up to either side of the raised platform and pulpit. Two more were polishing all the wooden surfaces in sight with large white rags that they occasionally dipped into big buckets of a dark, soapy solution. A pretty black girl was plugging in an electric guitar and fiddling with its knobs and buttons, while two teenagers slowly pushed a concert grand piano on rollers into position.

"We're going to have a treat today," Connie Bishop said, simultaneously waving to someone several rows away. "I heard through the grapevine—God rest you, Marvin—that Reverend Bob's going to be here today."

"You mean Robert Kaye? That Reverend Bob?"

"The one and only. The word's out that he just got back into town on a morning flight. He's supposed to be doing the service here and the evening devotional in the Faith Center. You ever hear him in person?"

Curt shook his head. "Only on TV. Any chance Reverend Bach'll be here?"

Scott laughed. "A chance, yeah, but don't bet the baby's college money. He doesn't do church anymore. Too busy taking care of business."

Curt closed his eyes and saw Bach—looking only a little younger than the Bach in the picture back in his room—standing at the pulpit of a small country church. One hand was holding the Bible high above his head and the other was punctuating his staccato speech. For a moment Curt was in that church, in the front row, gazing at the pastor with rapt, hero-worshiping attention. And Bach was looking back at him, speaking directly *to* him. He—

"Jesus, will you look at that?" Scott whispered, snapping him back from his daydream.

Curt looked and saw a disturbance in the row in front of them. Two teenage girls were leading a thin, pale man to his seat. The man was sick, no question about it. His face was china-white, empty of any emotion. His classy white sport shirt and dark gray corduroy slacks hung absurdly loose on his body, and his bones stood out sharply. He was whimpering softly through colorless lips that barely moved. The girls helped him along, murmuring apologies to the people they passed, who made way but kept their eyes averted in uncomfortable respect.

"Shit," Curt whispered, immediately sorry for using

that word in church, even such an unorthodox church as Worship Park.

But Connie Biship nodded. "That about says it, Mr. Potter."

"I think it's a real sign of faith," Scott said. "What a perfect example of what someone'll go through to hear Reverend Bob."

Curt nodded, but he was disturbed. "It's got to be a blood problem," he said softly. "Anemia or something, don't you think? Look at the way he's rubbing his arms. It's cool this morning, yeah, but that guy's freezing."

The bizarre party of three had found a place to sit, the two girls on either side of the sick man, and now the girls were leaning in close with their arms around him, each one whispering something to him, as though trying to provide comfort.

Embarrassed, Curt turned away. He was about to say something to Scott when there was a loud flurry of activity on the stage below. Before he could figure out what it was, the pale, sick man in front of them leapt suddenly to his feet and screamed. The sound that broke from his throat was a surreal, dreamlike wail that rose higher and higher like a siren. It echoed in the bowl, and suddenly people in all parts of the Park were on their feet, craning their necks, staring, pointing. The sick man screamed again, and Curt watched in growing horror as his breath started to come in short, ragged bursts. His eyes were locked icily on the stage. Curt stared at him, then turned to see what he was seeing.

Down below, the roadies were using a block and tackle to raise an ornate, beautifully carved wooden cross behind the pulpit. The morning sun was bouncing off the cross and sending spears of light dancing in a hundred directions at once. Confused, Curt realized that it was the cross the sick young man was staring at—and screaming in mortal agony.

The sick man's companions were frantically trying to get him seated again, but he remained on his feet. That awful, wounded cry broke from his lips again and again while his arms jerked out a terrifying, spastic semaphore.

Several people rushed over to help, and Connie Bishop was one of them.

"Hey, man, c'mon now. You're okay, pal, be cool, be cool." He put one of his huge arms around the man's thin shoulders and tried, as the girls had been trying, to get him seated. "You're okay, man, really now . . . you're cool."

It took several long, agonizing moments, but Connie, the girls, and several other willing bystanders finally got the man to sit down. He was no longer screaming, but that sad whimper still issued from his throat. Connie knelt beside him and put a hand on the man's scrawny forearm.

"You okay now, m'friend? You cool?"

The man looked at him with vacant eyes; he neither spoke nor moved.

Connie turned angrily to one of the girls. "What the hell were you thinking of, sister, bringing him here in this condition? You crazy?"

She spread her hands in an apologetic gesture. "We're sorry, hey, really. He's been feelin' down for a coupla weeks. We figured bringing' him here, y'know, to hear Reverend Bob and all, we figured that'd help."

Connie shook his head. "Crazy, that's what it is." He looked at the man, who was now utterly silent. "I guess he's okay now, though. You know what's wrong with him?"

The other girl said, "Uh-uh. Just that he's been like this for a while. We're gonna take him to the infirmary right after church."

"Yeah, you do that." He patted the man's shoulder and came slowly back to his seat beside Scott and Curt. "Good God," he said softly, "that fella's really in a bad way. It's no wonder he's rubbing himself; feels to me like his body temp's down twenty degrees." He glanced distastefully at his hands, as though he might have picked up an invisible coat of slime from the sick man. He sighed and repeated: "Good God."

Curt looked from the sick man to the stage, where the roadies were putting the finishing touches on the cross-rigging, securing it with several lengths of heavy cable that they anchored to the floor of the stage. A tenuous connection was made in his mind, but it was too sketchy to mean anything to him.

The roadies disappeared and were replaced almost immediately by a gaunt middle-aged man with a fringe of brown hair and thin wire-rim glasses who climbed to the stage and approached the pulpit.

"Here we go," Scott said.

"Who's that?"

"Reverend Welles, Jim Welles, one of the junior pastors. He usually does all the services here in the Park, but if it's true that Reverend Bob's here today, he'll probably just handle the introductions."

Welles tapped the pulpit microphone lightly, sending booming gunshots of sound around the Park. The pastor glanced up at the crowd and grinned sheepishly. Then his face grew serious.

"Let us pray."

The group bowed their heads in near-perfect unison, and when the short prayer was finished, they all murmured, "Amen."

"And now," Welles said. "I'd like to ask all of you to stand up and help us out with our first song of praise. I don't really need to introduce those who'll be supplying the music." He chuckled softly. "They've traveled the world over for the sake of the Universal Ministries cause, but at heart they're all just plain Chicago folks. Friends, my heart cries out in happiness as I present to you Marjorie Simpson and the Joy Reapers!"

The Joy Reapers? Curt thought. Are they serious?

The pretty black girl he'd seen plugging in her electric guitar suddenly appeared from behind the stage, followed closely by a black man with a violin, a red-haired girl who took her place at the concert grand, and a chunky man with a wide beaming smile who plunked himself down behind a drum set. Finally, a few feet behind the rest, came a tall man shouldering a Fender bass. The congregation fell expectantly silent. Then the violin player tapped his foot three times, and on the fourth beat the music kicked in.

While the congregation clapped and sang, Marjorie

and the redhead led them through several rocking verses about love and devotion and "battling for right with the might of the Lord." Curt was at first embarrassed and then surprisingly pleased to find his foot tapping against the grassy hillside. He even began singing along on the choruses.

Universal was definitely *not* a typical church. And, he thought, almost parenthetically, it wasn't bad at all.

When the Joy Reapers finished their number, Curt joined the Worship Park congregation in rousing applause. He turned to say something to Scott, but instead caught sight of the sick young man in the next row. He was not grinning and laughing like everyone else; he was still sitting quietly, staring ahead with that frightening lack of emotion—and rubbing his arms again. Curt shook his head and turned away.

Welles spoke: "Well, I'd say we're off to a pretty good start." There was scattered applause, and he waited for it to die down before continuing. "And now it's going to get even better. I know you've been hearing a rumor. I know it's been spreading around the compound all morning. And that's why I'm especially pleased to be the one to inform you that the rumor is true!" More applause, but the pastor pushed ahead, talking right over it: "Our special guest this morning is without a doubt our most honored minister. If you've been with us for any length of time at all, if you've followed us through our publications or on radio and television, if you've tossed your lot in with Universal in any way, well, then, you've fallen beneath the long shadow cast by this man. He's just back in town for a few hours, taking a breather between several of his many trips to arrange crusades and meet with people all around the world, and he's graciously—very graciously—agreed to speak to us this morning."

The applause was growing. Like a wave surging toward the beach, it was gathering strength and momentum.

"Friends! Please welcome! The Reverend! Robert! *Kaye*!"

The congregation exploded. Below, Kaye strode behind the pulpit, beaming up at them. He was dressed in an ordinary business suit, a blue jacket and blue pants with a white shirt and dazzling red tie. The large jewel-studded cross that Curt had always noticed on television was dangling around his neck, catching the sun and winking. He raised his hands over his head like a victorious politician, and the congregation answered with an even louder roar.

"Goooooooooooood *morning*!" Kaye cried, and the applause surged ever louder. It went on for a good three or four minutes, and the Reverend Kaye basked in its warmth until at last it began to dwindle and die.

"Good morning," he repeated. "It's good to see all of you here—real good! It's been a long time since I've been in Worship Park, and I've missed it . . . yes . . . yes,. I have. Sometimes it seems that I spend every Sunday of my life in a different church in a different city, and yet nowhere, nowhere is there a church as beautiful as this!"

Curt found himself nodding. It was the same captivating voice he had always heard on TV. Here it seemed to roll beautifully along the sloping valley walls. As Kaye enthusiastically preached on and on, Curt felt he could listen for hours—all day!—and never ever want to get up and leave.

His rapt attention was broken by a tap on his shoulder. He turned and saw Scott pointing down a row at the sick young man and his female escorts.

"Look at him," Scott whispered. "His face and hands . . . look!"

Curt did, and had to swallow back a sickened groan of horror.

The man's pale face seemed to have sunk; the flesh was now clinging to the skull beneath like wet cloth. Moisture was seeping from his pores, and blotchy red sores had opened up on his cheeks, hands, and forearms. His head lolled back crazily. His mouth was wide and gaping, but no sound came forth.

Apparently only Scott and Curt had noticed. Even the girls with him were so wrapped up in Kaye's speech that they were no longer paying attention to their companion.

"What's wrong with him? Jesus, Scott . . ."

Scott shook his head. "I don't know, but I think we

better do something damn quick. You go call a doctor. The nearest phone's at the library; just pick it up and ask for the infirmary. I'll— "

He was cut off by a high, thin scream. Behind them a girl had also noticed the sick man, and she was standing up and pointing at him, screaming incoherently. Down on the stage, Reverend Kaye stopped talking, his eyes searching the crowd for the source of the disturbance.

"Hey, call a doctor!" someone shouted from several rows away. "Lookatthisguywillyou? Call a doctor, quick!"

From everywhere people came scrambling to help. On the stage, Kaye said something to Welles, who frowned, passed a hand across his forehead, and ran from the platform, visibly shaken.

Connie Bishop leapt to his feet again and hurried to the sick man's side, while the two girls who were supposedly protecting him drew away in horror. One of them was looking around with trapped, desperate eyes, as though trying to scout the quickest evacuation route. The other was sobbing wildly and gesturing without words at the open sores on the man's flesh, which had begun to ooze blood and yellow pus.

"Never mind the doctor!" Scott told Curt. "Three or four guys already went to get one! Let's help Connie!"

They shoved people aside and joined Bishop in the next row. The sick man suddenly seemed to fold in upon himself, sagging, and fell over backward. His head struck the bench behind him with a sickening hollow *whap.*

Curt, Connie, Scott, and several others tried to raise him back into a sitting position. As he worked, Curt looked at the man's suppurating wounds and swallowed again, this time choking back a wave of vomit. The sores were actually deep furrows in the man's flesh. In places it seemed as though the skin was entirely gone. Dark blood trickled freely and mingled with thick pus as the sores began to grow, widening and spreading, consuming flesh.

A hand fell on Curt's shoulder and dragged him rudely out of the way. He turned to protest and saw Reverend Kaye move past him, the big cross around his neck swinging back and forth like a pendulum. The pastor knelt beside the sick man, pushing everyone else away at the

same time, and put his lips close to the man's right ear.
He whispered something, and for one terrible moment
Curt thought the man was actually going to explode from
within. The pale, thin frame jerked violently—once, twice,
three times. Kaye pulled the man's head even closer to
his own and continued to speak softly.

"What's he saying?" Curt asked, working his way back
to Scott's side again.

"I can't tell. I can't tell, but Jesus, look at that. I think
he's healing him!"

Indeed, the sick man's spasms began to subside, first
slowly diminishing, then turning into little more than a
slow twitching of his arms and legs, and finally trailing
away to nothing. He lay perfectly still, with his head
tilted back against Kaye's open hand, facing the sky, and
for the first time since his escorts had brought him into
the Park, his face showed an emotion other than pain.
He began to smile. At that same instant the growing
sores on his exposed flesh stopped spreading, and it
looked to Curt as though the slow oozing trickle of blood
and other fluids had stopped as well.

Kaye whispered a final word or two, then lowered the
man's head gently into the grass and stood up, smiling at
the crowd pressed close around him. "It's all right now,
friends. He's going to be fine. Please take your seats.
Please, sit down. Let's continue with the service."

No one moved away.

"Come now," he urged them. "I promise you, he's
going to be all right. Reverend Welles went to bring the
physician."

One by one, people started drifting away. A few went
back to their seats, but Curt noticed that many were
leaving the Park altogether, walking slowly back up the
hillside and disappearing down the main road that led to
Van Paris Hall. Connie Bishop came over to them and
sighed.

"Folks, I've never seen anything like that in my life.
And Lord help me, I don't ever want to see it again."

"Do you know what it was?" Scott asked.

Connie shrugged. "Not a clue."

"What about Kaye? Could you hear what he was saying?"

"I didn't hear a thing," he said, brushing past them. "And right now, all I want to do is sit for a minute. I'm feeling a mite dizzy."

They returned to their seats and watched the Park gradually coming back to order. People shuffled to their seats, and almost reluctantly the babble of conversation began to die away. Curt took a quick census and guessed that nearly a third of the congregation had left.

Reverend Kaye stayed with the sick man until two infirmary attendants arrived with a stretcher and bore him away. With one final glimpse Curt saw that he had been right: the sores *had* stopped spreading; some had even vanished completely.

The man had lapsed into a state of unconsciousness.

14

By dinnertime most of the residents of Van Paris Hall had tried to put the incident in the Park out of their minds. The afternoon had been filled with whispers—in the hallways, on the pathways, in the cafeteria and the lobby—all of it divided into two topics. The first centered around the young man's ailment. Speculation ranged from cancer to AIDS to epilepsy and even leprosy. The other topic was whether or not Kaye had actually healed the man. No one seemed to know. Despite the fact that people had been pressed close on all sides of Reverend Bob and the sick man, there wasn't a soul who had heard what he had whispered. Some said: Why, yes, of course Kaye had healed him. Others claimed that was patently ridiculous. Faith healing wasn't what a good Universal acolyte believed in—that was Pentecostal nonsense. Everyone, though, agreed on one thing: something very bad had happened in Worship Park that morning, and Kaye had quieted the man, however oddly.

The evening services in the Faith Center's main chapel were more crowded than usual, as hundreds of residents turned out to hear what Reverend Bob had to say. Kaye, however, gave only a standard sermon and made no mention of the morning's events.

At a quarter past nine, the Reverend Stephen Norris left his office in the Faith Center and strode briskly down to another office at the other end of the hall. He was a tall, very thin man, and in the empty building's night-shadowed corridors he looked like an insubstantial spirit. He opened a door, went through a darkened reception area, and knocked on another door.

"Come in."

Bob Kaye was seated behind his desk. His suit jacket was draped across the back of his chair, his tie loosened, his collar open to the third button. The only sign of his position in the church was the large jewel-studded cross around his neck, a cross that was just slightly larger than Norris' own. Kaye was leaning back, his feet propped up on the desk. There was a thin sheaf of papers spread across his lap. He flashed Norris a weary smile and told him to sit.

"You need a drink, Steve?"

"No, thanks, not tonight." Norris hesitated, as though unsure how to proceed. "I would have come by earlier, but I figured you'd be bushed after your trip. And after this morning, of course."

Kaye laughed colorlessly. "I am bushed. I'll tell you, I'd like nothing better than to put my head down on this desk and take a three-hour nap. Then I'd like to wake up, drive home, and go to bed. Unfortunately, some things take precedence over rest."

"Yeah, unfortunately. Do we really have to see the Master tonight?"

"I don't see any point in putting it off. Do you remember when this happened last time—February, was it?—and we waited two days to tell him? Do you remember how unhappy he was?"

Norris nodded. He looked down at his lap and was unsettled to realize that he'd unconsciously clenched his hands into tight fists.

Ten minutes later they had left the Faith Center and were walking through the quiet compound on an unlighted path that wound through dense woods toward the Reverend Arthur Bach's home. The evening had turned cold, and it was even colder in the woods, where the sun had not reached that day.

Kaye, who had not put his suit jacket on before leaving his office and was wishing he had, carried a file clenched

under one arm. The file contained everything that was
known about the young man who had collapsed in the
Park that morning. As they hurried along, he spoke in
rapid-fire sentences, filling Norris in.

The man's name was Thomas Chambers. He was twenty-
one years old, born in Seattle to an Air Force family. He
had come to Universal directly from failing out of the Air
Force Academy in Colorado Springs, a school he'd not
wanted to attend but which had been forced on him by
his parents. He had been in Chicago for three and a half
months. In the file was a photograph of Chambers. It was
a grainy, wide-angle-lens shot of the kind both Kaye and
Norris were used to seeing in their positions, taken by
one of the photographers whose job it was to wander the
compound snapping pictures of as many residents as possible, under the guise of assembling church publicity material. This particular shot showed Chambers diving for a
Frisbee, a happy, healthy grin on his face. It had been
snapped in August, a few weeks before Chambers had
become ill.

They broke out of the woods at the edge of a service
drive that skirted the far northern boundary of the church
property. Unlike the main roads in the center of the
compound, this drive was narrow, unpaved.

"You set everything up?" Norris asked.

Kaye nodded in the darkness. "I phoned Ray Bussey
earlier tonight. The Master will be there."

Norris grunted, but whether it was a grunt of satisfaction or dismay was not clear.

They rounded a final sharp bend in the road and saw
the house. It was a modest two-story structure that would
go virtually unnoticed by any residents who chose to
wander this far away from the heart of the compound.
Set back from the service drive several hundred yards, it
was surrounded by a rambling stone wall and an overgrown lawn. Two manicured gardens flanked the front
door. A single dim light burned in one of the downstairs
windows.

Stephen Norris drew in a deep breath and let it out
slowly. His muscles were tense, as they always were
when a meeting with the Master was imminent, although

why that should be, he couldn't say. He had nothing to fear. Neither did Bob Kaye. They were numbers three and four in the Universal hierarchy, after Bach and Richard Van Paris. And yet there was something about their bimonthly meetings that always made him terribly nervous.

"Come on," Kaye said, starting through the gate.

"Hold on." Norris pointed at the crosses that hung from their necks, then to a small wooden post near the stone fence. There were three pegs on top of the post.

"Oh, shit," Kaye said. "Sorry about that. I'm glad one of us is on the ball."

They slipped the crosses off and hung them from the pegs.

Together they started up the walk to the house.

15

"You look like shit," Curt remarked to Scott late that night as the three roommates sat talking.

"Well, thanks a lot. You're no movie star yourself. And for your information, I'm still kind of shook-up about the kid in the Park. I mean . . ." He hesitated, shaking his head. "Shit, what a mess that was."

"You guys been talkin' about it so much, I'm kinda sorry now I didn't go," Juan said.

As the evening had progressed, Juan had gradually come out of his shell. He wasn't completely comfortable with his two Anglo roommates, but both Curt and Scott sensed that that time was no longer far away.

"I'm not talking just about the Park," Curt said to Scott. "There's something else. You want to tell us about those dreams?"

Scott didn't say anything for a moment. "What do you mean?"

"You know what I mean. You've been having bad dreams. You said they were the cause of your falling-out with Brad. But you've been having them since you moved in here too. You had one last night."

"No I didn't."

"Don't bullshit me. Juan might have slept through it, after his trip and all, but I heard you mumbling and tossing. I heard you practically shout 'Shit, no!' at three in the morning."

"Look, Curt, I don't want to talk about it. All right? I

116

thought this was a friendly discussion here, not an inquisition. Besides, I'm sure Juan would rather talk about something else."

Juan leaned forward intently. "Uh-uh, not me. What dreams? What're you talkin' about?"

Scott slammed his fist on the mattress. "Dammit, will you get off it? What are you two, anyway, my guardians or something?"

"No," Curt said. "Just your roommates."

"They're not dreams," Scott said suddenly, so softly that the words were nearly inaudible.

Curt blinked. "What?"

"I said, they're not dreams. They're real. At least, it was the first time."

"Real," Curt repeated. "What do you mean?"

Scott stared at him. Then he drew in a breath and released it slowly. "All right, here goes. I hope you guys won't repeat this. All my life I've had trouble falling asleep. It's not really insomnia, because once I drop off I usually stay out until morning. It's more like a relaxation problem or something. Back in West Virginia, in my old life, I'd leave the house and go to a bar, knock off a couple of beers, maybe take a six-pack in the car and cruise the back roads, sometimes smoke a joint, whatever it took. But that's the old life. Obviously, I don't do that anymore.

"For a long time after I got here, the problem just vanished. Maybe it was because I was so happy to be here, or maybe I was working so hard that I was completely exhausted by nine every night—I'm not sure. But the problem went away.

"A couple weeks ago, it came back.

"The first few nights I'd get up and take the elevator down to the lobby, go outside and get a little air, maybe walk halfway to Worship Park and back. That worked fine until . . . well, it must have been the night after you got here, Curt, because you saw Brad and me arguing about it the next morning.

"That night I went all the way to the Park and still wasn't tired, so I pushed on. I'll tell you, guys, it's dark out there at night with no buildings or streetlamps or anything; after a while I had no idea where I was. But just when I'd think I was really lost, I'd come across an outdoor church that I recognized, or see a familiar picnic area. I figured that made it all right. I knew that I couldn't wander off the compound, because I'd come up against the fences. So I just kept walking, for half an hour, maybe an hour. I think I ended up on some road that runs along the northern edge of the compound. I think that now, I mean; at the time I didn't know. All I knew then was that I wound up in some part of the compound where nothing was familiar anymore—nothing at all.

"I came across a house back there. It wasn't real big, but it was ugly. It could've been the house where the Master lives; he's supposed to have a place here on the church property. Maybe it was just an old gardener's house. But I stood there looking at it, and it gave me a chill, being way out there by itself. Anyway, I kept walking, and about a half-mile later I hit the cemetery. It was right there, just—"

"Wait a minute," Curt said. "Cemetery? You mentioned that before. I didn't know there was a cemetery here."

"Neither did I—not for sure, anyway. I'd heard rumors about it. Supposedly it's for the foreign missionaries who die in the field and whose only wish is to be buried near the heart of the church, that kind of thing. Whatever. It's real. I saw it. It's a small place with a little hedge around it and a couple of stone posts with a metal gate at the entrance.

"So there I was standing there at the gate thinking: What the hell, you know, why not? I was already a long way from the Hall and I still wasn't all that tired, so I went in.

"It's really kept up nicely—the grass all cut, the flowers trimmed, the gravel paths all neatly raked—I could see that even in the dark. The main path goes about halfway back, and then it splits in two. I took the left-hand branch, but I didn't get too far, because . . . because of what I saw next."

He paused uncertainly, and Curt prompted him gently: "What was it?"

"It was a dog . . . a little black dog . . . a mutt, I think. It was lying in the middle of the path. Its . . . its belly had been cut open . . . slit from the throat to the crotch—cut with a knife, I guess, I don't know . . . The guts were everywhere. My daddy used to have a saying for a big mess. Strewn high and low. When I was little and he'd come home from the mine and I hadn't picked up my toys, he'd say, 'Jesus, Scotty, your crap's strewn high and low!' Well, this dog's guts were strewn high and low . . . all over the path, just . . . just *thrown* everywhere . . . It . . . it had been decapitated."

"Christ," Curt whispered.

"The worst of it was, it was so damn fresh. It couldn't have happened more than ten, maybe twenty minutes before. The blood was still fresh and the stink—it stank like new blood, like a slaughterhouse.

"I might've screamed. I don't really remember. I just stood there staring at it, and all of a sudden something hit me on the back of the head."

"Hit you? What—"

"It felt like a sock full of sand or something. It knocked me off balance and spun me around, and that's when I saw what it was. It was a bird, a huge damn bird, like a buzzard or vulture, flapping away into the night. I watched it flying away, listening to those big wings beating, and . . . and that's all I remember."

"All you remember?"

"Yeah. Next think I know, it's morning and I'm waking up in bed and telling Brad all about it and he's calling me a fool, saying it was a dream. We fought about it all day, not just that morning when you saw us in the hallway."

Curt frowned. "And you say you've dreamed about it since?"

"That's the crazy thing. I don't go back. I mean, I still have trouble falling asleep, but do you think I leave the room? No, sir. I stay put. Talking before bed helps a little, but when I finally drift off, I dream about it." He paused. "I don't go to the cemetery, but the cemetery comes to me.

"After the second night, well, that's when Brad and I fought so badly I had to move out. And it happened last night too, just like you said—the trouble getting to sleep, the dreams. I don't know what started it, and I certainly don't know what to make of what I saw out there. But I saw it."

When he had finished no one spoke for several moments.

"*Vampiro*," Juan said softly, speaking for the first time since Scott had begun his story.

"Vam*what*?"

"*Vampiro*," their new roommate repeated. "It's a legend. You know, vampires, like in the movies. They have the legend in Mexico too. I only been there once, but my mama grew up there, lived there till she was almost twenty. She told me the story when I was just a little kid. *Vampiros*. They come back from the dead, *de la ultratumba*, and walk the earth in search of blood. They hunt for man, but when no man is found they will kill small farm animals, cattle, sheep, goats—or cats and dogs. If they are discovered, they can change their shape. They become a wolf, *un lobo*, or take the form of a bat. Then they fly away into the night." He said nothing for a time. Then he simple repeated, "*Vampiro*."

Curt laughed. "Kind of impressionable, aren't you, Juan?"

"Hey, wait," Juan said quickly. "I don't believe that bullshit. Mexico has lots of superstitions like that. But I grew up here, I'm an American. I seen too many lame-ass movies to fall for that *vampiro* crap."

"I don't know," Scott said. His voice was soft, almost distant. "*Vampiro*, vampire. We had stories like that in West Virginia too. There's one about a young farmgirl in the 1800's. Her name was Blanche Kramp. How's that for a rib-tickler? Blanche Kramp. It's so silly, it's got to be real. Anyway, she got engaged to a rich landowner in the next county. No one could believe it. Poor little Blanche Kramp, whose parents never had a penny, getting married to this famous rich guy, like Cinderella or something. Everyone was excited—it was all the talk for weeks. Well, on the eve of her wedding, Blanche went to see her finacé. No one knows why, but she just left home, saying it was important that she go see him. When she got there, she knocked on his door like always, but there wasn't any answer. She knocked again, and still nothing. Finally she turned around to leave, but before she could take even a step, a hand fell on her shoulder and spun her back toward the door, and—"

"C'mon, Matheson, knock it off," Curt said. "It's late. We don't need a ghost story at this hour."

Scott grunted and lapsed into silence.

"It's weird how all different places got the same kinda stories," Juan said.

"Weird," Scott murmured, "yeah."

"Hey, folks, enough is enough," Curt said. "I'm sorry I brought it all up."

"Well, I'm glad I got it off my chest. I'm glad you dragged it out of me. Vampires? Certainly not. But the cemetery's real, and whatever I saw out there, whatever happened to me . . ." He didn't finish the sentence.

16

Newcomers to Universal were often surprised to learn that Anthony Smith and Rebecca Heller were not twins. Both were twenty-nine years old, both stood five feet seven inches tall, both had short curly brown hair, and together they ran the public relations department. But in reality their backgrounds were as disparate as could be. Smith had been with the church for eleven years, coming to Chicago as a disillusioned runaway from a wealthy Connecticut family. Heller, on the other hand, had grown up in a poor New Mexico farming community. She had fled to Chicago at the age of twenty-two, when her parents, husband, and three-year-old daughter were all killed in a fire that consumed the house trailer they shared.

"Glad you could make it," Smith said, shaking hands with Earnest Cummings and simultaneously glancing at his gold Rolex. "You're on time, as usual."

Cummings flashed a quick, meaningless smile. "Thanks. I always try to be."

"Of course you do. Coffee?"

"No, thanks. Actually, we're going to have to make this kind of quick. Two of my drivers are still down with colds, and I've got some newcomers to meet at O'Hare in a little while."

"Say no more. We'll keep it as brief as possible."

"Actually," Becky Heller said from her chair in the corner of Smith's office. "I'd want to keep this brief no matter how much time we had. The things we have to talk about aren't exactly high on my list of pleasantries."

Cummings arched his right eyebrow. "Really?"

"I'm afraid not. We have to talk about damage control. Nasty stuff, but it has to be done. Now. Before any more time goes by."

"I don't understand."

She smiled gently. "I'm referring to the Chambers incident."

"I gathered that, but . . . but I still don't understand. What do you mean, damage control?"

"Ernie, really, I'm surprised. You work with people every day. I'd hazard a guess that in your position you deal with more residents than any of us. The pastors are too busy. The Master and Dick Van Paris are out on the road too much. Tony and I get stuck behind our desks too often, writing and approving P. R. copy. But you . . . you deal with people all the time. I would have thought you'd know the term damage control by now."

"I know the term, Becky. I just don't see how it applies. Tom Chambers is very sick, but . . . Oh, my God. Are you telling me he's infectious?"

Smith laughed sharply. "Hardly. I've been conferring with the infirmary staff hourly ever since the collapse. They don't have an exact diagnosis yet, but they've assured me that it's not catching. As a matter of fact, at last report they've got him on lots of rest, a few antibiotics, and B-12 injections. They say he's responding nicely."

"Then—"

"I'm talking about damage control from our standpont —a public-relations standpoint. We've got to keep this thing on a short leash."

"We're talking about reporters," Heller said. "We get requests for interviews and background information all the time. My office fields almost a hundred requests a week, Tony's even more. And the reporters who request information are the good ones! Then there are the ones who sneak over the compound walls at night or who come in as part of a public tour group and then wander away from the tour and start snapping pictures of the cash room or the school or the Master's office"—she paused for effect—"or the infirmary."

"Ahhhhh."

She smiled. "You understand now."

Cummings nodded slowly. "I think so."

"There are just too many people who would love to grab hold of something like Tom Chambers' collapse and run with it, blow it all out of proportion. He's improving, but it's still a bizarre illness. And I can't even begin to describe what a field day they'd have with it. After a few vague or exaggerated stories popping up here and there, the evangelical raiders would be screaming 'Maltreatment!' or 'Abuse!' "

Tony Smith cleared his throat. "Do you know what happened to Alicia Chin last winter?"

Cummings nodded immediately. Alicia Chin was a fifteen-year-old runaway, a sophomore in the compound's school. One day she had slipped on a wet tile floor outside her classroom and had cracked her head against the cinder-block corridor wall. Bleeding profusely and slipping into a violent seizure, she might well have died had it not been for the quick thinking and rapid action taken by her teacher, David Rice.

"Well," Smith said, "as bad luck would have it, a reporter from some crackpot little conservative magazine— *The American Review*—just happened to wander into the building right after the ambulance was called. Alicia was just starting to have a seizure, kicking and flailing, thrashing from side to side. Dave Rice was doing his best to keep her still, but even at that she hit her head on the wall and floor a couple more times. Anyway, he was trying to keep her still at the same time he was using his own shirt to stop the poor girl's bleeding. And can you imagine what happened."

Cummings thought about it for a moment and shook his head.

"The next issue of *The American Review* came out, complete with a picture of Dave forcing Alicia to the floor. You could see a little blood in the picture—not much, just the right amount, really. Because the picture was accompanying an article about Universal's acceptance of sexual abuse and teacher-student rape."

Cummings gasped. "You're not serious. You—"

"Unfortunately," Becky Heller said, "we're both very serious. Which brings us back to the point I made before. We need to adhere to a strict damage-control plan for the Chambers incident. The young man is extremely sick. We don't know why. But maybe now you can understand why we can't afford to have reporters or anyone else running around trying to fill in the blanks."

"You're talking about a cover story."

"Exactly. And as much as I hate the word, I'm talking about stonewalling too. We don't talk about Tom Chambers at all. Not to friends or coworkers or newcomers. We don't say what we know, and we surely don't say what we don't know. We keep our mouths shut. But if asked by anyone—a newcomer, a long-timer, a junior staffer—we tell them this."

She handed several sheets of paper to him. He scanned them quickly. Within seconds the words "ARC (AIDS-Related Complex) was detected in . . ." leapt off the page at him. He put the paper down on Smith's desk and looked up at them in amazement.

"We're telling them Tom Chambers has AIDS?"

Becky Heller nodded. "And lest you think we're not serious about following through with this, we're adding a personal recomendation that he be moved to one of our AIDS treatment camps out west, *and* we've altered all his personal records to include several references to past homosexual encounters, and—"

"You can't do that!"

Tony Smith leaned forward again. "Of course we can do it. We have to do it."

"No . . . *no*! We're a church! Keeping quiet, okay, that's one thing, but lying? Tony, Becky, do you really expect me to be a party to this? This is nothing but a damn lie!"

Becky Heller shrugged. "You have to follow the story."

"Look," Smith said, "I don't understand why you're making such a bloody big deal out of it. If you love the church, then surely you can see that what we're asking makes sense. Who knows? Maybe we'll never have to use the story. Maybe we'll be able to get through it on stonewalling alone. But if one of us is ever in the position where he or she is forced to discuss the damn thing, then there's no contest; the reputation of one resident just doesn't measure up against the reputation of the entire movement. And Chambers' reputation isn't really at stake, anyway. Chambers can go out west and start over with the church out there . . . or do whatever he wants to do."

Cummings frowned. He put his thumb and forefinger up to the bridge of his nose and massaged it furiously. Twenty conflicting thoughts were swirling through his brain.

"I don't know," he said softly. "I just don't know."

Smith slammed a fist down on his desk. "You're wearing me out, Ernie. If it bothers you that much, then just refuse to talk about it. Say 'No comment' and send whoever's asking to Becky or me. But just be advised of this: Bob Kaye has stated that any failure to either keep quiet or use the AIDS story *will*—he guarantees it—result in dismissal from the church."

"But it's a lie!"

Smith and Heller exchanged tired glances, and Smith said, "I'm not going to argue with you anymore. You have your instructions. You know the consequences of not following them. Take that information back with you, think it over, and use it as you see fit. Understand?"

"No," Cummings murmured, so softly that he couldn't be heard.

"What's that?"

Cummings' smile was very thin. "I said yes, Tony. Yes, I understand."

17

At six o'clock Monday evening the Reverend Robert Kaye returned to the Faith Center office he had left on schedule at five.

He went into his inner domain and flicked a bank of switches, illuminating the room. From his top desk drawer, which he opened with a key on its own separate ring, he extracted the file he would be needing in a few minutes. He sat down, put the file on his lap, and closed his eyes.

It was now six-oh-four. At eight-thirty, according to the schedule the Master had laid out for him the night before, he would catch a commercial flight to New York, where he would connect with another scheduled flight to London. From there he would fly by private charter to Hamburg, West Germany, to meet with people high up in the European arm of the church. Before any of that, however, he had a meeting with Stephen Norris, and it was that meeting that had brought him back to his office after-hours.

He did not feel prepared for an overseas trip. If the truth were told, he didn't even want to go. It was too much travel, too soon. Beyond that, the purpose of this particular trip hadn't been discussed, or even thought about, until late last night during what should have been just a routine Tom Chambers briefing with the Master.

There was a soft knock on the door, and Norris came in. He was wearing his usual off-hours outfit—sweatpants and a tattered Gold's Gym T-shirt—and smoking one of his home-rolled cigarettes. He closed the door quietly and sat down, without saying hello to his host.

"You got your reservations all right?"

Kaye nodded. "I'm on an eight-thirty flight. My bags are already in the car."

Norris flashed him a sympathetic smile. "There are riskier jobs, I guess, but I wouldn't want to know what they are."

"Amen. I'd feel better if the Master had given us some justifiable reason. But no. He wants Germany. Case closed. I wonder if he's not getting just a touch too cocky."

"Arrogant," Norris whispered. Then, just slightly louder: "Who's your first contact over there?"

Kaye opened the file on his lap and extracted several loose pages. He skimmed them quickly. "A man by the name of Helmut Wilmar. He's ops manager in Hamburg. I talked to him briefly this morning—he arranged a charter from Heathrow to Germany for me—but I didn't tell him why I was coming. If we're lucky, he'll be sympathetic. We need someone of his rank to be the Master's familiar over there."

"And if he isn't? Sympathetic, I mean?"

"Then I get in touch with one Paul Josef Schroeder. He's a free agent, not a church employee, but he's done a lot of work for us in the past. After the familiar's been set up, we get to work on travel arrangements. That won't be easy either, but I managed to get to Van Paris last night after our meeting with the Master. He gave me carte blanche. In other words, I can grease all the palms necessary to assure success . . . and secrecy."

Norris laughed harshly. "That kind of thing still works?"

"It does. Or at least it had better. The way I figure it now, getting this done is going to require a minimum of eight connections. Minimum, Steve. Some we can almost surely rely on—Wilmar, Schroeder, a couple of others. The rest we can't be so sure about. If just one connection turns out to be a weak link . . ." He shrugged.

"And if this thing blows, we blow with it," Norris said. "We lose our ranking, and God knows what else. Right?"

"Yes. You might say that."

The two men looked at each other in silence for a long time. And when Kaye tried to insert the loose pages back into the file folder on his lap, his hand was trembling quite noticeably.

18

It was sometime in the darkest part of Monday night, between three and four, when Juan Jiminez awoke with a cry breaking from his lips.

"Gaaaaaa!"

He sat up in bed with a jolt, looking around at his surroundings. The light came on and Curt was standing over him, looking at him with concern. "What is it, Juan? Nightmare?"

Juan covered his eyes against the intrusion of light and nodded slowly.

"The same thing you told me about? Like before you met Pritikin in L.A.?"

"Don't know." He was quiet for several seconds, thinking. "No. Different—worse."

"You want to talk about it?"

Another hesitation—and finally another nod.

Curt glanced at the next bed, where Scott was sleeping soundly. "The first decent night's sleep he's had in I don't know how long. I hate to disturb him. Why don't we get some fresh air? You can tell me outside."

A few minutes later they were walking slowly down the big main path that led from the Hall to the Faith Center. It had rained a little earlier, and the night sky was still heavy with low, scudding clouds.

"Go ahead," Curt urged. "What was the dream about?"

Juan didn't look up from the path. He seemed to be concentrating mightily on every footstep, taking each one with great effort and studying it, as if he was just learning how to walk and wanted to memorize the mechanics. When he spoke, his voice was oddly muffled.

"*Muy malo*. It was bad. I was still in the barrio, only it was different. It was the barrio, but it was here. You know? How sometimes you're in two places at the same time?"

"I know."

"Okay, I was in the barrio—the barrio-here. I was up in our room and I heard this noise. It was outside the big window, so I went over to look. The curtains were pulled, and first I couldn't find the cord to get them open. Then I found the cord, but had a helluva time tryin' to pull it. It was cold. And it felt wet. And slippery. It kept comin' outta my hands, and every time I'd hold it tighter it would slip out quicker. But I finally got it.

"It was dark outside, like it is now, but I could see the barrio out there, way down below. All the houses and streets, the stores and parkin' lots and shit. Straight down was the dead-end street where I used to park my car and sleep. Way off in the distance I could see downtown L.A."

He stopped talking. Curt waited, but finally had to prompt him: "That's not all, is it?"

"No, no. I saw him too."

"Him?"

"Him. The man from my other dream. He was down there, way below our room, and he was lookin' up at me. He smiled. He . . . he came over to the side of the buildin' and started to climb. He—"

"Wait a minute. Climb? He had a ladder?"

"No! He didn't need one. He came straight up the side, like a spider or somethin'. He was movin' fast and he was comin' for me. I knew that . . . I felt it. He was comin' up the side of the buildin' to get me. I tried to turn away, 'cause I knew I had plenty of time—as fast as he was climbin', I still had time to run away if I hauled ass quick enough. But I couldn't move. There wasn't nobody else there, but I felt like someone was holdin' on to my feet or my legs, keepin' me from movin'. And then I saw why I'd had such a bitch of a time with the curtain cord. It was wet with blood, and the blood was all over the curtains too. They were soaked with blood! It was drippin' onto the floor in puddles! It was all over the room! And I tried to run again, but it still felt like someone had hold of me and I just couldn't move at all. And the man was gettin' closer, closer to the window, closer to me."

He looked at Curt and shivered. "Then I woke up. It . . . it was horrible."

Curt gently touched Juan's shoulder. He didn't know what to say, but gave it a shot anyway. "It sounds like it. But it's only a dream, Juan. I wouldn't worry about it too much. You've been through a lot in just a few days. The arson plan and going with Pritikin. Not to mention being put on a plane and sent here, so far away from home. It'll take time, but you'll get used to things. You might have dreams for a few more days. Who knows? I'm willing to bet they won't go away all at once, no matter how much you want them to."

"I know. Jeezus, I know. But that's not all. You know what else? You wanna know what I was thinkin' all the way through the dream?"

"What?"

"*Vampiro.* I kept thinkin' the man was a vampire, and he was gonna try to kill me. I knew he wanted to make me one of his livin' dead, just like in all the old stories."

Curt laughed, but it had an unexpectedly icy ring to it. Great, he thought, this is just super. Matheson's dream hysteria rubbing off on other people.

"You told us you didn't believe in those stories," he said, trying to keep his tone light and easy.

"I don't, but . . ."

"But what?"

Juan stared at him. After a time he said, "Nothin'. You're right. It was just a dream."

"Absolutely. At least you're thinking straight now. Anyone can have a nightmare, Juan, that's no big deal. It's when you start believing in shit like ghosts and vampires that you have me a little worried."

They had come to the Faith Center at last, and Curt seized the opportunity of their arrival to change the subject. He told Juan what he knew of the building and its history, trying to describe the offices and facilities inside. Juan listened attentively, and he seemed impressed with the Center's towering lines, but at the same time he still appeared troubled. His responses to Curt's descriptions were little more than one-syllable grunts, recalling the sullen and reticent way he had first entered room 1290 Saturday afternoon.

Curt felt at a loss. Not knowing what else to do, he put his arm around Juan's shoulders. "I guess this is no time for a tour, huh? Why don't we go back and get a little more sleep before morning?"

They had taken no more than a dozen steps in the direction of the Hall when Juan stopped suddenly. His eyes were lit with surprisingly fierce fire, and his right index finger jabbed at the sky.

"Look, Curt! There! It's like Scott said, man! Right there!"

Startled, Curt looked up and saw a large black bird taking flight from a spot in the path several hundred yards ahead. Powerful wings pumping, it flew over the trees in the direction of the library and Worship Park.

"Shit," he murmured. "What do you think it was? A crow?"

"Dunno. Looked kinda like a bat to me."

"A bat that big in the Midwest? Uh-uh, I don't think so." He wasn't sure if Juan had been serious or not, but even if it had been meant as a joke, he didn't quite feel like laughing, not after everything they'd been talking about lately. He thought about Scott's story, the dream he swore was real.

"Mighta been a crow," Juan conceded, to Curt's relief. "But it was awful damn big if—" He stopped. "Who's that?"

A figure up ahead was ambling slowly along in the direction of Van Paris Hall. Curt had the impression that it was an old man. He was bent at the waist, shoulders hunched forward against the autumn nighttime chill, head lowered.

"Hello!" he called.

The figure didn't stop, but continued plodding along ahead of them.

Curt took Juan's arm and pulled him forward, quickening their pace until they'd caught up with the man just outside the Hall's main entrance.

"G'morning," he said. "How you doing?"

The figure stopped and turned stiffly around to face them. Curt and Juan caught their breath sharply. The man wasn't old—twenty-five would have been an extreme-outside guess—but that wasn't the surprising part. He was asleep. Or at least he appeared to be. His eyes were heavy-lidded, half-closed. His face was pale and emotionless, the cheekbones sunken, the mouth slack. Although he was looking at them, both Curt and Juan had the uncomfortable sensation that he was staring at them without noticing them at all.

"My God," Curt said, "I think he's sleepwalking." He reached out to touch the man's shoulder, but Juan caught his wrist.

"Don't, man, it's dangerous!"

Curt paused. Yes, he'd heard that too, that it was dangerous to wake a sleepwalker and might throw him into some sort of irreversible shock. He had never put any stock in it, considering it just another old wives' tale. But face-to-face with this young-old man, he didn't feel inclined to put it to the test.

"What should we do?"

Juan shrugged. "Leave him go."

The man was still staring at them sightlessly, so they skirted around him to get inside the dorm, but once again Curt found himself hesitating. There was something on the collar of the man's shirt. He turned back, squinted, and saw a dark stain. He studied it and felt cool fingers creep lightly down his spine.

A dark stain.

He tried to take a step closer for a better look, but Juan grabbed his wrist again.

"C'mon, man," he said, dragging him roughly inside.

Once through the doors, Curt shook loose and turned around, looking back through the safety of the glass. Half-hidden by shadow, the man stood staring at the spot where they had been for another few seconds. At last he turned and shuffled off into the darkness.

"He's gonna be all right," Juan said. "Don't sweat it. He'll wake up soon. If he's really a sleepwalker."

"What do you mean, *if*? What else would he—"

"*Vampiro*," Juan said melodramatically.

"Shit. You and your *vampiros*. I'm sick of hearing about them."

Back in the room, Juan fell asleep almost immediately. Curt lay back with his eyes closed, but found sleep evasive. He tried to make his mind blank, but it kept replaying everything that had happened since Sunday night. One word kept coming back to him no matter how hard he tried to black it out. The most ridiculous thing, really, the stupidest. But he couldn't get it out of his mind.

Vampiro.

Vampire.

Riiiight, he thought, vampires in a church. Churches were supposed to kill vampires.

He reached up to scratch his ear and found that he was sweating.

Vampires. In the computer age. What a joke.

But he couldn't dismiss the images in his mind of hundreds of people walking about the compound with blank expressions on their faces, riding up and down in empty elevators, people who you could almost say went through the day like . . . like *zombies*.

My God. That word had occurred to him once before. Just as it had now, it had come to him as he'd been sitting on a bench outside the library, watching some of those people shuffle past. And wasn't "zombie" just another name for "vampire"?

Come on, he told himself. What you're thinking is lunacy. It's impossible. Flat-out impossible.

They come back from the dead, and walk the earth in search of blood.

Ha-ha.

When no man is found, they will kill small farm animals—cats and dogs.

Well, there was Scott's dream, his supposed walk in the darkness and the discovery of—

No! No, don't get carried away, for Chrissakes. A

dream, it was a dream, no different from Juan's nightmares or anyone else's.

They can change their shape. They become a wolf, un lobo, *or take the form of a bat.*

A bat. A huge bird flapping up and away into the night sky.

A bat.

A silent boy in an empty elevator, riding up and down, up and down, up and down.

A sleepwalker with an odd dark stain on his collar.

A bat.

And hundreds of zombies walking about the compound every day.

It was almost . . . No. There was no getting past the impossibility of such a thing. Why did he have such a difficult time accepting that all of a sudden?

A bat in the night, a boy in an elevator, a dark stain, a—

Noooo! his mind screamed. To slip away into superstitious nonsense, to get carried away by dreams, was dangerous.

It wasn't a dream, Scott had said. *It was real.*

II
The Fears of Autumn

A prophet is not without honor
save in his own country,
and in his own house.

—MATTHEW 13:57

It is not these well-fed long-haired men
that I fear, but the pale and the
hungry-looking.

—JULIUS CAESAR

19

Curt accompanied Juan to the offices of God's Hand Radio, where they met with the operations manager, a young black woman by the name of Laurie Campbell. Her office was large but not plushly decorated, and the only notable decor was a series of inspirational posters tacked on the walls, each one showing some scenic view (a waterfall, a wooded glen, a snowcapped mountain) and carrying some inspirational saying—"*The Journey of a Thousand Miles Begins with One Step!*" or "*Don't Pray for an Easy Life, Pray To Be a Strong Person!*" Campbell, who seemed friendly enough but nevertheless overworked and exhausted, listened to Juan and shook her head sadly.

"I'm afraid there just aren't any openings. We've been full for the last two months."

"I don't think you understand," Curt said. "Juan really needs to work. He's got a difficult past to get over, and work would be the best thing right now. It's what his counselors in Los Angeles recommended—get to Chicago and start working."

Campbell sighed. "I don't know. What kind of skills do you have, Juan?"

"Skills? Whaddya mean?"

"I mean, are you trained in anything? Have you ever worked in radio before? Ever done any type of broadcasting work?"

139

Juan laughed sharply. "Helped my friend's stepbrother on his construction crew one summer. That's it."

Laurie Campbell sighed again and cast both of them a rather irritated look. "That means you'd be starting as a gofer, and I just can't take on another one of those. If you had some strong skills or background, well, maybe, but for an untrained teenager I just couldn't—"

"What about in the Spanish-language department?" Curt said. "Couldn't you use somebody there?"

Campbell's irritation vanished; her expression changed to one of mild interest. "Spanish? Do you speak Spanish, Juan?"

"Hell, yes," Juan said, forgetting himself and stating what sounded like the most obvious fact in the world. "I talk Spanish better than I talk English."

"Can you translate?"

"Translate?"

"Yes. If I showed you a letter written in Spanish, would you be able to write down word for word what it said, in English?"

Juan glanced at the floor. "I don't know. I really don't read too good. Or write."

"Well, what about speech? If I said something to you in Spanish, could you turn to your friend here and tell him, in English, what I'd just said?"

"Sure. That's easy."

"Well, I guess I can use you after all. You'll be working with Cliff Alcock, the man in charge of our foreign-language division. If you're a good spoken-word translator, he can use you in putting together the satellite broadcasts to Central and South America. And if you'd be willing to take some evening remedial literacy classes at the school, there's no telling what might happen. Our Spanish department is rather small right now; you might move up quickly."

"You mean I got the job?"

She stood up and reached her right hand across her desk. "You do, my friend. Can you start right after lunch?"

He shrugged. "Sure, boss, no problem."

*   *   *

Phyllis Meyer also started work that day, side by side
with Scott in the Universal Ministries printing office. The
office, which was based in the library building and took
up the entire basement level, turned out hundreds of
pages of material each week—pamphlets, fliers, tracts,
and hundreds of fancy direct-mail pieces. While Scott
had worked his way up over the past year to first assistant in the graphic-design department, Phyllis began as so
many other newcomers did, as a clerk, a gofer. Her tasks
consisted largely of running from cubicle to cubicle with
documents and galleys and artwork. In her spare time she
prowled the corridors of the office, trying to learn her
way around and familiarize herself with the various publications, whose subjects included: the history of the church,
hunger programs, poverty, welfare, birth control, abortion, Bible history—

Birth control . . .

Abortion . . .

"Come on, now," she whispered, shoving the tracts in
question aside and picking up her cup of coffee. "Don't
get into that shit again, girl. It's over, right? It's done."

Of course it was. It was irrevocably in the past. And
yet she knew in her heart that while physically it was
indeed in the past, emotionally she would never forget.
She had bled her baby onto that doctor's table in that
sterile office, and the blood would always be fresh.

Okay, she thought, so it *won't* heal. But it's got to get
better, doesn't it? It's getting better already.

And it was, somewhat. Scott was seeing to that.

They met for lunch at noon—Scott and Phyllis, Juan
and Curt. Afterward they strolled slowly across the compound, enjoying the relative warmth of the October day.

"So tell me what you're going to be doing," Phyllis
said to Juan. "Whatever it is, it's got to be more exciting
than carrying camera-ready copy up and down cinder-
block hallways."

"Hey," Scott said, "I thought you liked your job."

She poked him in the ribs. "Just kidding, Mr. First
Assistant. It's great. It'll be greater when I get promoted
to something worthwhile."

"Well, my job sounds tough," Juan said, "but I ain't a

gofer, either. Laurie Campbell said I'm gonna be working with this Cliff Alcock guy, trans . . . trans*forming*
Spanish tapes."

"Transforming?" Phyllis said.

"Yeah. See, they got this guy, Roberto Fernandez,
from the Dominican. He makes all the tapes for the
Spanish-speakin' countries. But he's just a preacher, don't
know nothin' about radio. So when he's done, me and
Cliff Alcock, we gotta go through 'em all and put in the
radio stuff, all the . . . What did she call them, Curt?"

"Announcer cues."

"Yeah, announcer cues. Like where to put in commercials, where to have station breaks, that kinda thing. I
guess I also gotta watch close, 'cause this Reverend Fernandez gets all crazy sometimes when he's preachin' and
slips into English and stuff. If I catch that, I gotta take
the tapes back to him and make him record that part
over."

Phyllis nodded. "Sounds more interesting than my job."

Juan grinned. "That's 'cause you don't got the tongue,
señorita. You gotta speak the language."

Suddenly a girl ahead of them in the path stumbled
and fell. She had been coming in their direction, moving
slowly, when her knees had given way and she collapsed.
She swayed sickeningly for just the tiniest moment before
pitching face-forward.

"Jeezus!" Juan cried. "C'mon!"

They charged forward and reached her just as she
slowly rolled over and turned her face up toward the sky.
She appeared dazed. Her eyes were wide and staring, her
lips quivering. Dirt, twigs, and pebbles from the path
clung to her hair.

Curt knelt down beside her first, cradling her head
gently. "Are you okay? What happened?"

She didn't respond immediately. Then, just as he was
about to repeat the question, she nodded.

"You *are* okay?" he asked again, as though wanting to
be sure he'd interpreted the nod correctly.

"Y-y-yes. I'm just fine." Her voice was flat and lifeless.

"What happened?"

"D-don't know. Just . . . just fell."

In the time it had taken the girl to struggle through her brief answers, no fewer than ten people had clustered around them. One of these was Becky Heller, who had been rushing from her office in Van Paris Hall to her office in the Faith Center when she'd seen the accident. Quickly she took charge of the scene, brushing everyone aside, and leaning in close to whisper something to the fallen girl. In a moment the girl's lips stopped trembling, and her grimace was replaced by a small nervous smile. Heller whispered something else, and gradually the girl's smile became strong and bright and sure. Apparently satisfied, Heller turned to glare at the cluster of onlookers.

"Show's over, folks. She's okay. Just a little shaky, aren't you, Sally?" The girl nodded. Her smile was stretching into a dazzling grin. "You can all get back to work. Go on, now, all of you. God bless you. Go *on!*"

The bystanders broke up and began to drift away. Scott and Phyllis headed toward the printing department, and Curt decided to accompany Juan the rest of the way to God's Hand Radio. They had traveled most of the distance in a rather stunned silence before Juan turned to him and said, "I don't like it, man."

"What?"

"That girl. Didn't you see her neck?"

"No. What about it?"

"She had a cut on her neck, man, two of 'em." He spread his thumb and forefinger about a half-inch apart and placed them just above the base of his neck, to show Curt the location. "Like teeth marks. Y'know what I mean?"

"Oh, shit, Juan, you're not back on your *vampiro* kick again, are you? You said yourself they were just old stories, that they were impossible."

"I'm only tellin' you what I saw, *amigo*. I *don't* believe in vampires—really—but then, what in hell were those marks?"

Curt started to say "shaving nicks," but realized how ludicrous that was. He then tried to blurt out "acne" or "zits," but while that was not impossible, the fallen girl's pretty, unblemished face almost completely ruled that out. In the end, all he could do was shrug and laugh, although the sound that came out was really as far from a laugh as anything imaginable—it was a harsh, cold sound, like the crunching of broken glass underfoot.

Late that night, when room 1290 had been under the spell of sleep for four or five hours, Scott Matheson awoke suddenly from the middle of a black, dreamless unconsciousness. He rolled over stiffly and raised himself up. He had heard something, or thought he had. Yet as he listened he heard nothing but the heavy, steady breathing of his roommates and the distant, muted buzz of the fluorescents someone had left on in the bathroom.

He started to lie back down, but was stopped by an insistent pressure in his bladder.

"It figures," he whispered, forcing himself to get up, taking sleepy, unsteady steps toward the bathroom. Halfway there, he paused again.

This time there was no question of imagination. Something was at the window, and it was making a soft scraping sound, as though with fingernails.

He turned from the bathroom and shuffled past Curt's bed to the window. Behind the drapes he could still hear the scratching. It was such a small noise that it seemed almost imaginary, but he knew it was there and that it was real. He caught the edge of the drapes in his right hand and pulled them aside. His breathing stopped for a moment. He felt a sharp, cold stabbing in his chest.

There was a large object out there, moving quickly away through the night air. It must have been a bird, but it wasn't—at least not precisely. It was more the suggestion of a bird, a big amorphous patch of black, darker than the sky it was outlined against. A birdlike shape that didn't flap so much as pulsate, like a huge beating heart.

Scott was suddenly dizzy. His chest felt tight, and he had to lean against the window to keep from going to his knees. At last, when the shape had vanished, he felt his breath and some of his strength begin to flow back in.

Not a bird, he thought. But what the hell else flies like that, for Chrissakes? What else moves through the sky? Not a bird. Then what, dammit?

He took a deep breath and let go of the drapes. Slowly

he made his way to the bathroom, relieved himself, and returned to bed. He listened to the night silence for a long time, but heard no more scratching at the window. He briefly considered waking Curt and Juan and telling them what he had seen, but decided that wasn't a good idea. It was late, and anyway, they would only write it off as yet another Scott Matheson "dream."

He pulled the covers up to his chin and listened to the rapid pounding of his heart.

It wasn't a dream. He knew that. This was no more a dream than his walk to the back of the compound, his discovery of the cemetery and the butchered dog. He was absolutely positive of that.

He didn't fall asleep again for nearly three hours.

20

Ernest Cummings was late getting into his office Wednesday morning. He had been awakened just after six by a phone call from Tony Smith, requesting an eight-o'clock meeting. By the time he dragged himself into the office at ten-fifteen, Kelly Beckworth had been coping with his absence for more than two hours. She looked up from the phone and said, "Thank God, Ernie. Reuben Goldman's on the line. You remember asking him to handle the O'Hare pickups this morning? Well, he's broken down on the tollway. The engine in the van caught fire."

Cummings took the receiver and talked Goldman through the church procedure for off-compound vehicle repairs, then immediately hit the disconnect button and dialed a Van Paris Hall extension, arranging for Connie Bishop to take one of the spare vans and make the necessary airport runs. When he was done, he put the receiver down and smiled at Kelly wearily.

"Been like this all morning?"

"Worse. We had a flood in room 763, girls' side. We had a shipment of food show up at the cafeteria loading dock, but it was an order of prepackaged stuff for the burger place on Roosevelt Road, not us. We had a fight in the laundry room. And to top it off, we had two of the kids from the maintenance department get locked in the boiler room." She paused. "Where were you?"

He told her about his meeting with Smith. As with all his meetings with his superiors, it had followed a certain

146

pattern. It had opened with the usual compliments on what a fine job he was doing as director of housing, how Smith knew what a thankless position it was, and how they simply never seemed to have the opportunity to express their gratitude to him. Then it had soured, again as usual. Smith seemed to be blaming him for the number of severe illnesses in the church lately—Tom Chambers in the Park, Sally Morkowski, who had collapsed in the compound the day before. Since the director of housing was responsible for taking care of residents' problems, shouldn't these include the physical? Despite the probing questions he had asked Smith, he still wasn't sure if he was being ordered to start screening the kids in the Hall for medical problems. Rather, Smith seemed frustrated and had turned to Cummings, his usual whipping boy, to assuage those feelings.

"I just don't understand anything anymore," Cummings confided to Kelly when he was done with his story. "Nothing's been making sense lately. First Reverend Bob wants to pay me for my work. I turn him down, but he keeps pushing. There was a memo from him in my mail only last week, urging me to reconsider. Then I get some . . . well, I can't really talk about it, but there were some pretty bizarre orders that came down after the Tom Chambers thing. And now this. Medical checks. Physical screening. I don't know *what* they want. I just have a feeling that the movement's changing. Or that it's always been this way, but that I notice it more the longer I'm in this job."

Kelly, still a relative newcomer but loyal to her boss above all else, stared at him and shrugged. "What do you want me to say, Ernie?"

He blinked and smiled. "I don't know. Tell me it's my imagination. Remind me that the work I'm doing is good, that it's right, and that Tony Smith's just a distraction to put up with to get the work done."

"Okay, I'll say that."

Cummings laughed. "Maybe I just need a vacation. Do you realize that except for the pickup runs and driving the shopping-mall shuttle once in a while, I haven't been off-compound in almost four years?"

She studied him closely. After a moment she whispered the dreaded words: "Burn-out?"

He thought about that. A few months ago it wouldn't have seemed possible. Burn-out happened to others, those who came from shakier backgrounds or who didn't believe in the church with all their heart and soul. He closed his eyes momentarily to push the thought away, but all he saw was a mental replay of Tony Smith's lips twisted in a sneer as he said, *That Morkowski incident shouldn't have happened, Ernie.* He winced.

"Ernie?" Kelly Beckworth said gently, reaching across her desk to take his hand. "Do you need something?"

"Yeah," he said, squeezing her hand, grateful for the touch. "A friend."

After lunch, Cliff Alcock left Juan on his own for the first time in the day and a half he'd been working there. Telling him that there was a directors' meeting likely to last an hour or more, he left Juan in one of the production studios with two spools of reel-to-reel audiotape, an Akai tape deck, and the monitor board. His instructions: play with the tape deck and tape until he was comfortable with it. Record, play back, record some more, listen to himself through the monitor speakers mounted on the studio walls and through the headphones. In the end, if he felt really ambitious, Cliff told him to practice making some edits in his sample tapes.

"You're going to be doing a lot of this sort of thing," Alcock said as he departed for the meeting. "Roberto Fernandez is a long-winded son of a gun. You'll have to edit his sermons more than you know. Get used to it."

Alone in the studio, Juan sat back in his big comfy chair and looked around at all the equipment in the room. There was at least fifty thousand dollars' worth of high-tech production machinery. He reached out an overly careful rookie's hand and touched the monitor board lightly, allowing his fingers to move from the volume knobs (*pots*, Cliff had called them) up to the needles that showed you how loudly you were talking (*VU meters*), and back down again to the little plug (*jack*) where you snapped in the long, coiled headphone cord.

Suddenly he was overcome with a sensation of gratitude so immense that it almost brought tears. The thought that someone, for the first time in his life, trusted him to be all alone in a place full of impossibly expensive things—it was incredible! Once, when he had still been in school, his biology teacher had sent him across the hall to the small storage closet that housed the microscopes, scalpels, test tubes, beakers, clamps, stands, rubber tubing, and hundreds of bottles of chemicals that the science classes used. He was supposed to pick up two extra dissecting trays that the teacher had neglected to bring over before class, but once inside the closet he had paused, awestruck by the endless array of bottles and vials. Finally he had gotten the trays and had turned around, only to find his teacher standing three feet away watching him closely. Gone only a minute and a half at most, and he was a suspect. What a difference here.

He followed Cliff's instructions, playing with the big tape deck for a while, making several tapes ("Testing, testing," was the most inventive thing he could think of to say), and playing them back at various speeds and from various places in the tapes. At last, bored with the sound of his own voice, he went to the storage cupboards on the far wall, which Cliff had showed him housed stacks and stacks of old church sermons and radio broadcasts. He selected one with a bright red label:

SPEAKER: Bach
STATION: WGRI/Independent/Tupelo Mississippi
DATE: January 16, 1982

He carried it back to the Akai and threaded it on the way he'd been taught. He turned it on and listened as the voice of the church leader filled the room. The subject was the need to provide free, top-flight medical services to third-world nations.

At first Juan felt uncomfortable listening to Bach speak. Something about the voice of the man they called the Master bothered him, something slightly irritating and familiar. But soon he was lulled by the powerful, steady rhythms and even more by the hopeful, ever-optimistic message. He sank lower into his chair and closed his eyes.

Several minutes later he was in a sort of alert but dreamy doze when he heard the strangled cry. He leapt up right away, looking around the studio, but of course he was the only one there. The cry came again, and he pinpointed the source: directly outside the studio door. He ran to the door and threw it open and saw a boy several years younger than he slumped against the corridor wall, butt on the floor, head lolling to one side, breathing in harsh, ragged bursts.

"Hey, man, what's wrong?" Juan said, kneeling beside the boy. "What's the matter, *amigo*?"

The boy flinched at the sound of his voice, but then opened his eyes, saw Juan, and seemed to relax a little. His strangled cries had trickled away into soft moans, but one hand still opened and closed at his side, fluttering like a wounded bird.

"What's the matter?" Juan said again.

"That . . . that voice," the boy said. "Ahhh . . ."

"What voice?" Juan was momentarily puzzled, but then he felt a crushing wave of embarrassment. The boy was talking about the voice coming from monitor speakers mounted at regular intervals down the corridor. It was the voice of Reverend Bach, the same voice that was playing inside the production studio. Oh, God, he thought, I flipped the wrong switch. I turned that tape on all over the building. Did it just happen? Or did they all hear my stupid testing-testing shit too? Then the boy moaned softly again.

"What about it?" Juan asked, leaning close. "What about the voice?"

"The . . . the Master . . . That's the Master's voice."

"The Master, sure, that's him. What about it?"

"He . . . he comes to me at night . . . the Master at night . . . talks . . . that voice . . ."

Juan got scared. There was something really wrong with this kid. He gave up his feeble efforts at providing aid and ran to get help. It wasn't until the end of the day that he got the whole story from Lucinda Washington,

Laurie Campbell's secretary. The boy was Dennis Ryan. He worked in the maintenance department and had been at God's Hand Radio to return some expensive soldering equipment the department had borrowed a few days earlier. The report from the hospital was that Ryan's appendix had burst. It was lucky, Lucinda said, that Juan had discovered him when he did. Ryan was going to be all right, but only God knew how he would have fared if he had lain alone in that corridor much longer.

Juan left work that day feeling like a hero. It wasn't until much later that night that he began to think twice about the whole thing.

Curt broke out of a thicket of trees and stared at the fork in the road ahead of him. He had followed the trail from the Hall to the back of the compound, past the Faith Center, past God's Hand Radio, past the garage that housed the lawn mowers and pickups of the groundskeeping department. Now he didn't know which way to turn.

In a way it was a perfect metaphor for his state of mind, he thought.

He sensed his time at Universal winding to a close. He had come here with a course of action all planned out. He had expected to see Bach on his first day, his second or third day at the latest, and yet he had not been able to see him at all. Bach, Van Paris, and Kaye were guarded by hopelessly filled appointment calendars and strict secretaries.

Frustrated in his original mission, there didn't seem to be much point in staying. Life on the road beckoned him, and he found it bitterly amusing the way a wandering tramp's life could be both suffocating and powerfully addictive at the same time. He felt the urge to light out building steadily within his heart, and yet . . .

He didn't want to leave.

There. He had admitted it. In a bizarre way, he actually felt better.

He didn't want to leave. He had made friends here. Although he had not taken a job like the other residents, he took comfort in the sense of purpose he felt in the compound. The rhythms of church life were relaxing, even soothing.

Beyond that, there was something else holding him here. It was hard to put his finger on precisely what it was. It was a baffling, half-seen mystery, something he felt the urge to explore and expose. It was all tied up in confusing ways with Tom Chambers and Sally, the girl who had collapsed in the compound. Juan's dream and his obsession with old myths was part of it, too. And so was Scott. Scott's own dreams. The dead dog. The cemetery. Yes. The cemetery.

He sighed and followed the right-hand path. . . .

After what seemed like an hour, Curt rounded a final bend in the road and saw it. He almost missed it at first because it was set so far back off the road and masked by several tall trees and the murky light of late afternoon.

"Scott—" was the word that came through his lips unbidden.

And he thought: Scott, my man, I owe you an apology.

He stood there staring at it for a long time: the low stone wall with the iron gate set into it, the hedges that grew inside, the rows of stones.

"A cemetery," he whispered. "Jesus Christ."

He took a step toward the gate but stopped, casting a glance at the sky. He checked his watch: five-fifteen. Late for this time of year. It would be dark soon. Of course, darkness was only an imbecile's concern, something to trouble the minds of children and men with Stone Age superstitions. He took another step forward and stopped again. The iron gate seemed to wait for him to pull it open.

Curt looked up at the sky again.

Then, feeling more foolish than he had felt in a very long time, he turned around and hurried back to Van Paris Hall.

21

Stephen Norris listened to the voice coming through the receiver and nodded with apparent satisfaction. "That's pretty good news, Bob. I'm sure the Master'll be pleased."

"I hope so," Robert Kaye said through the static of three thousand miles of overseas connections. "When are you going to meet with him?"

"Tonight, I hope." Norris paused, and lit one of his home-rolled cigarettes. "I hear Van Paris is going to be there too."

"Excellent. We'll all be standing on first base together. You wrote down everything I told you?"

"Of course I wrote it down, Bob. The German connections are—or will be—ready. More than that, they're eager. Schroeder will set the ball rolling as soon as you leave to fly back home. They believe the number of connections needed to make the thing work can be kept to a minimum—half a dozen, maybe. Does that about sum it up?"

"Just about. Don't forget what I told you about the new man, Hans Lund. The Master will want to know everyone involved, and since Lund is new, make sure he at least has the name. We don't want Bach to think we're throwing surprises at him."

"Lund, Hans. Got it."

"Then that should just about do it. I'm leaving here in two days, but there's more business elsewhere. I'll be laying over in Paris for a couple of days, then off to

Stockholm and back to Paris again. P.R. meetings with local bigwigs. I won't be back in Chicago until next Friday."

"Friday. Okay."

"How're things there?"

Norris chuckled. "Could be better, Bob, but we're handling it."

Kaye wasn't fooled for a minute. "What's wrong?"

"Well, we've had a couple of incidents. A girl in the compound yesterday and a boy today in the radio office."

"Like Chambers?"

Norris sighed. "I don't have the medical reports yet, but they're similar."

"Damn. What're you doing about it?"

"Meeting with Tony Smith in about fifteen minutes, for starters. I'm squeezing him in before going off to see the Master."

"What else?"

"Bob, come on. Things are happening fast. I don't have a course of action yet. I don't even have all the facts. Just relax and I'll fill you in when you get back. Don't worry."

"Worry. Right. Not me. Things are going crazy at home, and we're still starting up the biggest logistical move we've ever undertaken. Why should I worry?"

They hung up a few moments later. Norris leaned forward and rested his elbows on his desk, his head in his hands. Bob was right. The European move was the biggest thing they'd ever undertaken. Problems at home or not, it was impossible not to worry about Germany. And yet it was the best thing. It had to be, because it was Bach's plan, and the Master didn't do things that were against their best interests. Sometimes his plans seemed odd; sometimes they were hard to accept; sometimes they even appeared to be mistakes. But mistakes to an ordinary person were not mistakes to Bach. That was something you learned quickly when you were in his service.

Norris still had his head buried in his hands several moments later when there was a knock on the door. Tony Smith.

"Come in," he called.

Smith was carrying several file folders and a bone-dry yellow slicker draped over one arm. He nodded to Norris and took a seat without waiting for an invitation.

"Okay, let's hear it," Norris said, in no mood for amenities himself.

Smith nodded again. He ran a hand through his curly brown hair and studied one of the folders on his lap. "Sally Morkowski. She's the girl who went down in the compound yesterday. She had all the classic symptoms. Fortunately, Becky saw it happen. She got there within a couple of minutes and shooed away the nosies. Morkowski is in the infirmary, recovering nicely, no problems."

"Do you have a list of residents who were there?"

Smith produced a sheet of paper from the folder and handed it across the desk to Norris, who scanned it quickly.

"Nineteen," Norris said. "Not good, but it could've been a lot worse. I'll want you to keep an eye on them, though. Just to be sure. What about this Ryan kid?"

"We were luckier there. There was only one person around, except for Laurie Campbell's secretary, who called the doctor. The resident and the secretary both got the same story—a burst appendix. It sat well with them, we think. Ryan's also in the infirmary, by the way, but he's not doing well. They're giving him blood and B12, so he might pull through. Dr. MacCauley says he'll know by tomorrow, but I'm telling you now: If things don't improve, the Master should be prepared to handle the case—induction."

Norris nodded thoughtfully. "I'll take a look at the prognosis reports tomorrow and make a decision then." He lit a cigarette. "The secretary was Lucinda Washington, I suppose?"

"Yes."

"And the resident?"

"A newcomer by the name of Jimenez. Juan Jimenez. He works—"

"Jimenez? Wait a minute. Wasn't he there when Morkowski went down?" Norris looked at the list of names again. "Yeah, right here . . . Juan Jimenez, room 1290."

"I know, we caught that, too. We're going to keep an eye on him, but I don't anticipate problems. He's too new. He's got fitting-in on the mind."

"Any way of knowing if he was in the Park the day Chambers—"

"Nope. Not there. Thank God for tiny favors."

"Yes, thank God for that," Norris said thoughtfully. He sighed. "This reminds me a little too much of the last time. Do you remember, Tony? It was five years ago, I think. The Master was being greedy then too, taking too much, too fast. That maintenance worker, Paul Hardy, started to catch on."

"I remember," Smith said, and nodded bitterly. "He ran, didn't he?"

"Snuck away in the night," Norris said. "We were lucky. I just hope . . ." He trailed away, shaking his head as if to dismiss horrible thoughts. "Enough," he said then. "We'll deal with things as they come. You'll keep me posted on all fronts?"

Smith rose and went for the door. "Of course. You'll have medical reports in the morning, and I'll try to get you watch reports on these residents every couple of days. It's all a problem, but I think we'll get through all right. When's Bob getting back?"

"Not for some time."

"And you can't tell me where he went? What he's doing?"

"Sorry. Not yet. But I *can* tell you that it's going to keep us all pretty busy for a while this fall. Actually, *very* busy."

Smith held up the folders and smiled crookedly. "Just what we need."

"Yes," Norris said. "Hard work. Noses to the grindstone and fingers crossed."

Smith's harsh laughter seemed to linger in the office for a long time after the man himself had left.

22

Scott was attending a screening of *Top Gun* in the Faith Center with Phyllis. Curt and Juan stayed around the room, but both were unusually silent. Juan was lying on his bed, hands folded behind his head, staring at the ceiling. Over and over again he replayed in his head his heroic rescue of Dennis Ryan in the corridor outside the production studio. But every time he ran through the scene again he felt less happy about it, and dwelled a little more on the strangeness of it all.

"He . . . he comes to me at night . . ." Ryan had said.

Who? Reverend Bach? The Master? At *night*?

That was kinda crazy, wasn't it?

He comes to me at night . . .

Of course, the kid had been really whacked out, in a lot of pain, and probably hysterical. Juan had heard junkies saying things that were a helluva lot more bizarre than that. He'd seen winos babbling about saucers from Venus, and bag ladies mumbling under their breath about the brain police who were only three inches tall and carried tiny needles full of mind-numbing drugs that they injected behind your ear if they caught you. This was probably the same thing . . . but did a busted appendix make you say wild things?

He comes to me at night . . .

Curt was buried in yet another of the church histories he had been reading obsessively since his arrival in Chicago. This time, though, he wasn't interested in the story

157

of Arthur Bach and Richard Van Paris, of Bach's rise from country pastor to powerful evangelist. This time he was desperately searching for clues that matched the strange thoughts swirling through his brain. He had planned his trip to the north of the compound that day as a way to banish those thoughts forever. He hadn't expected to find the cemetery.

At one point he put the books aside and closed his eyes like Juan, thinking. But when he did that, his mind immediately overloaded with hordes of stalking, flapping creatures with grinning faces and mouths with blood-red lips and long razor-sharp teeth glinting in cold moonlight. Birds soared off into the night on tremendously powerful wings, leaving decapitated dogs, gravestones hidden behind low stone walls, and zombielike children moving across the compound. He opened his eyes and sat up quickly, turning to Juan.

"Tell me again about the kid in the radio building," he said savagely.

Juan did, and when he was done he said, "Somethin' bother you about that?"

"I don't know." Curt sat up completely now, swinging his legs over the edge of the bed and staring across the room at Juan. He sighed. "That thing he said about Bach coming to him late at night, it's kind of strange, don't you think?"

Juan gave a small nod. "There's somethin' else too, Curt. I'll tell it to you, but you gotta promise not to think I'm psycho. Okay?"

Curt nodded. "What is it?"

"Well, I been sittin' here thinkin' about it all night. I was proud of myself, y'know? Shit, I still am. I mighta saved the kid's life. But I don't like that shit he said, either. And somethin' else, somethin' I didn't notice right off."

"Something he said?"

"Uh-uh. It's somethin' I saw when the medics was puttin' him on the stretcher. They'd unbuttoned his shirt to check him out, y'know? They'd been listenin' to his heart through one of them scopes, feelin' his belly, checkin' his ribs. When they lifted him up, the shirt fell open all the way and I saw 'em."

Curt leaned forward, suddenly very afraid of what he was about to hear. No, he was thinking wildly, he's not going to say it. He's not going to mention marks.

"I think I saw two of them little marks on his neck, Curt. I didn't think about it then, not with all the excitement, but now I'm almost sure I saw 'em. Just like the girl yesterday. Two little marks, right there on his neck."

"Like the girl yesterday," Curt repeated dully.

"Yeah! It's fuckin' weird, man. I mean, shit, I was just kiddin' about vampires—you *know* that—but what the hell're all these sick people runnin' around with little marks on their necks? Is it some kinda disease?"

Curt didn't answer. There was a distant roaring in his ears that seemed to be growing louder all the time. Arthur Bach, the pastor who was never seen. He thought of Van Paris—ditto, never seen. He thought of other things he had learned about the church—early assistants to Bach who had dropped out of sight when Van Paris came on the scene in the early seventies, and department heads who were in the compound one day, gone the next.

There was no denying where his thoughts were leading anymore. They might be utterly insane, but they couldn't be ignored. Two days ago he would have been shocked at the way all these things were fitting together in his mind, but now these crazy, ridiculous, childish, superstitious— pick your adjective—happenings had to be acknowledged.

"Is it some kinda disease?" Juan had asked.

And now he answered at last, in a whisper:

"I think it is, Juan."

"Jeezus, what if we catch it, man? What if it's catchin'?"

"I don't know. Look, you haven't talked to anyone else about this yet, have you? I mean the marks and things. You haven't mentioned it to anyone?"

"Shit, you kiddin'? You think I wanna look like an asshole?"

"Good. Keep it that way. I want to do a little research first, and when I find out, I'll tell you. Until then, just keep it quiet, okay?"

"Sure, you bet." Juan paused, letting a long moment of silence spin out. Then he said: "Hey, Curt, you don't look so hot, *amigo*."

"I'm okay."

"You sure? You look like you're about to take a dump in your pants. This disease, you afraid of it?"

Curt nodded. "I'm scared to death."

He slipped in and out of sleep a lot that night, chasing odd dreams and being chased by them in return. In one dream he was sitting in a dingy tavern in a small lumbering town somewhere in the north, sharing a beer with Tom Chambers. In another he was lying in the middle of a gravel path, his face turned toward the sky, while Becky Heller leaned over and whispered in his ear—strange, multisyllable words that he heard perfectly but couldn't understand. In another he and Arthur Bach were fishing from a small rowboat in the middle of a wide, sparkling lake. And in yet another the four of them—Scott, Phyllis, Juan, and he—were standing outside the gates of the Universal cemetery, talking about going in but admitting that they were afraid to.

He came fully awake after that dream, sitting up and wiping a sheen of cold perspiration from his forehead. He groped for his watch, found it, and squinted at the numbers on the face: three-fifteen. Shit. The night was going to last forever.

Was it possible? he wondered.

Of course it wasn't, not in the least, but how else to explain everything?

Vampires in a church.

Even given the fact (for the sake of argument) that he might accept the unacceptable concept of vampires, the thought that they would be hiding behind the facade of a church was laughable. The church was a force for good in the world, this church in particular. And if you believed the old legends, churches were vampires' oldest enemies.

He put a hand to his stomach and held it there, realizing for the first time that what he was feeling was no longer confusion but rather a crippling combination of terror and nausea that was sweeping through his body in cold waves. He felt dizzy. He felt as though he had been washed out from shore and cast upon the surface of a huge dark sea.

Vampires.

How could you rail against that one word with so much evidence flooding in, with so much—

Oh, God, he thought, please, God, if you're really here, if you're around this place at all, watch out for me, okay? Help me get through this. Take care of me.

He waited for a very long time, praying for an answer. None came. The silence of the night held sway, and haunting pictures of something far worse than clean, quick death capered madly within his troubled mind.

23

It rained on Sunday. As a result, the morning service in Worship Park was poorly attended. Among the few faithful, however, were Curt, Phyllis, Scott, Juan, and Connie Bishop.

Curt took the opportunity to study the other people in the Park as closely as possible. Since his discovery of the cemetery and his disturbing conversation with Juan, he had been counting every weary, blank-faced person he saw. In addition, he had been trying to unobtrusively get close enough to see marks on their necks. It had become an obsession with him, burning like a low-grade fever, something he had to do despite what it was doing to him. He stopped only when the number reached a horrifying two hundred.

Afterward, as the five of them walked back through the drizzle, Curt took the plunge he had been planning for all week.

"Do you guys think we could all get together this afternoon at four? For a little meeting?"

Connie stopped and looked at him. "What kind of meeting? Scripture reading?"

"Noooo, just a meeting."

"Who?"

"All of you."

Phyllis shrugged. "I don't have anything better to do, I guess." She turned to Scott. "What about you, hon?"

"Why not?"

Curt nodded gratefully to them and turned back to Connie and Juan. "Will you come?"

Juan nodded, but Connie was still confused. "It's important?"

"Yes. Very."

"Then I wouldn't miss it for the world. Besides, I'm riding in Phyllis' boat; I don't have anything better to do. As long as we're done by eight tonight, when my prayer group meets."

They headed toward the cafeteria to get some coffee. Phyllis and Scott made a few jokes about Curt's secretive behavior, and everyone laughed. Everyone but Curt, that is, who was lagging several paces behind the others now. He was wondering, as he had been for two days, if he was doing the right thing. There were moments when it seemed like the *only* thing to do, but at other times it seemed like the worst of at least a hundred alternatives.

He sighed. It was too late now. He'd committed himself.

Curt spent most of the afternoon alone in his room. He lay on the bed listening to the rain patter against the windows and reading from the stack of books on folklore that he had checked out of the library. Occasionally he glanced up at the picture of Arthur Tallman Bach hanging next to the door, and felt a slow shiver work its way down his spine.

At ten to four he went into the bathroom and splashed cold water on his face. After toweling off, he leaned over to comb his hair in the little countertop mirror Scott had brought back from the shopping mall a few days before. He always felt ridiculous bending over so far—it was a little like being in public and having to use the little kids' drinking fountain.

He froze. The comb fell from his fingers and skittered across the tile floor.

No mirror.

Oh, shit, he thought.

He bent down to pick up the comb and startled himself by speaking aloud: "Lunacy, Curt. Utter fucking lunacy."

But of course the whole world was a lunatic's twisted vision. Nuclear weapons in silos. Birth defects. Cancer.

Highway accidents that came out of nowhere. But vampires? Vampires are still just a bunch of goddamned nonsense, he thought.

He was still thinking those things—lunacy, nonsense—twenty minutes later as everyone settled in the room. Connie Bishop sat on the floor, his muscular legs stretched out in front of him, his back against the wall; Juan on his bed; Scott on his bed too, with Phyllis at his side. Curt perched on the edge of the desk so that he could look all of them in the eye. For a fleeting moment he thought about calling it all off.

"Well?" Connie said.

Juan lit a cigarette and leaned against his headboard. "Right. Let's hear it, *amigo*. What's so important you made us plan the day aroun' you?"

Curt smiled. "I'll tell you, but I want to make a couple of things clear first. We need to establish something. It's going to sound strange—hell, it *is* strange—but I need to know if you all think I'm sane."

"What?" Phyllis said. "What're you saying? Of course you're sane."

"Thanks, Phyl. I appreciate that more than you know. Anyone disagree with her?"

Scott, Juan, and Connie looked at each other. One by one they shook their heads.

"Good. I'm glad to have the support, because I guarantee you that by the time we're done today, you'll be calling for the guys in the padded truck. It makes me feel a little better to know that I'm at least starting in fair territory."

Connie opened his mouth to say something, but Curt rushed ahead:

"One more thing. I need a promise from all of you. I want you to promise that no matter what I say, you'll let me get through it. No interruptions. That's the only way I'll make it. Afterward you can say anything you want. But give me a chance to finish first. Okay?"

Again his friends exchanged baffled, troubled glances. Again he was answered with slow, thoughtful nods. Curt knew that if any of them had come here expecting a friendly bull session, those expectations had now been set aside. Good, he thought. It was just what he'd wanted.

"All right. I'm just going to start at the beginning and spill everything—what I've seen and read and thought. There are things that have been bothering me since the very first day I got here, and it hasn't gotten any better since then—only worse. It's been one thing after another, and I've been putting pieces together as they come. . . ."

By the time he was finished, more than two hours had passed. Late afternoon had given way to evening. The sound of rain pelting the windows had grown stronger. Curt leaned over from the desk and snatched a cigarette from the pack on Juan's bed—his fifth since he'd begun talking, only his seventh in the past four years.

"Okay, it's your turn. I appreciate you keeping the promise to let me finish the story, but now what do you think?"

No one said anything. They were too stunned to say anything.

"It's okay," he urged. "Hit me with your best shots. I think I can take it."

Scott tore himself away from Phyllis and moved to the edge of his bed. "What do you want us to say?"

"I don't know. Anything. Facts, opinions, dead-baby jokes. Let's hear it."

Scott shrugged. "Well, I'm not sure what you expect us to say. I mean, good God, it's all kind of crazy, isn't it? When we were lying in bed that night, talking about this stuff, about Juan's *vampiros* and everything, well, we weren't serious, you know."

"I know that. None of us were. But now I am."

Connie laughed sharply. "Curt, m'man, you keep saying that, but how can you be? Vampires? That's fairy-tale stuff."

"No arguments there, but all the same, the pieces fit."

Connie started to say something else, but before any words came out, he was seized by a look of utter confusion and closed his mouth in frustration.

"Anyone else? How about you, Juan, or Phyllis? Do you agree with them? Is it crazy?"

Phyllis was the first to answer: "Let's say, for the sake of argument, that there really are vampires. What're they doing here? This is a church. Churches are supposed to kill vampires, aren't they? Aren't churches the sworn enemies of vampires?"

Curt nodded. "That's one of the things I considered right from the start. All the legends mention it. But it's not the proximity to a church that matters, it's the amount of direct contact. Think about the vampire stories you know. Vampires can be as close to a church as you like—they can rise from a church graveyard with no problem—but lay a crucifix up against them, or splash them with holy water, and they're in real trouble."

"But—"

"Hang on, there's more. I mentioned Bach and Van Paris as the main vampires, right? How many times do you see either of them in direct contact with the church? How many times do you even *see* them? They're never at services or walking around the compound. They never do crusades. They don't even come into the cafeteria, for God's sake. They've got other people taking care of the public contact for them. How do we know where they're hiding?"

"But—"

"Just one more second, Phyl. Think about something else. Think about camouflage. When you come right down to it, what better hiding place for a vampire than right here, behind the facade of a religious movement? Even assuming that someone came here believing in all the old legends, or that someone nosy like me began to suspect things, they'd never dream there could be vampires here. Not inside a church. It's perfect."

Phyllis shrugged. "Point for you. But what about daylight? If all these tired people you kept calling the zombies are really vampires, how come they're out walking around all day, in the sunshine?"

Curt sighed, taking a last puff of his cigarette and stubbing it out in Juan's ashtray. "That's something else that threw me off the track for a while. But I didn't say those people are vampires, not necessarily. I think they're more like walking fast food for the real vampires. Maybe

Bach and Van Paris, or the others, if there are others, feed on those people, taking just enough to satisfy themselves without killing. It makes their victims weak and sick, but doesn't mean they become vampires. Although I do think the vampires go a little far sometimes. Look at Tom Chambers in the Park that Sunday. He was rubbing his skin and moaning a lot, as though the sunlight was too much for him. And when the workmen brought out the big stage cross, he went berserk. He wasn't a full vampire, but he was close."

"Oh, come on," Scott said. "If that's true, why don't these people talk? If they're being attacked by vampires at night, why don't they tell the rest of us about it? Why don't they just leave Chicago and run away somewhere? I mean, wouldn't you?"

"I would if I knew about it," Curt said softly.

"What's that supposed to mean?"

"It means you're not aware of being bitten by a vampire. Not according to the legends." He thumped the stack of books next to him on the desk for emphasis. "You might wake up the next morning feeling sick, or maybe you remember having a nasty dream, but you don't recall details of the visitation itself. I guess that the right circumstances might trigger something in you later on. Like the kid in the radio studio, the one Juan helped. He heard Bach's voice coming out from the speaker and started crying, saying the Master came to him in the night. A burst appendix? Maybe. But it's pretty damn strange, don't you think?"

"Strange," Connie muttered. "The only thing strange around here is you. But as long as everyone's humoring you, I don't want to be the one accused of not giving you a chance. I want to know where the other folks around here fit into your picture. What about the other pastors? The department heads? Ernie Cummings? Reverend Bob? Reverend Welles? Tony Smith? Reverend Norris?"

"I think they're the Master's human familiars."

"Human what?"

"Familiars. I'd heard the word only in connection with witches before, but when I started reading about vampires, it popped up again and again. See, a vampire keeps at least one normal human around him, someone to live in the real world for him, to conduct his business, get him whatever he needs, keep him safe from prying people, move him if necessary, sometimes even find his victims. Such a person is a familiar. Sometimes it's only one, but in this case I'm betting there are a lot more. I don't know about Cummings, or that Tony Smith guy you mentioned, but I can almost guarantee that Norris and Kaye are in on everything."

"Why? Why would they do it?" Scott said.

Curt shrugged. "A familiar is paid in various ways. Sometimes it's a simple matter of just staying alive—you know, the familiar's afraid that if he goes against his master, if he cuts and runs, he'll be tracked down and killed. Sometimes it's more complicated, kinkier. Sometimes a familiar gets to share the vampire's blood. Or maybe it's just a matter of earthly riches. Think about Reverend Bob. Wouldn't you say that getting to be the head pastor here, getting all the money, fame, fortune, and success, is a pretty good reward?"

"I don't like this, Curt," Phyllis said. "It was kind of fun when you started, but now it's all sounding real."

"Good! It better sound real. You better take it seriously. Because if I'm wrong, we won't be any worse off than we are right now—except for me, who will look stupid and probably lose your friendship to boot. But if it is real, even part of it, then we're all in a helluva lot of trouble. More trouble than you'd ever believe."

Scott smiled. "You mean we're in danger of joining the undead?" he asked, doing his best Lugosi.

"That, or becoming one of the zombies stumbling around the compound. Do the math, if you don't believe me. There are—what?—maybe fifteen hundred people here. Out of that number, at least four or five hundred are quiet, sick—zombies. Four or five hundred people who might have been victims of the Master. Not very good odds for us."

Connie stood up and started toward the door. "I don't have to listen to this. It was nice to meetcha, Curt buddy. Nice to know ya. But I don't figure we'll be talking anymore, not after this, although I might come visit you when they cart you off to the hospital.''

"Connie, wait! I'm not crazy. Just look around you. Jesus Christ, ask yourself the same questions I asked. Why are there five hundred dazed people out there? Why do they have two little red marks on their necks? Why can't any of us get in to see Bach or Van Paris? And why are there no mirrors in any of the rooms? Can you tell me that?''

Connie stopped and turned around. "Mirrors?''

"Yes! Don't you think it's just a little bit funny that they give us these huge luxury rooms that have everything we could ever need, but no mirrors? Don't you find it unusual that Ken Lambroux down the hall asked for a TV set and got one, but I asked for a mirror and didn't?''

"My God," Phyllis whispered. "I never thought about that. I mean, I thought it was a hassle having to use my little compact all the time, but I never would have connected that with vampires . . . not in a hundred years.''

No one acknowledged her. Curt and Connie were staring at each other levelly, like a couple of odd gunfighters trying to decide whether or not to draw.

"Connie?''

The black man ran a hand through his halo of hair, opened his mouth, closed it again, and shook his head. "Sorry, m'man, I can't. I just can't.''

He turned and left the room.

"Shit," Curt said, putting a hand up to cover his eyes. He knew that he should feel better right now. Spilling his fears into the open should have been a cleansing act. He had allowed himself that small spark of hope that they would somehow listen, consider, believe, and rally around.

He uncovered his eyes and looked at the remaining three. "So you all think I'm crazy, is that it? You think I took the big leap right off the deep end?''

Juan shook his head and spoke for the first time. "I didn't say that. I don't know what to think.''

"Yeah, well, don't forget that you were the one who first mentioned vampires.''

"Jeezus, man, I know, I know. But I was just kiddin', I never believed that shit.''

"And I never believed it either," Scott said. "I knew

I'd really been out to the cemetery and seen that stuff, long before you found it. But vampires? No way, Curt. Vandals killed that dog I found, not monsters. I never believed that, never. Even when we joked about it. Even when I heard the noise at the window and—" He broke off suddenly, looking away and down at the floor.

"What?" Curt demanded. "What noise? When?"

"Nothing. Forget it."

"What noise?"

"It was nothing, dammit!"

Phyllis touched his arm gently. "Scott, you never said anything about a noise at the window. What was it?"

Scott's eyes narrowed down to angry slits. His lips were tight as he said, "I didn't hear anything."

"Hey, cut the shit," Juan said. "If Curt can tell his story, you oughta do the same. No secrets. What's the deal?"

Scott shook his head miserably. "Honest to God, it was nothing. It happened a few nights ago. I woke up thinking I'd heard a noise . . ."

He told them the story of the scratching at the window, the black shape that had moved away—not a bird really, just a huge, indefinable shape. That was all.

"All?" Curt said. "What do you mean, that's all? How can you say that after everything we've been talking about? How do you know that wasn't Bach out there, trying to get in, trying to get at you—us?"

"Curt . . ." Phyllis said.

He ignored her. "Come on, Scott. Tell me. How do you know that wasn't Bach? Or Van Paris? Or one of the others? There were more, you know—someone named Walstein, and another guy named Paul Hummelt—friends of Bach in the early days, who disappeared after Van Paris came on the scene. How do you know it wasn't one of them?"

Scott flared, leaning forward, almost coming off the bed. "Because I'm not an idiot like you! I don't see things and immediately connect them to some wild old superstition!"

Curt shrugged. "You moved out of Brad's room because he didn't believe you'd seen the dog."

"That was different."

"How?"

"I told you. Dead dogs are real. Vampires are—are . . ."

"Crazy?"

"You said it, Curt, not me."

"Then tell me what you think. Not just about the zombies, Tom Chambers, the Ryan kid. Tell me why Bach was just a small-town preacher for so many years. Tell me why his parish was growing, but he wasn't big-time until he met Van Paris. Tell me why Van Paris shows up and bingo! a year later Bach's got one of the most successful ministries in the world. And tell me why Bach and his friends dropped out of sight. If Van Paris didn't turn them into vampires, then tell me what—"

"Stop it," Juan said. "Quit arguin', man, it ain't gettin' us nowhere."

"But what am I supposed to do? Throw my research out the window? Forget everything I've seen?"

"Well, whaddya want us to do?" Juan said. "What was you expectin'? You think we'd run out and buy a buncha garlic? Start sharpenin' stakes to drive into the Master's heart? Call the fuckin' Ghostbusters or somethin'?"

Curt shook his head. When he spoke again after a moment, his voice had dropped to a whisper. "I don't know, Juan. I just don't know."

No one spoke. For a long time the rain rattling against the windows was the only sound in the room.

"You know," Scott said at last. "Even assuming I could buy the vampire bit, I wouldn't sit still for this crap. Not when you're turning on Reverend Bach. To hear you sit here and badmouth the Master, calling the man we love, the man we came here for, a monster—I think it's sick. I worship that man, he's God on earth for me, and you come out with your maniac judgment against him. I think that's—"

"Shut up," Curt said softly.

Scott drew back. "What?"

"I said, shut up. You want to knock the vampire story? Fine, okay, that's your right. You want to call me crazy, you can do that too. But don't ever, ever, dare say I'm judging Bach too harshly. You can't say that."

"What're you talkin' about?" Juan said.

Curt turned away from them for a moment. When he faced them again, his eyes were red and moist. He spoke, but the words came out in broken, halting syllables.

"I . . . I didn't want to get into this, but I suppose you have to know."

"What?" Phyllis asked.

"It's Bach . . . your Master. Bach."

"Curt . . . ?"

Curt sighed. It had the eerie, rushing sound of a late-November wind gusting through leafless trees.

"Bach . . ." he said again. "The son of a bitch is my father."

24

For the majority of Van Paris Hall residents, Monday arrived like any other day. Cloud-muted sunlight filtered through the windows of their rooms. Roommates had sleepy conversations as they went off to breakfast. Even those who woke up feeling weaker than usual—whose eyes throbbed when they looked out the window, whose legs felt a little rubbery, unable to negotiate their first few steps very efficiently—saw nothing foreboding or out of the ordinary.

Yet to the four people who had attended Curt's bizarre meeting the day before, the morning looked quite different. What little sun there was seemed oddly comforting after a long night of cold, disturbing thoughts. It was not that they believed what they had heard, not at all. It was just a relief to wake up from the disturbed dreams Curt's troubled ramblings had given them.

Connie Bishop had slept better than any of them, but when he got dressed and prepared himself for another day of airport, bus-, and train-station runs, he found himself bemusedly thinking of Curt's frame of mind. Interesting, it was. But he didn't think it was anything to worry about. On and off, he had been at Universal longer than any of the others at the meeting. In that time he had seen plenty of strange reactions from newcomers— anger, bitterness, even paranoia. It was a kind of shock, or so he had always surmised. It hit you when the fact that you'd truly left the old behind and begun a new life came home to stay. Sometimes that was in the first few days, sometimes after weeks, or even months. Obviously that was what they had seen in Curt last night, the shock. The man's intangibles had become tangible—he was here, and he knew it—and his mind was playing tricky games with him.

Vampires, he thought.

Well, it was probably the wildest reaction he'd seen yet. It was one for the books. But Curt was basically a good guy. He'd pull through.

But if Connie was sanguine about the whole affair, Scott Matheson was not. He didn't like it, not at all, any of it. He was concerned for his roommate, wondering if he'd brought this weird emotional baggage with him or if something in the Universal life-style had created it. But it was more than that. Try as he might, he couldn't dismiss the mental picture he had of Curt's dead-serious face. Lurking just behind it, however, was something still worse. Since the meeting it had been coming back to him repeatedly—a recurrence of the icy chill he had felt when he'd discovered the butchered dog, when that huge bird-thing had gone flapping away into the dark sky. Leaving the room early, with the cobbled-up excuse of a huge print run pending at work, he ate alone in the cafeteria, picking at his food.

At noon he searched the print shop until he found Phyllis in a back-corner storage room, sorting huge sheets of rub-off transfer lettering by point size. They went to the cafeteria together, moving silently through the line, agreeing without speaking on a table near the big picture windows. They sat down and looked at each other, struggling for words, uncomfortably aware of the clatter of dishes and the happy babble of voices surrounding them.

"We can't avoid it," Scott said suddenly.

"Last night?"

He nodded. "We're going to have to talk about it. What do you think?"

"Jesus, Scott, what *can* I think?"

"Well, you don't believe him, do you?"

"About what? The vampires? Or about him being Bach's son?"

"Either."

"The vampires . . ." she said. "No. No, I couldn't believe something like that. The other? I don't know. The story he told was pretty believable, and—"

"Wait a minute, hold on. Believable? Let's reconstruct what he said. Bach's a little nowhere pastor in a small Wisconsin town, right? He falls in love with one of his parishioners, a young farm girl. Curt's mother. They have an affair for almost two years, until she gets pregnant and confronts him. Details accurate so far?"

Phyllis looked at him strangely and nodded.

"Okay. She confronts him. He goes crazy. Cuts her off, rigs it so that she's embarrassed in front of the whole town, holds her up in front of everyone as a whore, a slut. She leaves, hits the road. Drags herself and baby Curt all over hell and back, all around the Midwest, the East. Still accurate?"

She nodded again. "Yes, Scott."

"Mom dies when Curt's fourteen. From there he takes off on his own, moving here and there. Different schools, different jobs, West Coast, East Coast, North, South. Starts trying to get in touch with old pastor Dad back in Wisconsin. Nothing. Letters go unanswered, phone calls go unreturned. Then Dad gets suddenly famous. Now Curt's really cut off. He tries a few more times to get in touch but he finally gives up."

"Yes, Scott," Phyllis said again, with more than a trace of irritation.

"Curt writes him off for years, but never stops thinking about him. Finally, six or eight months ago, he's in some dive in northern Michigan, right? He sees a crusade on TV, Reverend Bob, the choir, all that. He decides then to come back and confront Dad face-to-face, although it takes him a long time and a couple more moves to work up the courage. And, of course, when he finally *does* get here, Dad's impossible to reach."

"And you don't believe any of that?"

He shrugged. "Not really. It's a little too pat, you know? All a little too good to be true."

"A *Scarlet Letter* of the eighties?"

"Something like that, yeah." He paused. "Although, if

it was true, it would explain how he could flip out, I guess. It might just be the reason he started seeing vampires everywhere—the strain of it all, I mean."

"Then you're saying it's possible?"

He nodded. "The father-son part, Phyl, not the vampires. Let's get that straight."

"And you say there's no chance he's right about the rest of it?"

"Be serious. Vampires?"

She put her fork down and sighed. "I know what you mean. I really love this place. It's probably the best thing that ever happened to me. I mean before . . . before the baby, I wouldn't have come here in a million years. But now I'm here, and I love it. The church, the job . . . you. It's saving me. I guess I just assumed that Curt felt the same, that everyone did."

"So we agree. The only question is—"

"Stop. We agree. Yes. I know that what Curt said is crazy, but I can't stop thinking that we're condemning him without a trial."

"What? You—"

"Can I sit down?"

They looked up and saw Juan standing next to them, lunch tray in hand, smiling emptily.

Phyllis nodded and pushed a chair away from the table for him.

He slid in next to her and looked uneasily down at his tray, as though the thought of food made him ill. Then he looked up at Scott and Phyllis. "I bet I know what you're talkin' about."

"Yeah, I'll bet you do," Scott said. "How about you? What do you make of the whole thing?"

Juan grimaced. "The guy's my roommate, man. What am I s'posed to say?"

"What you think," Phyllis said. "What you feel."

He laughed. "I think Curt's *loco*. No shit. But it's kinda my fault too, know what I mean? I'm the one first said *vampiro*, I gave him the idea."

"But you were kidding!" Scott said.

"Sure, yeah, I guess I was. You see a cut-up dog, I make a joke out of it. Big birds flyin' around, I make

another joke. Marks on necks, another fuckin' joke.
Jeezus, I didn't 'spect him to start takin' it serious."

"You can almost see how he'd made the connection,
though, can't you?" Phyllis said, her voice softer and
lower than before.

They turned to her, startled, "Don't tell me you—"

"Believe him? No, I'm just defending him. Take everything he's seen or heard about Bach's past, his meeting with Van Paris and the way he drops from sight, the
zombies, marks on the neck. You look at those things
and you can almost make the connection Curt made."

Juan snorted. "Maybe you can. Not me. Uh-uh."

"That's because you're not keeping an open mind.
You keep thinking and saying it's impossible. But throw
that word out, pretend for a minute there's no such thing
as impossible. Then what does it all look like?"

"It looks like vampires," Scott said with a sigh. "But
that doesn't mean—"

"Obviously not. I'm just trying to understand Curt.
We've all got fears, but that doesn't make us crazy. And
if you take everything at face value, Curt made a pretty
convincing case. I know he didn't have any real facts. But
what if he did have some facts? What would the two of
you do then?"

"I'd start shinin' up my crucifix," Juan said, drawing
laughter from Scott.

That was the end of it, as Scott and Juan took off on a
string of puns and jokes on the subject, one feeding the
next, humor they hadn't been able to find during the
meeting the day before, or during their long, restless
night of unsettled sleep. But Phyllis didn't join their
laughter.

She looked around uneasily. Maybe three hundred faces
in all. Most of them were smiling or chatting calmly with
their lunchtime companions. But others were sitting by
themselves, picking at their food. Their expressions were
dull, their eyes vapid, their clothes wrinkled. They were
pale.

Pale.

She wished Scott would stop laughing. She wanted him
to take her hand.

Pale.

Why did she find that word so troubling? Why did the very thought of it reverberate in her mind and send a creeping chill down her arms?

Pale.

Oh, for Chrissakes, Phyl, knock it off. You're getting ridiculous.

She rose from the table and started making her way across the crowded room, vaguely aware of Scott and Juan calling out to her, asking her where she was going. She didn't answer, but instead headed straight for her intended target, a young man in his mid-twenties seated near the main exit. He was dressed in a dirty flannel shirt and blue jeans with holes at each knee. His blond hair was disheveled, his face unshaved for at least a week or two. He was not eating, but rather staring morosely into a bowl of tomato soup. A cigarette was burning away, apparently forgotten, between his pale fingers. She approached him cautiously, trying to get a look inside the unbuttoned collar of the flannel shirt. She almost found the right angle for the peek she wanted, but got too close, brushed against the young man's shoulder and neck. She jerked away convulsively.

"Ooooh, excuse me. Kind of clumsy today, I guess."

The young man didn't say anything, didn't even turn around.

Phyllis hurried away, shivering, as though she'd just touched the thin wall of glass that separates the pythons from the people in the snake house at the zoo. She left the room, and once outside in the lobby leaned against the wall and drew a deep breath.

Pale.

Yes. And more.

Distracted, she glanced at the spot on her arm where she had brushed against the young man's shoulder. It itched. Of course, that was just her imagination, but knowing that didn't help a bit; the urge to scratch was almost overwhelming.

Get a hold of yourself, girl. You're slipping.

But the itch was very bad now. It felt like a slowly healing wound. She reached to scratch it and stopped.

She couldn't, didn't want to touch that particular spot on her arm, although she didn't know precisely why. It just seemed like a bad thing to do. Suddenly it seemed like a very bad thing.

Kelly Beckworth looked up with a grin as Curt entered the office. She hit a couple of keys on her computer, saving whatever file she'd been working on, and said, "Hi. You looking for Ernie?"

Curt nodded. "I know it's kind of late, but—"

"No problem. You picked a good time. He's been out most of the day but he got back about ten minutes ago, Let me buzz him."

Curt nodded, and waited for her to take care of the formalities.

He had been lying on his bed, unwilling to get up or go out, alternately browsing through the books of folklore and myths he'd kept close at hand and staring quietly at the two pictures he had brought with him to the compound, the only two pictures of his father and mother he'd ever had. One showed the couple standing out back of Bach's church in Wisconsin, apparently taking a break from a busy day of raking leaves. The rakes were leaning against the white clapboard building behind them, and a tremendous pile of red and orange leaves was just off to the left. The other picture was of his mother and Bach sitting on a dilapidated wooden pier on the edge of a small lake. In both pictures Bach looked surprisingly as he looked in the picture hanging near the door of the room—youthful, strong, powerful, always in command. His mother looked young and happy in a way he had never seen her look during his lifetime, when she had seemed ever weary, older and weaker every day. The pictures, apparently snapped by some willing and discreet friend, were faded now. The colors were washed-out, the paper growing brittle after . . . What? Thirty-one years?

He studied those pictures intently, until in an odd way he felt fulfilled and satisfied by the ache that settled in the center of his chest.

Then and only then had he headed for Cummings' office.

"He's tied up with paperwork, but he'll see you," Kelly said now. "Go on in."

Curt thanked her and slipped through the door to the inner office. It was a small spartan room.

Cummings put his pen down and looked up. "Hello, Curt."

Curt grinned foolishly. "Hi, there."

"Have a seat, please. I'd offer you coffee, but my machine went to Mr. Coffee Heaven a couple of weeks ago." He paused, flashed a quick but weary smile, and said, "I expect you're here to talk about the Master?"

Curt's eyes widened. He tried to say something, but could produce only a sharp clicking noise in his throat.

"I had a talk with Connie this morning. Before he took off for O'Hare. He mentioned your little meeting yesterday."

Now Curt found a word. "Shit," he said.

"He indicated that you have certain . . . 'apprehensions,' I guess is the word, about the Master. Accurate?"

"Apprehensions. Yeah, that's right."

"He said that you're worried by the fact that you're unable to see Reverend Bach. He said you feel deceived, that perhaps the Master doesn't exist, or that if he does, he's not exactly the wonderful man we've made him out to be. Also accurate?"

"To a point."

"Well, I hate to argue with you, but you must realize those are completely unfounded statements. Of course Reverend Bach exists. He's very real, and as good and benevolent as the church says he is. Could a man who doesn't exist, or is somehow a fraud, create all this?" He swept a hand through the air, indicating, Curt supposed, the entire church.

"I don't know," Curt said. "Could he?"

Cummings frowned. "I don't really understand where you're coming from, Curt. Did someone in the Master's office offend you somehow? Did you see something that upset you?"

"You could say that. Lots of things."

"Then I'm very sorry. What would it take to make you change your mind?"

"Seeing Bach would be a big step. In the daytime."

"In the . . . ? I don't think I understand."

"Have you ever seen him, Ernest? Have you seen Bach? Have you seen him during the day?"

"I don't . . . No. No, I haven't. Not during the day. Or at night, for that matter."

"Then how do you know?"

"I'm sorry. How do I know what?"

"That he isn't a vampire?"

"Cummings' face flushed, then went dark, becoming almost purple. His throat visibly tightened and a single blue vein rose from his temple, throbbing. "What are you talking about, Mr. Potter?"

"Just what I said. If you haven't seen Bach, how do you know he's not a vampire? Or Van Paris? How do you know?"

For a moment Curt thought the man was going to pass out. Then, in a matter of seconds, he regained a remarkable composure. His muscles relaxed and he almost smiled. Almost.

"Apparently Connie didn't tell me *everything* about your meeting." He reached over and picked up the phone on his desk, punched a single button. "Kelly? Can you come in here and join us, please?"

"You—"

"Bear with me, Curt. I'd like Kelly to hear this too. And I think you'd better tell us everything. Let us know just what it is that's rattling around inside that head of yours. Please."

And so Curt pulled two battered pictures from his back pocket and told them.

25

It was eleven P.M. and Curt Potter had left in the company of Kelly Beckworth hours earlier, and yet Ernest Cummings was still sitting at his desk, his head resting in a natural cup formed by his hands, his eyelids beginning to sag. Strange words and dreadful accusations still echoed in his mind. Occasionally he would jump a little, as though he had just heard something outside his window. The minutes ticked stealthily by.

Vampires. In his church. Blood-subsisting demons. The Master the father of an illegitimate child. The Master a *vampire*. Cummings' own superiors the vampire's familiars. His own friends here in the Hall, victims. His beloved movement just a shoddy front for something evil, something beyond human imagination.

He felt a tight hand squeezing around his heart.

The thing he kept coming back to was Curt's admonition that he keep an open mind. When he did that, the theory almost made sense. It explained his strained relationships with Reverend Bob and Reverend Norris, with Heller and Smith, something that had always baffled him because he always felt like an adversary when talking to them. It explained the illnesses among the membership, and the extent everyone seemed willing to go to in order to cover up those illnesses. It answered questions, too, the questions that everyone in the Hall asked: *Why don't they let anyone go see Reverend Bach? Why doesn't the Master show up at church on Sundays?* It even explained his own perennial question to his superiors: *If this is a direct order from the top, why don't I get it from the Master himself?*

Except that he knew better.

Vampires were impossible. As were other things of that ilk: ghosts, demons, wraiths, fairies, bizarre psychic powers. Spectral shapes were impossible, and blank-eyed zombies, and . . . and Christ rising after three days? Was that impossible too? No, no of course not, absolutely not. And if you bent the boundaries a little, what happened to the "impossibility" of modern high technology? Long ago, who had thought that flying was possible?

Cummings nodded slowly, although he hated himself for doing so. He couldn't give in to Potter's accusations so easily. He had to study the problem scientifically, objectively, first accepting the possibility of the vampires' existence, then disproving that existence with facts.

To begin with, there was one very obvious argument: he had been with the church for six years. Wouldn't you think that in all that time he would have noticed something before? Then again, why hadn't he ever noticed marks on the necks of residents?

The answer to the first question was unfortunately simple. The reason he hadn't suspected anything before was that he hadn't been looking. Elementary. When your mind never even thought about, let alone credited, the possibility of the existence of vampires, how could you see any? The same was true for the little red marks Curt had described. Had he been searching for marks? Had he *ever* searched for marks? Of course not. Were the marks there? That was another matter entirely.

He groaned softly, terrified to realize how easily things fell into place when you looked at the matter with an open mind.

"You and Kelly, go to the coffee shop," he had told Curt. "Get a snack, talk about work or football or something, anything but this. Give me some time to mull it all over, and I'll get back to you. Okay?"

But what now? Now that he had mulled it over, what should he do?

His first instinct was to call Reverend Norris, or even

Reverend Bob if he was back from overseas. He had a duty to protect the church, to warn them that there was a potentially dangerous, deluded young man in their presence. And yet if even half of what Curt had said was true, wasn't his duty completely the opposite? Wasn't his duty, then, to *fight* the church, combat the evil?

What then? Call Tony Smith? Perhaps. But if Smith was also a human familiar for the inhuman things, what would that accomplish?

"Kelly?" he had said as she and Curt had left his office. "I'm leaving you in charge of Curt for the next few days. Be his friend, watch out for him, keep his mind off this until I decide what to do. Be his custodian, his strong shoulder."

But who was going to be *his* friend? Who was going to tell *him* what to do?

If he called Smith and reported, in abbreviated fashion, everything that he'd heard tonight, perhaps he could pick up some more clues. There might be something in Tony's reaction to the story—humor, anger, discomfort—that would help him piece everything together.

Or you might get fired from your job, he thought, get thrown back out on the same streets you couldn't handle six years ago, let alone now.

But he doubted that would happen. After all, he was doing what was expected of him, being a good soldier and reporting trouble before it reared its head even higher and got out of hand.

Call Smith, then. And play it by ear from there.

He sighed again, picked up the phone on his desk, and dialed.

Kelly and Curt didn't make it very far. In fact they got only as far as the first couch in the Hall lobby, where Kelly urged him to sit and rest a few minutes before going back to his room for the night. Reluctantly he agreed, plopping down and staring blankly at the huge potted plant to his left.

Kelly didn't say anything either. She was remembering a recurring nightmare she'd had as a little girl. Not a nightmare about vampires, oddly enough, but a dream in which her father had abandoned her and her mother in a vast snowy land that was remarkably like the Antarctic in her father's picture book. She and her mother would be struggling forward, heads down against the driving wind, the impossible cold, periodically pausing to raise their heads and call for him, shrieking into the teeth of the gale, "*Daddeeeee!*" and "*Thomas! Thomas Beckworth! Where are you?*" Every time she would wake up, she would get out of bed and carry the memory of that arctic cold down the hall with her to her parents' bedroom, where she would open the door with a nudge and stand watching her mother and father as they slept side by side, wondering what she would do if he ever did leave them.

This was the first time in more than ten years that she had recalled that dream, because of what Curt had told them in Ernie's office. If Bach was really his father, and the Master had cut Curt and his mother off, she didn't find it surprising at all that Curt was seeing vampires around the compound. To her, the vampires didn't seem nearly as terrifying as the loss of a father.

"You know," Curt said suddenly, startling her out of the depths of her thoughts, "you don't have to worry about what Cummings said back there. All that about watching out for me, being my friend. It was nice of him, but it's not necessary. I'm doing fine. You don't have to waste your time chasing me around."

She smiled. "It's not a waste of time."

"You mean you'd actually enjoy chasing me around?"

"I'm not sure I'd think of it as chasing. More like . . ."

"Stalking?" he suggested.

They stared at each other. Then they both burst out laughing.

"Not that either," she said. "I guess it would be a job, since Ernie asked me to do it, but it wouldn't seem like a job. Definitely not like filing and punching things up on that crazy computer in the office."

"Gee, that's encouraging. I'm more exciting than a stack of filing."

Again they exchanged a brief, unusual expression before laughing.

"Sometimes," she said slowly, "I get the feeling that I'm not doing all I could for the movement. Holed up in the office with my nose pressed up against a monitor, taking messages for Ernie, answering the phone. I tell myself it's important—I know it is—but it still feels so pointless sometimes. But helping you, that might be really vital. It—"

"Watching over the crazy man?"

She frowned. "You're not crazy."

"Thanks for the vote of confidence, but don't you think you ought to line up with everybody else before it's too late? After all, a guy like me who runs around talking about vampires, there's no telling what he might do. You better turn against me while I'm still around, or before I go off the deep end altogether."

"Self-pity doesn't cut it with me," she said. "And I couldn't care less about your vampires, anyway."

"You couldn't—"

"I may not believe you, but you must have good reasons for saying everything you did."

"You—"

"I'm more interested in the other things you were saying. I'd rather hear about your relationship with your father."

Curt blinked. "My father?"

"The Master."

"Wait a minute." Curt looked down at his hands, which had knotted themselves together into a single tight, twisted fist. "Are you saying you believe what I said about Bach and my mother?"

"Why not? You had that picture. I'd believe you even if you didn't have a picture. You don't have any reason to lie."

He shook his head, taken aback by her trust.

"The fact is, Curt," she went on, "I think you're an honest guy."

That *really* startled him, but not nearly as much as he was startled a moment later when she asked to hear the story of his years on the road.

Overwhelmed with gratitude, he was only too happy to comply.

*   *   *

Ernest Cummings put the receiver down and shoved the phone to the far side of his desk. He stared across his office at an indistinct spot on the opposite wall, a spot that might have been dirt, discolored paint, or merely night shadow.

Smith had kept him on the line for a good twenty minutes. After eliciting several sober reassurances from Cummings that this was serious business and not some kind of wacky, elaborate joke, he had made him repeat the overall gist of Curt Potter's story twice. And yet he had taken it well. He had been mildly distressed, but in the end more amused than anything else. He had told Cummings not to worry. He would look into it. If there was anything to be taken care of, he would take care of it immediately. No problem, no sweat, no strain, no need to be concerned.

And yet, Cummings thought now, he didn't feel placated at all. Quite the opposite. He was even more unsure of himself than he had been before placing the call. Smith's reaction had been . . . unusual. Concerned and carefree at the same time. Unusual. Difficult to understand, or to pin down. And as far as leaving it all up to Smith? Well, if Curt was even one-third correct in what he'd said . . .

There was a sudden scraping sound outside his window. Cummings turned rapidly, his heart leaping wildly. He thought he caught a glimpse of a vague, indeterminate shape in the blackness out there, but he wasn't sure. He leaned forward, squinted, but whatever had been there (if anything at all) was gone. The shrubs that surrounded the building rustled in the night breeze, like restless, shifting sentries.

He turned back to his desk and sighed. He was tired but unable to even entertain the thought of sleep, frightened but unable to consider any reasonable courses of action. He knew he should lock up the office and go to his room, but that seemed like too much work and . . . too dangerous. He stayed at his desk instead, lingering for a very, very long time.

By the time he finally got up to leave, dawn was tinting the eastern sky red with the promise of the first sunny day in quite a while. He stood at his window for a time, greatly disturbed to realize that even with the arrival of the sun, even with morning just an hour or so away, none of the vague terror he was feeling had left him. Apparently, there would be no rescue by a tired cliché. Things did *not* look any better with the coming of the morning light.

26

Curt was thankful for the knock on the door. It chopped off the beginning of what was blossoming into a full-scale argument between him and Scott. Alone in their room, Curt had asked Scott what bothered him most about the story. Scott began to answer, started to say something about feeling let down by a roommate he had liked and enjoyed living with, and Curt felt his temper starting to slip, wondering why it always came back to his personality—why they couldn't just look at the facts. He was about to say so when the knock rescued him.

"Yes?"

The door opened and Becky Heller came in. She was carrying a clipboard to which was attached the most incredibly thick sheaf of papers either of them had ever seen.

"Hi, guys. Room 1290, right?"

Scott nodded. "You're Becky Heller."

"That's right." A quick glance down at her clipboard. A rapid shuffle of paper. "I'm looking for a Curt Potter. Are you—"

"That's me," Curt said. He stepped forward, but didn't hold out his hand. A soft whisper of suspicion stirred in the back of his mind.

"Well, Curt, I'm the assistant director of public relations, second in command to Tony—"

"Tony Smith, I know. What do you want?"

Another glance. Another shuffle of paper. Meaningless gestures, really, since a moment later she set the clipboard down on the desk as though she didn't need it, never had. "Do you mind if I sit down? I've been on my feet a lot today."

Curt didn't move, but Scott hurried over to pull out one of the desk chairs for her.

"What do you want?" Curt said again before she was even settled.

She grinned at him. It was a broad, almost wild smile, and Curt heard the whisper again, slightly louder this time.

"You do want something, don't you?"

"Of course," Heller said. "Yes. Something awfully important, really. It's a business proposition. I've just come from a meeting with Tony Smith and some other folks—Laurie Campbell from God's Hand Radio, and Stu Gallagher from the television department. We're developing a program to use newcomers in our TV crusades, as witnesses. That's why I came to see you. If you're interested"—she paused as though expecting him to jump in with something, but eventually went on—"I can tell you more."

Curt shrugged, trying to look casual despite the fact that the whisper was now a steady chant. "Go ahead."

"Well, we've wanted to involve the residents in our crusades for a long time—above and beyond the technical work and support they provide, of course. We've wanted to put them in front of the cameras. Tony and I feel that some personal witnessing from people other than Reverend Bob or Reverend Norris would be a big factor in drawing some undecideds into the church, those who maybe like what the pastors are telling them but aren't convinced, or think it's too show-biz. Some witnessing from a good old everyday resident at Universal might be just enough to sway them, if they could hear how that resident's life had been changed or—"

"Could you get to the point?" Curt said. Scott flashed him a startled, angry look, but he ignored it. "What are you here for?"

Heller was flustered. "I'm sorry, I thought I was telling you that. We want to start resident witnessing next week, with the big crusade from Golden Gate Park in San Francisco. If everything goes well there, we'll be expanding the program a little at a time, maybe using it every second or third crusade, bringing it in more often, until finally it becomes a regular feature of every broadcast. It'll start as a test, but I can almost guarantee it'll grow quickly."

"You still haven't explained why you're here."

She nodded quickly. "We want to start in San Francisco," she repeated, "and we want to use one long-term compound resident as well as one newcomer. The long-term person will discuss why he came to the church and what Universal has meant to him, how it's changed his life, what kinds of good works he's been able to accomplish, and how much he owes to the whole movement. The newcomer will pretty much just discuss the reasons he joined the church and what he hopes to gain from it.

"We went to the main computer to find our people. For starters, we asked it for the name of a relative newcomer who hadn't signed up for a job yet, someone with the free time to take a few days off for rehearsal and most of next week off for the trip to California." She paused, her smile brightening again. "It spat out your name, Curt, right off the top. And that's the reason I'm here."

"You're offering me a job."

Heller shrugged. "Not a job, exactly. A temporary position."

"On camera."

"Yes."

"In front of millions of people coast to coast."

"Worldwide."

Curt smiled. The whisper was almost a shout. "A lot of people would really like that, wouldn't they? I mean, TV, San Francisco, a chance to be famous for a few minutes. A lot of people would think that was great."

Pleased, Heller said, "Many people would, you bet. It's a big chance for the right person, Curt. What I said is true—everything's real up in the air right now, it's still very much in the testing stages—but if everything goes well, who's to say what might happen? There might be more TV shots, maybe some worldwide travel, a chance to be side by side with Reverend Bob. It could really grow into a top position for the right person."

"Being on television," Curt said, seemingly marveling at the improbable news, still smiling. "I should be thrilled, right? It was really something, wasn't it, the way the computer just kicked my name out? I was really lucky, right? Wasn't I?"

Heller laughed and turned to Scott with a confidential aside: "We knew he'd be happy. This is really a once-in-a-lifetime shot. He's a lucky man."

"Television," Curt repeated, as though he simply couldn't get over it. "What an opportunity."

Heller leaned forward. "It's not only your chance to advance yourself and have a little fun at the same time, but think of what you'd be doing for the movement. It's a chance most of the people here in the compound would kill for. And it's *your* chance, Curt, yours alone. You get to help the movement, help yourself, and launch what could be the hot new trend in televised crusades. Think of it as the inauguration of personal witnessing on a large scale—mega-witnessing."

"And all because a computer kicked out my name."

"That's right."

"And because you talked to Ernest Cummings."

"That . . . What?"

"You talked to Ernest Cummings, didn't you?"

Curt watched her face closely, was convinced that he saw her go a degree or two paler. In his mind the whisper was wailing and yammering.

"I haven't seen Ernie in a couple of weeks," Heller said. "Not since the ventilation system in the cafeteria broke when Reverend Bob was out of town. Why?"

"No reason . . . just wondering."

"But just wondering what? Do you—"

"When do I have to give you an answer?"

Heller started to speak, but got out only about half a strangled word before stopping in utter surprise. Now Curt was sure of it, utterly convinced: she was paler, much paler. When she spoke, a large measure of confidence had vanished from her voice. "You mean you're not decided?"

"Not quite. Oh, I know it should be a real honor. I believe what you said about that. But frankly, the whole idea kind of scares me. I've got stage fright. I'll need to think about it."

"Stage fright? Stage fright can be worked around, Curt. Don't let it stop you, or even make you think twice. We can have you talk to Reverend Norris, and he can help you overcome your fear. I don't think you should let a little case of nerves ruin your chance to be a Universal Ministries' groundbreaker."

Curt flashed a sheepish grin and spread his hands apologetically. "I hear what you're saying . . . I understand. But I'll still need some time to think about it. When do you need to know?"

"The crusade's a week from tomorrow," Heller said with a sigh. "I guess I'd need to hear from you by Friday at the latest. Preferably much sooner."

"Friday. Got it."

"Is there anything I can do to get your answer now? Anything I can tell you or show you?"

Curt's sheepish grin became sad and troubled. "Afraid not. I just need time to think."

Heller stood and shook her head slowly. "You've got till Friday, then. Don't be foolish, Curt. Join the crusade. You'll be glad you did. I can guarantee it."

When Heller was gone and they were alone again, Scott turned to him with an astonished grin. "I don't believe that! You lucky son of a bitch! I can understand your being nervous, but if you pass this by you ought to have your head examined and . . ." He trailed away unsteadily. He looked at Curt closely and said, "What's wrong, Potter? You don't look nervous, you look angry."

"Of course I'm angry. You heard her. You sat here while she threw me her line of bullshit. What do you think that was? A genuine offer? Do you really believe that shit about the computer tossing out my name?"

"What else?"

"What else? What else? They're trying to buy me off, Scott! They come around and offer me a nice little TV appearance in the hope I'll forget all about vampires. They figure I'll be so grateful for my chance to be famous that I'll stop investigating the church. Or that I'll be so busy being their big personal witness that I won't have time to go after vampires . . . or my dad."

Curt paused a moment, staring across the room. Then, while Scott looked on in amazement, he began to laugh. It was a cold laugh, utterly humorless.

"Who would ever believe it?" he said, almost to himself. "It's like a bribe or something. Who would ever believe vampires could be so goddamned subtle?"

27

Phyllis couldn't wait any longer. If she was going to get this nonsense over with, put her mind at rest, now was the time to get moving.

Damn Curt Potter. Screw him and his goddamn rambling about vampires. Didn't he know what an idiot he was being?

Ah, her mind shot back, if Curt's such a fool, why are you scared? If he's just rambling, why can't you get it out of your mind?

She sighed, then quickly glanced across the room to see if she'd disturbed her roommate, Carole Vance. She hadn't, thank God. Carole was still bent over her New Testament, scribbling down red-letter passages for future reference. Her other roommate, Paula Harpool, was working late in the office at the school.

Good point, she thought again. If Curt was so wrong, what was *her* problem?

This evening had been a textbook example. She had eaten dinner with a handful of friends from work, laughing about trivial things, clothes and shoes and hair, all the usuals. Vampires had been the farthest thing from her mind. But then later, walking back through the lobby, she had felt a finger of fear trace its way down her spine. The fear had grown to a low-grade terror as she waited for the elevator, and then, riding up, she kept glancing nervously at the car's paneled ceiling, as though expecting one of the panels to pop open and something to appear up there and drop down on her.

By the time she reached the sixth floor, she had chosen her course of action. She was going to spend a night out in the compound. If she saw something, if something happened (ha-ha-ha), she would have an answer. If the night was uneventful, she would also have an answer.

She had watched the sun vanish in the west, seeing the light become shadow, the shadow become a cloak, the cloak become a smothering blanket of darkness. The fear in her rose and fell like surging waves, one moment just a mildly worrisome thing, the next an all-out assault on her nerves and senses. Finally, afraid that if she kept hesitating she would back out altogether, she went out into the hallway.

Riding down again, she refused to look up at the ceiling panels in the car, keeping her eyes focused instead on the bank of floor buttons to the right of the door. She didn't allow herself to think about vampires at all until she had crossed the lobby and gone out through the main doors. When the chill night air struck her, though, she hesitated.

"Get moving," she murmured.

Right.

She started walking.

After more than two hours in the cold and the dark, she felt sure that all her fear had been unjustified. There wasn't anything to be frightened of, never had been. All her original assumptions had been right; Curt was wrong.

For the first half-hour or so she had stayed close to "civilization," circling the buildings in the general vicinity of Van Paris Hall. Then, feeling courageous, she had struck out on a path leading past the library to Worship Park. Finally, feeling triumphantly brave, she'd allowed herself to leave everything behind and head into the very heart of the compound, walking in a northerly direction on a series of trails that wound through trees and heavy undergrowth.

Nothing. Not a scary thing within sight or earshot. So much for Curt and his ghouls.

Gleefully she realized that while the others had grumbled and made jokes, while Curt had worried himself sick, she alone had done something. It was actually kind of easy to take care of problems like this when you went about it scientifically. Wait until Juan and Scott found out, wait until she told Curt. They would thank her. They would praise her. That alone made the hours in the cold worth it.

A rustling in the bushes to her left made her whirl quickly, eyes darting wildly from side to side, searching for any signs of movement.

Whatever had been there was gone. A squirrel, she thought, or a field mouse. A stray night breeze. She shrugged and started walking again, maybe just a bit faster than before. Occasionally she glanced at the luminous dial of the Seiko she'd gotten for her birthday a year ago. When it got to be eleven-thirty and none of Curt's horrors had appeared, she would go back to the Hall and go to bed. She was looking forward to her first good night's sleep in three days.

Another rustling noise, louder than the first.

She turned again, surveying the bushes, and felt the first traces of uneasiness since leaving the safety of the main buildings behind. Not that she saw anything, because she didn't. Not that the rustling sound continued for more than a moment; it stopped almost as soon as it started. It was just that hearing the noise twice like that in the space of a few moments, hearing it and yet being unable to spot anything . . .

She checked her watch again. Eleven-twenty-three. Well, that was certainly close enough to eleven-thirty, wasn't it? She could go back now with a clear conscience and celebrate the success of her test.

When she started back in the direction she'd come, she heard the rustling noise again, but refused to stop and look a third time. She already knew what she would see—absolutely nothing. Why waste time on a stupid squirrel? It was a long way back to her room, and she was suddenly much colder than she had been all night.

She quickened her pace—

—and the shifting, stirring sound of vines and branches came to her once more, louder than ever—

—and the fear heightened a notch or two.

She hurried along, not running, but walking steadily. For several moments she thought she was imagining things. She told herself: the rustling *isn't* following me. No. There is *no* animal or person moving along through the darkness, just out of sight. The rustling has *stopped*. Yes, indeed. It has *stopped*.

The cold notwithstanding, a thin sheen of sweat broke out on her temples and the backs of her hands. She brushed a loose strand of brown hair out of her eyes and walked a little faster.

The rustling grew louder, closer, and seemed to reach a peak at the precise moment she came to the branch in the path. In front of her, the trail suddenly split in three directions. One veered sharply left; the second also angled to the left, though not quite as severely; the third bent hard to the right. She stood there staring, utterly nonplussed.

Damn. Which way had she come in?

The rustling stopped.

Two left, one right . . . Which way?

She had a vague idea that she had come straight in, that to get back to the Hall she must go straight. *But there was no straight path*! Two left, one right . . . Shit.

Behind her, just to her left, the bushes moved stealthily again. She tasted fear when she swallowed, warm and coppery, unpleasant. Her stomach did a slow roll.

C'mon, Phyl, nothing to worry about, remember? You've been out here two hours and you haven't seen a thing. Just stay calm and head home . . . head home.

She chose the path that cut to the right only because it seemed to have less of a curve than the others and she was hoping it would straighten out within a hundred yards or so. Without being aware of it, she was almost jogging now. To her relief, the path she'd picked did indeed curve back to the left and head approximately south after a short distance, and to her even greater relief the rustling noise seemed to have stayed behind, back at the intersection, and—

"Excuse me, miss."

Phyllis jumped, uttering a high-pitched squeal of terror. She pivoted sharply and gasped when she saw the man standing there. He was two or three feet behind her, just at the edge of the path, where the gravel underfoot gave way to soft earth and the start of the underbrush. An ordinary man: not terribly tall, but not short either; average weight; thick dark hair streaked with the tiniest traces of white or gray; a bright, refreshing smile. Completely ordinary. The only unusual thing about him was the fact that he was out here, almost a mile away from the center of the compound, with nothing but a sport coat and slacks to protect him from the cold. They didn't look nearly warm enough, not for a clear, chilly night like this. And yet he wasn't shivering. He was smiling. Then he spread his hands wide to show that he meant her no harm.

"I'm sorry, I didn't mean to startle you. I only wanted to ask directions back to the building they call Van Paris Center."

"Hall," Phyllis mumbled, barely recovered from her shock.

The man's brow creased. "I beg your pardon?"

"Hall. Van Paris Hall, not Center."

The man threw back his head and laughed. "Sorry. Stupid of me, wasn't it? Van Paris Hall. Of course."

His voice was interesting. Low without being soft, flat without being dull, accentless but somehow richly midwestern. It was a voice she found vaguely, troublingly familiar, but she couldn't say where she'd ever heard it before.

"That's okay," she said, shrugging off his mistake. "You must be a newcomer."

Another laugh. "Me? A newcomer? More like an oldcomer, I'm afraid. I'm far too old to be considered a newcomer anywhere . . . at anything."

"No, I mean a newcomer at the church. That's what they—we—call the new arrivals. I'm a newcomer myself, and I figured with your Van Paris Center mistake and everything . . . well, I figured you must be pretty new too."

"Not new, just a bit confused," he said, and smiled in a way that made her doubt he was ever confused about anything.

It was funny, but standing here talking to him—looking at him—she felt herself growing tired. It was hard to believe she could be sleepy out here in the depths of the compound on a chilly night, talking to a stranger who had just scared the hell out of her a few moments before, but she was. Her eyelids were suddenly heavy and her brain seemed to be tingling and numb. She struggled to bring herself back to full attention.

"Do you think you can direct me to Van Paris Hall?" he asked.

"I . . . I think so. I mean, I hope so. I'm sort of lost myself. I think we're on the right path, but I'm not sure."

The man's smile became a full dazzling grin. "Then we'll walk this path and see where it leads. Agreed?"

Phyllis felt another wave of drowsiness wash over her. She tried to remain alert, tried focusing on the man's face, but the more she did that, the more tired she became.

His eyes. His eyes were interesting. It was hard to believe, actually, that she'd found his face ordinary at first glance. There was really nothing ordinary about his eyes at all. They were deep and very dark and rather secretive. She felt good when she looked into them, relaxed, comfortable. Sleepy or not, looking into the man's eyes took away all the fear she'd felt just a short time before when she had been trying to choose the proper path.

It's just like the old New England gentleman said, she thought foolishly. You take the less-traveled road, and lord, what a difference.

She giggled.

The man's brow creased again. "Did I say something funny?"

"No!" she said quickly. "Not at all. I was just thinking."

She flashed an embarrassed smile and looked into his eyes again, sighing as warmth and drowsy comfort settled deeper into her bones.

"Thinking," the man echoed. "I see. I hate to interrupt your thought process, but don't you think we should be off? Don't you think we should hurry if we hope to find the elusive Van Paris Hall?"

"Yes," she said, her voice sounding impossibly faraway and dreamlike in her own ears.

Without another word the man started quickly down the path with short but efficient strides. She looked after him for a moment, then sprinted to catch up, like a small child afraid of being left alone. Oddly, movement did nothing to chase away the foggy, sleepy haze that had taken up residence inside her. If anything, it increased it, and she fell into a kind of automatic, somnambulistic rhythm behind him.

They walked for almost half an hour, through deep woods and across the occasional open field. She had long since given up trying to spot familiar landmarks or places she had passed earlier in the evening, and instead was content merely to follow the stranger and let him show the way. Several times, when the path they were on would take an unexpected bend or follow a rise or fall in the terrain, she would stumble, catching herself just before she fell.

Finally a building rose out of the darkness. She noticed it over the man's shoulder, a house set back off the trail and surrounded by a stone wall and a large overgrown front lawn. A house? she thought. In the compound? And for the shortest of moments she felt a twinge of her previous fear. Then the man stopped in front of the wall, and she almost ran into him. He turned and gave her another of his bright smiles.

"Van Paris Hall?" he asked.

She shook her head dumbly.

He laughed. "Hardly. But do you know what it is?"

She tried to speak, uttered a little dry squeak. "No."

"It's my home. A retreat from the trials of my hectic life."

"Yes," she murmured, completely confused, not understanding anything anymore and yet not caring, either. Van Paris Hall seemed impossibly distant to her now; the whole concept of Universal Ministries and her room, her friends, her job in the print shop, seemed like something from another, long-ago life. Now there was nothing but the man, his smile, his eyes.

"You'd like to come inside, wouldn't you?"

Dazed, she whispered, "Oh, yes."

The man shook his head. "What a shame that I can't ask you in. But I think you understand. As disappointed as you might feel right now, I think you know that if you are good and loyal, if you are true, then someday you *will* be allowed in. Someday you will see everything in that house, everything in this church. You do understand that, don't you?"

"Yes."

"So insightful," he said gently. "I knew you must be. You proved your wisdom and your worth the day you decided to come join us." He paused and studied her closely. Minutes ticked by like years. "You have led a tragic life for one so young, haven't you? It's hard to imagine the sorrow, seeing an innocent life ripped from your womb. The pain you must have felt! The anger!"

"You . . . you know about that?"

"Of course." He laughed yet again, a pleasant, comforting chuckle. "I know everything about everyone who comes here. It's my business to know. I know what's gone on in their minds before, and what they're thinking now. I know how to approach them. I knew, for example, to come to you in confusion. I knew your compassion wouldn't allow you to turn away from a stranger in the dark, seeking directions. I was right about all of that, wasn't I?"

"Y-yes."

"Then you see what I mean. I know everything."

"Everything," Phyllis whispered.

"You chose to come here because of the pain in your past. That's why I came to you. I wanted to assure you that from now on you're safe with us. You'll never again know the horrors you endured before. From tonight on, you'll be walking down a new path. You'll know only glory and comfort and peace. You'll live in the arms of the eternal powers. One day . . . one day, you shall know the absolute triumph of those powers."

"Triumph," she repeated—or had the word only echoed in her mind?

"You do want that, don't you? You want to know the peace of the eternal powers, don't you?"

"Yes!" she cried, moaning the word with something like ecstasy. Her past had never seemed further away than it did right now. Her anger, her bitterness, her fear, all of that had drowned in the deep pools of comfort she saw in this man's eyes. He spoke about eternal powers. She didn't know what he meant, but she sensed the truth in his words. She felt it, felt the undeniable strength and beauty in what he promised.

"Do you?" he asked again, challenging her.

"Yes! *Yes!*"

His smile seemed to shrink, collapsing in on itself and becoming a slick grin of eager passion. He chuckled deep in his throat. He took a step closer and reached out to her. She felt his hands close over her shoulders. For a moment she drew back, startled by a sharp jolt that coursed through her body, as though his hands were conducting a strong electrical current. But then she felt the jolt turn to surging warmth, felt a tingling in her arms and legs, a gentle thrill of readiness in her breasts, her loins.

"Then you shall have it—everything," he whispered.

He inclined his head toward her, and she saw teeth as bright as a dazzling summer day. She relaxed completely, sagging against him, and when his lips touched her neck she slipped into a world of soft darkness, where everything but time ceased to exist, and where even time was changed into something utterly unknowable.

She stayed in that world for a very long time.

28

As Ernest Cummings had told Curt, there were several
ways to get to Fox Valley, the closest shopping mall. You
could take the shuttle bus on Saturday or sign out one of
the ten cars available to residents from the Universal
motor pool. When Scott, Curt, Juan, Phyllis, and Kelly
Beckworth went there on Wednesday evening, they arranged through Kelly's connections with Cummings for
the largest vehicle in the loaner system—a Ford Country
Squire station wagon that had seen better days but was still
quite functional.

The trip was Kelly's idea in the first place, and she had
taken it upon herself to get in touch with Scott to see if
he too thought it might be good for Curt, a diversion to
take his mind off his gloomy thoughts.

Curt hadn't wanted to go. As soon as the idea had
been proposed, he'd guessed the reason behind it and
had immediately resented it.

"C'mon, *amigo*," Juan had said. "You can't just hang
around here all the time with your ass draggin' in the
dirt. Put it aside, why doncha? Have a little fun."

Fun, Curt had thought. Great. But he relented and
began to develop a plan.

When they got to the mall, they initially stuck together
as a group, helping Juan find some socks he needed to
buy in J. C. Penney, following Scott to the Footlocker to
price a new pair of running shoes. Curt tried to lag
behind the others, but Kelly wasn't about to let him get

away with that. While Scott and Juan led the way and Phyllis, who had been oddly quiet all evening, stayed close to Scott's side, Kelly remained several paces back with Curt, pointing out amusing window displays or interesting customers, trying to lighten his sullen mood.

Finally, after about an hour, Curt made his move. "You know, we've probably all got things we need to buy. Since the place is going to close in a couple of hours, why don't we split up? We can meet somewhere at nine and head back to the compound."

Scott and Kelly exchanged a worried glance. "You sure?" Scott said. "If you've got to get something, we can tag along and— "

"Let's split up," Curt repeated. "It'll be faster. And less boring for everyone."

They talked about it, and finally agreed to go their separate ways. There was some discussion about where to meet, but since Scott and Phyllis were the only ones among them who had been to the mall before, it fell to him to choose a location—the little court in front of Sears, on the mall's lower level.

Curt watched them go, and when he was certain of being left alone, found the nearest set of cushioned benches and sat down. A few feet away, a fat young woman in jeans and a sweatshirt was trying to quiet her baby while juggling a huge armful of packages. Two young boys, no more than ten or eleven, trotted by arguing about the way to the Radio Shack. A bearded man in an expensive-looking business suit paused, glanced at Curt, then looked off in several different directions, trying to orient himself. A black teenager dug his cigarette pack out of his coat pocket, found it empty, balled it up, and threw it across the concourse with a curse. A mall on a quiet week night. *Middle America Goes Shopping*. An eighties version of a Norman Rockwell scene. Wonderful.

He took a deep, relaxing breath and pulled his wallet from his pocket. There was more than three hundred dollars in there, mostly in tens and twenties, the remains of his final paycheck from his last job on a New Jersey loading-dock. That was one good thing about Universal, he thought crazily: the place might be run by the undead, but it was easy on your pocketbook.

He counted the money twice. Just over three hundred dollars. More than enough to buy the things he needed, with plenty left over for any future contingencies. He checked off his mental shopping list for the tenth time, trying to satisfy the nagging doubt that he was forgetting something. If so, he thought, too bad. You can only do so much, anticipate things only up to a point. It's not as though there's a store in here called Vampire Hunters Ltd., a one-stop outfitting shop for the things I need.

That phrase ran through his mind again: *You can only do so much.*

He sighed, and wondered if it would be enough. Then he got up and headed for the first stop on his list—a budget jewelry store.

When he arrived at Sears at ten to nine, the others were already there waiting for him, comparing their few purchases and trying to decide whether or not to visit the Fannie May store nearby. Curt hesitated, shifted his incredible collection of shopping bags—marked "THINGS REMEMBERED," "GNC," "BROWN'S SPORTING GOODS," "KOENIG ART EMPORIUM," and even "SEARS" itself—to more comfortable positions, and went over to them.

"Son of a gun," Scott said when he saw him approaching. "What the hell'd you do, Curt? Buy the whole mall?"

Curt laughed. "Just about. As much as I could afford."

Kelly got up and came over, putting a friendly hand on his shoulder. "What'd you get?"

"You'll all see soon enough. Are we leaving?"

"Not yet," Juan said. "We was just talkin'. You wanna get some candy before we go, or you wanna go to that restaurant down there and have a drink?" He pointed to a place called Fitzhugh's a few hundred yards away, by the closest exit.

Curt shifted the packages again. "A drink sounds fantastic right now."

Inside the dark restaurant a few minutes later, they

found an out-of-the-way table, ordered a round of drinks and sandwiches, and immediately turned to Curt.

"So what'd you get?" Kelly asked again. "Something special for your new best friend? Hmmm?"

"What new best friend?" Juan said with a laugh. "Curt knows who his pals are, ain't that right, *amigo*? What did you get me?"

Curt held up his hand. "Take it easy, guys. I didn't . . . well, actually, I did. There's stuff in here for everyone."

"Everyone?" Kelly said. "Let's—"

"But first I want to see what all of you got."

"Uh-uh, you're not dodging us that easily," Scott told him. "We just got little things. You've got three thousand sacks under the table. What gives? Christmas?"

"I got a lot of things," he said. "These first. There's one for each of you."

He reached down to his feet and brought up the bag marked "THINGS REMEMBERED.". He reached inside and drew out a tangle of silver crosses on fine link chains. Separating them carefully, he laid them in the middle of the table, where they caught the light from the muted overhead fixtures.

"Crosses?" Kelly said. "I don't get it. Why crosses? We can get those back at the church, from the resident-support department. They give them away to anyone who wants them."

"I know. But I didn't want Universal crosses. They're . . . they're frauds. I wanted different ones . . . clean ones."

"What do you mean?" Phyllis reached out a hand to touch one of the crosses, but stopped herself just short of actually doing it.

"I know what he's saying," Scott said. "I get it, I understand perfectly. Crosses. Vampires. Right, Curt? You're still on that jag, aren't you?"

He nodded. "Crosses keep vampires away. That's why I got one for each of you. I want you all to start wearing them right away, tonight."

"Oh, shit, man, you ain't serious," Juan said.

"That's where you're wrong. I'm dead serious."

"Five crosses?" Kelly said, as though all the implications of the discussion hadn't reached her yet. "Wasn't that expensive?"

"Money's not the problem. I mean, let's face it, Things Remembered isn't exactly Tiffany's. These were on sale, eight bucks apiece."

Scott leaned forward, an angry flush rushing up his cheeks. He was about to say something when the waitress appeared with their drinks. He waited until she'd put them down and disappeared again before saying, "Damn you, Curt. You—"

"I know what you're going to say," Curt told him. "Don't you think I anticipated your reaction to this? I don't care. I want you to take the things anyway, wear them—"

"I thought you were going to forget about this!"

"I never said that. I never even suggested it. Oh, I know that's what you had in mind when you brought me here tonight. Humor the poor guy, take his mind off his troubles. But I never said anything about forgetting it."

"This is getting out of hand," Scott said.

Juan muttered. "I agree. Way outta hand, if you ask me."

Curt sighed deeply and turned to him. "You're telling me you won't wear one of these either?"

For a few seconds Juan appeared torn. Then he shook his head firmly.

"Phyl? What about you?"

She didn't answer right away. Her hand strayed toward the crosses in the middle of the table again, and just as before, stopped a few inches short of actually touching them.

"Sorry, Curt," she said in a voice so soft it was almost impossible to hear.

"Kelly?"

She groaned, as though hating the decision she was about to make more than the idea of actually taking one of the crosses and wearing it.

"I don't think I can, Curt. It . . . it doesn't seem right. I have a cross back in my room, one that Ernie gave me

after I'd put in one month on the job. If I took this, it
. . . it would . . ."

Curt angrily swept four of the crosses back into the
bag, dropped the bag at his feet, and picked up the
remaining one from the tabletop. It was two inches tall
and of sturdy design, dangling from the end of a twenty-
four-inch chain. Holding the chain in one hand, the cross
in the other, he murmured, "Bless this cross. Bless it in
the name of the Father and of the Son and of the Holy
Ghost. Amen." He started to slip it over his neck, but
paused, holding it away and staring at it in frank
amazement.

There was a slight tingling in his fingertips, a pleasant,
pulsing current that ran through him, almost as though
the cross was generating a subtle current.

But it was gone after just two or three seconds. He
wondered if it had really been there.

He slipped the cross over his neck, letting it dangle
outside his shirt.

Scott watched this ritual with thinly veiled disgust.
With the defeated manner of a man who hates to bring
the subject up but realizes he must get it out of the way,
he asked, "What else did you get, Curt?"

"Garlic," Curt said. "I thought that'd be impossible to
find in a mall, but they had it at the vitamin store, of all
places. I bought ten boxes. I was going to give a box to
everyone, but I guess it's safe to assume you don't want
them. And I also got these—"

He bent below the table again and came up with the
largest bag of all, the one from the art store. Reaching
inside, he came out with a piece of wood nearly three
feet long and more than an inch wide. There were grooves
in the wood, and at each end a sharp forty-five-degree
angle.

Kelly gasped, but it took Juan to say, "What the fuck
is that?"

Curt couldn't resist a smile. "It's called a stretcher
strip. I guess you use it to hold and frame your canvas, if
you're a painter. These are the biggest they had—number
fifties, they're called. I bought twenty. Cut each one in
half, and that makes forty. Forty stakes."

"Stakes!" Scott cried, his voice much louder than he'd intended. He glanced around in embarrassment, then repeated more softly, "Stakes? For God's sake, Potter, what next? This little game of yours is getting dangerous."

"It's not a game," Curt said. "Dangerous, but not a game."

"But if you think you're going to run around and drive those things into people, you—"

For the second time, he was interrupted by the arrival of the waitress, this time as she brought their hamburgers and club sandwiches. Scott was going to continue when she departed, but Curt didn't give him the opportunity:

"As long as you're pissed off, you might as well know that I went to the sporting-goods store and got a knife too, a big hunter's gutting knife—in case the points on these strips aren't strong enough and we've got to carve new ones. And to help cut the strips in half, of course."

"Knives, Curt? You've got—"

"And my last stop was Sears." He paused, suddenly finding perverse pleasure in the others' distress. "I bought a nice Craftsman hammer to pound the stakes in. And I'm almost looking forward to the chance to use it."

He regretted that last almost immediately—Kelly went pale, Juan looked sick to his stomach—and it wasn't true by a long shot, but there was no taking it back. He was about to apologize when he stopped and stared at Phyllis.

There was something about the way she'd been acting all evening that had been bothering him. She had been restless since they'd first gotten together, and as he stared at her now, he saw her hand stray idly to a spot on her throat just below the jawline. She rubbed the spot for a moment or two, as though it irritated her, and then put her hand back in her lap. A moment later the hand was straying upward again . . .

"Phyl? What is it? What's wrong?"

She blinked, as though coming out of a light doze. "What?"

"I asked you what's wrong."

"Nothing. Why?"

"Your neck. You keep scratching it."

She seemed flustered. "My neck? It's nothing . . . I

don't know, not really. It itches a little, that's all. I had a rash there when I got up this morning, and I guess it's starting to act up."

That tidbit of news meant nothing to the others, but Curt leapt out of his chair as though he'd been jabbed with a goad. Scrambling around the table, he elbowed in between Phyllis and Scott and knelt beside her. "Let me see."

She frowned, but took her hand away slowly and allowed him to look.

"Oh, God," he whispered. "Oh, my God."

"What is it?" Scott demanded, half out of his chair but unable to see with Curt blocking the way.

Curt ignored him, looking squarely at Phyllis. "Where were you last night? What happened to you?"

"What do you mean? Nothing happened. I went out, took a walk, and came home to bed."

"That's all?"

"Dammit, Potter, what's wrong?" Scott asked.

"I think so . . . yeah, that's all," Phyllis said. "I went out and took a walk."

"Did you meet anyone outside? Think. Hard. Did you meet anyone?"

"No, I don't think so. If I did, I sure don't remember. What the hell does any of that have to do with my rash?"

Finally Scott grabbed Curt by the shoulder and forced him aside. He took Phyllis' chin in his hands and tilted her head back. He peered at the spot Curt had been studying. For a moment his eyes seemed to swim out of focus. His mouth dropped open. A tight choking sound escaped his throat. Then he whirled and faced Curt.

"This is some kind of goddamned cheap joke, isn't it? It's some kind of half-assed trick to get us to believe in your stupid vampires. You even dragged Phyllis into it, didn't you?"

Now Kelly was studying Phyllis' neck, and Phyllis, upset by all the fuss, was trying to get out of her chair.

"What is it?" Juan said. "What's goin' on?"

"She's been bitten," Curt told him. "She's been attacked. She's got the marks."

He went back to Phyllis' side and tilted her head as Scott had, only at an angle so that everyone could see.

Phyllis swatted his hand away. "Would you just leave me alone?"

"There they are," Curt said, for everyone's benefit. "Two teeth marks."

They were starting to draw the unwelcome attention of the other tables, and the waitress hurried over.

"Is something wrong? If you're gonna fight, you better settle it somewhere else. Not that I could care, but the manager's actually working tonight, and he'll toss you out on your—"

"It's okay," Scott snapped. "We're leaving. How much do we owe you?"

She was taken aback. "I don't know. They're all on separate checks."

"Well, *about* how much? Hurry. We've got to leave."

"I . . . I'll have to add them."

"Never mind that." He pulled out his wallet, peeled two twenties off the stack of bills inside, and dropped them on the table. He grabbed Phyllis by the arm and led her, protesting loudly all the way, out of the restaurant. Curt, Kelly, and Juan followed quickly behind.

The waitress stared after them. "You didn't even touch your food! What about your food?"

Outside, Scott dragged Phyllis across the parking lot to the station wagon. They were almost there when Curt and the others caught up. Curt grabbed his arm and spun him around.

"Would you just wait a minute, Scott? Calm down. You know this isn't a trick. You know it proves everything I've said."

"What do you mean, proves? It doesn't prove anything. You and Phyl got together and cooked the whole thing up."

"It's not a trick! Ask Phyllis if you don't believe me. Ask her!"

Before Scott could say a word, Phyllis snapped, "Listen to him, Scott. It's not a trick."

"Okay, so it's a rash. You said yourself that nothing

happened." He looked at Curt and repeated, "It's just a rash."

Curt sighed and said softly, "You know better than that."

Without thinking, Scott aimed a punch at him. Curt's packages slipped from his grasp and fell to the pavement as he threw up a blocking hand. Trembling, Scott stared at him; a single teardrop trickled down his cheek.

Phyllis put an arm around his shoulder. "Scott, it's all right, don't worry about it. It *is* a rash. Nothing happened last night. I swear."

Curt knelt to pick up his packages. "At least nothing that you remember," he muttered.

"Nothing," Phyllis insisted. "Period. Case closed."

"Okay, fine, it's a rash. And nothing happened. You just happened to be walking around the compound late last night, all alone, and today you just happen to have a rash that looks exactly like two sharp teeth marks. But nothing happened. Fine. So be it." He turned to Kelly, who was standing a few paces back, next to Juan, wide-eyed, her face pale and ghostlike in the unnatural glow of the parking-lot arc lamps. "Will you carry some of these?"

She nodded wordlessly, picking up the art-store bag and the package from Sears.

Scott sighed, a soft and weary shushing noise. "I thought you were in your room last night, Phyl."

She looked startled. "I . . . I was. Yeah. I was in my room."

"Then what's this about walking around the compound?"

"I . . . I don't remember."

"You don't remember? But you remember being in your room, don't you?"

"Yes," she said, as though trying to convince herself.

"So you must have gone for a walk later, right?"

"I guess so. Yes."

He seemed satisfied. "Let's go. It's time to head back."

"Wait a minute," Curt said, getting back to his feet with his parcels clutched protectively to his chest. "No one believes me yet? Even after this, nobody will take me seriously?"

He was met with four silent stares. Only Kelly looked as though she might have been about to speak.

"Damn," he said, defeated. "Okay, let's go."

They rode back to the compound in absolute silence. Curt was close to tears. He couldn't think of anything but how close it was all getting, how stiflingly, chokingly close. Phyllis now. Bach or one of his seconds had reached inside their little group. It still wasn't too late for her, but if she didn't begin to take it seriously . . .

Oh, God, when are they going to believe? What is it going to take?

In addition to coping with the clinging, crawling fear that he'd been living with for a long time, he now had to deal with his cold, dark, and overpowering sense of desolation. He was utterly alone, and he saw nothing that would change that.

But a few moments later he discovered how wrong he was.

They had just pulled into the parking lot at Van Paris Hall. Scott was busy shutting off the engine and logging their mileage into the record book kept in the station-wagon glove compartment, while the others were gathering their purchases together. Curt was making sure he had everything when he heard his name whispered softly and turned to see Kelly leaning close to him. Her eyes were wide and fearful, her lower lip quivering.

"What is it?"

"Curt," she said again, still whispering, "can I . . . can I still have one of those crosses?"

29

It was twelve-twenty-eight A.M. and Ernest Cummings was alone in his darkened office, sipping coffee. The words he'd exchanged with Becky Heller more than two hours earlier were still vibrating in his mind.

They were hiding something.

Heller had come to him fresh from a meeting with Reverend Norris and Tony Smith. They were formulating big plans for a true-testimony segment in each crusade, and had sent out tentative feelers to a number of residents about participating in the project. A certain Curt Potter had refused. Would Cummings be willing to speak to Potter, try to make him see what an important opportunity it was?

Cummings had heard her out, but only with difficulty; her words were almost drowned out by the alarm buzzer blaring away in his head. Odd that this should come up two days after he had reported his conversation with Curt to Tony Smith.

And so he had asked her why, with nearly two thousand people to choose from, Potter was so important.

Heller's eyes had narrowed. "I hope you're not refusing this order, Ernie."

He had pulled back. "I didn't realize it was an order."

She smiled. "Maybe 'order' was the wrong word. Call it a favor. We'd appreciate it if you'd have a talk with Mr. Potter. We hate to see anyone miss a chance like this."

215

"Then you're not thinking of forcing him to participate?"
Her smile faltered. "Of course not."

"Then why not move on to someone else? Forget Curt
and offer it to someone who might be dying for the
chance?"

She mumbled something about the computer and a list
of newcomers who hadn't yet settled on jobs, and reiter-
ated that phrase—big opportunity—adding something
about advancement and promotion. She finished by saying,
"I think it's a communication problem. Obviously, something I said triggered some hostility. When you talk to
him, I'm sure you'll be able to make him change his
mind."

"All right, I'll do what I can. Does this have anything
to do with the talk I had with Curt on Monday?"

Softly she said, "I know of no such talk. I have to run
now. Be in touch by Sunday. We're counting on it."

Now the thought rose once again: they were hiding
something. It was simply too large a coincidence.

Damn. What was he working for? A church? Or the
CIA?

Wearily he turned and looked out the window. Was
there something lurking out there now, slowly destroying
everything he had ever believed in? Was there *anything*
out there? It was a ludicrous question, but it stayed with
him for a long, long time.

Kelly waited a long time for sleep to come. She stared
at the ceiling, its smooth surface becoming a screen on
which she saw projected everything that had occurred
since Monday evening in Ernie's office. When she closed
her eyes to shut the pictures out, they followed her.
What of all the purchases Curt had made—the wood and
garlic, the knife and hammer, the crosses on their fine
link chains? It should have been comical, really, but she
was unable to smile. All she felt was fear.

Phyllis had marks on her neck.

Well, so what? Didn't everyone get cuts or sores or
blemishes? Of course. But these marks weren't like that.
They were neatly spaced, even, precise. Sharp punctures.

In Detroit, two months before she had met the church

worker who had changed her life, she had cut high school
and gone into the city for the day. No reason, no plan. It
was simply something to do. She wandered for hours
through good neighborhoods and bad. At one point she
had spotted a bone-thin, tired young woman sitting on
the front steps of her building, holding a wailing infant in
her arms. Something in the child's cry had drawn Kelly
over to see what the matter was. The baby was sick, the
thin woman told her. The night before, he had been
bitten by a rat. Then the mother had pulled away the
blanket in which she'd wrapped her son, showing Kelly
something on the infant's hand—two sharp, even wounds,
slightly puffed, slightly red.

"See that?" the woman had said. "Y'see that, girl?
Thas where the bastard bit 'im. Thas his teeth marks
right there, the motherfucker."

The marks on Phyllis' throat were almost exactly like
the teeth marks on the baby's hand. A little larger, a
little farther apart, but otherwise identical.

Thas his teeth marks right there, the motherfucker.

Kelly sat up abruptly, looking at the window. The
drapes were closed, but not entirely. A sliver of a cold
autumn moon hung in the sky, and its weak light was like
some kind of message. She groped on the desk next to
her bed, coming away with the cross Curt had given her.
She held it up in front of her and stared at it. She slipped
it over her neck. With her hand still touching the smooth,
gleaming symbol, she fell asleep.

Dark shadows, swirling shadows. They reached out for
him as he walked, as though they'd become tangible. He
walked faster, shrinking from the touch. Behind was
darkness. Ahead was darkness. To each side lurked the
capering shadows. He was lost. Lost in a place he had
never seen before, never been to or even dreamed of. It
was not the menacing barrio of his previous dreams. Not
those streets, but new dream streets.

Something was following him.

He could hear no footsteps, no muffled breathing,
nothing of the sort. But as certainly as he knew his name,
he knew that something was behind him, stalking.

218 Paul F. Olson

And still the shadows tried to ensnare him in their freezing, dead embrace.

He walked for a very long time, his fear growing stronger. It wouldn't be so bad if he could tell exactly what was happening, where he was, when the dream was going to end. It was the confusion, the goddamned un-knowing, that terrified him more than anything else.

At last he saw dim forms outlined, trees and shrubs and autumn-dead flowerbeds beside the path he was on. He began to run. It didn't matter now what was ahead. It had to be better than this. When he broke out into a moonlit clearing and a landscape that he knew, he stopped dead and started to laugh. He wasn't in a land of terrors, after all. This dream world was not one of fear but one of familiar places and things.

He was standing in Worship Park, high above the rows and rows of amphitheater benches. The floorboards of the stage down below gleamed in the moonlight as though they were made of bone. There was nothing frightening about this at all. It was like coming home.

But then he heard something that struck a new chord of fear within him. It was a loud flapping noise of gigan-tic wings coming from behind, from that eternal world of darkness he'd just come through. It was the sound of air being displaced with a great *whooosh, whooosh*.

Juan whirled around and saw at last what he'd sensed in the darkness—a huge bat with mighty stretched wings and long razor-sharp teeth. It arrowed down at him from a vast height, zeroing in on the hillside, on *him*.

He screamed. He had never screamed before in his life, and the high, terrible sound of it frightened him almost as much as the sight of the bat. He threw himself to the ground and covered his head, sensing certain death. He no longer was convinced that this was just another of his dreams; it was too real.

He heard the pounding of the wings on the night air, heard the high, grating sound of the bat's radar keening, coming closer, almost above him now and ready to—

The noise ceased.

In one moment a quiet peace replaced the sounds of

onrushing death. There was only the rasp of his own breath and the rapid drumming of his heart.

Was the bat gone? Could it be gone?

Slowly he uncovered his head and looked up. He was still in Worship Park, but he was alone. He struggled to his feet and looked all around, not yet willing to believe that he was no longer in danger. But it was true. The bat had vanished even more rapidly than it had appeared. He sighed. It was gone. Oh, thank God, thank—

A hand closed upon his shoulder.

He froze, but it didn't matter whether he could move or not, for the hand was turning him around, rudely twisting him and compelling him to look at his captor. He tried to protest, but the words died when he found himself face-to-face with the man from his previous dreams.

"You—" he started. His vocal cords seized up, his throat felt as though it were clogged with sand.

He recognized the man for the first time. It was someone whose picture he had seen many times. Keith Pritikin had shown it to him with pride. It was hanging in the lobby of Van Paris Hall. Hell, it was even hanging next to the door of room 1290.

Arthur Bach.

His head began to spin, and strange lights danced before his eyes, but through it he saw that Bach's teeth were as long and sharp as those of the monstrous bat. Somehow, impossibly, they gleamed even in the dark of night.

Bach's head inclined toward his. The lips drew back to reveal the full length of the incisors, teeth so long and sharp they could never, ever have existed on any human being. Juan made one last effort to pull away, but in vain. The lips touched his throat. He felt a nip of stinging pain and woke up.

His eyes snapped open and he sat up in bed, looking every which way. All was still. When he squinted, he could see Scott in the next bed, his mouth slightly open, his eyelids fluttering ever so slightly. Across the room he saw Curt, also asleep, his hand dangling over the edge of his bed, his fingers twitching nervously.

Jeezus.

A dream. Of course it had been a dream. In originality and terror it put all his earlier nightmares to shame, but it was just a dream nevertheless.

Vampires, he thought. Jesus goddamned Christ, *vampires*. He turned to glance at Curt again and summoned an additional thought: No, man, no way.

But suddenly he was more unsure than he'd ever been before.

Phyllis came instantly awake and sat up. The room was silent. Carole and Paula were asleep. Everything was normal, just as it should be in the middle of the night, except there had been a noise at the window.

That was stupid, impossible. Her room was on the sixth floor!

Yet as she sank back onto her pillow, she heard it again. A muffled scratching at the window, like long fingernails on glass, which had always bothered her to distraction. She rolled over and looked at the closed drapes. Fingernails on glass? What a joke.

But she heard it again. A distinct though distant scratching at the window.

Irritated, too bone-tired to be scared, she got out of bed and padded across the room. She pulled the drapes back with her right hand and recoiled in shock. She didn't scream. She couldn't. The strong hand of fear had smothered all screams.

There was a face at the window, hanging there as though the person it belonged to had somehow rigged a tall ladder and was standing on it. The face was vaguely familiar to her, an ageless face. The hair was thick and dark, streaked faintly with shots of gray. The lips were full, parted slightly in a bitter grin.

A hand with long, delicately thin fingers emerged from below the window frame and scratched the glass, making the noise she had heard before. The lips drew back, but it took her a moment to realize that the man out there was speaking to her.

"Phyllis, open the window. Let me in. I have to speak to you again." The voice, like the face, had a fuzzy familiarity to it. "Let me in. We have a great deal to discuss, don't we?"

She found a single word hidden amid her fear: "No."

The face drew back a little, and she saw at last that it was indeed connected to a whole body. She also saw with a burning rush of panic that the body wasn't standing on any ladder—it was clinging to the side of the building. It was hanging on by its hands, as though it were some kind of insect or . . . or monster.

"Please, Phyllis, let me in."

"No!" she said again. "Go away!" She glanced at Carole, but the girl wasn't stirring.

"Phyllis, what's wrong? I thought we were good friends. You don't have to be afraid to open the window. You don't have to be afraid of anything. Now let me in."

Phyllis felt herself weakening. Looking into the man's eyes was like swimming in cool, deep water. It was refreshing but relaxing at the same time, mesmerizing, lulling, almost hypnotic. She was suddenly weak, sleepy.

"Yes, Phyllis, that's right, open the window. Let in the night air. Let *me* in. It's what I wish. It's my command."

She swayed on her feet, her hand going out automatically to brace herself. It caught the lower edge of the window frame.

The thing outside smiled fully, revealing long, sharp canine teeth. "Yes! Open it!"

Phyllis felt her hand moving independently of her brain, moving across the glass toward the sliding catch on the side. Her fingers touched the latch and closed over it.

"Yes, Phyllis, yes! Open it! Now!"

At that moment it seemed like the only thing to do. Caught in a web of warm, fuzzy drowsiness, she wanted the window open, wanted more than anything to let the man outside in. She began to move the latch to one side, and the man's smile turned into a blazing grin of triumph. She almost had it open and—

—hesitated.

The man's lips and teeth were smeared with blood.

She stared at the man's teeth, his lips, and was suddenly jolted back into consciousness.

"Please, Phyllis, don't stop. Open the window now. Let me in. I'm your friend."

She drew back and secured the latch again. "No," she said, "never!" She glanced at Carole for the second time, and then at Paula. They were still sleeping soundly. *My God, is this whole conversation going on inside my head?* "Go away!" she cried.

The man, or whatever it was, hissed and vanished into the night air. There was nothing remarkable about the disappearance. He was there, and then he wasn't.

Phyllis staggered back into the room, collapsing across the foot of Paula Harpool's bed. Paula sat up, saw her, and uttered a sharp cry.

"Phyl? What's wrong?"

Carole woke up then and stared at them. "What is it? What's going on?"

"I don't know," Paula said. "Phyllis! What's wrong?"

Phyllis stared at her, her mouth moving, trying to form words. The only sounds that came out were short, hitching little gasps.

"Phyl, my God, are you sick? What happened? What is it?"

The tears broke free at last, and Phyllis lay there, her head cradled in Paula's lap, sobbing great heaving tears of fright and shock.

30

Curt, Juan, and Scott were about to start down for breakfast when they heard an urgent knock. Curt was closest to the door and pulled it open, moving back a step when he saw Phyllis standing there. She looked ragged and worn out. Her hair was sloppily combed, her yellow blouse buttoned one button off all the way up. Her eyes were red and puffy.

"Phyl, what—"

She brushed past him into the room, going over to Scott and saying, "It's true! All of it's true, every bit of it!"

Scott took her by the shoulders. "What's wrong? Did something happen?"

She didn't hear him. "It's true," she said again, dangerously close to tears. "Everything Curt said is . . . It's . . ." She did cry then, her head falling against Scott's chest.

Scott held her tightly, glancing sharply at Curt, whose eyes were wide and his face pale. Juan too seemed to have lost much of his color, and he backed up to the far side of the room one unsteady step at a time.

"Phyl, don't cry," Scott said softly. "Talk to me. What is it? What happened, hon?"

Her body racked with ceaseless shudders, Phyllis said, "He came last night."

"Who came? Curt—"

"Not Curt. Bach. I . . . I think it was Bach."

A thin stream of air escaped Curt's lips. Juan uttered a small childlike squeak. Scott only stared at her and repeated, "Bach." It was not a question or a statement but just a word, a word that came out sounding cold and dead.

She nodded. "I think so. Anyway, it was a v-vampire."

Curt's hand went to the cross at his neck. He twisted the chain nervously.

Scott pushed Phyllis away, holding her firmly by the shoulders at arm's length. "What do you mean, a vampire? Tell me what happened."

And so she told them everything from the time she had awakened to the scratching at the window to the time an hour later when she had tried to get back to sleep with a copy of the Bible clutched against her chest.

"But I couldn't . . . couldn't sleep . . . not for the rest of the night. I kept seeing that face, th-those eyes. I kept seeing those teeth and the b-blood. I kept hearing his voice. I kept thinking about how . . . how close I came to opening the window, and I . . . I just couldn't sleep."

Scott grunted. "You're getting as bad as the rest of them. You had a nightmare. Juan was just telling me about *his* nightmare. That's all it was."

She shook her head. "It was real."

"You mean, you thought it was real."

"It was, Scott, you've got to believe me. A vampire came to my window! He tried to get in! Ask my roommates!"

"I thought you said they slept through it."

"They did, but they were up afterward. I woke Paula up when I fell across her bed. Does that sound like a fucking dream to you?"

"All right, so it was a sleepwalking dream. Those aren't so uncommon, you know. It—"

"*It was real!*" Phyllis shrieked, lurching toward him and pummeling his body with her fists. He reached up, defending himself, deflecting the punches before they could do much harm, but Curt noticed that he had begun to cry as he did so.

"Phyllis," he said, "hold on, hon, stop it, please. I believe you. I do. I believe everything, goddammit. I believe it all. Now stop, please. I believe you, just stop, baby, stop."

Juan stepped forward, gently took her flailing arms, and pulled her away from Scott. Curt came over too, and the two of them took her to Scott's bed. She was crying fitfully. Juan too had bright tears trickling down his cheeks. And Scott still stood in the middle of the room, sobbing fiercely.

Curt stared at all of them and felt his own emotional dam beginning to give way as well. He swallowed hard, but that did nothing to hold back the tears that suddenly overcame him.

Belief had finally come.

By ten that morning they were all gathered in the room—Curt, Scott, Kelly, Phyllis, and Juan. They had debated calling Connie Bishop, but had ultimately decided against it. Connie hadn't been with them for the past three days. He was an outsider now and hadn't gone through the painful process that had built them into a small, close-knit group of believers.

Curt's purchases from the mall lay in the middle of the floor. Except for the crosses. The crosses had been distributed to everyone present.

"I don't understand," Scott said after hearing Phyllis' story repeated for Kelly's sake. "If Bach's so powerful, why didn't he just break into the room? Couldn't he have smashed the glass or something?"

Curt shook his head. "That's part of the old legends. Outside, if you meet a vampire, he can do anything he wants to you. But inside your home, you've got control. You have to *invite* him inside. Once you do it the first time, he's free to enter and leave at will, but he has to be invited to begin with." He paused and looked at Phyllis. "You were damn lucky you said no."

"How many of those legends are actually true?" Kelly asked.

Curt shrugged. He glanced wistfully at the cigarette Juan was smoking and at the pack lying on the bed, but didn't take one. "As far as I know, all of them. After all, what're legends but old truths handed down through the generations? And what we've seen so far seems to back that up."

"Then the crosses and garlic will work?"

He grinned crookedly and pointed at the paraphernalia scattered across the floor. "We're sure betting on it, aren't we? I know a lot of books and movies try to change the myths around. They say vampires really can come out in daylight, that sometimes garlic doesn't keep them away. They say that vampires aren't scared of crosses or wild roses or running water. They say vampires can see themselves in mirrors. I don't know why they change everything. Maybe they're trying to make it all seem more real. But ask Phyllis. I don't think we need to make it any more real."

Phyllis shivered. "Do you think I was really bitten when I went for my walk?"

He nodded. "Yeah. I think you met up with Bach, that he took a little bit of blood. That's why he came back last night. I'm not sure, but it's probably his method of operation. He catches you outside first, then tries for a repeat in your room."

"But why don't I remember it? Why is the whole night so fuzzy?"

"Another part of the legend. A victim rarely remembers an attack. You remember what happened last night because you weren't actually attacked. You were awake during the whole episode at your window. But during a real attack, you're under the vampire's spell, and when it's over you can't remember any of the details."

"Is he gonna come back?" Juan asked.

"Probably. He might come for the rest of us too. But we've got these now." He held out his cross. "And I'll give everyone some garlic to rub around your windows." He turned to Kelly and Phyllis. "Try to do it when your roommates aren't around. We don't want everyone in the compound to think we're insane."

The room fell silent. A minute ticked by, then two. The atmosphere was heavy with unanswered questions.

Finally Scott said, "Curt? There's one part of this I can't get around. I keep trying to convince myself of it, but it's hopeless. I can't fit it into my thinking."

"What?"

Scott sighed. "Bach's dead, isn't he? He's like the things in the movies you were talking about, right? The undead? The living dead?"

Curt nodded slowly. "I think so. He's been dead since 1969, when he met Van Paris. I think Van Paris was a vampire. Bach was killed but rose again. Just like you said—the undead."

"Oh, shit," Scott said. "I don't feel too well. I'm . . . I'm dizzy."

"How do you think I feel? That fucking monster's my father."

Everyone stared at him. Kelly put a hand on his shoulder and squeezed gently.

Curt drew in a slow, steady breath. "Do you realize that if this thing goes the way it should, that if we're able to fight it, I might end up driving a stake into my own father's heart?"

Again no one spoke. Someone in the room uttered a sharp gasp, but that was all.

"How do we start?" Juan said after a long time. "Where do we go from here, Curt?

Curt looked at him for a moment, then seemed to pull himself together. "I think we're going to find out where the vampires are. Would anyone like to visit a cemetery?"

31

They took some time to tidy up their personal affairs—commitments to work and friends—and reconvened in room 1290 some hours later. After everyone had sat down, Curt asked, "Did you all use the garlic?"

Kelly nodded. "I waited until my roommates went out to lunch. Then I rubbed it all around the window frame, like you said. The little bits of peel kept falling off, and there I was down on my knees, scrabbling around trying to pick them all up. I felt like a thief getting rid of fingerprints on the furniture."

"What about you, Phyl?"

"I used it," she said. "I even took the screens off and rubbed some outside."

Curt smiled. "Good. Rub some more tonight, just to be sure. And keep the crosses near you, keep them around your necks. If you see something, hold it up and . . . well, we've been through this already, haven't we?"

Everyone nodded, and Juan said, "We still gonna visit the cemetery tonight?"

"We have to," Curt told him. "But right now I want to make a visit to Ernie. Kelly swears he's not a familiar, that he went to Smith and Heller out of love for the church. I believe her, and I think we need him on our side. He knows the workings of this place better than anyone else. Even though he's a real outsider, he might still be able to save us time by pointing out which officials *are* in on everything. And, Phyl? I'm going to want you with me when I talk to him."

Scott frowned. "Why?"

Curt ignored him and said to Phyllis, "Will you come?"

"I could," she said softly, looking at the ground between her feet. "I mean, I guess I could. But why?"

"You've got solid proof. You've got a firsthand account of an attack—or an attempted attack, anyway. And you've still got the marks."

Her hand drifted to her throat. The pinpoint punctures there were healing, the red fading, the swelling going down, but they were still easily visible. She touched the wound and shivered. "Why don't we all go?" she asked.

He shook his head. "Kelly told us he's safe, and from talking to him before, I tend to agree. But if we're wrong, if he's really an insider like we think Kaye and Norris are, I don't want him knowing how many of us are onto him. It would be exposing too much of our hand to the enemy. It's better to keep it down to just Phyl and me."

Phyllis looked at the others and finally at Curt. Her hand strayed once more to the marks at her throat. Her eyes narrowed and she grimaced.

"Yes, I'll come," she said. "I'll talk to him."

Cummings was on the telephone when they got there. He looked tired, but more than that he looked frazzled. He finished up with the call and said, "Curt, I'm glad you're here. Have you seen Kelly?"

Curt shook his head. "Not since yesterday."

"I don't know what's happened. She hasn't been in all day. That's not like her, and the extra work is wearing me out." He leaned back in his chair with a hefty sigh. "Anyway, I'm glad you're here. You must have ESP. I was going to contact you tonight and . . . I'm sorry. It's Phyllis, isn't it?"

She nodded and took a seat beside Curt. For several moments there was awkward silence. Then Curt cleared his throat.

"I'm here about the vampires," he said.

Cummings put a hand up to his head and massaged his right temple. "So I gathered. What's up?"

"We've got some things to tell you, and show you. More things have been happening. Phyl's been—" He stopped abruptly, as though uncertain how to proceed. "I'll let her tell you."

Her story took less than ten minutes, but Cummings stared at the wound on her neck for a long time, not saying anything, his expression absolutely unreadable. At one point she tried to pull her collar back into its normal position, but he stopped her and examined the marks some more. At last he sat back in his chair and began massaging his temple again.

When she was done, Curt jumped in and went over briefly the other things that had passed since their last conversation. He mentioned his purchases at Fox Valley and some of the plans they'd been making, leaving out any reference to Scott or Juan or Kelly.

When he'd finished, the room fell silent once again. The electric clock on the wall behind Cummings' desk hummed loudly, but that was the only sound.

After almost a full minute, Cummings murmured, "I'm sorry. In God's name, you can't imagine how sorry I am."

Curt's breath caught in his throat. "What do you mean?"

"I'm sorry," he repeated. "For what happened to you, for what this church—the church that I supposedly represent—did to you."

"Are you saying you believe us?" Curt asked cautiously.

"Of course I believe you. I . . . I almost did after we talked before. Then Becky came to me and told me about the TV offer—and she was so insistent that you take them up on it. I kept thinking that she and Tony were trying to hide something. The only thing I could possibly connect it with was your story, the vampires and . . . and your relationship to the Master. I still wasn't sure, but now . . ." He shrugged helplessly.

"Will you help us?" Phyllis said.

"H-help? Yes, of course I will. But how? What can I do?"

Curt smiled. "You can do a lot, more than any of us, I think. First, answer some questions."

Ernest nodded. "Go ahead."

"Okay. You've been here a long time. You deal with the high officials every day, don't you?"

"Almost every day, sure."

"Can you say with any certainty who knows about the vampires and who doesn't? We need to know who we can trust and who to watch out for."

"I . . . I don't know. I only just found out about this. How could I possibly know—"

"Trust your feelings, Ernest. Who gives you orders?"

At that, Ernest chuckled. "Many people. Most days I think too many. Reverend Bob, Reverend Norris, some of the junior pastors. Tony Smith and Becky Heller, of course. A few of the other department heads."

"Did any of them ever ask you to do anything strange? Something that seemed unusual?"

Another laugh. "All the time."

"Anything that seems to make sense now that you know about the vampires?"

As Ernest pondered that, he happened to gaze outside. In the late-afternoon sunlight a Frisbee sailed past the window and someone chased it. "I suppose, when you look at it that way, yes, quite a few of the things make sense. Mostly, my orders come from Tony and Becky. When I question them, both Reverend Norris and Reverend Bob back them up. I'm usually told that the orders come from the Master and I *must* follow through."

"Then doesn't it seem like—"

"Of course! Yes, I see what you're getting at. All four of them." He paused, and then repeated, marveling, "All four of them are in on it."

"And what about the others?" Curt said. "The department heads, the junior pastors? Do any of them do the same thing?"

"No. Never. The orders from those people are menial things. Photocopy this, mail that, pass this around, call so-and-so. The policy decisions all come from Heller and Smith and the two senior reverends."

Curt looked at Phyllis and grinned. "We're lucky, then.

It's a limited group we're dealing with. Vampires are nothing if not smart; they keep their inner circle as small as possible."

"What about the vampires themselves?" Ernest asked.

"We're not sure," Curt said. "That's next on the agenda. We can count Bach and Van Paris for sure. Maybe some of the early ministers like Hummelt and Walstein, and possibly some of the residents the vampires have accidentally killed, the way they almost killed Chambers and Ryan. We still have to find that out."

"You mentioned 'we,' " Ernest said. "If I had turned you away, were you and Phyllis prepared to fight this alone?"

"No," Curt said. "Thank God, no." And he told their new comrade about the others in their circle.

Ernest rubbed his temple again. "It's still a tiny group against something like this. I'm ready to help."

"Are you? I'm sorry, but I don't think you are. I don't think any of us really are. I know I'm not. We're talking about my goddamned father! And what about you? You've been here a long time. Do you really think you could drive a stake into the chest of the man you've worshiped?"

"I worship no one but Christ," Ernest said coolly.

"Okay, call it 'admired.' You've followed Bach for years. Can you really turn all that admiration, respect, and love around and do what's going to have to be done to get rid of him?"

"Wh-why must I be the one?"

"You might not be, but then again, you might. We all have to be ready for the possibility. Can you handle that?"

Ernest thought for a moment. He had been a textbook teenage alcoholic. He had come to the growing compound of Universal Ministries fresh from Boston's Roxbury district. The church had dried him out first, then taught him, supported him, set him on the proper path. He had worked hard to repay that, and had been rewarded with the promotion to his current post. Throughout all of that, the bad times and the good, the Reverend Arthur Bach had been a beacon to him. He had read the Master's words with awe, listened to his tape-recorded sermons with something like hypnotic ecstasy, loving Bach second only to God himself. But it was all deception. Fraud. Lies.

He glanced at Phyllis Meyer's expectant face, and the thought of the bestial masks on her neck made him shudder. "I can handle it," he announced firmly.

Outside Ernest's office widow was a large grassy expanse of lawn. In the spring and summer, and even on warm fall days, it was a haven for baseball players, Frisbee tossers, suntan fanatics, and those who just liked to sit on the grass for a while and talk to friends.

Among them was a muscular bearded man in his early thirties who was sitting with his back against the building's brick wall, alternating glances between the sky above and the closely printed pages of the Universal Ministries' Bible open across his lap. Clipped to his belt was something that, at a quick glance, looked like a Walkman-style cassette player. Upon closer examination, someone would have noticed an odd appliance attached to the unit, something that looked like a TV satellite dish shrunk down five hundred times—a small metallic cup. The man was using a set of headphones and listening to this unit attentively, sometimes cocking his head to one side to hear a bit better, other times jotting quick notes in the margins of Leviticus, Chapter 4.

When Ernest's meeting with Curt and Phyllis was over, the muscular young man stood up, stretched, and removed his headphones, letting them dangle around his neck. He snapped his Bible closed and slipped it under his arm. Then he stretched again, glanced casually around, and hurried across the compound to the Faith Center.

The Reverend Robert Kaye got back into town just after three that afternoon. He hoped to be in his office just long enough to grab his messages and then go home to sleep off the jet lag. He had been at his desk barely long enough to find the stack of mail that had been building up during his absence, however, when there was a knock on his door and Reverend Norris came in without waiting to be invited.

"So it *was* you," Norris said. "Tony called me and said he thought he'd seen your car coming into the back lot. What're you doing here? You weren't due back till tomorrow."

Trapped, Kaye sighed and lowered himself into his chair. "We wrapped things up early in Paris. I was able to catch a flight out early this morning."

"It went well?"

Kaye nodded and proceeded to discuss his trip to Germany and the Master's move there, which was now to be known as Project Far Horizon.

"Well, I can't say I'm too thrilled about the whole thing, but at least I know where we stand," Norris said.

"You understand the Master's desire to travel abroad?"

"Understand it? No. But I do understand that it's what he wants. Why he'd want to head for Europe when we have things laid out so perfectly here . . . Christ, Bob, he's got the cream of American youth to choose from! What's so damned special about making German vampires? I—" He paused, and shook his head angrily. "Forget it. It's his command and our duty to obey, right? The move begins December first?"

Kaye nodded. "We'll leave the compound, travel to O'Hare, and set the whole operation rolling. We'll be responsible for getting him as far as Hamburg, and from there it'll be in the hands of Wilmar, Schroeder, and the other Germans. The Master will be traveling under an alias, and . . . Well, I don't think we have to discuss this now. We'll have plenty of time for it later." He paused. "You want a drink?"

Norris accepted a bourbon and water, lit one of his home-rolled cigarettes, and said, "I have to tell you, I'm glad you made it back early. I've been trying to reach you for several days, but couldn't get through."

"Not surprising. I was in and out of Paris a lot. Besides Stockholm, I managed to hit Brussels, London, and Vienna. I'm worn out. Why? Something wrong?"

Norris' expression clouded and his jaw tightened perceptibly. "There's a new Enemy of the Lord," he said.

Kaye paled. "Go on."

"It's rather like that episode with Paul Hardy five years ago. Of course Hardy was a touch crazy to begin with. He saw things and started babbling about were-wolves and flesh-eaters. In the end he ran from the compound like a whipped dog. It was a scare, but we never even got around to considering induction. It never got that bad."

"Dammit, Steve, I know all that. It's in the past. Who's the *new* Enemy?"

"A newcomer, some guy by the name of Curt Potter. He got wind of a few things. He put them together and came up with the idea that this church is being run by vampires."

Kaye gasped, and his face turned a sickly ashen color. When he leaned forward in his chair he felt suddenly dizzy.

"Vampires," he repeated dully. "You're sure?"

"A hundred percent. He took his story to Cummings, who had the presence of mind to call Tony. Tony brought it to me. According to Ernie, Potter's been spreading it around, too, telling others."

"Others." Kaye murmured the word as though it held no sense for him. "Others? Jesus Christ, Steve, how'd this happen? No sane resident of the church would cook up a vampire story on his own. We're too careful!"

"Maybe," Norris said, sounding unconvinced. "You know as well as I do that lately the Master's appetite has become insatiable. My guess is that Potter just saw a few too many things. As far as we know, he was in the Park the day Chambers went down. He was also there when Morkowski had her problem. And his roommate is Juan Jimenez, the Hispanic kid who found Dennis Ryan in the radio studio. Maybe he saw other things too. We have no way of knowing."

Norris sighed. "And there's more. Potter's claiming that Bach is his father."

Kaye laughed. It was sudden, surprising, and completely without humor. "Well, now we know he's not sane. The Master couldn't be his father. He was never married . . . Oh, shit." He looked down into the dregs of his Scotch and water. When he spoke again, his voice was soft and shaky. "Illegitimate? Is that possible?"

"Not only possible, probable," Norris said. "I did some research. It seems our beloved leader did see a little action back in his pastoral days, particularly when he was at Faith Lutheran in that pissant town in Wisconsin. He knocked up at least one local lady, maybe more. Of course, the trail's so faint after all these years that there's no way of confirming any of that, or finding the names, or discovering what happened to any offspring. But it's likely that Potter's story is true. He's thirty-one. That fits the time frame of Bach's tenure at Faith Lutheran perfectly."

"That puts a different spin on things," Kaye remarked. "All by itself, it could be disastrous. But when you combine it with the vampire mess, it could serve to point out Potter's unstable mind. You know what I mean? A long-lost child seeking vengeance, and walking the sanity tight-rope at the same time?"

Norris frowned. "You're not suggesting releasing the father-son story as a way of covering up the other, are you?"

"Hardly. But having it in the background could create a fall-back position for us later, if worse comes to worst." He rose and mixed himself another drink. While he stirred, he said, "What precautions have been taken?"

Norris smiled faintly. "We've done all we could in light of your absence. We went to Potter and offered him a television spot." He quickly explained the offer Becky Heller had made to Curt. "He balked at it, but we're going to keep the pressure on for a while and see if he can't be persuaded to change his mind."

Kaye's brow wrinkled, as though he wasn't convinced of the success potential in the plan. "Anything else?"

"Not really. We're watching him carefully, along with his roommates, the Jimenez kid and a one-year resident named Scott Matheson. Also Connie Bishop, and a couple of girls named Meyer and Beckworth. Beyond that, it's anyone's guess how far it might have spread. Every one of them except for Potter works and is in a Bible-study group. That gives them a wide circle of contacts. If even one of those contacts has been spoken to, it wouldn't do to have Potter suddenly drop out of sight; it would raise too many suspicions."

Kaye nodded and took a long swallow of his drink. "You're sure he really believes this, Steve? This isn't some kind of elaborate joke being played on Ernie? Something like that?"

"I don't think so. And even if it is, I think we have to take it seriously."

The door opened and Tony Smith swept in, looking panic-stricken. "Steve, I just learned some very bad news. You know Howard Crisp, that observer we planted outside Ernie's office? He was outside the window using one of our listening devices when Potter and Meyer came in to see Ernie. He didn't get it word for word, but apparently the Master had paid that Meyer girl a visit earlier in the week, before she got wise. She had marks to show Ernie. And after he got a look at them, it seems like Ernie promised to do whatever it takes to stop Bach."

Woodenly Kaye said, "That's a straight quote?"

"Straight enough. But I'm not done yet. We had other observers checking out Potter's room. He and his friends have stockpiled crosses and garlic. They even have wooden stakes."

"Son of a bitch," Norris murmured.

Kaye looked pale. "If Ernie's turned, a little educated guesswork should tell us what comes next. He'll start meeting with other residents, spreading the word. He's a popular figure, and what he says carries a lot of weight. Most of the people he talks to will think he's slipped a screw, but if even one in ten believes him . . ." He hesitated. "There might be press leaks. There will certainly be wild debate here in the compound. At its worst, we'll have a small army waving stakes in our faces and demanding to see the Master. With Ernie, a group of five kids could easily grow to two dozen or more."

Smith nodded. "That's exactly what I'm worried about. There's always the chance that he was bluffing Potter, pretending to go along with him but secretly thinking he's insane. Maybe he plans to arrange counseling or spiritual help. But I don't think we really want to take that chance, do we?"

"Absolutely not," Norris said. "We've got a minor risk on the verge of being multiplied God knows how many times. We have to act now."

Kaye and Smith nodded.

"If you want, Bob, I'll set up a meeting with the Master. We'll go together and bring him up-to-date."

"And?" Smith said.

Norris sighed. "And do whatever the hell he tells us to do."

32

It took them much longer than planned to find the cemetery. Four times they chose the wrong trail from among the network of footpaths in the back of the compound. At one point they had even circled back to within a few hundred yards of the television broadcast offices and had been forced to head back into the woods again, virtually starting over. At last, with the afternoon waning and the autumn evening rushing on, they found it.

"There," Curt said, pointing at the low stone wall with its iron gate. "Finally."

The little group paused just outside the gate, more than one of them glancing up at the sky. Rain had fallen on and off during the day. It wasn't raining now, but the sky was still overcast, the road they were standing on muddy and wet. The lack of sun made it seem even later than it was.

"What time is it?" Scott asked, his voice low.

"Five o'clock," Phyllis said. "What does that give us? Half an hour?"

"Probably less," Curt said. "Let's go in."

He approached the gate, trying to ignore the chill that had overtaken him as soon as he spotted it. When his hand touched the iron, he thought it felt much colder than it should have, and he struggled to keep his imagination in check. He knew this scouting mission was going to be difficult enough without giving in to superstition and wild thoughts.

239

He expected the gate to squeal when he pushed it open—that would have been so appropriate—but it swung open soundlessly on well-oiled hinges. He took a step forward, paused, and looked back over his shoulder at the others.

"Are you coming?"

No one spoke, but as soon as he passed the stone wall and set foot on the gravel path within, they followed, keeping close, keeping silent.

A short distance inside, the path split, and Curt chose the branch that went to the right. He followed it until he came to the first row of stones. They were all identical, like the markers in a military cemetery—low stone affairs with simple inscriptions bearing only name and date of death. In that first row there were ten stones, with dates as early as September 2, 1971 and as recent as February 9, 1984. None of the names was familiar.

They moved along from row to row, not spending much time on any of them, but checking each stone nevertheless. There were clues to be found here, they knew, if only they could recognize them when they saw them.

In short order they had followed the path all the way to the back of the cemetery, to the point where it joined the left branch and headed back toward the gate. Curt paused and, from this vantage point, surveyed the entire graveyard. It was certainly small enough, and contained few graves by the standards of most cemeteries. One hundred? That was a good guess. The rows were well-spaced and held as few as three plots up to a maximum of twelve.

"There," Scott said suddenly, breaking the silence that had held them all for the last ten minutes or so.

They turned and saw him pointing to a row of stones forty or fifty yards ahead of them.

"What is—"

"That's where I saw the dog. Next to that end stone. It's where I saw the bird—the bat—flying away."

He spoke softly, but his voice had a quavering edge to it. Phyllis moved closer to him and saw that he was trembling. She put an arm around his shoulders and pulled him close to her.

Just a few moments after that, they had their first real success.

"Lookit this!" Juan said, kneeling by the third stone in a short row of six.

They hurried to his side and looked at the inscription:

CHRISTOPHER WALSTEIN
November 17, 1969

"Walstein," Scott read. "Wasn't that one of—"

"My father's early friends, right. Some of the histories say he was one of the ones responsible for him making the decision to leave his country parish behind and try for bigger things. That was in 1967. They'd made a little progress—a small-time radio show in Milwaukee, a national revival-style tour every summer—when Van Paris arrived on the scene and Walstein dropped out of sight, along with all the other friends and business partners."

He paused, knelt by the stone, and read aloud: " 'November 17, 1969.' Jesus Christ. According to what I read, my father met Van Paris in October 1969. Just a month before this."

They checked the other three stones remaining in the row, but didn't see any familiar names. In the very next row, however, they found more.

"Oh, my God," Curt said, "they're all here, look! David Alonzo Brandon: November 29, 1969. Paul J. Hummelt: January 17, 1970. Randall Walter Breuhauser: January 19, 1970. All of Bach's early advisers, all dead within three months of Van Paris' arrival. And here's another one. I haven't heard the name before, but he must have been somebody. Edward Lucas: February 3, 1970. That's about three weeks before Van Paris turned this land over to the movement, maybe *six* weeks before they broke ground on the Faith Center."

"What about all the other graves?" Kelly asked. "You

didn't know those names, and the dates were all across the board—1972, 1978, 1983, you-name-it. Victims?"

Curt shook his head. "I don't know. Some of them must be. They could be the ones who weren't as lucky as Tom Chambers and Sally Morkowski. The ones who really died."

One by one, they turned and looked around the cemetery. The thought that there might be a hundred vampires beneath their feet suddenly gripped them. They were up against more than they had originally thought, more than they could ever hope to stop, even if they were an army instead of just five bewildered people—six if you counted Cummings.

"Anyway," Curt went on before his fear could stop him cold, "they have a rationale for this place. They say it's for foreign missionaries and outpost directors who die but want to be buried near the Master. We have to give them the benefit of the doubt on that, I guess. Some of the graves could be legitimate."

"You mean some of the dead people here are really dead," Juan said, and laughed once, sharply.

Curt looked at the sky. "Shit. We've been here longer than I thought. It's almost dark."

"But we haven't found Bach or Van Paris," Scott said.

They stared at each other. Then, hurrying, they began to move down the few remaining rows, scanning each marker for the names of the church leaders, or even possible pseudonyms, since it was unlikely the officials would take the stupid risk of burying the Master under his own name in a place that any of his faithful could stumble across at any time. They came up with nothing, and stopped again by the last row.

"I don't get it," Phyllis said. "Where is he? If he's not here, where—"

"His house!" Curt said, inspiration dawning. "They say he has a house here in the compound, right? Scott, you said you saw it, the night you found the decapitated dog. I'll bet he's there, along with Van Paris. The Masters removed from their flock." He shook his head, as though amazed he hadn't thought of it before. "In the legends, the king vampires are never kept in the same place as the others. They're kept in safer surroundings. Which is exactly what Bach's house would be—safer."

"His house," Phyllis repeated softly. She was frowning, as though something about that phrase troubled her but she couldn't say what. "His . . . house . . ."

Curt swore. "I should have figured it out. But at least we accomplished something today by proving Walstein and—"

He broke off suddenly, his eyes darting left and right, scanning the cemetery nervously.

"Curt?" Kelly said, touching his arm. "What's wrong?"

He didn't answer directly. Instead he said, "Time! What time is it?"

Phyllis gasped as much at the implication of his question as at the fact that she had to bring her watch nearly up to her face in order to read it. In the absorption of their discoveries, they had failed once again to notice the vanishing daylight.

"Close to five-thirty. I . . . I can't . . . I can't tell!"

"Do you feel it?" Curt said, with awed fascination in his voice. "It's that time, it's getting ready. Oh, Jesus, *do you feel it*?"

They did. The air in the cemetery had grown stale and warm. In addition, there was a current tingling around them, causing the fine hairs on their arms and the backs of their necks to stir and rise. It was as though some invisible but strong force had charged the air with pulsing electricity.

"Let's get out of here," Curt said. "Now!"

They sprinted down the gravel path. The gate was close, but not close enough, so they headed for the nearest wall. They leapt at it, scaling it easily and tumbling into the grass on the other side. There they lay, breathing hard, ready for anything. They weren't sure precisely what was about to happen, but they didn't doubt for a moment that something was on the way.

Curt got up, crouching on his hands and knees, and peered over the wall. Scott joined him first, then Kelly, Phyllis, and finally Juan. The cemetery was almost invisible in the gathering darkness. The split, curving path was just an ill-defined trail; the headstones were vague blobs of grayish white.

And still the atmosphere around them was changing. The air became heavier, warmer, and carried still more of that oddly pulsing electrical current that now brought gooseflesh to their arms and legs. More than one of them sniffed the air and caught a whiff of something foul, like the scent of faraway death.

They watched and waited, an almost maniacal sense of curiosity seizing all of them and keeping them there despite the fear they felt.

The ground under their knees seemed to pulse in much the way the air around them did, as though the earth was about to split open and expel something.

"*Jeeeezus*," Juan hissed, his voice equal parts terror and wonder.

And then the last trace of daylight was gone and total darkness fell. In that instant the warming air grew instantly colder by as much as twenty degrees. The drop was so sudden that several of them stopped breathing for a moment in shock. As the temperature fell, the tingling current flowing around them increased in equal measure.

Curt, for one, was certain that all of his hair was now standing on end.

Then they watched the vampires begin to rise.

33

The clock read five minutes past two when Juan awoke from a restless sleep plagued by dreams. Images of insubstantial shapes—twenty or thirty—rose from the ground like smoke and took to the air with rapid flapping movements. The shapes whipped away into the night while he and his friends watched in stunned horror. In the dreams, as it had been in reality just hours before, the whole thing was over in seconds.

He bolted upright in bed and gazed with sleep-hooded eyes at the darkness of the room. Curt and Scott were asleep, both of them tossing beneath the covers. Scott was uttering low sounds from deep in the back of his throat.

Juan lay down again, but knew as soon as his head hit the pillow that he wouldn't sleep for some time to come. He was too frightened by what had happened to them earlier, and equally fearful that a return to sleep would bring a return to his terrible dreams.

Surrendering, he cursed softly and got out of bed, crossed the room to his dresser, and started pulling on clothes. Not sure what he had in mind, he started toward the door, but hesitated near the head of his bed. The cross Curt had given him was dangling from the edge of the headboard, ready in case he should need it in the middle of the night. His hand moved toward it, almost touched it, but stopped. He didn't need it. He couldn't say with any certainty where he was going, but he surely

245

had no intention of leaving the Hall. And as long as he stayed inside the building he would be safe, wouldn't he?

Of course you'll be safe, he thought. Don't be *estúpido*. Ain't no fuckin' vampire gonna come inside the Hall.

He opened the door and slipped out into the silent corridor. He hurried to the elevators and took one down to the lobby. Now he knew where he was going. He was going to the lounge, where at this time of night he could be completely alone and watch TV until he felt relaxed enough to return to an untroubled sleep.

On his way through the lobby, he passed a Japanese man in his late twenties curled up on one of the couches and sleeping with an open Bible in his lap. Looking around, he assured himself that no one else was there. That was good. He needed a little time away to think. Although he missed precious little of L.A. and the barrio, he did miss the chance to enjoy nobody's company but his own.

When he reached the darkened lounge, he passed by the light switch and instead went directly to the television in the far corner. He turned it on and flipped from channel to channel, running across static, test patterns, old movies, an aerobics show, more static, more movies. He settled for a slapstick comedy starring a not-very-funny team of actors he'd never seen before, and settled down on the couch to watch.

The minutes dragged by, and so did the movie. He considered getting up and changing to something else, but was starting to feel sleepy. His limbs became heavy and his eyes grew grainy and dry. As bad joke followed bad joke, he closed his eyes altogether and started to drift. At one point he was startled back to alertness by some half-comic reference to Los Angeles, but the line was gone before he could home in on it, and he lay back again, still drifting.

As the movie wore on and the commercials came with increasing speed, Juan slept. This time there were no dreams to chase him, no awful memories of their expedition to the cemetery. It was a good sleep, and if he could somehow have been awake to comment on it, he would have said it was goddamned well-deserved.

*   *   *

An unknown time later he awoke, coming around with such an incredibly violent start that he almost tumbled from the couch, as though someone had come into the room and kicked him in the ribs.

He jolted upright and discovered that he was sweating. There was a burning sensation in his stomach and a tight prickling in his chest. He looked around quickly, his body coiled into a street kid's defense posture, just the way he had been that morning in L.A. when Keith Pritikin had shaken him awake in his car.

The movie was over, the TV station off the air. Idiot static hissed, the only noise in the room. Then what had awakened him? He glanced around the room again, and his gaze paused on the sliding doors, now covered for the night by thick, heavy drapes.

Something out there? He didn't think so, but maybe.

"Yeah," he whispered to no one but the empty room, "*vampiros* out there, right?"

He tried to laugh but couldn't.

That was when he heard the slow, deliberate scratching on the glass.

His blood changed to thick sludge in his veins. The metallic taste of fear flooded into his mouth. His right hand closed over the arm of the couch, gripping it in a death lock.

He waited, terrified.

The scratching noise came again, a little louder.

He got up, ignoring the crackling of bones in his back, the stiffness of his joints and muscles. Something was out there and he had to see what it was.

He approached the sliding doors and paused, raising a hand hypnotically to open the drapes.

Don't! a voice within him shrieked. *No!*

But he had to see. He grasped the drapes with a slow, dreamlike motion and pulled them back.

He froze, all his breath leaving in a quick, shocked gasp. Time stood still for just an instant, and he could hear the death-march pounding of his heart.

Then the instant was past, and Juan screamed into the empty Van Paris Hall night.

There was a dead, fish-white face peering at him through the glass.

Curt stirred in bed, groping for consciousness. He hung teetering on the edge of a dream, almost slipped back in, and then awoke. He brought one stiff clawlike hand up to his face, rubbed his eyes, and sat up.

Shit, he thought, the middle of the night again. He wondered if he would ever again know a night of uninterrupted sleep.

He lay down again and threw an arm over his eyes, thinking without trying about the nightmare he had dodged—the cemetery and the rising of the vampires.

As they had huddled close to each other and watched, the vampires had come out of the ground. They had come from Walstein's grave, and Hummelt's, and Brandon's. They had come from the graves of Edward Lucas and Randall Breuhauser, and from the other parts of the cemetery where there had been no recognizable names. Not from all of the graves, no, but from many. They rose in insubstantial form, not man shapes or beast shapes, but swirling smoke, dark and slowly moving clouds. Within seconds, before they could even think of fleeing, the vampires had taken off, flapping up into the night, until they could be seen no more. As soon as they were gone, the atmosphere had changed yet again, becoming normal. The temperature had warmed a few degrees and the pulsing current in the air had stopped. Beneath their feet the ground had stopped its terrible movements.

And then they had run home, the five of them, charging along with their crosses held out to ward off anything they might see, like medicine men being chased by demons.

Curt was certain that he had narrowly escaped reliving all of that in his dreams, and even thinking about it now, he knew that he would not dare return to sleep for the rest of the night. He had lived the nightmare once. He could not face it again so soon.

He got out of bed and stumbled into the bathroom,

relieved himself, splashed cold water on his face, and started back. Halfway across the room he stopped.

"Oh, shit." His voice was a husky, choked whisper.

Juan was not in his bed. Scott was still asleep, albeit restlessly, but Juan was gone. Foolishly Curt looked all around the room, as if expecting the boy to be hiding under the dresser or cowering in the shadows next to the bookcase. Of course he wasn't.

Curt felt a wave of nausea sweep over him. Where would Juan have gone? Outside? No, not after the cemetery trip. Then where? Where would—

His thoughts snapped off abruptly, replaced with a fresh wave of terror, when he saw Juan's cross dangling from the headboard.

With fear striking mighty blows inside his skull, Curt pulled on his jeans too quickly, getting the legs mixed up and nearly sprawling on the floor. He took a deep breath, calmed himself, and got it right. Then, barefoot and bare-chested, he grabbed his own cross from his bed and raced from the room. He didn't know where to go, had no idea where to begin, but he knew he had to find Juan.

"Come out, young friend. I need to talk to you. We have many things to discuss."

Juan didn't reply. He was still paralyzed, riveted by the intense power of the voice that belonged to the man outside the window, hopelessly caught by the man's eyes, which gazed passionately in at him and seemed to command him to do many things at once. The face didn't really look dead or fishlike anymore, as he had thought at first. It seemed warm and friendly, almost jovial. It seemed vaguely familiar, not threatening at all.

"Please, Juan. It *is* Juan, isn't it? I hear you have some misconceptions about my work. I think we need to talk and clear some of the misunderstanding away. I have to show you I'm not what you think I am. Please. Listen to me. Come outside."

Juan nodded. He felt drawn, aware of a hypnotic force pulling him. Go outside, the man had said. Yes. It seemed right to do that; it seemed like the only thing to do.

The man smiled. "Good for you, Juan. You're thinking properly now. Go ahead, open the door. The latch is simple. Come join me, let me show you how wrong you and your friends are. I'll show you how caring I can really be.''

Like a bothersome gnat that can't be chased away, a small part of Juan's mind tried to warn him again. It sketched a picture of immense and horrible pain, great suffering, the torture and torment that would result from obeying the man beyond the glass. But that picture was weak and distant. It seemed almost pathetic in comparison to the glory he saw in the man's eyes. Staring into them, he felt himself floating away on soft clouds of pure pleasure unlike anything he'd ever dreamed of.

"Yes, Juan, the latch! Do it! If you come out here now, I have huge rewards for you. You'll never again know the life you knew on the streets. Never! Join me! Come follow the High Church, *true* church!''

The man smiled again, and Juan felt the last traces of resistance being blown from his mind.

"*Yes, Juan, yes! Open it!*''

And with all reason gone, Juan's hand closed over the latch on the sliding glass door.

The elevator was too damn slow, Curt thought, wishing all the way down that he had taken the stairs. Every time he considered the question of where Juan could have gone, cold panic racked his body. Juan was smart. He wouldn't have gone for a walk tonight, not without his cross. But then where was he?

The elevator finally reached the lobby, and Curt leapt out like a cartoon musketeer, holding his cross high. There were no vampires waiting for him. The place was deserted except for a Japanese man sleeping on a couch across the way.

"Juan!" he called. "Hey, Juan!"

The Japanese man grunted in his sleep, did a half-turn on the couch, and began to snore softly.

"Juan!"

No answer.

Running, Curt made his way across the lobby to the corridor of small offices. He tried each door as he raced past, but each one was locked, the lights within turned off for the night. He spun around and hurried back in the direction of the cafeteria, peering in through the high, narrow windows at the shadowy shapes of the tables, salad bar, and other fixtures. He searched for signs of movement in the darkness in there, saw none, and changed direction again.

He skidded to a stop in the center of the lobby and looked in all directions. Without going to every floor in both wings of the Hall, there were only three places left to check: the laundry rooms, the cluster of conference rooms and meeting halls down the two long corridors to his left, and the lounge.

"Juan!"

The Japanese man grunted, as if to point out to Curt that he was wasting time.

He spun around and took off at full speed again for the lounge.

The door slid open on its greased track without a sound.

"Good for you, Juan. You're a smart young man. You deserve the reward you're going to get. Come outside and claim it."

Juan gazed into the man's deep eyes and stepped forward, oblivious of the cool night air. He stopped just inches away and smiled. The man smiled back.

"You've done well. Tonight I'll give you true peace and induct you into the ranks of my church, and then we can work together. We'll stand side by side and induct your friends too. You'll be a group again, all happy and safe. Would you like that?"

Juan murmured, "Oh, yes."

The man laughed. It had a warm, full, pleasant sound to it. Juan continued to gaze into his eyes, watching them turn from deep pools into warm, fiery lakes, then into broad oceans of soothing water. He was no longer floating, but sinking, falling gratefully down and down into a place where street life meant nothing, where there was no more fear, where time and even life itself were completely meaningless and ultimately useless, where existence held one meaning only.

And it was good . . .

. . . it was right.

The man reached for him and took him by the shoulders with fingers that were long and delicate but very powerful.

"Yes, Juan, tonight you'll feed me, and then your friends will feed you. It's a circle." He chuckled again. "A wonderful circle."

The man inclined his head forward, drawing his lips back in a kind of canine snarl and revealing long—

"Bach!"

The man hissed sharply and pulled away, looking past Juan at the source of the disturbance.

Curt was standing in the entrance to the lounge, his feet planted firmly, his shining cross held up in front of him.

The man pushed Juan aside and advanced into the room, smiling so broadly that he was almost grinning.

"Well, Curt Potter." In a rapid, uncanny transformation his voice lost all its commanding power, becoming instead casual, conversational, almost folksy. "Funny. It seems almost like Old Home Week in here all of a sudden."

Curt's mouth opened slightly. The hand holding the cross trembled but didn't drop. "Stay back," he warned. "Back!"

"Now, Curt, you don't mean to say those things. Not to your father. I think we ought to get to know each other, don't you?"

"Get back," Curt repeated, but his voice seemed to have lost much of its earlier power.

Bach laughed. "You mean to stand there and tell me you don't feel like catching up, filling in the missing years? Now, that's a pity. I'd kind of hoped we could become friends before I took you. It seems right that we should."

He took three slow, steady steps toward Curt. "I tried to follow you off and on during the years. Did you know that? No, of course you didn't. It wasn't always easy, even for someone in my position, since I didn't want to bring my inner circle in on my private family history. I had to be cautious and secretive, and you were hard to keep track of, moving here and there, changing schools, changing jobs, but I caught bits and pieces of it. I knew when your mother died. I celebrated the occasion. I went on a frenzy that night and made my first actual kill in quite a long time. I—"

"No!" Curt cried. "Don't say that, you son of a bitch, you *can't* say those things! And don't come any closer, either."

"But, Curt, give me a chance. Please?" He took another two steps closer to the door of the lounge.

Curt's arm trembled again. The fight seemed to have gone out of him. It was only with very great effort that he mustered the strength to say, "Give you a chance? You've got to be kidding. Give you a chance after what you did to us? Give you a chance, knowing who you are, what you are?"

Bach continued to smile. "I'm still your father. Whether or not I'm something else is irrelevant, isn't it?"

At the mention of the word "father," something clicked in Curt's mind. Once again he drew himself up and raised the cross higher. He was still just a shadow of the warrior he had been when he'd entered the room, still pale and fighting furiously to keep his legs from shaking, but when Bach took yet another step closer, he yelled savagely, "Get back! Now, damn you! Get out of here and leave Juan alone! Go!"

"Curt, really, I—"

Curt leapt forward, brandishing the cross like a sword: "In the name of God the Father, get back! In the name of Christ, get out of here!"

Bach hissed again, and a low animal snarl crawled out of his throat.

"*In the name of God, I command you to leave!*" Curt rasped.

There was a momentary flash of light, and the vampire was gone. It happened so quickly that he might as well have been an image from a movie projector suddenly turned off.

In the same instant Juan's eyes cleared and his body sagged, as though he'd been released from a physical hold. He looked around the room, blinking stupidly at the open sliding glass door, at Curt standing with the cross grasped in his quivering hand.

Curt dropped the cross and stumbled toward him, his arms held out and seeking the comfort of an embrace.

"Curt! What is it? What happened in here? What—"

Curt tried to speak, but burst instead into great gasping sobs. He started to sag to his knees. Juan reached out, caught him, but was carried with him to the ground, and the two of them lay there on the floor of the lounge, trapped in a state of bewildered terror.

III
War

Into the eternal darkness,
into fire and into ice.

—DANTE ALIGHIERI

Two evils, monstrous either one apart,
Possessed me, and were long and loath at going:
A cry of Absence, Absence, in the heart,
And in the wood the furious winter blowing.

—JOHN CROWE RANSOM

God's Hand can touch you too!

—UNIVERSAL MINISTRIES

34

Ernest wasn't in his office when Curt and Kelly got there shortly before ten that morning. According to his temporary receptionist, he was on the fourth floor, checking out a newcomer's complaint of a faulty toilet. She got them both a cup of coffee and bade them wait.

Kelly looked at the growing mountain of unfinished paperwork, unentered data records, unfiled folders on her old desk, and whispered in Curt's ear, "I feel so bad leaving Ernie stranded like this." She tried to smile, but it looked more like a grimace. "I used to be so reliable."

Curt squeezed her hand. "I think he understands."

Ernest got there a short time later, saw them sitting in the corner, flashed a quick smile, and ushered them into his inner office.

"I thought you'd be here. What's the pleasant news this time?"

Quickly Curt told him everything that had happened the day before. During the account of the cemetery visit, Ernest looked troubled, shifting in his chair as though he was sitting on a tack, but when Curt came to the story or the assault on Juan, the director of housing seemed to fall apart. His hand moved to the small pocket testament on his desk, clutched it tightly for a moment, let go, and clutched it again. He repeated that sequence three or four times, while his eyes widened and a small vein in his temple popped out and began to twitch.

"An attack right here in the Hall," he said hoarsely

when Curt was through. "By Bach . . . oh, Curt, by your *father*." He drew a long, shaky breath. "Juan's all right? You're sure he wasn't harmed?"

"Not this time," Curt said.

"He was lucky. Both of you were." He clutched the testament again, but suddenly noticed what he was doing and shoved the book away roughly, as though that small volume was responsible for everything that was happening. "I find myself wanting to apologize, but I can't anymore. What this church has done to you, it's also done to me. For years I've been lied to, led by the nose, *used* in this . . . this nightmare. I think of how many innocent people I talked to, picked up at the airport, drove to Fox Valley, sat with in the lobby or in their rooms, witnessing about glorious Universal all the way. It makes me want to put a gun to my head."

"Then you're still willing to help us?" Kelly said.

"Yes, of course. I thought carefully about everything you said, Curt, about the hurt it would cause me to go after my former leaders. I worried about that. I even prayed over it. But you know something? I don't care. Something's snapped inside me. I've been hurt and I find myself wanting to hurt back. Tell me what you need of me and I'll be there, I'll do it."

Curt took Kelly's hand again and held it tightly. He told Ernest their plans.

"Do you want me to go with you to the cemetery?" Ernest asked.

"If possible."

"And what else?"

"Shovels."

"Shovels?"

"It's the one thing I forgot at the mall, and I doubt I could have found them there anyway. We'll need several— four or five, if possible. Can you get them?"

Ernest nodded. "That won't be hard. Is that all?"

"What about a pick?"

"I can try."

"Then that's it. I think we can get everything else we need. We're going to just go down the line, do as many as we have time for. I doubt we'll get more than one or two today. Walstein first. He's the first one we spotted. We'll play it by ear from there."

"Okay," Ernest said. The word was spoken softly, but with an incredible amount of strength behind it. "I'll be at your side. Check back with me after lunch, and I'll have your equipment."

"How do you keep from being scared?" Kelly said several hours later.

Curt stared at her. Then he laughed. "What makes you think I'm not scared?"

"I don't know. You seem so calm,"

Curt had asked for these moments alone with her, sending the others to Ernest's office to fetch the supplies they would be needing. He wasn't sure of his feelings toward her, but he did know that something might go wrong when they visited the cemetery again. He or any of the others could be killed. And talking to Kelly was the only way he would be able to steel his nerve to face what might come next.

"I'm scared," he said. "I'm scared to death. Maybe I'm just hiding it better than the rest of you."

"But you—"

"I think it's *good* to be frightened right now. If what we're going to do this afternoon didn't make you want to run screaming out of the compound, I'd have to say you were insane. I've got through this thing so far by thinking as little as possible. I'm moving on instinct, you know what I mean?"

She nodded slowly. "Well, you make a good leader. Can you imagine seeing the vampires come out of the cemetery yesterday and having *me* in charge? Or Scott? We would've run away first thing. But you held your ground, and so did the rest of us. You're the one who's keeping us here. We'd've left already without you; we'd be scattered to the four winds right now."

Curt didn't answer, but took her hand, pressing it gently between both of his. At that moment he knew exactly how he felt about her.

"Curt?" she asked, as though she had picked up those feelings herself and wanted to urge him on.

"I love you," he said.

She pulled back abruptly, taking her hand away from him and cradling it in her lap, as though he had injured it. "No you don't. You don't even *know* me."

"I don't care. I love—"

"Curt, why are you saying that? You can't possibly—"

"I've felt it for a while now, ever since that first night, when you were with me in Ernie's office. Afterward, when we sat in the lobby and talked, you didn't call me crazy, or try to convince me there weren't such things as vampires. You didn't even make a joke out of it. You wanted to know about my mother and father. You were concerned. You knew it had to be tearing me up inside, and that's what bothered you. You *cared* about me."

She hesitated. "How do you know I wasn't doing what Ernie told me to do? Watching out for you? Being a friend?"

"I knew."

She turned away from him, and when she looked back, her face was a mask of warring emotions. She was smiling, and yet there were tears trickling down her cheeks. She put a hand on his shoulder and moved in closer, kissing him just above the jaw. He lifted her chin in the cup of his right hand and returned the kiss.

"Curt . . ." she said again, her voice barely a whisper.

"Shhh. Don't say anything."

It took a long time to obtain the last of their equipment, and it was after three o'clock when they left Van Paris Hall. Each of them carried a box or a knapsack containing the tools they would be needing. They had a dozen red roses and a dozen white. They had fifteen or twenty small vials of holy water and a small velvet bag containing ten holy wafers, none of which had been easy to charm out of the extremely recalcitrant priest at the Wheaton Catholic church Curt and Juan had visited. They had garlic and about ten of the stakes made from the sharp wooden stretcher strips. They had the shovels and a large pick Ernest had gotten for them. They had the hunting knife Curt had purchased, and the Craftsman hammer too. The assorted paraphernalia earned them quite a few strange glances as they made their way toward the back of the compound, but they simply smiled, nodded, and kept on moving like people on a perfectly public, perfectly ordinary mission.

When they arrived at the cemetery, they scouted the road for a hundred yards or so in each direction, but the only things moving were the shadows created by the late-afternoon sun and the breeze as it moved through the pines, cedars, and scattered hardwoods around them.

It was now almost four.

"It's hard for me to believe this place actually exists," Ernest said, gazing at the stone fence and iron gate. "As long as I've been here, I've never seen it—only heard rumors."

"I'm not surprised," Curt told him. "The way those trails and roads twist and turn, it's well hidden. Even if you were looking for it, you might end up doing what we did the other day, going around in circles."

"C'mon," Juan said. "You guys can talk later. Let's get movin'."

They went in and headed down the left-hand branch of the gravel path. They stopped before the first grave. The stone said:

THEODORE D. WILLIAMSON
July 16, 1974

"Williamson," Ernest said softly. "There's a Theodore Williamson science lab in the school building, with a little brass plaque outside the door. Something about the room being dedicated to the memory of a devoted church founder. He was an architect, I think, helped design some of the buildings in the compound."

"Until the compound was finished and he'd outlived his usefulness," Phyllis said.

Kelly shivered. "He probably would have preferred a gold watch."

"Very funny," Scott said. "So, is this it? Is he the one?"

Curt shrugged. "We've got a lot to choose from. Might as well start here."

Slowly everyone nodded.

They worked in teams, three at a time, Curt, Kelly, and Ernest first, the others taking over at approximately the midway point. The digging was more arduous than any of them had expected. Every time they made some progress, portions of the grave wall would give way and a trickle of dirt, sod, and gravel would run back into the hole. And yet they worked as though possessed, driving the pick and their shovels deeper and deeper, not pausing between strokes. There was very little good daylight left when Juan's shovel plunged deep into the earth and struck solid wood.

A small cheer rose from the graveside, and the diggers hoisted themselves up and out, stood looking down at a two-foot section of gleaming casket.

"Oh, Lord," Kelly breathed. "Don't you . . . do you think the sun will kill him, or are we going to have to use the stakes?"

Curt wiped perspiration from his forehead and shook his head. "I wish I knew."

They stood staring into the grave for several moments more. Now that their goal was finally within reach, they seemed unwilling to take the next step.

"An architect," Phyllis whispered, almost to herself. "You said he was an architect. Just a guy who designed buildings. An artist."

Curt turned away, suddenly unsure he had the heart to continue.

"My daddy used to know a guy in Wheeling who was an architect," Scott remarked. "He designed hospitals and research clinics, places that help people. He had a knack for medical buildings."

Curt groaned. Even with his back to the grave, he could picture the shiny casket top, could imagine the way it would feel in his hands.

"Do you think—" he heard Phyllis say, but then heard no more. He angrily thrust his hands into his pockets, and they touched the picture he carried with him everywhere these days, one of the photographs of Arthur Bach and his mother.

"I don't give a fuck if he was an architect or a saint," he snapped, whirling back to face the others. "He's not an architect anymore." He challenged them with an accusatory stare. "You *know* what he is now."

He picked up the hammer and lowered himself into the grave.

At the very moment his feet touched the wooden casket, the sky grew dark. Curt glanced up fearfully and saw a towering bank of clouds blocking the weak sun. Black and ferocious, their edges were limned in orange and gold, like a romantic portrait of Armageddon. He shook his head, fell to his knees, and began rapidly brushing away dirt and sod and gravel.

The casket felt even worse than he had imagined. Hard and almost distastefully slick, it was aged wood with all the properties of cold metal. As he scrabbled around on top of it he had to fight back several waves of dizziness that threatened to overwhelm him.

When he had revealed the locks along the side, he picked up the hammer and began driving it down again and again, not allowing himself to think of the thing he was about to expose.

"You need help?" Scott called from above.

"No," he snapped, without looking up.

The hammer continued to pound, and the wood around the locks began to splinter and crack. Sensing completion, he mounted a final explosive flurry of blows and the locks gave way. He immediately tossed the hammer out of the grave and began to dig along the sides of the casket, gouging out footholds and making a place to stand. When he had his niche, he stood staring down, wiping streaks of dirt off his face and streaming perspiration away from his eyes.

"This is it," he said, as much for his own benefit as for the others'.

He raised the lid.

All of them stared at the body of the vampire Theodore Williamson. He was a short balding man with a

heavy paunch and a moon-faced puffiness that reminded
Curt of a chronic heavy drinker.

When the filtered sunlight struck the body, its eyelids
snapped open, revealing sunken bloodshot orbs. It began
to twist and writhe upon its gray silk bed, and its throat
muscles worked convulsively. At first it emitted nothing
but a gasping sound, which then became a thin keening
that rose higher and higher, like a cry of mortal agony.
Its hands reached up, groping blindly.

With a sickened groan, Curt scrambled out of the
grave. He slipped halfway up, and would have fallen on
the body below had not Phyllis and Juan caught him and
pulled him to safety. He stood looking down at the
monster, holding his cross out in front of him.

The vampire's chubby hands jerked and fluttered like
injured birds, occasionally striking the walls of the grave
and knocking dirt loose. The dirt fell across Williamson's
fat fish-white face like large sprinklings of pepper. The
vampire's feet drummed against the casket and produced
sounds like gunshots.

But after half a minute or so the wailing cries and
thrashing movements ceased. Its eyes closed and its body
lay twisted like a corpse flung willy-nilly into the casket.

"The daylight didn't finish him," Kelly said. "I mean,
he *is* still alive, isn't he? Or dead? Undead? Whatever he
was before?"

Curt nodded, picking up one of the sharp stretcher
strips and the hammer. Before he descended again into
the grave, he also picked up a white rose, a red rose, a
vial of holy water, and a box of garlic. Then he looked up
at the sky, searching for the right words. He finally said,
"Help us, God. Help us do what's right."

He threw the two roses into the casket. They landed
on Williamson's chest.

The vampire's eyes snapped open again, and an other-
worldly shriek filled the air. It clutched the roses slowly,
trying to rid itself of them.

Curt uncapped the vial of holy water. "Help us, God,"
he said again, sprinkling the water on the thing below.

Williamson's body exploded in violent spasms. The
vampire sat up, but got only halfway out of the casket

before it slumped back again and lay motionless. The shrieking ebbed to wounded sobs and sniffles.

"Oh, my God," Ernest said. "Look!"

The front of Williamson's dark suit jacket, as well as the silk shirt beneath, had been burned away. They could see the thing's pale chest covered with the red, blistered flesh of a burn victim.

"Gone," Scott said. "That stuff was like acid."

The vampire was completely silent.

"I'm going down," Curt said before his fear got the better of him, and he lowered himself into the grave.

He stood for a moment, one foot on either side of the casket, heedless of the dirt and gravel filling his shoes. Then he moved several steps forward, maneuvering for position, and got on his knees.

The others stared down at him.

"C'mon, pray. The Lord's Prayer . . . something . . . anything."

They looked at each other, confused.

"Pray, goddammit!"

Still no one spoke, and so Curt searched his memory, and a prayer from Sunday school years ago flooded into his mind. A psalm. He began to speak the words, not even sure if they were correct: "To thee, O Lord, I lift up my soul. O my God, in you I trust. Let not my enemies exult over me. Consider how many are my foes, and with what . . . with what violent hatred they hate me. Oh, guard my life and deliver me . . . deliver me, O God."

He finished, tears streaming down his face, and looked up at the others again. "C'mon," he said. "Follow me. Repeat it." He hitched in a breath and began again: "To thee, O Lord, I lift up my soul. O my God, in you I trust. Let not my enemies exult over me."

Haltingly the others spoke the words: *"To thee, O Lord, I lift up my soul. O my God, in you I trust. Let not my enemies exult over me."*

"Consider how many are my foes, and with what violent hatred they hate me."

"Consider how many are my foes, and with what violent hatred they hate me."

"Oh, guard my life and deliver me, O God."

"Oh, guard my life and deliver me, O God."

The world seemed to be spinning off-center, whirling Curt with it, around and around in helpless circles. Colorful pinpoints of light danced before his eyes. He pulled in a long, deep breath and lowered the stake until it rested in the center of the creature's burned chest. He pressed just hard enough to dimple the flesh. He raised the hammer.

"One more time," he said. "O God, let not my enemies exult over me."

The others came through, loud and strong and clear: *"O God, let not my enemies exult over me!"*

"Now," Curt whispered, and struck hammer to wood.

This time Theodore Williamson's eyes rolled open slowly. As the stake went in a half-inch, the vampire's mouth opened too, showing glistening incisors.

Curt brought the hammer down again . . . again . . . again. The stake sank through flesh and muscle, glancing off bone, seeking its target.

The vampire moaned, its voice at first like that of an animal, then like a sobbing child's, finally like nothing Curt had ever heard before. Its shrieks rose and fell, one moment so loud they were ear-splitting, the next like a whisper of wind through a grove of trees.

Again.

Again.

Again.

And still the creature shrieked.

"Pray again!" Curt cried. *"Pray loud! Drown out the son of a bitch!"*

His friends answered his plea, and the air above the cemetery was filled with the preternatural sounds of frightened prayers mingling with dying screams.

Again.

Blood welled up around the stake and ran down the vampire's chest. Blood trickled from its nose, the corners of its mouth. Blood filled its staring eyes.

Again.

The creature's cries became hoarse. Its hands reached for the hammer, trying to knock it away, trying to grab the stake and pull it out of its chest, trying to take Curt by the arm.

Again.

Suddenly the blood pouring from Williamson's chest turned black. Curt knew what that meant. The job was almost done.

Again.

The stake hit home.

The vampire's mouth opened wider, but this time no sound escaped. It twisted in the casket, but the effort was a feeble, pathetic one. Its eyes widened momentarily, and then snapped closed for the last time, for all time.

Curt dropped the hammer. Above, the prayer petered out in the middle of its fourth repetition, and his friends knelt on the edge of the grave, hands reaching down to pick Curt up and lift him from the hole.

One less vampire would rise with the coming of night.

35

Silence filled Kaye's office. He and Norris had just finished listening to Howard Crisp's account of what had taken place in the cemetery. Norris leaned back and lit his third home-rolled cigarette of the last half-hour. He looked at Kaye questioningly, but Kaye just frowned and gave a halfhearted shrug.

Crisp cleared his throat. "You need me for anything else?"

Kaye shook his head, but before Crisp could get out of the office, he stopped him. "That prayer, the one Potter used. You said it was a psalm?"

"Yeah," Crisp said. "A psalm of David. The twenty-fifth." He laughed. "Funny thing about that one. I had to learn it in church school back when I was a little kid. Everyone in the class had to memorize one psalm. There were about twenty of us, and I'll bet nineteen learned the twenty-third, you know, 'The Lord is my shepherd' and all that. Not me. I had to be different. I flipped a couple pages and learned the twenty-fifth. I'd forgotten all about it until Potter started saying it tonight."

Kaye nodded and thanked him.

When they were alone, Norris said, "I know what the Master told you last night, Bob. Move slowly, proceed with caution. Induct the Enemies one at a time, to avoid raising suspicions among their friends. But, dammit, look at what happened! We had them in the cemetery! We missed a perfect chance to take them all at once, away from the Hall, where nobody would ever see it! And we lost a flock member. Okay, so Williamson wasn't hot shit. I still think—"

"I know what you think," Kaye said. "I'm well aware of exactly what you think."

Norris crushed out the butt of his cigarette. "And the Master failed last night. I can't believe that either. A textbook-simple induction, a fucking stupid spic!"

Kaye tried to calm him down. "Don't forget, it would've worked if Potter hadn't shown up. Don't worry about one failed attempt. It's not the first time an initial induction move's been botched. The Master'll get them, all of them, even the stupid spic."

Norris frowned, unconvinced. "What about Ernie?"

Kaye nodded. "Ernie's our big problem now. I've given it a lot of thought, and I've decided to go to the Master again tonight."

"You mean—"

"Tonight we'll have the pleasure of seeing Mr. Cummings inducted."

For the first time, Norris' mood lightened. "Tonight?" he repeated hopefully.

"I don't see the point in waiting any longer. When we're done here, I'm going to have a talk with Becky. I'm sure she can locate another housing director and cook up a story. Maybe Ernie was a closet drinker. Perhaps, after years of hostility, he finally renounced the church and left town. If Becky can act as quickly as I think she can, we ought to be ready for a public announcement tomorrow morning."

Norris laughed. "I like it."

They couldn't stop talking about what had taken place in the cemetery earlier.

After they had recovered from watching Williamson's gory demise, Curt, Scott, and Juan had undertaken the job of using the hunting knife to sever the vampire's head from its body. It was tough, grisly work. When they were done, they pried the vampire's mouth open and stuffed in several garlic bulbs, then turned the head upside down in the casket. Finally they placed several red and white roses into the box and sprinkled it with holy water before closing it and sealing it with holy wafers. Then they climbed out and shoveled half the dirt back into the grave, stopping only when total darkness was imminent and they were too exhausted to do any more.

"What now?" Phyllis had said as they stood together staring at the site of their first victory.

"Now?" Curt had said, surprised. "Now we go back to the Hall."

"But the other vampires—"

He shook his head and pointed at the sun, a frightening few degrees above the horizon. "No time. We'll come back tomorrow."

Now, hours later, Juan said, "Are we gonna go earlier tomorrow?" as though one conquest made him eager for more.

Scott shrugged. "We might as well. If we go at noon tomorrow, or even earlier, like ten or eleven, we might be able to get three or four of the bastards."

"Will they . . . ?" Kelly began. She paused, gathering her thoughts together, and continued: "Will they all be like Williamson?"

"Probably," Curt said, and felt a tight, painful stabbing in his stomach at the thought of repeating their afternoon's ritual . . . how many times? Ten? Twenty? *A hundred?* Could they possibly do what they had done to Williamson a hundred times? He doubted it. It would drive them to madness. On a more practical level, it would take too long. They would still be here in ten years, exhuming the undead and driving stakes, and all the while, his father would be creating new vampires for them to hunt. Madness? Yes, indeed. And it left them only one real option.

"Bach," he whispered.

"What?" Juan said.

Curt started, surprised that he had spoken aloud. "I was just thinking," he said, and slowly he outlined for the others what was on his mind.

Ernest leaned forward. "You mean you want to go after him right away?"

"It's all I can think of," Curt said. "We can't keep moving around the outside of the whole mess; we've got to strike at the heart. If we can somehow get Bach and Van Paris, they . . . well, maybe the rest of it will disintegrate. I don't know. I can't even guess. But I do know that we won't get anywhere doing what we're doing now. Who the hell is Theodore Williamson to Universal? Nobody. We have to get the leader. And fast, before Kaye and Norris find out."

The group was quiet. After a while Phyllis said, "You're right."

Scott nodded. "Tomorrow we should find Bach." He paused, laughing. "I don't imagine that's going to be very easy, but go straight to the top—that's what I always say."

At a few minutes to eight there was a knock on the door. They stared at it, startled and suddenly afraid.

"Who—" Scott said, but Curt was already on his feet. He stopped with his hand on the knob, drew the silver cross out of his shirt, and opened the door a crack.

He relaxed instantly. It was just a frantically excited teenager.

"Is he here?" the young man said.

"Who?"

"Ernie. I gotta see him right away."

Curt started to say something, but Ernest pushed past him and positioned himself between Curt and the boy.

"What is it, son? Who are you?"

"Terry. Terry Arbogast. Your receptionist sent me to get you."

"My receptionist? Liz? What does she want?"

Still a little out of breath, the boy explained that there had been a flood in the cafeteria. Some old piping connected to the big industrial dishwashers had given way, and the entire kitchen area was now under two feet of water, the dining area swamped by at least a foot.

"Maintenance is down there, but they can't get into the back room to shut off the supply. Key broke in the door. You gotta come right away and bring your master set. They can get the broken one out with a pick, but—"

Ernest nodded. "I understand. Go tell them I'll be

down in a minute. My master keys are in my office. I'll get them and go right to the kitchen."

The boy nodded and fled down the corridor. Ernest turned back to the others in the room and shrugged. "It's my job."

Curt shook his head. "I don't think you need to—"

"It won't take long. I'll be back in an hour and we can talk about tomorrow."

"But—"

Ernest left the room and shut the door behind him. Terry Arbogast was already out of sight, hurrying on to the kitchen to carry word of impending rescue. Ernest smiled faintly. A few days ago a flood would have been a disaster of epic proportions, but after what they had been through late that afternoon, it would almost be a pleasant diversion.

As he hurried down the corridor, he listened to the soft conversation and distant stereo music that came from behind closed doors. There had been a time, he thought, when hearing those sounds would have made him happy, would have made him think of residents whose lives had been saved, improved, who were now in a place where all was right for them and always would be. Tonight, however, he could only think of those residents and feel his fear return. As he rode down in the elevator, he replayed some of the talk of the last hour.

"We know there's a house in the compound," Curt had said. "I've seen it, Scott's seen it. Is it *his* house? The Master's? I don't know, but I'm willing to bet it is. At any rate, I want to find out one way or the other, so we can move when we have to."

Ernest had frowned at that. "I don't know of any way to find out. There's no one to ask, at least not anyone who would give us a straight answer."

"Then we'll pay a visit," Phyllis had said. "You know, trial-and-error."

Scott had laughed at that—a sour, bitter sound. "Only problem with that, Phyl, is that around here trial-and-error can be a one-shot deal."

Now, as Cummings stepped out of the elevator and made his way to his office, he thought about how true

Scott's statement was. He thought about the quaint legends of Stoker's *Dracula*, and about another book he had found in the library as a boy, something called *Varney the Vampyre*. In comparison to what they were facing, those books seemed tame, and not only because they were confined to the safety of the printed page, but also because the vampires in those stories were only that—vampires. They weren't creatures surrounded by a host of human familiars, guarded by the front of an internationally famous religious movement. He almost laughed. *Universal Ministries*, he thought crazily, *Or: Curt and His Friends Meet the Vampire Mafia*.

In his office he found his big ring of master keys and hurriedly started for the door. He was almost there when he paused, almost as an afterthought, and reached up to tear another page off his *Inspirational Thought a Day* calendar.

The message for the next day stared down at him: *The light is with you. Walk while you have the light, lest the darkness overtake you.* John 12:35.

He shuddered and shut off the lights. He reached for the door but paused again, his hand frozen in midair, inches from the knob, his heart thudding mightily.

There was a noise at the window.

Or was there?

Had he really heard a soft scraping noise, like sand against glass, or was his imagination running away with him?

With fear building in his chest, he forced himself to take a deep breath and turn around. He stared at the window, but saw nothing there. Nothing at all. Just darkness, barely lit by the thin sliver of the moon.

Nothing, he thought, and tried to muster a smile at his foolishness. It felt more like a cockeyed grimace.

He turned and left the office, noticing for the first time that the lobby seemed exceptionally quiet for so early in the evening. No intramural athletes coming back from a game, no prayer group meeting in the corner, no friends standing around and chatting. In fact, the place was more than quiet. It was absolutely, unnaturally empty.

Well, not quite.

He was no more than halfway across the room when he saw a man standing by the main entrance. He mumbled a greeting that was far from cheery, and was about ready to turn toward the cafeteria when he stopped.

The man was older, with a full, luxurious head of silver hair and a bushy white mustache. His face was well-lined but ruddy, and the overall effect was one of vitality and wisdom, not old age.

Ernest felt dizzy, wishing suddenly he had something nearby to grab on to.

He knew who that man was. He had seen his picture on TV and in various Universal publications. It was a man they were all taught to venerate. He wasn't a pastor, but that didn't matter; for his contributions to the movement, he was second only to Arthur Bach himself. In honor of that, the residential hall where they stood right now was named for him.

It was Richard D. Van Paris.

"Hello, Ernie," Van Paris said.

Ernest uttered a single startled exclamation.

"Working late? That's good. Dedication is so hard to find these days, don't you think?"

"You . . . you're . . ."

"Tired? Having trouble making the connection? Unfortunately, that's the drawback to all that hard work. You wear yourself out, start saying foolish things and acting . . . well, let's say unwisely."

"You . . ."

"Don't strain yourself, Ernie," Van Paris said, taking a step closer. "I understand your exhaustion. The Master and I both sympathize. You've been working yourself to the point where you feel as though you're going to drop any moment. You need a rest. We think you've more than earned it."

"A . . . rest?"

"Of course. Call it a well-deserved break."

"I—"

"You don't have to be modest, Ernie. Everyone needs a rest once in a while. A long time ago I needed one, and a foreign acquaintance of mine was pleased to be of service. I met the Master, and he needed one—all that hurrying about, trying to build a worldwide movement from the ground up—and I serviced him. Paul Hummelt, Ed Lucas, Chris Walstein, Ted Williamson, and many others: they needed their rest too. Now it's your turn."

"I don't—"

"Are you familiar with the concept of induction? No, I suppose you're not. You've been too preoccupied with all your meaningless little chores to consider the finer things. Well, induction's a wonderful event, Ernie. It takes you beyond the drudgery of this paltry church and places you into the *real* church, the High Church. What do you think of that? Sound interesting?"

Ernest tried to speak but faltered again. Listening to Van Paris speak was like listening to Reverend Bob when he was fired up. Some of the emotion was missing, but not the hypnotic, mesmerizing rhythm. It pulled you in effortlessly, made you forget whatever troubles were on your mind and—

"Ernie? Answer me. Wouldn't you like to know the beauty of the High Church?"

"I . . . don't know."

Van Paris chuckled. "I guess not. You're still so blinded by things around you that you can't see the truth. But induction takes care of that for you. That's the beauty of it. You don't have to do a thing but relax—relax and let the truth flow over you, fill you. That's why we're here tonight, the Master and I, to do that for you. Call it our way of thanking you for all that hard work."

Ernest didn't want to, but he felt himself nodding. "Yes," he whispered.

Van Paris took another step closer and clapped his hands together joyfully. "You mean you accept? You're ready to join the High Church?"

"Yes . . . yes, I th-think so . . . oh, yes."

Van Paris beamed. "Then you shall meet the Master," he said, and came still another step closer.

Immediately there was another presence in the lobby, and again Ernest had no trouble recognizing him. The awe that swept over him as he stared at that man made him want to fall to his knees and call out his praises.

"Bach," he said wonderingly. "The Master."

Bach laughed. "Hello, Ernie. You spoiled my entrance. Usually, when we work together, Richard has the pleasure of announcing me like royalty." He raised his voice in a parody of Van Paris: "Announcing the Reverend Arthur Bach, the Master of the true High Church." He laughed again. "But you already knew me. Ah, well."

Ernest looked from one to the other, Van Paris to Bach to Van Paris again, and felt great warmth spreading through his body. Their eyes . . . *his* eyes . . . the Master's eyes . . .

"Are you ready for the High Church?" Bach asked him. "Ready for induction?"

Ernest nodded dumbly. The warmth spread through him faster, farther, and he could only revel in the sensation and await the induction they spoke of.

"Then you must do one small thing," Bach said.

Ernest nodded again, ready to do anything to please.

"You have to take off that cross you're wearing and throw it away, get rid of it."

His hand strayed to the shining silver cross around his neck. His fingers closed around it.

Van Paris nodded. "That's right, Ernie. Rip it off, dispose of it. You won't need foolish little symbols like that in the High Church."

Ernest pulled. The link chain snapped and dangled loose in his hand. He held the cross up and stared at it, blinking.

"Good man," Bach said. "Now throw it across the room. You don't need it anymore."

But Ernest didn't obey immediately. He blinked again and stared at the cross, feeling some of the warmth in his body receding, being replaced by a slow, stealthy chill. Throw it away? Why? Why wasn't it a necessary object in this High Church they were talking about?

"Come now, Ernie, get rid of it. It's nothing but a pagan symbol in the High Church. You won't need it, I promise."

Ernest nodded. He tried to pull his arm back, but it wouldn't move. He tried again, but it was as though he had been paralyzed. Dimly he heard familiar voices chanting words he couldn't quite understand.

"Ernie . . ." Bach said, and his voice was no longer friendly. Now there was a note of stern anger in it. "You've been given an order. Throw the damn cross away now!"

Ernest frowned. The chanting voices in his head were growing louder.

"Please," Van Paris told him, "we're doing you a favor, Ernie. Don't you see that? You said you wanted the joy of induction, but we can't give it to you if you insist on clinging to that silly charm. You have to throw it away if you want to experience everything we promised."

Ernest tried to move his arm again, but again was unable to do so. The voices in his head were almost blocking out the Master and Van Paris and . . . There! He could almost understand them now, almost hear what they were chanting.

"The cross!" Bach commanded. "Get rid of it now!"

Ernest began to smile. At last he could make out everything those voices in his head were saying: *To thee, O Lord, I lift up my soul. O my God, in you I trust. Let not my enemies exult over me.*

"The cross, Ernie," Van Paris said, sounding a million miles away.

To thee, O Lord, I lift up my soul. O my God, in you I trust. Let not my enemies exult over me.

"Please. It's such a simple command, and a small price to pay to know the beauty of the High Church."

Slowly Bach and Van Paris advanced across the room, reaching out as though they meant to take the cross away themselves. Three steps away, then two, then one.

And suddenly the light flooded back into Ernest's brain. His smile became a broad grin. He knew! He knew what those words meant, and he spoke them out loud:

"To thee, O Lord, I lift up my soul. Let not my enemies exult over me."

Bach and Van Paris hissed, a horrible sound that was almost a shriek.

Ernest's arm swept forward in a ferocious downward arc. He slammed the cross against Van Paris' shoulder.

The vampire screamed and vanished like a light extinguished.

Bach took a shambling step back, holding his hands in front of him, and when he spoke his voice was no longer strong and commanding. Suddenly the Master sounded like a pleading supplicant. "Ernie, you don't understand. We don't want to hurt you. We want to help. Now, put the cross away, won't you? The High Church is waiting, but—"

Cummings lunged forward and thrust the cross into Bach's face. *"In God I trust! Let not my enemies exult over me!"*

Bach screamed. There was a single bright flash of light and he was gone. For a moment a corrupt odor of death and decay lingered in the lobby, but then that too vanished.

Ernest looked around, the cross still gripped in his hand.

"Let not my enemies exult over me, let not my enemies exult over me, let not my enemies exult over me, let not . . ."

He was still saying those words, repeating them again and again, when two of the shadows across the silent lobby—the shadow of a potted plant and the shadow of a padded, high-backed chair—detached themselves from the wall and moved forward. As they moved, they revealed themselves as two short young men dressed in dark blue jeans and black shirts.

"Let not my enemies exult over me," Ernie was still mumbling when the men came up behind him.

He never heard them.

He never saw them.

When they struck him on the back of the neck, he fell first to his knees, then collapsed face-forward on the tile floor.

36

By ten o'clock, after phone calls and discussions and several group forays into the shadowy corridors of the Hall, they were forced to admit the truth: Ernest was missing. It was too early, perhaps, to assume that he had fallen prey to Bach or Van Paris, but the end result was the same. Maybe he had seen too much in the cemetery. Possibly his fear—or, as Scott wryly suggested at one point, his good sense—had finally gotten the better of him. He might be boarding a plane at O'Hare right now, or thumbing his way toward Iowa.

Curt was counting vials of holy water to keep his mind off it when he stopped in frustration and said, "This is ridiculous! Inventory! I've got us doing a fucking inventory now! Let me see, we've got seven boxes of garlic, twenty-one stakes, three dozen roses . . . Shit. It's nonsense! What good is any of this going to do? How is a goddamned inventory possibly going to help us?"

Kelly sat next to him on the bed and reached out to comfort him. She held her ground when he tried to push her away. "Calm down. You had a good idea, taking inventory. We've got to know where we stand."

He looked at the vials and laughed. "I'll tell you where we stand," he said hoarsely. "We're standing in our own graves. All we're doing is waiting for someone to come along and close the lid on us, shovel in the dirt. I'm sorry, guys. Inventory. Jesus. Now I *know* I'm crazy."

"It's not so crazy," Scott said. "If nothing else, it helps

279

fill the time, right? We have to do something until Ernie gets back. Look, you've done a good job leading us so far—"

"A good job? My God, Matheson, how can you say that? I've gotten us involved in madness! I've got us lurking around graveyards and pounding stakes into monsters! I'm risking our lives chasing a nightmare. And now Ernie's missing. You say he's coming back, but how do you know? How do any of us know what happened? Maybe he went off-compound for something—but maybe not." He slammed his fist onto the bed. "A good job. Christ, yes. I'm the all-time champion leader, aren't I?"

Phyllis knelt on the floor in front of him. "You didn't do anything wrong," she said softly. "The vampires did. You can't blame yourself for seeing the evil and trying to stop it."

But suddenly he was on his feet. Scott called after him. Juan tried to stop him. Kelly tried to take his hand. But he pushed past all of them and stormed out of the room.

Kelly caught up with him in the lobby. In one corner of the huge room a group of girls from a scripture group sat reading aloud from the Bible. Near the corridor that led to the offices, a teenage boy was leaning on the wall reading the new edition of *Praise!*, the compound news letter. Well apart from them, Curt was standing by the main doors, gazing out into the night. Kelly came up behind him and put a hand on his shoulder.

"Curt? Tell me something, okay?"

He turned around. There were tears still damp on his cheeks.

"Tell me you know how wrong you were up there. Tell me it was just irrational anger talking. Tell me you don't really blame yourself for what's happening. Will you do that?"

The corners of his mouth twitched. "That's *three* some-things. And, no, I can't tell you that."

She put her arms around him and pulled him close. "It's crazy to blame yourself for what the vampires caused. Look at the *good* things you've accomplished. You kept us together, for starters. We would have run away days ago if it hadn't been for you. You got Williamson almost single-handedly. And now you've decided to go to your father's house, when we would have just kept running around in circles at the cemetery."

"You don't understand. Christ, the real point is that I'm the one who got us involved in this in the first place. If it hadn't been for me, you'd all be happy and safe right now. Ernie would still be here, and we'd all—"

"We'd all be zombies."

He stopped, puzzled. "Zombies?"

"We'd be part of the sickies wandering around the compound, not smiling, not talking, maybe having seizures like Tom Chambers, having our blood taken from us every now and then. Oh, maybe not all of us right away, but eventually. We'd be feeding the vampires instead of fighting them. Phyllis was first, but who would've been next? Juan? Scott? *Me?*"

"I—"

"Curt, you did the only thing you could. You did the *right* thing."

He shook his head, but broke off in the middle of the gesture. Then he seemed about to smile, but couldn't quite accomplish that either. Finally he just hugged her tightly, as though he never wanted to let go.

"Come on," she said, kissing his cheek. "We don't have to go back right away. Let's go to my room. We've got some more talking to do."

There was a note on Kelly's bed. She picked it up, read it, and handed it to Curt.

Kelly:
   Where you been keeping yourself, girl? Haven't seen you in *decades!* In case you decide to grace us with your presence, Lonnie and I went to see *Jewel of the Nile* in the Faith Center. Back around midnight, I guess. Hope to see you then, stranger. God bless you!
                                                              Kim

"My roommates," Kelly said, shaking her head and smiling. "I think I'll keep 'em."

Curt smiled. "You're a witty soul, aren't you?"

They looked at each other, and a moment later were laughing. Kelly hugged him, saying through her laughter, "That's better. I'm glad to see you're not blaming yourself anymore." He stiffened. "What's the matter? You *aren't* still blaming yourself, are you?"

Slowly he pulled back from her embrace. He didn't say anything right away, but after the passage of perhaps a minute, sighed.

"Curt?"

He sighed again. "I can't stop thinking how much better it would be if I'd never come here. I mean, the hell of it is, I still don't know what I hoped to accomplish. Bach wasn't going to embrace me—I knew that; he'd made it abundantly clear over the years. Look at what he did to my mom. Look at the way he ignored my letters and calls. I'm not sure what I expected. I didn't want his money. I didn't want him as a father. I . . . I don't know *what* I wanted. To make a public scene? To score some points off him in my mother's memory? *Prove* something?"

She embraced him again, holding him tight and absorbing his tears and the painful shudders coursing through his body.

"And if I hadn't come . . . if I'd stayed there in Michigan doing odd jobs, or stayed in New Jersey on the loading dock, I . . . it . . . none of this would have happened."

She ran a hand through his hair. She put her lips close to his ear and said, "Did you ever think you were brought here for a reason?"

He pulled away from her again, but now he wasn't looking at her in torment, but with the sudden inquisitiveness of a man groping for the answer to a dark secret.

"What?"

"Did you ever think some other power put that crusade on the barroom TV for you to see? That you were led here to fight your father? To kill the vampires?"

He seemed ready to object—he *wanted* to object—but couldn't.

"You'll never know why you came here," she said. "But we are going to save people. Forget the rest. We're going to save people, Curt. That's the only thing you have to know."

This time he put his arms around her. "I love you," he whispered, a tremor passing through his frame. "Jesus, Kel, I love you so much it feels like I'm splitting apart."

She put a finger to his lips. "Shhhh."

The exploration and discovery that followed flowed out of their embrace naturally. Their lovemaking was quick, urgent. It was a blessed catharsis—beautiful and warm.

"I'm getting worried," Phyllis said.

Scott shot her a startled glance. "What do you mean?"

She shook her head. "Where are they? They've been gone over an hour."

"They're together," Juan said. "So long as—"

"How do you know that?" she asked. "How do you know they're together? Curt ran out of here alone and Kelly followed him. If she found him, fine, but what if he's wandering around in the compound someplace and she's still looking for him?"

Juan sighed. "It's okay, Phyl. They're together."

"How do you *know*? How can you be so goddamned sure they're—"

"Phyl, please!" Scott said. "Let's not talk about it."

"What's the matter? Are you afraid too? You are, aren't you? You know I'm right and—"

"I'm not afraid! They're fine. And what could we do, anyway? Go out and look, so there are five targets out there instead of two? What would that accomplish?"

"You *are* afraid," Phyllis said. "I can see it on your face."

Scott leaned back on his bed, refusing to answer. He scratched his beard and tried to hide his face from her. The truth of the matter was, she was right. He was terrified. If Curt and Kelly weren't together, the results could be . . . well, he couldn't allow himself to think about it. Besides the eloquently simple fact that they were friends, Curt was more: he was their leader. If he was lost, their little ship of vampire fighters would be rudderless, and then how would they ever find the direction or power to finish what they'd started?

By eleven-fifteen the lights were off in Kelly's room, and they were sleeping a well-deserved, peaceful sleep. After making love they had gotten dressed again, but had fallen back into each other's arms. Loving embraces and murmured words had lulled them, taken them away. Now the only sounds were their deep, steady breathing and the faraway hum of Lonnie's clock radio across the room. The only sounds until:

"Kelly. Come on, Kelly. Wake up and let me in."

Kelly snapped awake instantly, felt her gaze being drawn toward the window.

"Good girl! Come let me in. I've got something for you."

The drapes were only half-closed, and through the glass she could see a dim, wraithlike form. It was someone she thought she recognized. A pleasant face, masked by darkness and distance, but still friendly, still familiar. Even from here she could see his smile and his eyes dancing merrily, urging her to action.

"Hurry, Kelly. There's not much time."

Moving as carefully as she could so as not to disturb him, she disentangled herself from Curt's arms, got up, crossed to the window, and stopped. Joy exploded within her heart.

"Ernie! My God, Ernie, you're here! You're alive! Curt, it's—"

"Shhh! Don't wake him up! He needs his rest."

This close, Ernie's blazing eyes seemed to penetrate her and take total command. In that moment they became the most important things in the world. She forgot all about Curt and his love, her love for him. She forgot about the bliss of their lovemaking less than an hour before. She forgot about her friends back in room 1290. She forgot about her past in Detroit. All that mattered were—

"My eyes," Ernest said. He smiled, his lips drawing back in a sharp grin. "Tell me what you see in my eyes, Kelly."

She tried to speak, but failed. Her joy at their friend's return was suddenly mixed with layers of confusion and doubt. If Ernie was here, why had he come to her window and not the door? Had he sneaked back into the compound, perhaps, afraid of being spotted by the vampires or their familiars? Was he here to join them again, or to urge them to run away with him? And what—

"My eyes," Ernest prompted. "Do you see beauty there?"

She nodded mechanically.

"Do you see truth?"

Oh, yes, she thought, nodding again.

"Peace? Is there peace there?"

Another nod.

"What about the wonders of belonging to a miraculous church? Do you see that?"

"Church," she whispered. "Y-yes."

Ernest's grin stretched. It became a surreal expression of maniacal happiness. For the first time she noticed that he didn't seem to be standing on anything outside. Rather, he appeared to be hanging from the side of the building, clinging to glass and stone. But of course that couldn't be. Ernie had sneaked back to talk to them, and he had brought a ladder—

"I'll tell you a secret, Kelly. If you open the window and let me in, I can give you all those things. That's right. The beauty, the peace, the wonder of the High Church—it can all be yours."

"The High Church? I don't understand."

"Not yet, maybe, but when you let me in, I'll explain everything."

Of course, she thought. He must be exhausted, standing out there on the ladder like that. Her fingers searched for and found the latch. The joy and doubt and confusion had merged in her mind into a sensation of terrible relief, monumental *rightness*. Ernie was back. And now, for a reason she could think of only in a disjointed fashion, the long darkness was at an end. Once she let Ernie in, the nightmare would be over and blessed peace would be at hand.

"C'mon, Kelly, open the window. Now."

Without knowing why, hardly aware of her actions, she cast a look back over her shoulder at the man sleeping in her bed. There was a faint angelic smile on his face. It was funny, but she couldn't even remember his name. Floating in her mind somewhere was the knowledge that he would somehow be as interested as she in Ernie's return. But she could feel his presence flying away from her until he had become a stranger.

Ernest hissed, "Forget him! He's nothing! He violated you. You don't owe him anything. Forget him and open the window now!"

Her gaze lingered on the trespasser for one moment longer. Then she turned away, disgusted. She flicked the latch and slid the large glass window back along its greased track. Ernest uttered a small triumphant cry. The sound of it made gooseflesh break out on her arms, but before she could step back, before she even realized what was happening, he stood next to her. He seemed taller than she remembered. And his eyes no longer danced merrily, but glowed with savage fire.

"Ernie? Is something—"

"You did a good job, Kelly. And now I'll do mine. Now you'll get your reward."

His arms opened wide, encircling her. A split second's shock and revulsion gave way again to that newfound sensation of perfect peace and righteousness. She slipped into his grasp and felt herself melting against him. A warm and comfortable dizziness claimed her, and she thought briefly and for no apparent reason of the stranger in her bed. Then Ernest's head moved forward and his lips parted.

"Yes," she murmured. "Oh, yes."

Her head lolled back on her shoulders rolling slowly from side to side. As she faced the window, she saw that there was no ladder out there after all. Just the sheer brick wall. This time it made perfect sense to her. It was right that there should be no ladder. It was more than right; it was the only way.

When the sting of pain came, a delightful shudder racked her body. It wasn't pain at all, really, but the end of the nightmare and the beginning of that perfect, unending peace. She moved into him and slipped down, down, sinking, sinking farther, vanishing, disappearing, drowning.

When it was done, Ernest released her and stepped toward the sleeping figure on the bed. He was halfway across the room when he stopped and cocked his head at the sound of soft footsteps approaching in the corridor. He waited, poised in absolute calm. He listened a second longer and turned away just as the door began to open.

He took Kelly's hand.

The two forms slipped through the window and into the night.

Meanwhile Curt slept soundly, two small silver crosses still lying beside him on the bed.

The scream woke him a moment later. He sat up, terrified, and found himself face-to-face with two frightened girls. He recognized them as Kelly's roommates, and was about to say something when the one called Kim screamed for the second time. It was then he realized that he was alone in the bed.

Kelly!

He scrambled to his feet and grabbed Kim by the shoulders. "Where is she? What happened to her?"

Doubtless thinking him insane, Kim slapped him viciously and pulled away. "What're you talking about? Where's *who*? And what're you doing in Kelly's bed?"

"Never mind that. Where is she?"

The other girl, Lonnie, came forward, placing herself between them. "You mean you don't know? You're sleeping in her bed; you must know something."

Curt shook his head frantically and turned, scanning the room. He saw the open window, the drapes stirring in the breeze. He felt the chill of the night filling the air.

"Oh, my God," he said. "Oh, no. No!"

He ran to the window and leaned out. The compound was empty.

"Hey," Kim said, "I know you. You're Curt, the guy Kelly's been hanging out with. What I *don't* know—and believe me, I'm dying to find out—is what the hell you're doing here. You—"

"Shut up!"

Kim drew back, eyes wide and affrighted. She clutched Lonnie, and the two of them hugged each other, as if to protect themselves from Curt and the evil he represented.

"What's the matter with you?" Lonnie said. "If you're trying to scare us, you—"

But Curt wasn't listening. His head was filled with roaring, ringing noises that drowned out everything else. He doubled over, clutching his stomach, and vomited.

"Hey, man, you—"

He vomited again, choking and gagging, heaving in great gasping bursts. He looked at the floor, where the sickish contents of his stomach lay steaming. Then he saw something else and screamed.

On the floor were three or four drops of bright, fresh blood. Kelly's blood.

"*Nooooooooo!*" he wailed, and fled the room.

He charged down the corridor and punched the elevator button. When the car didn't materialize immediately, he began to pound the wall, alternately kicking the elevator doors and stabbing the button again and again. When it finally arrived, he staggered in and rode down to the lobby, sobbing, pummeling the ornate paneled walls of the car with ceaseless fury.

Five minutes later he burst into room 1290. Scott saw the anguish on his face and was at his side immediately, supporting him, leading him over to his bed.

"Curt? What happened? Where's Kelly?"

"No," Curt muttered. "No. Oh, God, no, no . . . God, no!"

"C'mon, Curt, talk to me. Tell us. What is it? What happened?"

Scott's words didn't penetrate. Curt continued to sob, repeating the word "no" over and over.

Scott shook him, hard.

Curt rocked back on his heels and raised one clenched fist. He didn't strike, however. Instead, oddly, all the anger seemed to go out of him. His body sagged. He lowered his fist and relaxed it. He stopped crying. His breathing slowed, and he seemed almost calm.

"Okay," Scott said, "now tell us. Did something happen to Kelly? Is she all right, or—"

"They got her," he said in a dead voice. "One of them took her. And I slept through it. Jesus, Scott, I killed her."

Phyllis said, "*What*?"

The story spilled out of him, everything from the time Kelly had caught up with him in the lobby to his finding her blood on the floor. As he spoke, Phyllis began to cry softly. Juan lit a cigarette but never smoked it, letting it burn out between his trembling fingers. Scott listened, showing no expression, staring straight ahead.

When the story was complete, they looked at each other in silence. That Kelly Beckworth was gone was impossible to accept. She had been taken from them when they needed her most. She had been taken after bravely rescuing Curt from his despair.

"That bastard," Curt said after a long time. "That motherfucking son of a bitch, that cocksucking bastard . . . I'm going to kill him. I'm going to put the stake right through his goddamned shriveled heart. I'm going to look into his face and laugh when I do it. I'm going to say 'Hey, Dad, fuck you! How do you like this, shithead?' I'm going to put the stake on his chest and take that goddamned hammer and he won't—"

"Curt," Scott said softly, "it's all right, partner. Calm down. You're right. We're going to get him, all of us, just like you said."

Curt turned slowly and looked at him. Then he turned to Phyllis and Juan. His eyes were gleaming. "Yeah. We're all going to get him. Tomorrow. You can count on it."

37

Sometime during the course of that long, long night, the weather had turned. In a matter of hours, fall was gone and an early winter—maybe a false winter, maybe not—slammed into the area. Icy rain was driven forward in the teeth of a northwest wind. The last of the autumn leaves were ripped cruelly from the trees and sent cascading wildly across the compound.

Perfect, Curt thought as they left Van Paris Hall the next morning. It's almost as though the Master knew we were coming, as though he arranged this. For a few moments, his frustration and despair threatened to overwhelm him, but then he pulled himself together.

Okay, dad, he thought. If that's the way you want it, fine. We've made it this far, and I'm warning you: you're going to have to do better than this. It's going to take a lot more than the weather to stop us now.

Even weeks afterward, Scott's memory of his night walk to the house at the back of the compound and the discovery of the decapitated dog in the cemetery was still fresh in his mind. If anything, the recent visits to the burial ground had only succeeded in strengthening his recollection.

When they broke out of the maze of trees and trails at the back of the compound and stood at the edge of the gravel service road, Curt and the others automatically

looked to the right, toward the cemetery, but Scott shook
his head and pointed in the other direction.

"The house is over there."

"You sure?" Juan said.

He nodded. "That night I was coming from that direction. I passed the house first, before I got to the cemetery. Of course, we're still not sure it's Bach's house, but
what else have we got?"

A half-mile along they came to a rambling, run-down
stone fence surrounding a large overgrown lot. The house
was set at the back of the lot, and their immediate
impression was that it wasn't anything like what they had
expected. No sprawling mansion or stone keep. It was
just a two-story house surrounded by weeds and rocks. It
looked dilapidated, and the only signs of occupancy were
the curtains in all the windows.

"That's it?" Curt said. "That's where the high, exalted
Master lives?"

Seeing it again in the daylight, even Scott seemed
uncertain. "That's the house I saw, I guess—"

"That's the place," Phyllis said suddenly. "I know it."

They turned to stare at her. She was leaning against
the stone fence, eyes riveted on the house. It was hard to
be certain in the gray morning light, but she looked as
though she had grown quite pale.

"How do you know?" Curt said.

"My walk. The night I got the marks. He . . . he met
me in the woods and he brought me here." She paused,
shaking her head, as though the sudden flood of memory
amazed her. "He told me it was his house, but that I
couldn't come in. He asked me if I understood. He said
someday, if I was loyal, I could come in, but not that
night . . . not yet."

"Jesus," Curt whispered. He looked from Phyllis to
the house and back again. "Is everyone ready?"

They approached the gate, but paused before passing
through it, puzzled by something there. It was a short
wooden post set just outside. At the top of the post were
three short wooden pegs.

"Whaddya think . . . ?" Juan asked.

Scott laughed colorlessly. "A hitching post. A hitching post for vampires."

They stared at it a moment longer. Then Curt turned to Juan. "You know the plan?"

Juan nodded. "I look around back. Quick. Super-fast, just like you say. I meet you back here in five minutes. *Sí*?"

"Be careful."

Juan's dark eyes darkened further, and he nodded solemnly. When he took off for the side of the house, the others slipped through the gate in single file and started up the walk. When they reached the front steps, they hesitated again.

There was something in the air here, Curt thought, and he was not the only one who felt it. It was akin to what had come over them at the cemetery just before the vampires rose—a tingling in the atmosphere. Curt looked up at the upper floor of the house and felt a wave of vertigo, as though the building was leaning forward and was about to topple over, crushing them beneath it. He felt a powerful urge to turn around and hurry off the property, but stifled it. They were too close now. Instead of running, he turned to the others, his eyes asking a silent question.

No one answered, not with words or nods, but one by one they mounted the set of three steps onto the front stoop and waited. Curt briefly touched the cross at his neck, then reached out and knocked. The sound his knuckles made on the wood was unnaturally loud. He jerked his hand back as though he'd been scalded.

They waited again. A full minute passed. Then two.

Curt knocked again.

They heard shuffling footsteps inside, approaching the door slowly. Curt took an involuntary step backward, bumping into Phyllis and almost knocking her off the icy stoop. Scott caught her, kept his arm around her shoulders. They held their breath as the steps came up to the other side of the door and stopped. Curt imagined he saw the knob beginning to turn, but blinked and saw that he was wrong. Nothing at all was happening.

At last the door swung open, revealing a young man

with shaggy blond hair and a thin, almost nonexistent mustache. He was huge, his body that of an iron-pumper. He was wearing jeans, Reeboks, and a sweatshirt that said "I USE MY MUSCLES FOR GOD." The familiar church cross hung around his neck, smaller than the ones the ministers wore on TV but similar—gold studded with tiny, glittering jewels.

He smiled. "What can I do for you folks?"

Curt tried a harmless smile of his own. "Hi there. We, uh, we're residents over at Van Paris Hall. We'd like to see . . . well, we'd like to see Reverend Bach."

The big man blinked once. "Reverend Bach," he repeated. "You mean the Master."

Curt nodded. "Is he in?"

"Yes."

Curt faltered. There was a sudden loud roar in his ears, and he felt his chest tighten painfully. Somehow, of all the possible scenarios he had envisioned when thinking about this visit, this one had not been among them. Were they really going to get to see Bach, who, if he was a vampire, must still be sleeping his daylight sleep?

Battling to regain his composure, he said, "He's here? Right now?"

The big man nodded pleasantly. "He sure is. But I'm afraid he's too busy for visitors."

Curt felt the tension go out of him in a rush. There had been no mistake. "I know he's a busy man, but I'm sure he'll see us if you tell him we're here. It won't even take long. Just a minute or two and then we'll leave. We—"

"I'm sorry," the big man said, "but you're wasting your time. The Master never sees visitors here at the house. This is where he does most of his work, where there's peace and quiet. I couldn't disturb him. Maybe I could help you? My name's Ray Bussey, by the way. I'm Reverend Bach's housekeeper."

Curt frowned, but stood firm. "That won't do it. It has to be Bach."

Bussey spread his hands wide and shrugged. "I don't know what to tell you. You know, you really should have checked with someone at the Hall. They would've told you the rules about seeing the Master at his house. You could've saved a trip."

Phyllis stepped forward. "It's not the trip we're worried about, Mr. Bussey, it's the Master. We really—"

"Sorry," Bussey said firmly. "No dice, no chance."

"Never?"

"Afraid not. Your best bet is to catch him after church some Sunday. Any other time and he's much too busy."

"After church," Curt repeated. "After *church*? How many times does Bach do services? How many times is he in the Park or the Faith Center? There are people here ten years or more who've never seen Bach do a single church service anywhere!"

For a fraction of an instant Bussey seemed caught off guard. Then he recovered, saying, "I'll be honest with you. You're right. The Master doesn't do many services these days. It's the same problem again—his schedule. He's in and out of town so much that his workload here piles up until it's just ridiculous. But he told me just the other day that he wants to start doing church again real soon. Maybe you'll get lucky."

"Lucky," Scott said dryly. "Yeah."

Bussey flashed a cheerful smile. "Well, you never know."

"Then there's absolutely no chance that you'll let us in to see him today?" Curt asked.

"Nope. Sorry."

"We're sorry too," Curt said. "Let's go, guys."

He turned around and started down the steps. They had gotten no more than ten feet away from the door when Bussey called after them, his voice carried by the wind: "If there's anything else I can do for you, you just give me a shout, you hear?"

They ignored him, and a moment later heard the front door slam shut.

"Strikeout," Scott muttered.

"Not quite," Curt said. "We learned a few things. We know this really is Bach's house. We know how to get here quickly, or as quickly as possible through those damn woods. We know Bach has a giant goon for a housekeeper. All of that . . . well, it's more than we knew an hour ago. And we still haven't heard Juan's report from around back."

"Maybe." Scott sounded unconvinced. "We don't know for sure if we were getting a straight story. Maybe Bussey, *if* that's his name, was lying. Maybe it's not Bach's house, maybe the Master isn't anywhere around here or—"

He stopped suddenly, looking left and right, the color draining from his face.

"What is it?" Phyllis said. "Scott . . . Jesus, what's wrong?"

He shook his head. "Curt, you mentioned Juan. Well, where the hell is he?"

Startled, the others joined him in frantically scanning the landscape. Juan was supposed to meet them back at the gate after five minutes of snooping. Five minutes.

But more than five minutes had passed while they were at the door.

And the storm-swept stretch of road in front of them was completely empty.

38

Curt's hand went automatically to his cross. Five minutes, he thought dazedly. He was only supposed to take five minutes.

"Juan?" he called uncertainly. "Hey . . . Juan!"

The howl of the wind was the only response.

He tried again, slightly louder: "Juan!"

Silence. Seconds knit themselves together, forming a long and painful minute.

"He's dead," Scott said suddenly. "They got him. I don't know how, but they—"

"Shut up!" Curt snapped. Then: "*Juan!*"

From the side of the house came the sound of running footsteps crunching on gravel. Curt imagined the towering form of Ray Bussey charging at them with a gun in his hand, and his own hand went to the cross again and closed around it tightly.

"Jimenez? Is that you?"

"Yeah, man" came the response. "Hang on, don't leamme here, okay?"

He appeared at the side of the house and charged headlong through the weeds and brush that choked the front yard. He reached the road and skidded to a stop beside them, puffing fiercely. His eyes were wild, his hair a tangled mess. Rain water streamed down his face. He put one hand on Curt's shoulder and sagged against him, slowly catching his breath.

"Christ," he said, "it ain't much of a house, y'know?

But it's bigger than it looks. I got all the way around, then hadda bust my ass to get back here. I figured maybe you was gonna ditch me."

"What did you find?" Curt asked, and immediately Phyllis and Scott were peppering him with questions too. He seemed flustered, taken aback by the flurry of queries.

"I hate to interrupt," Curt said, "but I'd feel better about this if we weren't virtually standing in the front yard. Let's head back to the woods."

They hurried down the service road. When they reached the twisting series of wooded paths, they took the one that offered the straightest route back to the Hall, but stopped several hundred yards along it, picking out seats on large rocks and stumps.

"So let's hear it," Scott said. "What did you see?"

Juan grinned. He was extremely proud of himself. "It's Bach's house, all right. And the bastard's there, too."

"You're sure?" Curt asked. "How do you know?"

Juan held up his hand. "Lemme tell it my own way, *amigo*." He paused, took a deep breath, and began: "After I left you guys, I stuck close to the house. I figured, hey, if I'm pressed up against the side, nobody can see me, even if they're lookin' out, y'know? I made it all the way to the back, and that's where I come up against this iron fence. It was maybe, I dunno, five feet tall, and had big spikes on top. Almost tore a hole in my jeans. Shit, what am I sayin'? Almost tore a hole in my fuckin' *leg*. The ramp was on the other side."

"Ramp?" Curt said.

"Yeah, y'know, like a delivery ramp or somethin'." He used his hands to make a forty-five-degree angle in the air. "It went down a ways, like to the basement. Maybe eight feet down in all. I looked at it, but I couldn't decide if I should go down there or not. I was startin' to get kinda scared, and I didn't know how much more of my five minutes was left, but I finally decided, why not, what the hell? I was there, I might as well go all the way."

"Pretty brave," Curt remarked.

Juan snorted laughter. "Brave, hell. Curious, man, curious."

"I don't care *what* made you do it. It's still brave."

"You wanna hear the story or not?"

Smiling faintly, Curt waved him on.

"Okay. So I walk down this ramp, and shit if it ain't gettin' colder all of a sudden. I mean, it's a nasty day, right? What is it? Forty degrees maybe? thirty-five? At the top of the ramp it feels like twenty. And every few feet goin' down, it gets even colder. By the time you get to the doors at the bottom, it's fuckin' below zero. *That's* how I figured out I wasn't just chasin' shadows. I knew I was gettin' onto somethin'.

"Down at the bottom, like I said, there's these big metal doors. Two of 'em, chained and padlocked and all. And they're decorated! Somebody carved this pattern of twistin' lines goin' around and around in circles. Y'know what I mean? Circles inside of more circles, gettin' smaller. But they wasn't *perfect* circles. Really, they was kinda lopsided. It was fuckin' bizarre. But the strangest thing was this head carved in the middle of the patterns, one on each door."

"A picture of someone?" Scott asked.

Juan shook his head emphatically. "An animal. A sheep, I think it was."

"Could it have been a goat?" Curt said.

He thought about that. "Yeah. It had horns and all. Maybe it was a goat."

"Pan," Curt said. "The human god with the goat's head."

"Maybe, maybe not. I was too fuckin' cold to pay all that much attention to it. I was shiverin' like all hell—I'm from L.A., remember, I ain't used to *that* kinda shit—so I just wanted to check it out as quick as I could, then meet you back around front.

"I tried touchin' the door, but got burned." He raised his right hand and showed them a series of small round blisters, one on each fingertip. "I couldn't figure that out. It was cold back there, but I got burned. Didn't make no sense. Then I got it. Them metal doors was so cold, I got a fuckin' burn from 'em, like you get from liquid nitrogen or somethin'. These are goddamned *freeze* blisters."

Phyllis gasped.

"Then I knew the Master hadda be down there in that basement. I didn't wanna spend no more time hangin' around, so I started back. I barely got over the fence when I heard somethin' in the woods. A noise, like somebody walkin' along—somebody clumsy. I snuck up behind some trees and saw him. A man, a gardener or somethin', collectin' firewood."

Curt started to say something, but Juan never gave him the chance. He was beaming from ear to ear now as he said, "There was somethin' really weird about the guy, but I couldn't figure it out right away. I mean, a guy collectin' dead branches and logs in the woods is weird enough, right? But then I knew what it was. He had a bulge underneath his coat."

Scott grunted. "You mean he was fat?"

"Fat, yeah. But that wasn't the bulge I'm talkin' about."

"Then—"

"Hang on, *amigo,* lemme finish, okay? I picked up a piece of wood off the ground and snuck up behind him. I didn't know if I was doin' it right or not. Shit, I'm a street kid, not no fuckin' Indian. All I knew was if I made any noise I'd be dead, and I did my goddamn best to be quiet. Didn't matter. Storm was makin' so much noise the guy didn't hear a thing."

"You—"

"I bashed the sucker on the head, put him down cold. And I took it."

Irritated now with Juan's roundabout way to the point, Curt said, "Took *what?*"

Juan laughed. He opened his jacket and from the belt of his jeans pulled out a gleaming handgun. It wasn't particularly large, but to the rest of them it looked murderously threatening.

"Jesus," Scott whispered. "What—"

"It's a thirty-eight-caliber service revolver," Juan said proudly. "A cop gun. Not the best fuckin' piece I ever had my hands on, but hey, you take what you can get, am I right? Better yet, the thing's loaded, and the idiot even had these on him." He reached into his jacket pocket and pulled out a box of bullets. "Can you imagine someone stupid enough to carry bullets in his pocket? I mean, unless you're goin' off to war, that's about as lame as it gets." He laughed merrily. "But I ain't gonna turn down a gift like that. Jeezus, we're set now."

"Are you crazy?" Curt said. "We don't need a gun!"

"That's what you say. If them guys're gonna carry, *I'm* gonna carry."

"But vampires can't be hurt by—"

"Vampires can't, but men? Hey, that's a different story. Take it from a kid who knows what he's talkin' about."

Curt was shaken. Guns? Had it really gone that far?

Juan put a hand on his shoulder. "Relax, *amigo*. It'll be cool. Trust me, okay? You never know. We might need it. And believe me, man, then you'll be glad I did what I did."

Curt simply shook his head in dismay.

"So you guys gonna tell me what happened to you?" Juan said, seeing his friend's distress and artfully changing the subject.

Scott and Phyllis quickly sketched in the events at the front door.

"Yeah," he said when they were done, "that Bussey guy, he was tellin' the truth, all right. Bach's there. He's down in the basement."

Phyllis said, "It makes sense. Wasn't Dracula always in the castle cellar, or whatever they call basements in castles? Van Paris is probably down there too."

Scott nodded. "I can't believe it, but things are going our way." He touched Juan's shoulder. "You done good, roomie. Gun and all. You helped us prove that Bach was there more quickly than I ever thought we could."

Juan puffed out his chest, polishing his knuckles on his jacket. "It was nothin', man."

"Oh-oh. I see a swelled head in the making."

Everyone laughed. Even Curt chuckled a little. For the first time in days they seemed almost ready to relax, as though the proof of Bach's residence was enough to keep them going.

"We're going back to the Hall to get our stuff," Curt

said, "and we're turning right around and going back to the house. We'll go to the basement doors and—"

"They're locked," Scott said. "You heard Juan's story. They're locked, and cold—so cold he *burned* himself."

"So? Williamson's coffin was locked too, and buried under six feet of dirt. We didn't stop for that. We'll see how cold the doors are after we sprinkle a little holy water on them."

Everyone nodded slowly, not sure if the holy water would do the trick or not, but knowing that the house and the basement doors were their best chance for victory.

Scott patted Curt on the back. "What do you think, Potter? Think your dear papa will be surprised to see you walking into his basement with a stake in your hand?"

Curt looked startled. He didn't say anything, but after a few seconds began to smile—an expression of grim determination.

39

Kaye scrambled to his feet as Norris entered the office.

"Jesus Christ, I was beginning to think my secretary would never find you."

Norris sat down and immediately lit one of his cigarettes. "Sorry about that. I was late getting in today. It's getting colder out there, almost feels like snow." He paused, taking a long drag of smoke. "So go ahead and fill me in. I haven't heard you use the words 'code red' in years."

Kaye lowered himself back into his chair and quickly summarized his reports from Ray Bussey and Howard Crisp, including Crisp's word-for-word account of what he had heard the Enemies talking about in the woods after their visit to the house.

"Shit," Norris said when he had finished. "It's too soon. If they know about the cellar doors and they plan on using them, we're backed right up against the wall. We can't move the Master, but we don't have the time to take care of the Enemies."

"Exactly. As you know, the Master's induction plans were to be played out over the course of five or six days. That allowed time for a few second chances. But now . . ."

Norris crushed out his cigarette. "Your secretary mentioned something about new plans."

"Yes. You know what our main objective is: to protect the Master. We can lose the flock if need be, some of it or even all of it. It's a horrible thing to think about, but if it came down to a choice, there wouldn't be any question. Protect Bach first, Van Paris second, and leave the rest to whatever fate might come."

"So we have to get the Master out of the way."

Kaye nodded slowly. "It's our only remaining choice."

"Move him where?"

"Germany."

"You mean Project—"

"Far Horizon, yes. Now, I know it's more than a month ahead of schedule, but I don't see any other options. We've never developed contingency plans for an all-out assault like this. We probably should have created a plan to send Bach to one of the domestic offices in the event of emergency . . . New York, maybe, or L.A. But that's hindsight. With time running out, we'll have to fall back on the only plans we *do* have. Germany. Far Horizon. We'll have to push the whole operation ahead to this afternoon. With the Master safe with our friends in Europe, we'll have the time we need to remove the Enemies slowly, without pressure."

"Can we work it out in time?"

"If we have to. We have our connections. Schroeder and Lund and the others can be notified to go into action on their end, and we'll just have to wing the rest of it. At least we have most of the groundwork laid."

Norris frowned. "I don't like it. Why don't we go after the Enemies in force?"

"You're kidding yourself. We can't murder them. We have Connie Bishop, who knows what they're up to. He thinks they're crazy, but if they all vanished at once, his suspicions would be . . . well, we'd be back to the problem we've had all along."

"But, Bob, the High Church is a mighty power!"

"Do you think I'm enjoying this? I don't like it any more than you, but there's no other way. The Master's facing an unprecedented threat. If we pull this off, if we keep him safe from the Enemies . . . Jesus, Steve, if we do that, we're in. Everything we've always worked for will be ours. The Master will reward us. I'll be inducted and you'll be the new senior pastor. After that, you'll be next to join the flock. We'll have what we always wanted, the immortality, the power. But if we risk the Master just because your pride says we should stand and fight, it'll all go down the drain. Don't you see that?"

Norris nodded wordlessly.

"I thought so," Kaye said. "I want to join the flock. So do you. Well, dammit, let's do what it takes to get there."

The phone rang. Kaye picked it up, listened to his receptionist, nodded, and punched one of the intra-compound lines.

"Kaye."

He listened for a while, then spoke cryptically to the person on the other end.

He hung up the phone and turned back to Norris. "The Enemies are at the Faith Center. We're not sure why, but Crisp overheard something about preparing to attack."

Norris sighed. "They don't waste any time, do they? What's the procedure?"

"Crisp's sending a team to the house with the aim of helping Ray Bussey. They understand they're allowed to remove the Enemies, but only if the Master is directly threatened, which both Crisp and I take to mean an assault on the cellar. It's tying their hands—we all know that—but a direct threat to his existence is the only way the Master will allow a removal."

"And if that doesn't work?"

Kaye frowned. He rummaged through the drift of papers on his desk, found several that were clipped together, and handed them to Norris. "This is a list of names and numbers, some in Chicago, some in New York, the rest overseas. Go back to your office right now. When you get there, send your receptionist away and notify all these people."

"Notify them of what?"

"Tell them that unless they hear otherwise, Far Horizon will begin this afternoon."

Without discussing the matter, they had hurried straight to the Faith Center. There they entered the largest church and took a pew in the back. A service had ended several minutes before, but there were ten or twelve residents lingering behind, heads bowed in silent prayer.

They prayed with them, in whispered unison. At first it seemed to be doing no good. The true nature of the church polluted and diluted everything. It cast a pall over the room that only they could sense. It made the already darkened chapel seem darker still. The ornaments of faith around them seemed like relics of evil.

But gradually they felt a change occurring, a sense of power and strength creeping over them. To Curt it seemed as though great invisible fingers had grasped the fabric of that gray pall and started pulling it apart. For almost half an hour the light that broke through was weak and ineffective, but slowly it grew, steadily it mounted, until not just Curt, but all of them could feel it, even see it. It manifested itself in a new determination, and in a firm but steady tingle that spread from their hearts outward to their arms and legs, their hands, their fingers.

"D'you feel it?" Juan whispered. "Mother of God, d'you feel it?"

Nobody spoke. Nobody had to.

They stayed in the chapel for another hour, savoring the light and strength, absorbing it, reveling in it. At last, feeling reborn, they returned to Van Paris Hall.

They began packing their equipment into knapsacks.

They prayed together a final time—*Let not my enemies exult over me*—and when they were done, held hands, all four of them, until they were ready.

"Now?" Phyllis said, rising.

Curt studied all of them carefully. He nodded.

"Yeah. Now."

40

The weather had deteriorated by the time they left the Hall. The wind was blowing harder and there were now stony pellets of snow mixed with the flying sleet. Although it was barely past one, the sky had the dark and angry look of onrushing night. Most residents were staying in, giving the compound the appearance of an abandoned estate.

When they reached the woods beyond the main group of offices, they paused and rested in the shelter of the trees. Even here, however, the wind had sharp teeth and dead leaves whipped past like small animals scurrying before the wrath of a monstrous predator.

But there was something worse than the weather, Curt thought. The farther they got from the Hall, the less he could feel the power they'd found in church. It hadn't left them completely, but it was fading with every passing second.

He looked at the others and knew they were all thinking the same thing.

When they reached the house some minutes later, Curt stared at it, trying to visualize his father's face, picturing the act of plunging a stake into his undead heart. All he felt was a cold internal chill that seemed the perfect complement to the weather. *Soul-sleet,* he thought, and laughed. The harsh sound of it snapped all of them out of their reverie.

"We gonna get to it?" Juan said.

Curt nodded. "You know the plan. Scott and Juan, we'll go around back. Phyl, you go to the door. You're our cover." He paused, taking her hand and squeezing it. "Remember, without you, that Bussey goon will get us for sure. Do it up good."

She smiled. "Good. You bet. That's the only way I know how to work."

Scott hugged her, kissed her, held her for almost a minute. He let her go only when Juan touched his shoulder and said, "C'mon, time's flyin'."

He pulled away from her, kissed her on the cheek a final time, and nodded. "All set."

Phyllis waited by the gate, pretending indecision while they left her and headed east down the service road, as though going to the cemetery. When they were certain that nobody would be able to see them from the house, they left the road and doubled back through the woods.

Wind-whipped branches slapped them as they hurried along. Here and there they had to scramble over deadfalls or negotiate muddy low spots in the forest floor. They were beginning to think they were off course when they broke out of the trees and saw the back of the house.

It was just as Juan had described it. An iron fence with spikes ran from one corner of the building to the property's back wall, blocking them off from the driveway and the paved delivery ramp that led to the basement doors.

They approached the fence and flung their knapsacks over to the other side. Juan used the fence-top like a gymnastics horse. Wary of the way he'd almost hurt himself climbing over before, he placed his hands between the spikes and lithely vaulted the fence in one smooth motion. Scott then grasped two of the spikes and pulled himself up and over.

When Curt's turn came, however, he was only halfway across when his grip on the ice-slicked metal slipped and he felt a sharp pain on the inside of his right leg. He heard a ripping noise and looked down just long enough to see a gaping hole in his jeans. He hesitated, one foot atop the fence, the other still dangling, caught his breath, and pulled himself the rest of the way across.

Side by side, they walked to the edge of the ramp and started down.

"You feel it?" Curt said softly. "It's just like you said, Juan . . . it's colder."

Scott grunted. "Bach's here all right. Jesus, what a difference."

When they got to the bottom of the ramp, they stared at the two steel doors and the network of concentric circles etched on their surface. In the center of each door was the perfectly carved likeness of a bearded goat-god. Curt reached out to touch the door on the right, but his fingers barely brushed the surface before he jerked back with a strangled cry.

He held his hand up. Tiny gray-white blisters had already popped out on his fingertips.

Shaking his head, he unzipped his knapsack and rummaged around inside until he had found two vials of holy water. He gave one to Juan, kept the other for himself, and muttered an improvised prayer. When he was done, he uncapped his vial and held it out in front of him. Juan did the same.

"Now?" Juan said.

Curt nodded. "On three."

He counted slowly, and at the designated number they splashed each door with the water.

Immediately there was a magnesium-bright flash of light and a tremendous thunderclap of sound. They were knocked back almost five feet, buffeted by a rolling wave of searing heat. Curt heard a sizzling and realized that the hair on the top of his head was singed. They lay on the wet ramp, faces pressed to the concrete, until the heat had subsided. Only then did they dare look at the doors again.

"Son of a bitch," Juan whispered.

The doors were charred and the etched steel wrinkled from the intensity of the heat. Near the hinges and where they met in the center, the doors had actually buckled. The chain that held the padlock in place was now solid black, and the padlock was just a melted, almost unrecognizable lump of metal on the ground.

"Can you believe it?" Curt said.

Scott shrugged and picked himself up. "I saw it, didn't I?" But despite the casual tone, his face betrayed his awe and bewilderment.

Carefully, as though expecting another thunder burst, they approached the doors again. Curt reached out and touched them tentatively, ready to pull his hand back if need be. But the metal was no longer burning cold, nor was it hot. Now it was just cool, reflecting the chilly air temperature.

"It worked," he said. "It really worked."

He grabbed the right-hand door and attempted to pull it open, but it didn't budge. He tried the one on the left, with the same result. Maneuvering his fingers for better purchase, he took hold of one of the places where the steel had buckled, but pulling there produced nothing.

"Think they got it locked from the inside?" Juan asked.

"I don't know. Get me the hammer."

"What?"

"The hammer, dammit! It's in your backpack. Hurry!"

Juan fumbled in his bag and found it, handed it over, and watched Curt place the clawed end into the space between the doors.

"Scott, come here. Juan, take the gun and cover us. Get about halfway up the ramp and be ready to shoot if there's trouble."

Juan was surprised. "Trouble? What kind of—"

"I don't know. Just get ready."

Juan took the gun and crouched on the ramp like a sniper. Scott and Curt started working on the doors together. With their hands and the hammer, with strength and desperate hope, they began forcing their way into the domain of the Master.

Phyllis' last thought before the front door swung open was to wonder if her friends were all right. She hoped she'd given them enough time to get back there and get started. She had waited an extra four or five minutes just to be sure.

"Yes?"

She looked up as Ray Bussey towered over her. Fighting back the urge to flinch away from him, she smiled shyly. "Hi there. Remember me?"

He laughed. "Sure. My memory's not always the best, but a few hours aren't enough to forget a pretty face."

"Thanks," she said, remembering Curt's advice: *Slow answers, one-word answers. That's the best way to draw everything out and buy lots of time. Keep it slow.*

Bussey laughed again. "That's all you have to say? I'm sure you didn't come here just to be complimented. I hope you're still not expecting to see Reverend Bach."

"Maybe."

His smile faded. "Maybe what?"

"Maybe I am. That's part of it, anyway. But I also have a complaint, Mr. Busford."

"Bussey."

"Excuse me?"

"Bussey. Raymond Bussey. What kind of complaint?"

"Well . . ."

"Yes?"

"Well, frankly, I'm not real happy with the way you treated us."

Bussey looked troubled. "Because I wouldn't let you see the Master? I tried to explain that—very politely, let me add. It was you and your friends that got upset, not me."

"Well, it wasn't fair."

"Now, hang on, miss. I've got a job to do. Part of that job is keeping house, making sure everything runs smoothly around here, but that's not all of it. When the Master's here, I'm the one in charge of keeping his schedule. I'm supposed to make sure he's not disturbed. That's what I'm paid for."

Phyllis nodded. "I'll buy that, I guess, but that doesn't excuse rudeness."

"Rudeness?" For a second he looked ready to hit her. Then his eyes cleared, and he said, "I'm sorry you think I was rude. I don't happen to think I was, but I'll apologize anyway. Now, you'll have to excuse me. I've got things to take care of that—"

"Hold on," Phyllis said quickly, afraid the door would

be shut in her face and she would lose her chance. "Aren't you going to ask me what you can do to make it up to me?"

"Of course," Bussey said, suddenly smiling again, as though she amused him. "How stupid of me. What can I do to make it up to you?"

"Simple. Let me in to see Reverend Bach right now."

Bussey's eyes widened. "Are you crazy? What do I have to tell you to get you to understand? Nobody sees the Master at his house. If you can't get an office appointment, you have to wait until you see him in church. It's that simple." He paused, studying her closely. "Anyway, I couldn't let you in even if I was allowed to. The Master left half an hour ago for a commuter flight to St. Louis, something about a crusade at Busch Stadium next summer. So you see, I can't—"

"You're lying!"

"No, I'm not," Bussey said, shaking his head firmly.

"You're lying!" Phyllis repeated. "I come here to see the head of the church—*my* church . . . it's just as much mine as yours—and you won't let me. What is it with you? Is it me? Or do you just hate all residents?"

"I don't hate you . . . I don't hate anyone. The Master's gone."

"Yeah, right, and he's going to be doing a service in the Faith Center real soon, right? Right. And I'm the ghost of Anne Boleyn. I don't know why you're doing this to me, but it's not fair, any of it. I'm a resident here, and I demand my rights as a resident! *I demand to see the Master!*"

Flustered, Bussey said, "Young lady, I suggest you calm down. Maybe you ought to think about going back to the Hall and getting some rest before you say anything you'll be sorry for later. And before you go, let me say again that the Master simply isn't here. I don't hate you. The rules apply to everyone, and there's nothing I can do about them. That's all there is to it."

"If the Master's gone, when's he coming back?"

"I . . . I couldn't say for sure," Bussey said, faltering. "Two days . . . maybe three or four. It depends on how his plans—"

"Liar! Fucking goddamned liar! You hate me! You hate me! You hate me!"

Letting herself go at last, she launched herself at him. Despite the obvious difference in size, Bussey stumbled back, caught off guard by the force of her attack. She threw herself against him and began flailing, pummeling him with her open hands, her fists. He tried to get away from her, but she clung to his shirt, terrier-tough, as he dragged her into the entryway of the house. They struck a small decorative table and knocked the telephone on it to the floor with a crash and clang.

"You hate me, you son of a bitch, you hate my fucking guts, and it's not fair! All I want is to see the Master, but you won't let me!"

Bussey's face was contorted with shock. He reached down and tried to flick her away like a bothersome insect, but still she hung on, connecting with blow after blow.

"You hate me, God damn you!" she shrieked a final time, releasing her hold on him and scrambling past, making a break for the interior of the house.

She almost reached the living room. She caught a glimpse of a red velvet couch and something that might have been an ornate Bible stand minus the Bible, when he dived for her from behind and caught her legs. They crashed to the floor together, Bussey panting, Phyllis moaning in a burlesque of great pain.

"You can't come in here!" he said. "It's against all rules! It's against every reg—"

"Shut up, bastard!" she cried, pulling herself up and slapping him hard across the face.

He recoiled and struggled to his feet, grasping her by the sleeve of her jacket and dragging her with him. He pulled her, kicking and screaming, back into the entryway, lashing out with his foot and knocking the front door closed. Then he bent down and picked the telephone up from the floor.

"I've had it with you, bitch! I've tried to be nice, but you don't understand nice!"

Phyllis screamed on and on, still flailing away but no longer connecting.

Bussey punched two buttons on the phone. "Franklin, get up here now. I've got a lunatic on my hands, and . . . What? Shit, Frank, I don't care what's going on outside. You've got enough men down there. I want *you* up *here*! Listen to her. Hear that screaming? I need help!"

He slammed the receiver down and turned full attention back to Phyllis. "You've got one more chance to cool down, but if—"

"*Fucker!*" she cried, and spat in his face.

Bussey swore and pushed her up against the front door, pinning her there. Now that he had the advantage at last, he seemed content to wait for help to arrive.

She glared at him, watching, fascinated, as her phlegm clung to the side of his nose.

Then she heard footsteps racing toward them from the rear of the house and knew that it was almost over.

Had she given her friends the time they desperately needed?

Even in the cold, Scott and Curt worked up a tremendous sweat. Their hands were blistered and sore. After several minutes, Curt stopped, puffing hard.

"Juan, give me the gun. You help Scott. Maybe you guys can get it."

"You sure you want this?" Juan said, handing the weapon over gingerly.

Curt nodded.

"Know how to use it?"

"Believe me, if I have to, I'll figure it out."

They traded places, Curt guarding from the ramp, Juan joining Scott below. Slowly, the door began to move. As it did, they realized it had just been sticking, was not in fact locked from the inside. Over and over again Scott would slip the clawed end of the hammer into the gap they were gradually creating. Then he would lever it back while Juan pulled, until the space was larger. Then he would take the hammer out, reposition it, and try again. At last, when the gap was too large for the hammer to do any good at all, he threw it aside and pulled along with Juan. The screeching grind of steel on the concrete ramp was nerve-jarring and horrible.

"Dammit, c'mon," he said, breathing hard. "We're almost there. Another foot or two and we can fit through."

With one final furious tug, the barrier gave way and the door swung open at last.

"That's it!" he cried. "We—"

His cry of triumph was cut off by a sharp report.

From halfway up the ramp, Curt saw a blur of motion and heard a second explosion. Dizzily, as though everything was tilted to one side, he noticed a short, rotund man standing in the doorway his friends had just succeeded in opening. The rotund man was pointing a handgun at the spot where Scott was standing. Only Scott was not standing there anymore. And neither was Juan. They were lying almost three feet back from the doors, their bodies sprawled at bizarre angles on the concrete ramp, crimson stains spreading across the fronts of their jackets.

Dreamily Curt stared at them, trying to absorb what he was seeing. Then he pivoted back to face the man with the gun—just in time to see the man turn the gun in his direction.

His confusion exploded in panic. He turned and fled, not even aware that he scooped up the hammer and knapsacks as he ran. He slipped and stumbled his way up the ramp, pausing at the top and looking back.

The man was gone—and his friends were lying in growing pools of their own blood.

Scott was dead. He knew that immediately, beyond doubt.

But Juan . . . Juan was moving.

His hands were twitching, his legs bicycling, as though he was trying to flee from his pain.

Instantly Curt started back down the ramp. He held the gun in front of him, determined not to get caught off guard this time.

Juan heard him coming. His head rolled to the side and his wide, dark eyes gazed up beseechingly.

"Curt . . . Jesus, man . . . *Jeeeeezus* . . ."

And suddenly, before Curt could get to him, there

were men in the doorway again. He saw the short man
who had shot his friends, and beside him a taller figure in
a rain slicker and a Los Angeles Raiders cap. A gun was
pointed in his direction. It went off.

He threw himself against the concrete wall and fired
two shots in return. They went wild, one hitting the
metal doors and zinging off in the opposite direction, the
other going somewhere wide of its target.

The air was filled with gunfire. He saw sparks jumping
off the concrete at his feet, on either side of his head.

"Curt!" Juan gasped through the volley of shots. "Run,
man!" As he reached for the short man's ankle, trying
desperately to trip him, an expression of exquisite agony
contorted his face. *"Run!"*

And Curt did.

He raced back up the ramp and headed for the iron
fence.

As if from a great distance, he heard two more shots
fired in rapid succession and felt an odd nip of pain in his
thigh. Then he was over the fence, crashing through the
bushes and weeds along the side of the house.

When he reached the front, he kept running, heading
for the safety of the woods. But as soon as he was
through the gate, something stopped him, held him back.

Phyllis.

Where was she?

It was hard to remember, difficult to think of anything.
The picture of Scott and Juan sprawled across the ramp
blotted out everything else in his mind. Scott was dead.
At least he was safe from *them*. But Juan . . . Oh, Jesus.
He knew the men would drag Juan into the cellar, hold
him there until the Master awoke and—"

Phyllis. Think about Phyllis.

It came to him. She was in the house. Of course. She
was creating a diversion, buying time for them. Time for
what? Why, for Scott and Juan to get shot, of course!

He went to his knees at the edge of the trail, partially
from weakness, partially to hide himself behind the low
stone wall that surrounded Bach's property. He hun-
kered down there and waited for Phyllis to come out. He

didn't know how long he waited, but it seemed a very long time indeed. After a while he became convinced that not only had Scott and Juan been shot by the men in the basement, but also something else had gone wrong. As more minutes passed with no sight of Phyllis, he was sure that Bussey had gotten her. And yet he continued to wait. It was the only thing he could do.

When the front door of the house opened an eternity later, he didn't hear it. Nor did he hear Bussey and his assistant throw Phyllis out onto the front stoop with a warning never to return. Nor did he hear Phyllis' footsteps hurrying down the walk. He was too busy thinking about Juan with blood pouring from his chest, urging Curt to save himself even as he lay wounded and trapped—a prisoner of the vampires. He didn't hear anything at all until she came through the gate and saw him hiding there behind the fence.

"C-Curt? Where're the others?"

He looked up, startled. He didn't think he had ever been so happy to see anyone in his life. "Thank God, you made it! I didn't know—"

"Where's Scott?" she said again. "Where's Juan?" Her voice was rising, growing panicky. "I gave you enough time, didn't I?"

Curt swallowed hard. When he spoke, his voice sounded like the voice of death in a nightmare, hollow and flat and utterly lifeless.

"Phyl . . . Scott's dead. A fat guy shot him."

"Curt! Don't joke, dammit! What happened back there?"

He rose and gathered her in his arms. "I told you, Phyl. We got the door open, but there was a man with a gun waiting for us. Scott's dead. He got shot. Juan was wounded, and I tried to rescue him but I couldn't. They shot at me. I got hit, but it just grazed me. Scott got it right in the middle of the chest, and Juan . . . Juan . . ."

Phyllis pulled away from him. "God damn you, don't say that. Scott's not . . . not . . . he's not dead. Curt, *why are you lying to me*?"

"Phyl . . ." he said, but could say no more. It didn't

matter. For the first time since she'd come through the gate, she saw his face—really saw it—and understood.

"Oh, God, no."

Curt pulled her close again, and the tears broke from both of them. They stood holding each other, sobbing, gripped by feelings of loss beyond comprehension. The wind and sleet were not enough to move them.

Only two left.

And it was far from finished.

41

The four of them—Smith, Heller, Norris, and Kaye—were in Kaye's office, having a drink and discussing recent developments. Top on the list was the disturbing report from Howard Crisp and his observers: the two remaining Enemies had entered the woods near the house and disappeared. They had not returned to their rooms. Everyone's best guess was that they were preparing to go forward. It looked as though the events of the afternoon had not slowed them down at all.

Tony Smith ran a hand through his hair and frowned. "Given the news," he said, "I can only assume that what Steve's been telling me is actually going to happen. You're going to go with Far Horizon, am I right?"

"You are," Kaye said. "Now, I know the whole operation was originally considered to be an offensive maneuver, placing the Master in Germany, which would then become the beachhead for a whole European flock formation. That's changed a little. The beginning of the move will now have to be considered defensive. But only the beginning. Once Bach's in Hamburg, everything will revert to its original conception."

Heller cleared her throat. "Excuse me for interrupting, but I'm a little lost. Apparently I've been left out of a few meetings. Are you saying we're moving the Master overseas today?"

"In a half-hour," Kaye said. "We'll move the casket by panel truck to O'Hare. Once there, it will be packed for

318

overseas travel, following all the usual airline standards. It will be loaded onto an American Airlines flight to La Guardia. By tonight, it should be aboard a British Airways flight to Heathrow, where it will be met by a chartered German plane that will fly it to Hamburg. In Hamburg, our European contacts will assume all responsibility. Although we'll have to escort the Master that far, once the Germans step in, the escort will be free to turn around and come back to Chicago."

"And who's the lucky soul who gets to do all that traveling?" Norris said.

Kaye smiled and turned to face Heller. "How about it, Becky? You wouldn't object to a little night flying, would you?"

She flushed. "That's not funny, Bob. I just told you I haven't been kept up-to-date on this operation. I—"

"There's nothing to it. We have people behind the scenes every step of the way. They're going to be doing the real work. Actually, the less you know, the better. You're supposed to be in mourning. If you look a little confused or frightened . . . well, it's all for a better effect."

"Mourning?"

Kaye nodded. "Your name is Sandy Gottlieb. The man in the casket is your grandfather, Joseph. He suffered a massive heart attack two days ago, died before the paramedics even arrived. Now you're taking him back to his hometown, Hamburg, for burial."

"Shit, Bob, I—"

"We've already taken care of your passport, and there's a whole folder of necessary paperwork for you to flash around if need be, although that isn't likely; we've greased too many palms to have glitches now. Don't worry."

She grimaced. "Me? Worry?"

"And of course you'll be well-rewarded. We've already arranged for a five-thousand-dollar deposit in your checking account. For services rendered, you might say."

Now she seemed embarrassed. "That isn't necessary, Bob. You know I'd do anything to keep the Master safe."

"Yes. Of course. Nevertheless, it seems a small-enough amount to say thanks for taking all of this on yourself on the spur of the moment." He turned to the others. "Any questions?"

"Will the Master sleep the entire way?" Norris asked.

"Just as we planned when the German move was first discussed, yes. Bach understands Far Horizon completely. It was his idea, remember. There won't be any nocturnal activities over the Atlantic. He'll be a perfectly believable corpse."

"Thank God," Becky said.

"Anything else?" Kaye asked. "No? Well, then I have some more bad news. I found out just before you got here. It seems Van Paris is gone."

The room erupted in disbelief. It took Kaye several minutes to calm his three associates down so that he could continue.

"My plan was to move Van Paris at the same time as Bach. The idea was to have them be Becky's father and uncle, killed in a car crash. But apparently Crisp's men were checking the cellar to make sure things were ready for the move. They discovered Van Paris' casket empty."

"But why?"

"Nobody knows, Tony. Van Paris is older than any of the others in the flock. Seven hundred years? Possibly. Probably older than that. He didn't survive that long by being stupid. It's possible he sensed things running too much against him and left last night, while he could. Maybe he didn't want to return to his European homeland. Maybe he was afraid of losing Bach and thought he'd go create another world leader somewhere else. It could be any of those things, or a hundred others. He started everything when he met Bach, and in that way he was the King of Kings around here. But he didn't run the church. He didn't even run the flock itself. My guess is he knew we'd kill to save the Master, but was less sure of how far we'd go to protect the Master's maker. He was always strange. I could never read his mind or predict his movements, and I certainly can't at this point. All I know is what Crisp told me: Van Paris is gone, and with so much else happening so quickly, we'll have to accept it and just march ahead. The Master is still our number-one priority, just as he always was. The only difference is, our number-two priority is no longer around."

Bringing the meeting to a close, Kaye handed a fat file folder to Heller. "Everything you need's in here, Becky. Keep the passport and traveling papers, obviously. The rest of the information is your itinerary, your list of contacts, a packet of faces, names, and profiles you'll need to know. Memorize them. Know them forward and back. Then destroy them."

Heller took the folder. "Shred, baby, shred," she murmured.

"You'll have to pack in a hurry," Kaye told her. "Just a change of clothes and a toothbrush. No luxuries. I want everyone back here in fifteen minutes. From there we'll go to the house, where we'll meet Bussey and the truck driver. As it stands now, we'll escort them as far as the side service gate. From there, Becky and the Master are on their own. Understood?"

Everyone nodded.

When he was alone again, Kaye poured himself another drink and gulped it quickly. He thought about Van Paris and Bach, about Far Horizon. He thought about the Enemies and their seemingly unstoppable determination. He sighed, realizing that the remainder of his living days and any future he would have in the High Church would be decided in the next hour.

The clock was ticking.

And it was ticking fast.

"I loved him," Phyllis said.

Curt didn't respond. He had made a compress from his shirt and was pressing it against the bullet wound in his thigh, which throbbed with dull, hot fire.

"I really did," she said. "And you loved Kelly. They're gone, and Juan's gone, and so is Ernie. Curt . . . Jesus, Curt, we're alone now. We're the only ones left."

Without answering, he turned and looked around. The afternoon was slipping away. The storm was still howling. Their hiding place in the woods barely protected them from the sleet and wind.

"I want to quit."

He didn't seem surprised. "You can't," was all he said.

"I *have* to. You don't understand. I can't do this anymore. I'm going back to the Hall. And I'm leaving the compound this afternoon."

He kept his hand pressed to his thigh and was silent.

"Don't shut me out," she said. "Listen to me, understand what I'm trying to say. It's no good. Haven't you seen that by now? We can't win."

He nodded slowly. "You're right."

"Then how can you argue—"

"You're right," he said again. "We'll probably be killed. But I don't care. I don't even think of it in terms of winning or losing anymore. I just know that I have to do what I can. I've got to stop my father, and if he stops me too . . . then that's the way it'll be."

"But that doesn't—"

"Jesus Christ, Phyllis, don't you realize we're not doing this for ourselves anymore? We're doing it for the people in the compound. We're doing it for Scott and Kelly and Juan, trying to make sure they didn't die for nothing. We're doing it for Ernie . . . for whatever happened to Ernie. If we quit now, it'd be like saying, well, you know, Kelly became a vampire and Scott took a bullet in the heart, but so what? I'm going to cover my ass. I can't say that, and I don't think you can either." He paused, looking at her for the first time. "Can you?"

She put her head down and covered her eyes, staying that way for a very long time. When at last she looked up, there was a new light of determination in her eyes. It was barely a flicker, but it was there.

"Curt . . . I'm afraid."

"Oh, well there's a new thought. Stop the presses. Phyllis is afraid."

"I . . . I'm scared to death." She hesitated. The flicker of light grew brighter.

It was the only answer he needed.

"We're going to pray," he said.

She took his hands and waited for him to begin.

Kaye's associates made it back to the office in less than fifteen minutes. They looked nervous, jittery, eager to begin. Kaye put down the phone and turned to them. "That's it," he said. "Crisp and his observers have been officially relieved of their duties. If the Enemies decide to move again, it's going to be us against them. From here on out, we're on our own."

"The airport?" Heller said.

"They're ready for us."

"Then we'd better get going," she said. "Lord knows this is one flight I don't want to miss."

They stood, Norris hurriedly lighting one last home-rolled cigarette. Heller hefted her tan suitcase and shifted it back and forth until the grip was comfortable in her hand.

"Ready?" Kaye said.

They nodded.

A moment later they left the Faith Center and took Kaye's car across the compound.

"The crosses!" Phyllis cried.

Curt stopped in the middle of the Twenty-third Psalm. He looked down and felt an atavistic sense of awe. The crosses around their necks had begun to glow. They didn't just shine in the weak gray light. They actually *glowed* with their own internal power.

"That's it," he said. "We've got to go now."

They grabbed their knapsacks and stood. Curt started forward, hesitated, and patted his back pocket. A faint frown creased his face. Something was missing. Then he remembered. He'd put it in his front pocket that morning, before the first visit to the house. He shoved his hand deep and found it—the picture of his mother and father together. He held it momentarily and nodded with surprising determination.

"Whatever happens . . ." he began, not sure he had the words to express what was racing through his mind.

She shook her head. "Don't say it. Let's just go while the power's here."

They left their hiding place and started back through the woods for the final time, heading for the home of Arthur Bach.

42

As they hurried along the maze of paths that led through the woods, Curt's leg began to ache steadily, fiercely. He didn't want to slow down, but found pushing ahead at full speed maddeningly difficult.

Both of them were lost in their own private thoughts. As they neared the service road, Curt had an image of his father standing in front of him, just the way he had been that night in the lounge when Juan had almost been lost. Tall and graceful, utterly ageless, he was grinning his sharklike grin, his hands spread apart as if in benediction. No words came with the picture, but Curt sensed his father was trying to say something to him. He chased the image away and hurried to catch up with Phyllis before he fell too far behind.

When they emerged from the woods, the freezing rain had lightened and the snow pellets it had been mixed with had changed to lighter, fluffier flakes that melted when they hit the ground. For the first time that day they were able to glance at the sky without getting their faces stung by sleet. The wind seemed to have eased, too, almost as though the worst of the storm had moved on. And yet the sky was still dark, too much like nightfall for either of their tastes.

They began to run. Curt was limping badly, and by the time they reached the house he had to stop at the front gate and lean against the fence to catch his breath and let the throbbing pain subside.

"What about Bussey?" Phyllis said after a moment.

Curt drew a deep breath and let it out slowly. "To hell with him. We'll shoot him if we can, but I'm not going to worry anymore about things I can't control."

They cut to the right across the overgrown lawn, heading for the side of the house, but had made it only about halfway when Phyllis stopped and held up her hand.

"Listen. What's that?"

They could hear engines running behind the house. From the sound of it, there were several cars back there, or a car and a truck perhaps. In addition, they could hear several people shouting back and forth to each other, giving orders or directions. Although Curt couldn't make out what they were saying, he thought they sounded a bit frantic.

He put a finger to his lips and motioned for Phyllis to follow. Taking one stealthy step at a time, they approached the back of the house. A moment before they got there, car doors slammed and engines revved. They heard the sound of tires spinning on wet pavement.

"C'mon," Curt said, and led Phyllis to the back corner just in time to see a shiny black Lincoln and an unmarked panel van pulling away from the rear delivery ramp. Both vehicles had their headlights on and wipers going, and both were moving slowly in the opposite direction, following the gravel drive around the far side of the house and out onto the compound service road.

"What the . . . ?" Curt muttered. Fingering his cross through his wet jacket, he watched the gleaming taillights disappear down the road at a speed of no more than five miles an hour.

"Delivery?" Phyllis said.

"Probably. You see anyone else back there?"

She craned to catch a glimpse of anyone moving on the ramp or near the basement doors, and shook her head. "It's quiet."

"Probably getting supplies. We'll have to be especially careful. If they just got a delivery, there'll be people in the basement for sure."

They helped each other over the iron fence and stayed as close as possible to the side of the house as they made their way to the ramp. They glanced at each other uncertainly and started down.

Phyllis gasped when she saw the damage to the doors. She reached out gingerly, wanting to touch the twisted, blackened steel, but Curt caught her wrist.

"Don't. You'll burn yourself."

"You . . . you three did this?"

"We didn't, the holy water did." And as if he wanted to prove it, he reached into his knapsack and pulled out a fresh vial. Urging Phyllis to stand back, he uncapped it and splashed its contents on the doors, ready to duck for cover in the event of another thunderclap and heat flash.

Nothing happened.

The water ran freely down the doors, trickling into the minute channels that were the remains of the etched circles and carved goat heads.

Suspiciously Curt reached out and allowed his fingertips to brush against the steel. It was cool to the touch, almost cold.

"I don't get it," he said.

"The holy water you used before?"

"Maybe, but I'm not sure." He put his fingers in one of the buckled spots in the center and pulled. The door swung open easily. "Oh, shit, this can't be happening. No locks, no stickiness? That doesn't make any sense. Even with the padlock off this morning, it took us ten minutes to get the door open. This is too easy."

"You think it's a trap?"

"I wouldn't doubt it. Let's go, but be careful, okay? Don't leave my side."

Phyllis made a small sound that was almost a laugh. "Don't worry."

They went in.

Once through the doors, they entered absolute blackness. Curt had seen such darkness only twice before in his life—once in Mammoth Cave in Kentucky and once on a camping trip in Canada, late at night, zipped into his sleeping bag and secure in his tent. Never had he been in the middle of pure, untainted dark inside a house or any kind of manmade dwelling. In that kind of setting it was worse than unnatural—it was almost perverted.

"Wouldn't you know it?" he said. They had loaded the gun again in the woods, and now he held it in front of him like a shield. "We've got everything in the world in our knapsacks. Everything *but* a damn flashlight. Can you find a light switch over on your side?"

Phyllis tried. "Nothing. How about you?"

"Uh-uh. Come on, take my hand. We'll have to go this way, in the dark."

One step at a time they made their way into the basement. They kept their free hands out in front of them to feel for obstructions, and Curt had to struggle against the feeling that someone was going to take his wrist at any moment and drag him off to certain death. When he was able to dismiss that thought from his mind, he imagined instead someone sneaking up behind them.

The air was cold and stale, heavy with an odor that reminded them of dead mice rotting in the walls or meat gone bad on the kitchen counter during the course of a hot summer day. It was a thick, sweetish smell, horrible, unshakable.

"The crosses aren't glowing anymore," Phyllis said suddenly, making him jump.

"I noticed. Shhhh."

After several long moments they bumped against the wall and realized they had come to a corner. There was cold, sweating stone in front of them and to their left. The way to the right was clear, however, and they turned in that direction, wondering if the cellar was really as big as it seemed, or if it was just the darkness, the slow pace of their advance.

Suddenly they saw a dim glow up ahead. It grew brighter as they approached, and at the same time the corridor they were in widened considerably, becoming almost a room unto itself.

Eventually they came to an immense room with a high, vaulted ceiling. Curt was confused until he realized that all the while they were fumbling in darkness they must have been going down as well as forward. They weren't in a cellar proper, but rather some kind of underground vault dug well below the house.

The air here was colder than it had been outside. The stench of death was stronger here too. Curt tasted bile in his mouth, and had to swallow it back to keep from choking.

"Curt, look at the walls."

He did, and saw what Phyllis meant. The light in this room, as dim as it was, didn't come from any kind of lamps or fixtures. It was the stone walls themselves that were glowing, lit by a weird, flickering light with a greenish tint.

And then they saw the coffins.

They were across the room, arranged side by side along the far wall.

Fourteen of them.

Curt stared at them. For a moment he was positive that his heart had stopped, but then he realized how foolish that was. Stopped? Hardly. It was hammering triple-time. He swallowed and squeezed Phyllis' hand.

This is it, he thought. We've come this far and we're at the end of the road. This is where we're going to die.

He wasn't sure how long they stood there staring, but finally he summoned the courage to carry this suicide mission to its final stages. Before they could back down, they hurried across the room and stopped beside the first in the long line of caskets.

Curt handed the gun to Phyllis and practically tore the zipper off his knapsack in his hurry to get it open. He took the hammer and attacked the coffin's locks. It took only seven or eight blows to shatter them, and he lifted the heavy lid to look inside.

It wasn't his father, wasn't Van Paris, wasn't anyone he recognized.

"Who—"

"I don't know," he snapped. "Let's go."

They moved to the next coffin and broke the locks on that one as well. Again, the body inside was that of a stranger.

"Shit, where is he?"

They attacked the third coffin, the fourth, and the fifth. Inside every one was an unknown vampire.

On the sixth coffin they finally found someone they knew. The shock of it knocked Curt back several feet. His vision spun wildly. He groped for Phyllis, trying to find support, but missed and went down on his knees on the stone floor of the vault. When at last he was able to stand, he approached the coffin and looked inside again.

"Oh, Christ," he whispered. "Kelly."

She was beautiful. Her face was smooth, lovely, free of all blemishes. Her blond hair shone with a luster he found difficult to understand. Her eyes were closed, making her look as though she was enjoying a pleasant, restful, well-deserved sleep.

He thought about the way he had seen her last, after they had made love, and tried to speak her name again but couldn't.

Phyllis touched his shoulder. He turned. She was holding one of the sharp stretcher strips and the hammer.

His eyes widened. "Are you crazy? Did you lose your fucking mind? It's Kelly! It's—"

"That's all the more reason," she said softly. "We should put her to rest."

He grabbed her by the shoulders, shook her hard. Then, just as suddenly as the rage had come upon him, it left. His body slumped. He released his hold on her.

"Yeah," he said. "You're right. We owe her that much at least, don't we?"

Phyllis nodded.

"But not now. Now we've got to find my father."

One after another they attacked the coffins—seven, eight, nine, ten—but didn't find Bach or Van Paris.

In the eleventh coffin they found Juan, still wearing his bloody jacket and shirt. His throat had been torn out. The flesh of his neck lay open and exposed. Bone and cartilage had been shattered. The silk lining beneath him was soaked with brownish-red splotches, still wet. Curt turned away and swallowed hard.

Too late, he thought. We're always too late. Too late for Kelly, too late for Juan . . .

He felt himself going slowly crazy and began to work

like a madman, wielding the hammer like a murderous
weapon. He attacked the locks on each coffin with a
lunatic rage. He hammered, he pounded, he destroyed.

The last coffin, the fourteenth, was empty. Its silken
bed glistened in the greenish light of the vault. Curt
stared at it, trembling with anger, fighting the urge to
turn and throw the hammer across the room.

"He's not here! Jesus, Phyl, he's gone! *My father's
gone!*"

They stared at each other. It seemed utterly impossible
that they could have gone through so much, suffered so
much loss, battled so much terror, and have it end like
this.

"All my life he's avoided me," Curt said, tears running
down his face. "He's done more than avoid me—he's
escaped me. And now he's escaped again. How'd he do
it? Where'd he go? Where—"

"Curt! You just said it!" Her eyes flashed fire. "He
escaped!"

He frowned. "I know. What does—"

"Think about it! Jesus, Curt, *think*! What was happening when we got here? The van! The van was taking him
away! He's in the goddamned van!"

He was stunned. "The van," he murmured. "He's in
the van."

"*Yes!*"

The spell holding him broke. He grabbed his knapsack, took Phyllis' hand, and dragged her running across
the vault, back toward the black corridor and the doors
that led to the outside.

We lost time, he thought. Maybe too much. But maybe
not. The van was moving slowly, and we lost only ten
minutes or so. There might still be a chance.

He clung to that possibility as they charged through the
damaged doors and up the delivery ramp. He *had* to
cling to it. It was all he had left.

The muddy road that wound along the western boundary of the compound had not been designed for rapid

travel, but meandered in stately dips and curves. Once they had Bach safely away from the house, around the back side of a hairpin turn, the familiars pulled their vehicles over and got out. Standing sheltered from the wind alongside the van, they compared last-minute notes. Routes to the airport were confirmed. Instructions were repeated. Only when he was sure that everyone from himself down to the van driver was on the same wavelength did Kaye order the procession to begin moving again.

Norris lit a cigarette and inhaled slowly, finding himself lulled by the metronomic click of the Lincoln's wipers. "So this is Far Horizon."

"Is *that* what it is?" Tony Smith said from the back seat. "I thought it was a joy ride in the country."

Kaye laughed and peered over the steering wheel, trying to see better in the gathering gloom. "It is rather anticlimactic, isn't it? I wonder what the Enemies are going to think when they get to the house and find it abandoned."

Norris grunted. "Maybe they'll finally realize they were way over their heads all along."

Nobody replied to that. Norris turned around and looked at the panel van following close behind. Through the dusk and sleet-streaked glass he could barely make out the shapes of the driver in his Pathway Delivery Corporation costume overalls and Becky Heller sitting next to him. It looked as though they were engaged in deep conversation. In the back of the van, he knew, riding with the Master, was Ray Bussey.

He turned forward again, smoking in silence and enjoying the sense of peace that had settled over him as soon as they had pulled free of the house. It was almost over now. Within a few days or weeks, Kaye would join the High Church. He thought about that, and a phrase ran through his mind: *Stephen J. Norris, Senior Pastor.* He liked the sound of it.

"Almost there?" Smith asked.

"Not quite," Kaye said. "A few more minutes. Remember, we deliberately put the service gate as far away from the Hall as possible."

"It's taking forever."

"Don't worry," Kaye said. "We'll be there soon."

But none of them had any way of knowing what still lay ahead.

Curt had never known such physical exertion—the throbbing in his wounded leg, the stabbing pains in his chest, the dizzying headache and lack of breath. Yet he forced himself to run faster, faster, following the muddy tracks that pointed the way they had to go. Somehow Phyllis managed to lag only five or six paces behind, forcing herself, like him, past her limits of endurance.

As he ran, a huge roaring filled his ears and he kept seeing a mental image that he tried to shake but couldn't. He was running in the image too, but he was a little boy, running to catch a football thrown by his father, a father that never was or would be. He charged forward to catch the ball, afraid to let it fall untouched. He wanted to please that image-father, wanted to please him more than anything in the world, desperately wanted to make him proud. His father . . . a real father . . not a monster. The image made no sense at all, and yet he couldn't get rid of it.

"Curt!" Phyllis gasped. "Curt, I can't . . . keep . . . up!"

He waved her on, not wanting to waste words, not sure he had the strength to utter them.

"*Cuuuuuuuurrrtt!*"

He pushed himself still faster. The pain in his leg was deadly serious now. He wasn't sure if he was drawing full breaths or not. He slipped on a patch of ice, barely caught his balance in time, and knew he was close to utter collapse. In his mind, the image of the father had been replaced by one of the underground vault with greenish-lit walls, the football gone in favor of fourteen open coffins.

How much longer? How much farther?

"*Curt! Pleeeeaaaase!*"

He spared a quick glance over his shoulder. She had fallen farther back, was now almost twenty yards behind. He waved her on again and kept running.

They were passing parts of the compound he had never known existed—outdoor parks, wide sloping meadows, dense groves of trees, and small outbuildings that might have been storage sheds or might have been abandoned years before. The service road twisted right and left, took a sharp bend westward, and straightened out at last.

Through the gloom and the haze of his exhaustion he saw the most remarkable sight he had ever seen. Not far ahead, a black Lincoln and an unmarked panel van moved slowly along. They might have been going ten miles an hour, but that didn't seem possible because he and Phyllis were gaining on them, closing the gap between them inch by inch, foot by foot.

"*There!*" he cried, the effort sending fresh waves of agony screaming through his body. "*Hurry!*"

Closer. They were even closer now. But they were still too far away. He tried a fresh burst of speed, but felt his feet almost go out from under him. The world tilted wildly, and he nearly dropped his precious knapsack as he threw his arms out to save himself from a brutal fall that miraculously never came. He managed to right himself in time, and charged ahead regardless. Phyllis was at least fifty yards back, struggling.

Now he could hear traffic passing on Butterfield Road and realized that the car and van were going to leave the compound, taking the Master with them. He could glimpse the compound walls through the trees and brush.

Time, he thought, there's no time.

But then the taillights of both vehicles flashed, and he saw them coming to a stop in front of a towering iron gate he'd never seen before. It was similar to the main entrance, farther to the east, but not quite so ornate. Rather than fancy, intertwined patterns of wrought iron, this gate was utterly functional.

And there was one other difference, he saw now.

This gate was locked.

As the car and van ground to a complete halt, he slowed to a walk and waited for Phyllis to catch up. Together again, they leaned on each other to keep from falling. Their sides heaved, their pained breath whistled through dry throats. The rest was brief. A moment later,

they limped forward, closing the space between them and
the vehicles to a scant twenty feet. They fell on to the
ground, waiting to see what was going to happen, and
except for the sound of traffic beyond the walls, the
world seemed to wait with them. The sleet and snow had
stopped. The wind had died.

Curt took the service revolver from Phyllis. Trembling,
he clicked off the safety, cocked it, and held it up.

The front passenger door of the Lincoln opened and a
tall figure unfolded from within. The figure was laughing,
responding to a joke told by someone else in the car, and
Curt recognized that laugh. He had heard it on TV many
times. Then the figure turned, and he saw the face,
confirming it. It was the Reverend Stephen Norris.

Norris turned to the van and held up a hand, as if to
say this would take only a minute. He reached into his
pocket. Curt couldn't see what he pulled out, but he
could hear the jingling of many keys.

"The gate," Phyllis whispered.

Norris strode to the gate, fumbled for the right key,
found it, and inserted it in the padlock.

Curt moved. Leaping forward half a dozen steps, he
brought the gun up again and somehow found a measure
of strength to bark:

"Norris! Stop!"

The minister spun around. He saw them, saw the gun,
but if he was surprised, he didn't show it.

"Don't move!"

Norris laughed. "Hello, Curt. We were just talking
about you, but who'd have thought you'd show up here?"

"Shut up!" Curt snapped. "I want my father!"

"Now, really, you don't expect—"

"*I want my father!*"

There was movement inside the vehicles now.

"Look out!" Phyllis cried.

Then everything seemed to happen at once.

43

A second after Phyllis uttered her warning, the muddy road was filled with scrambling figures. Curt was barely able to count them—two more from the car, three from the van. He noticed that one of the figures was Ray Bussey, and he was holding a handgun almost twice the size of the .38.

Unthinking, Curt fired. The report was deafening. He staggered back a step, felt a hot throbbing in his hand and arm. The flesh on his palm felt scorched.

Ray Bussey dropped his weapon and stumbled back drunkenly. He bumped against the side of the van and crumpled, his head striking the fender with a dull thump.

"Potter," Norris said, his voice more urgent all of a sudden, "you're mistaken, son. If you'll take a moment and listen to us, we'll explain what's—"

"I told you to shut up!" Curt cried, pivoting and firing again.

Norris screamed. It was a strange sound, high and shockingly girlish. The minister recoiled, clutching his shoulder.

"You really better stop now. You—"

The gun went off again, snapping Norris' words in half. He reeled around in a complete circle, stopped, swayed back and forth, and finally pitched face-forward into the mud. His hands came up, groping blindly, closing on empty air, while his entire body twitched and jerked spastically. Then he lay still.

By that time Curt had already pivoted and found himself face-to-face with Tony Smith. Smith was waving his arms in some kind of weird semaphore, pleading almost incoherently for Curt to stop, stop what he was doing, stop now.

Curt pulled the trigger again. Smith flew backward and landed like a rag toy in the snow.

Then a man in work overalls was charging him. The man hit Smith's sprawled form and went sailing through the air. Curt stepped back, and the man landed where he had just been standing, the air going out of him in a rush.

"You . . . son . . . of . . . a . . . bitch," he heard the man mutter, struggling to pull himself up.

Curt waited until he was almost on his feet, until he was half-walking, half-crawling forward, until he was a threat once again. Then he fired. The man's eyes widened and he collapsed, motionless.

Curt heard pounding footsteps, a strangled shout, and turned around to see Phyllis in action, chasing Rebecca Heller as she fled across the open meadow to the east. He hesitated, but not for long; Heller was moving too quickly and Phyllis was too tired; Heller was getting away.

He pulled the trigger, amazed at the way Heller seemed to fly forward, arms and legs splayed at bizarre angles. She landed in the snow and didn't move again.

Phyllis stared down at the body. Then she turned and looked back at Curt. Her eyes flashed with dark, angry fire. She began to scream. He fought the desire to go comfort her, assure her that they were doing the only thing they could. There would be time for that later, but not now, not while there was still one left.

He turned back to the Lincoln and faced the Reverend Robert Kaye. For a moment he was confused, because the man confronting him was not what he had expected. Gone was the powerful, beatific smile. Gone was the confident posture. Gone was all the commanding presence of the TV celebrity, the minister who captivated newcomers and longtime residents alike with his fiery sermons. Gone was the all-mighty vampire's familiar.

Reverend Bob was terrified. He stared at Curt with wild, affrighted eyes. He was crying.

"Potter," he said, and gone as well was the mighty voice, changed into a quivering, pleading whimper. "Potter, you've got to understand something. This isn't my idea, none of it . . . it's not my fault. I approved this plan, sure, but you've got to understand it wasn't mine. I'm just doing my job—"

"Shut up," Curt said softly.

"I . . . I've got to make you understand." Kaye had backed up slowly until he was pressed against the rear of the van. "Let me go. I'll do anything. Anything you want, anything you say. I mean, Jesus, man, it's hardly fair, is it? You with a gun, me with nothing?" He was sobbing now. "Anything, Potter . . . Jesus Christ, I'll do anything you want."

Curt smiled. He felt something he hadn't felt in a very long time. An odd confidence flowed through his body. This was Robert Kaye? This was the church's highest human leader? This was the vampires' strongest ally?

"Are you listening to me, Potter? I'll do anything!"

"Good. You can start by getting away from the van. Or better yet, open it for me. Unlock it, bring my father out here."

Kaye swayed on his feet. "I couldn't do that. Just let me leave. Let me go through that gate, and I swear I'll leave the church. Forever. I'll get on a plane and—"

Curt laughed. "You really think I'd let the number-one public figure in the church go free? Now, open the van and watch me kill your Master."

"I can't! I have to protect—"

"Oh, you're doing a fine job of protecting him, all right." He paused and steadied the gun. *"Open the van!"*

"I can't! My God, don't you understand that? I won't willingly participate in the death of my leader. I—"

Disgusted, Curt pulled the trigger. The hammer fell on empty chambers.

Kaye uttered a triumphant cry. "There! You see? It's fate, Potter, you *can* let me go!" His cries changed from fear and self-pity to relief. He leaned against the back of the van and sobbed gratefully.

Curt stared down at the empty gun in his hand. Confused, he had a distant thought that he needed to find the knapsack, but he couldn't remember where he had left it. He turned to his right, looked to his left, but didn't see it anywhere.

"Do you need these?"

He spun around and saw Phyllis standing there. She didn't look angry with him now, only weary, worn out. She was holding the box of bullets that had been in the knapsack.

He nodded, took the box, and filled the chambers of the .38 with hands that were numb from the cold, trembling with fear. Kaye saw what he was doing and began to whimper again.

"Open the van!" Curt commanded.

Kaye's whimpers turned to blubbering. "Please . . . Christ, c'mon, Potter, I can't . . . I told you. Look. Listen. If you're going to make me do that, just kill me. I'd rather be dead than betray the Master. *Please!*"

Curt stared at him. He turned to Phyllis, seeking an answer, a way out, but she had none to offer. Her expression left the call up to him. He glanced up at the cloudy sky, wondering how long till dark, the Master's time. Then he looked back at Kaye.

"You bastard," he whispered, and pulled the trigger.

Kaye began a scream that he never finished. His arms flew apart in an insane parody of the blessings he gave at the end of his sermons. He stood there like that for an eternity, not moving, not saying anything. A thin trickle of blood appeared at the corner of his mouth. At last he toppled over, pitching forward onto the ground.

"That's it!" Curt cried, rushing forward. He sidestepped Kaye's body and tried the back doors of the van, but they were locked from the inside. Cursing, he ran around to the front and climbed in the driver's side. He emerged a moment later, wild-eyed.

"It's locked in there too! They've got him locked in!"

"The hammer—"

"No time. Get back."

She stared at him, not moving, not comprehending.

"Go on! Get back!"

Still she stood rooted to the ground.

"Dammit, Phyl, *get back*!"

He half-pushed her, half-dragged her away from the van.

"What're you doing? We've got to—"

"Get down! Lie flat!"

When she didn't move quickly enough for him, he planted a hand between her shoulder blades and pushed her down into the mud, where she landed with a grunt.

Quickly he turned and crouched. They were only ten feet away from the van. He didn't know whether that was a safe distance or not, but he didn't trust his aim enough to move farther back.

He brought the gun up before him. He leveled it at a spot somewhere below the rocker panels. He closed his eyes and drew a deep breath.

"Let not my enemies exult over me," he murmured.

He squeezed off his five remaining shots.

On the third one the van's fuel tank ruptured.

There was an ear-splitting roar, and Curt threw himself to the ground, shutting his eyes tight and throwing his arms up over his head. Even at that he saw a flash-image of the fireball, and felt the tremendous wave of heat surge over them. Hot shards of metal rained down all around them, landing on the wet ground with serpentine hisses. He was about to look up, when there was a smaller, secondary explosion, and they were buffeted once again. A door hinge landed on his back, making him wail in pain.

When at last he dared to look, he felt weak at what he saw.

The explosion had destroyed the van, which now looked like some strange modern sculpture. It had tipped over onto its right side, and he could see that the back doors had blown completely open. In addition, the left side had been peeled back, as if by a giant can opener, and the cab up front had separated and lay canted at an impossi-

ble angle. Flames licked around the wreckage, lighting
the sky, creating twisting, writhing shadows on the ground.

Picking himself up, Curt crawled forward a few feet
and peered through the hole in the back of the van.
Inside, tipped over, almost upside down, a huge wooden
coffin was engulfed in flames.

His breath rushed out of him.

It was over. Thank God, it was finished at last. Somehow, they had come through the darkness and made it to
the light on the other side.

Phyllis touched his shoulder. "Will . . . will that do
it?" she asked, pointing at the burning coffin.

He nodded. "Fire. Yeah. That'll do it. Fire's cleansing.
He's dead now, he's finished."

He took her hand and held it, staring into the flames
and savoring the relief that spread through him like numb-
ing anesthetic. But then an odd thing happened. As
though the dancing flames were pen on paper, he saw a
picture being drawn there. It took him a while to understand what it was, but when he did, he felt tears spill
down his cheeks unbidden, uncontrollable.

It was the same image he'd had as they had chased the
car and van through the compound. A little boy racing to
catch a football thrown by his father, reaching, stretching, afraid to fail and disappoint the man he loved. The
image confused him even more than it had before, but its
power was undeniable, because the little boy was Curt
himself, but that father had never existed.

He reached into his pocket and pulled out the creased
and tattered photograph. He stared at it in the light of
the fire. Arthur Bach smiling. His mother smiling. Happy
days. Days gone by. Days that, like the boy and the
football, might as well have never existed.

"No," he said then. "No way."

He got to his feet and limped over to where the knapsack lay. He unzipped it, pulled out the hammer, pulled
out a stake.

"Curt, what—"

"It's not going to end like this. Fire's too good for that
bastard."

"You can't!" she cried. "The flames—"

"I don't care! He's not going to get off that easy!"

He approached the van, squinting against the heat that seared his face. He shifted the stake and hammer to his left hand, and with his right made ready to reach into the flames and drag out his father's coffin.

"*Curt!*"

And then she was beside him, one arm around his neck, the other around his waist, trying to pull him back. He whirled on her, slapped her, pushed her away.

She slipped and fell to the ground. "Curt, no, please don't! You said the fire's enough. Let it do the job, don't go in there, Curt, don't—"

"I have to," he said simply, amazed in a distant sort of way at the calm power in his voice.

"Curt . . ."

He ignored her and stepped into the flames. He saw nothing, heard only a crackling roar, felt a searing pain engulf his arms. He groped blindly and felt his fingers close over the scalding metal that was the coffin's brass handle. He screamed in pain, but hung on. He pulled. The coffin moved only an inch.

"C'mon. Now!" he told himself, and pulled again, willing himself to find the reservoir of strength he needed to finish the job.

The coffin moved perhaps another inch, perhaps less.

Now he could hear the sizzle of his own hair burning, and felt something wet trickling down his cheek, his jaw.

He pulled. It did no good. The coffin was too heavy. It wasn't going to move. He couldn't free it, and was going to die trying.

"Please," he whispered, and pulled again.

As if the coffin had suddenly grown fifty pounds lighter, it slid toward him. Confused, he turned and saw Phyllis standing next to him, flames licking around her, her hands closed over the brass handle next to his.

"*Pull!*" she said, and working together, they did.

The coffin bucked, jerked forward. They pulled again, and tumbled backward as it came free of the van and fell to the ground outside.

Scrambling to their feet, they dragged it safely away from the inferno. When they tried to remove their hands from the handle, they came away with searing jolts of pain and the sickening sound of ripping flesh; the heat had fused them to the brass.

And then they were rolling on the ground, hugging each other, putting out their burning clothes and hair, pushing each other down and slapping at the flames like children engaged in a bizarre and dangerous game.

When they were free of the fire, they turned back to the coffin. It sat there in the mud, its own flames dying slowly, the wood charred and smoking, smoldering.

Curt took the hammer and approached slowly. Ignoring his pain, he brought the hammer down against the first lock, which broke off freely from the damaged wood. He nodded, satisfied, and turned to the second lock, which also shattered with startling ease.

He grasped the lid with both hands, felt the charred wood crumbling away beneath his fingertips, and lifted. The hinges in the back ripped free with a crunching, tearing noise, and he used all his strength to push the lid aside. It tumbled into the road and split in half.

He looked down at Arthur Bach, the Master, his father.

He seemed to be sleeping peacefully, his eyes closed, his lips slightly parted in what was almost a half-smile. The silk lining of the coffin had turned from gray to black, and apparently even Bach's clothes had begun to smolder from the heat, but he seemed not to notice. His undead sleep was perfect, undisturbed.

"Let not my enemies exult over me," Curt murmured again. He took the artist's stretcher strip in his hand and raised it high above his father's body. "O my God, in you I trust."

He plunged the stake into the center of Bach's chest.

Bach's eyes flew open. He saw Curt, and for a moment his expression was so startled that it was almost comical.

"Hello, Dad," Curt said, and brought the hammer down onto the stake.

Bach wailed. It was a sound similar to Theodore Williamson's cry, but much worse. It had a quality that seemed more real than Williamson's shriek, much less unnatural, and in that way it was infinitely more horrible.

Curt brought the hammer down again.

"*Nooooo!*" his father wailed.

Curt laughed. "Oh, yeah. This is for you, you son of a bitch! All for you!"

Again the hammer fell.

Bach began to writhe and twist, his hands coming up like grappling hooks, reaching for Curt's throat. Curt knocked them away with the hammer and struck the stake again. Bach bucked like a wild animal.

"*Noooo! You can't!*"

Just watch, he thought. Without thinking, he climbed into the coffin and planted his knees on his father's stomach, pinning him.

"*Nooooooooooooo!*"

Again and again he brought the hammer down, driving the stake home, and still the master vampire fought him. His claw-hands came up and tore Curt's burned face, ripping away pieces of skin, but Curt was beyond any pain now. He was running on an inner current of sheer terror. He barely felt his father's claws on his cheeks, was hardly aware of the vampire's wail in his ears.

The hammer fell again. The stake moved toward its target. Bach's breath began to come in rapid, ragged spurts.

"*Curt . . . no . . . no . . . no . . . no!*"

"Yes," Curt said, and continued to hammer.

"*I'm the Master!*"

"Tough shit."

"*I'm your father!*"

Curt nodded, and hammered still.

"*Nooooooooooooooooooooooooooooooooooo!*"

The cry split the air more completely than the explosion of the van, rending sky and shadow, shaking the earth beneath them.

And then Curt hesitated for the first time.

Something was happening.

He paused, the hammer raised over his head. His father was changing shape.

The monster left his father's features. The face that had just an instant before been contorted with an utterly inhuman rage became not a vampire's face but a man's. At the same time, Bach aged, decades flashing by in heartbeats. His hair turned snow white, his smooth face seemed to crumple in on itself, becoming lined with wrinkles. His mouth opened, and Curt saw the sharp incisors actually shrinking, drawing back into the gums, becoming blunt and harmless. But the eyes . . . It was the eyes most of all that changed. All traces of fierce, bestial anger left them. All signs of vampiric hunger fled. In the span of time covered by a single blink, the eyes became sad, pitifully tortured, completely human.

Curt began to tremble. With the hammer still raised over his head, he stared at the stake, which was no longer driven into a monster's chest, but into the chest of a melancholy old man.

It was his father, his real father. It was the man in the faded photograph come back to life.

"Curt . . ." the old man said, his voice little more than a husky, croaking whisper. "Curt . . . forgive me."

The world began to slip away from him as he realized what he had done. His vision whirled crazily, going dim, going gray, going black.

. . . *forgive me* . . .

He lowered the hammer and began to cry.

Curt . . . forgive me.

His body shaking all over, he raised himself and started to get out of the coffin. He had one leg over the side when his father's hand closed on his wrist.

"Curt!" Phyllis shrieked.

He looked down into the face of the vampire.

His vision swam again, but he saw that his father was gone once more. He had vanished as quickly as he had arrived, disappearing forever. He saw Bach's lips flash toward him, saw a glint of teeth, and heard the vampire's deep, chuckling laugh, pleased at how easily the charade had been accomplished.

With a wrenching cry he pulled away from the clawlike grip on his wrist and threw himself forward. His momen-

tum almost carried him across the coffin to the ground on
the other side, but he managed to hang on. He turned,
slapping Bach's hand away, and brought the hammer
high overhead for the final blow.

"*Now!*" he cried—and brought the hammer down.

The stake plunged home.

The end was almost an anticlimax. There was a brief
flash of light, a single clap of sound, both of which might
have terrified Curt and Phyllis at one time but had no
power to frighten them now. As Curt scrambled out of
the coffin for the last time, his father's body rose several
inches off its charred silk bed, and there, in midair,
changed from flesh and blood to ashes. The ashes fell
back into the coffin, stirred slightly in a breeze that
seemed to come from nowhere, and then were still.

Curt took Phyllis in his arms and pulled her against
him. They stood there like that for a long time. They
weren't crying anymore. They weren't trembling.

"It's over," he said at last.

It was almost two hours later when they started back
for the Hall. They limped across the open meadow, past
the body of Becky Heller and toward the woods that
separated the main cluster of buildings from the remote
site of the final battle.

They had checked to make sure all the familiars were
dead. They had checked Bach's coffin several times, but
the ashes were still there, hadn't moved. They had waited
until the fire in the van had burned itself out completely.
And only then had they considered going back.

They entered the woods with no fear whatsoever, picking their way along instinctively. It was now full dark,
and no doubt there were vampires roaming the compound, but like the Master's final dissolution, that thought
held no power to disturb them.

There was still much work ahead of them, but for the
first time they were in command.

"Curt?" Phyllis said after a long time in silence.

"Hmmmm?"

"Which one was real? At the end, I mean. Which one
was real? The vampire? Or the old man?"

He stopped and turned to her. He wanted to give her an answer. He wanted it more than he had wanted anything else in his life.

His eyes filled with tears. He shook his head.

"Both, I think." He took her hand. "Both."

Epilogue

*There the wicked cease from troubling; and
there the weary be at rest.*

—Job 3:17

Taking a cab out from O'Hare, he was surprised at the
number of changes in such a short time. On his first trip,
Ernest had told him about the ever-increasing development, but now it seemed as though there wasn't a square
inch of open land remaining west of Chicago. Every lot
had either a completed development or the beginnings of
one.

He told the driver to wait by the front gate. The driver
frowned.

"Really. I'm not going to be long. Just wait and you
can take me back to the airport."

He hadn't seen or heard a thing on the entire trip that
convinced him the driver understood English, but apparently his request was clear. The driver frowned again and
motioned at the meter, which already showed a considerable fare.

"It's okay," he said. "Just wait."

The driver shrugged, and said in perfect English: "It's
your dime."

He nodded, and started walking up the driveway.

It was a college now.

He had known all about that, of course, had followed
the story in *Time* and *Newsweek* and the Chicago papers
he picked up in California from time to time. He had
read all about the mysterious disintegration of what had
once been the most powerful religious movement in the

world. The stories had always been written with a curious, breathless quality, as though the reporters didn't understand what they were writing about but relished it nevertheless. There had been the unexplained disappearance of the church leader, the Reverend Arthur Bach, and the murders of several other high officials, including the beloved Reverend Robert Kaye, known to his followers and fans simply as Reverend Bob. None of it made any sense. There was no motive, no explanation. All the financial accounts, on paper and in the movement's vast computer system, were in order. There were no missing funds whatsoever.

Slowly, over the course of the next two years, the church had broken up bit by bit and fallen apart. Crusades had come to a standstill, of course, as had publication of new books and pamphlets. There had been no direct-mail campaigns. Newcomers had stopped arriving, and older residents had grown disillusioned over the lack of leadership and had drifted away a few at a time. The compound had been sold to a corporation that ran computer and technical colleges in various big cities around the country. The Faith Center had been turned into a tower of classrooms. The Hall housed programming geeks and other silicon-heads. The radio and TV studios were now broadcast-training facilities.

The religion of world change had been replaced by the religion of high tech, and certain wags, sectarian and otherwise, had trumpeted their joy at the death of what was most assuredly just a faddish cult that had been doomed to failure from the very start.

He came to a stop in front of the Hall and stared at the brass nameplate mounted outside the doors: "WILLIAM DUNBAR RESIDENCE CENTER." He glanced up, craning his neck to see the window of room 1290, and swallowed hard, surprised at the strength of his emotions.

The church was dead. Universal Ministries was gone. On occasion, he would see an ad for it in the back pages of the Sunday newspapers, but the ads meant nothing. They were just desperate attempts by a few scattered people who couldn't let go of the past. The real church, the High Church, was dead.

He walked around the Hall and took the main road to the Faith Center, which was now called simply Academics and Administration. As he strolled through the crowds of young people hurrying to and from their various classes, he thought about Phyllis. She was living down south now, in a Dallas suburb, sharing a two-bedroom apartment with her boyfriend of more than a year. She had passed her high-school GED on the first try and was now taking classes in architecture, planning on going all the way for her master's degree. They corresponded regularly, talked on the phone at least once a month, but rarely mentioned the past.

She had refused to come with him on this trip.

Standing outside the old Faith Center, he closed his eyes and remembered the dark times he had shared with her. It had taken them more than two weeks to finish the vampires. The actual battles had been quite easy, as though the creatures had had no life or fight left in them after the death of their Master, but the logistics had been staggering. He had estimated that by the time they were satisfied their work was finished, they had driven stakes into perhaps one hundred of the undead, old church officials and innocent residents alike. Kelly had been the worst, but giving her the peace she had worked so hard to earn while alive had almost been worth the pain. Almost.

Through that entire two-week period, staying in a hotel each night and returning to the compound by day to do battle, they had never found Van Paris. He had speculated that perhaps the oldest of the vampires had fled when things had turned against him. Phyllis thought perhaps finishing the Master had also finished the vampire who created the Master. Neither of them could be sure, and sometimes at night he still awoke from vivid dreams in which Van Paris chased him across shadowy landscapes, terrible and unconquerable.

A student hurrying past on the way to some class or other bumped into him, rushing on without an apology. He opened his eyes and realized that he was trembling.

The High Church was dead.

Yes, of course. The new look of the compound, the new names, the new faces told him that.

The High Church was dead, and coming here today had proved that to him as nothing else could have.

He turned his face up into the bright May sunshine and tried on a smile that felt stiff and rusty.

"I'm here," he said. "I'm alive."

He reached into his back pocket and pulled out the photograph that was always with him. He stared at it for several minutes, letting the fingers of his free hand brush the images of both people in the picture. Then he closed his hand around it, crumpling it into a ball, and dropped it on the sidewalk. He ground it under the heel of his tennis shoe.

From somewhere not quite in the compound but not quite in his head either, he heard a voice. It spoke three words to him. Three simple words. Three words that chased him through his dreams more often than the shade of Richard Van Paris.

Curt . . . forgive me.

He inclined his head slightly, listening.

. . . forgive me.

A single tear rolled slowly down his cheek.

He shoved his hands deep in his pockets and started back toward the gate.

ABOUT THE AUTHOR

Paul F. Olson spent thirteen years managing bookstores in the midwest before breaking into the horror field full-time. From 1986 to 1988 he was the editor and publisher of the award-nominated *Horrorstruck* magazine. Thirty years old, he lives in Wheaton, Illinois, with his wife and their new twin daughters. *The Night Prophets* is his first novel.